{Pictured below}

Billie Holliday
Dexter Gordon
Jules Broussard
Art Blakey

Wynton Marsalis
Dizzy Gillespie

John Coltrane
Elvin Jones
Sonny Rollins

Detail from "Jazzed Up" by Kelly Sullivan
12.5' X 5' Oil Canvas, 1993
On Display at the Fillmore Grill

FILLMORE GRILL

2301 Fillmore Street
San Francisco, CA 94115   415•922•1444

PAGES FROM OUR GUEST BOOK:
[#2. JEAN CLAUDE CARRIÉRE, APRIL 3, 1989]

TOSCA
SAN FRANCISCO

The dreadfull discord which did drive The noble Argonauts to outrage fell.
–Faerie Queen iv,i,23[1593]

ARGONAUT

NEW SERIES No. THREE   VOL. 138 No. 4214
SAN FRANCISCO CALIFORNIA

Since its first issue in 1877, the Argonaut has published this symbol. The bear, washed out to sea, is floating on the back of a walrus in the Pacific Ocean. He is thinking that if he devours it he will drown, if he remains on the walrus' back, he will die of starvation! What to do?

TABLE OF CONTENTS

LEADING ARTICLES

Table of Contents

FICTION

POETRY

CRAZIES: IS AMERICA GOING NUTS?

Argonaut (Spring 1994 ISBN 1-882206-04-5) is published quarterly by the Argonaut Press Inc., The Argonaut Building, 2250 Geary Blvd, San Francisco, CA 94115. (415)563-6033 Fax (415)563-5934. Subscriptions: $32 one year, $52 two years. Add $15 per year for first class mail. Britain, £28; Canada and other foreign, $37; add $25 per year for airmail. Application to mail at Second Class Postage Rates pending in San Francisco. POSTMASTER: Send address changes to: Argonaut, The Argonaaut Building, 2250 Geary Blvd., San Francisco, CA 94115. Argonaut does not encourage the submission of unsolicited manuscripts or artwork and will not return them. Distributed by the book trade by Publishers Group West, P.O. Box 8843, Emeryville, CA 94662; Contents Copyright ©1994 by Argonaut Press, Inc. Printed in the U.S.

Table of Contents

CORRESPONDENCE AND REVIEWS

ARGONAUT

WARREN HINCKLE, Editor & Publisher
JOHN J. SIMON, Senior Editor
MARY O'DONNELL, Managing Editor
ISHMAEL REED, Literary Editor
ALEXANDRA ANDERSON-SPIVY, Art Editor
MATTHEW NAYTHONS, Photo Editor
CICELY NICHOLS, Copy Editor
MARIANNE HINCKLE, Production Manager

ROGER BLACK, Design Director
RONA MICHELE, Art Director
JOHN MILLER, Design Consultant
THOR MULLER, Senior Designer
KAROL BARSKE, TERRY CUNIFF,
MIMI HEFT, WENDY WONG, Production
CANDY BRUCE, LOTHLORIEN B &
CATHY MILLER, Editorial Assistants

Advisory Editor: Alger Hiss,   Argonaut Bear illustration: WARD SCHUMAKER,
Contributing Editors: Joanne Grant (Biography), Fredric Hobbs (Multimedia),
Barbara Stauffacher Solomon (Architecture), Studs Terkel (Americana),
Sally Belfrage (London), Hunter S. Thompson (4th Amendment),
Ron Turner (Small Presses), William W. Turner (Intelligence Community), Sidney Zion (Law).

Drop us a line or subscribe via Internet: argonot@crl.com

FOURTH PRINTING!

ISHMAEL REED'S

Japanese By Spring

*"Mr. Reed constructs brilliant verbal
fusillades that reduce his targets
to their most ridiculous components."*
—The New York Times

*"Like verbal bebop, artfully staccato
sentence fragments—fast-paced, abruptly
changing rhythm and direction."*
—The Washington Post

"Japanese By Spring *carries the day
on the strength of its
humor, insight and boldness."*
—The Philadelphia Inquirer

PUBLISHED BY ATHENEUM
MACMILLAN PUBLISHING COMPANY
866 THIRD AVE., NEW YORK, N.Y. 10022

[SELF PORTRAIT BY RALPH STEADMAN, ISSUE TWO]

AUTHOR! AUTHOR!

ARGONAUT AUTHORS, WHO REFLECT THE SENSIBILITY OF THE BOOK, WHICH IS TO CHALLENGE THE NUMB-ING SAMENESS AND POLITICAL PRECON-CEPTIONS OF CONTEMPORARY AMERICAN MAGAZINES WHILE STRETCHING THE ENVELOPE OF IMAGINATION AND WIT, INCLUDE RALPH STEADMAN, STUDS TERKEL, ALAN GINSBERG, CURT GENTRY, ERICA JONG, PAUL KRASSNER, SHANA ALEXANDER, ISHMAEL REED, EVE BABITZ, SUSAN CHEEVER, SIDNEY ZION, HUNTER S. THOMPSON, FRANCIS COPPOLA AND JERRY BROWN

Prattle

Burying Nixon, The Nation, Alas,
Forgets Bebe Rebozo; Nixon *Was* A
Real Crook, Who Dined With The Mob
On The Sauces of Cuba; He Was Better
Interned Than Interred

WHEN NIXON KICKED, the Brit Defence Minister sought
words for the occasion. 'He was Lear, Othello, Hamlet, Brutus
all rolled into one,' Jonathan Aitken said on BBC Radio 4. The Tory
forgot Iago. Nixon flowered in revenge -- his life may best be understood
as a masterpiece of getting even for the inadequacies with which his cre-
ators endowed him. When he laughed, which even his haigographers
allow was infrequently, it was with the sneaky whoopee of a capuchin
monkey ejaculating on his betters through the bars of his cage. Nixon
was far and away the most miserable, miserly, scheming political miscre-
ant (had he lived in this city by the Thames in the time of the man who
owned the English novel, Nixon would have lived forever in the vocabu
lary of the language as a Dickensian adjectival noun of the distinction of
a Pekinsniff or a Fagan) ever to sup and slurp at the public trough while
injustly enriching himself through the petty, brackish alliances the
second rate invariably tend to forge in the crucibles of political power.

No more than Iago, Nixon resembled most his late-blooming pallsy-wallsy, the Arkansas traveller Bill Clinton. Both men were black lotuses pushing up through the mud of American politics. Nixon's attraction for the lowlife and the greasy little men in cheap shiny suits and florid Hawaiian shirts pressed open at the neck whom he choose to hang around in leisure hours — one thinks of his Key Biscane boarder, Bebe Rebozo and other confidents who caused the Secret Service men guarding Nixon at the Florida White House to chew the rug in anxiety and warn the White House about the

DRAWINGS BY KRISTEN WETTERHAHN

unsavory character of the president's entourage — has not escaped the notice of his biographers, who either puzzle over it — Gary Wills just couldn't understand how a big strategic thinker like Nixon surrounded himself with thugs — or attempt to explain it away. Earl Mazo duly recorded that Nixon's long acquaintancewith the rotten underbelly of life began when he worked as a kid as a barker for a crooked wheel-of-chance operation. Mazo tried to put a happy face on this: "Nixon barked for the *legal* front of the concession, where the prizes were hams and sides of bacon, which was a 'come on' for a back room featuring poker and dice," he wrote in the 1959 bio *Richard Nixon*.

Nixon benefited personally from the mob's looting of Cuba and the shower of wealth it rained on southern Florida (to borrow Thomas Macaulay's descriptive phrase about Britian's plunder of India.) There was even a dark mob cloud over the title of the Florida White

House at Key Biscayne which was brokered by Keyes Realty of Miami, the firm that many mob seraphim and crooked Batista government officials fleeing pre-Castro Havana with shopping bags bursting with cash choose to invest their ill-gotten gains in Southern Florida real estate. In one of those smary coincidences that defined Nixon's life, one of the Watergate burglars, Eugenio Martinez, was a vice president of Keyes in 1971 and help establish in the Keyes Building the real estate firm, Ameritas, which employed another Nixon campaign burgular, Bernard Barker, and was used as corporate cover by the Watergate break-in gang. Barker's partner in real estate deals was the ubiquitious Bebe Rebozo, who was also a silent partner in Nixon's tainted real estate ventures. A Keyes Realty officer was a director of Rebozo's Key Biscayne Bank.

That the 37th president, Tricky Dick, and the 42nd president, Slick Willy, became enamoured of one another prior to Nixon's death in April is unsurprising considering the commonality of their experiences. Both "came from dirt," as Nixon's advisor Roger Stone said, and neither of them in Nixon's memorable phrase on the Watergate tapes gave a shit about the Italian lire, or cared for little else save their own relentless self-advancement. They were made for each other. As Brando playing Stanley says to Blondre in the pre-rape scene in *A Streetcar Named Desire*, "We've had this date from the beginning." Both took their low life connections with them on the trip up the scarlet lane to the Oval Office, as the acid rain of Whitewater has made clear in the case of the Clintons and their conniving, stonewalling, cheating, polluting, document shreding, gum-chewing, bottom-pinching and bottom-feeding country cousins from the Snoppes-lookalike state of Arkansas. Clinton apologist Joe Klein tried to put some gloss on Clinton's association with unsavory types in his *Newsweek* column by comparing the president to Tonya Harding, the fallen Olympic skater who had her Goody Two Shoes competitor whacked on the knee with a pipe. Wrote a desperately seeking Klein: Clinton, has "a Tonya side" which is reflected in "his love of the precipice." Wibbledy, wobbledy.

Nixon has lived all his life in the shadow of felony. I know something of the unexplored side of Nixon's dark star. Because of the necessities of self-defense, I began researching Nixonian secrets in the

early 70s, when a magazine I was then publishing made Nixon's enemies' list and soon thereafter went out of business courtesy of the White
House dirty tricks squad. The magazine was *Scanlan's Monthly*. It was a
sucessor to *Ramparts*, an antiwar slick which I edited in the 60s and had
experienced a few body blows from the government in the form of moles
infiltrated into the staff, IRS hassling of investors and the like. But
Nixon made LBJ look like a piker in terms of retaliation for editorial

criticism. My partner on *Scanlan's* was
Sidney Zion, who had quite his job as
legal editor of the *New York Times* to
lauch a muckraking journal. The Nixon
administration presented us with a lot
of mud to rake and we went after them
with a passion, accusing the president
of high crimes and misdemeanors of
raping the economy and conduciting an
illegal, unconstitutional war in
Cambodia. An early *Scanlan's* cover
showed a fist punching Nixon's face in
and carried the headline, "Impeach
Nixon." That was in 1970 and we were
two years premature. The thing that

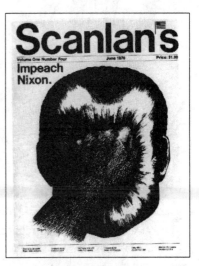

ON NIXON'S ENEMIES LIST

apparently provoked Tricky Dick to call for our heads was an editorial
with a photograph of Nixon with a bunch of east coast hardhat labor
goons visiting Nixon in the White House. These goons had been sending
their hardhats to beat up people protesting Nixon's escalation of the
war he had promised to end. The editorial which was titled "The Great
White House Tea Party" detailed the criminal records of most of the
labor leaders pictured around a wheyfaced Nixon and pointed out that
the travel restrictions on their bail meant they were breaking the law by
leaving New York City to visit the White House. The editorial and the
photography, captioned "Nixon and The Bums," also ran as a full page
Scanlan's ad in the *New York Times*.

Strange things then began to happen to *Scanlan's*. The strangest
of all—the entire 200,000 press run of the magazine which had been

FERAL HOUSE — THE TOAST OF THE COGNOSCENTI

PUBLISHER OF:

COSMIC RETRIBUTION: THE INFERNAL ART OF JOE COLEMAN
SECRET AND SUPPRESSED: BANNED IDEAS & HIDDEN HISTORY
APOCALYPSE CULTURE
KOOKS: A GUIDE TO THE OUTER LIMITS OF HUMAN BELIEF
NIGHTMARE OF ECSTASY: THE LIFE AND ART OF EDWARD D. WOOD, JR.

For a free catalogue, write PO Box 3466, Portland, OR, 97208 printed in Canada was arrested and confiscated by the Canadian Royal Mounted Police as the truck carrying *Scanlan's* neared the U.S. border. The printer was also raided and his men roughed up. The Canadian press reported that the Mounties had acted at the request of the Nixon White House.

 Scanlan's had to cease publication, and a few years down the line Zion and I were interested to read in John Dean's book about his high times as the White House lawyer, *Blind Ambition*, that Dean's first assignment as counsel to the President was to "get *Scanlan's*." He had difficulty accepting the contract until he was told that the order came from Nixon directly. Dean was told among other things to sic the IRS on us. This so upset Dean's still-virginal conscience that he went to Murray Chotiner, Nixon's old California hatchet man, for advise. "If the President wants you to turn the IRS loose," Chotiner said, "then you turn the IRS loose. If you don't, he'll find someone who does." wrote the man who ratted out the White House.

'It All Goes Back To The Bay of Pigs'

 Quoting Nixon, credit the Watergate tapes: *Look the problem is that this will open the whole, the whole Bay of Pigs thing...very bad to have this fellow Hunt, ah, he knows too damned much, if he was involved, the Cuba thing, it would be a fiasco; it would make the CIA look bad.... and it is very likely to blow the whole Bay of Pigs thing... the problem is it tracks back to the Bay of Pigs.*

 In other parts of the Watergate tapes, Nixon made reference to the same problem as "the Cuba thing." Cuba — pre-Castro Cuba — was the black hole that sucked an observably willing Nixon into the orbit of such rouge planets as Meyer Lansky, Norman 'Roughhouse' Northman and gang and Howard Hughes, all of whom either simply stole, or cheated the government and others, and gave Nixon the benefit of their dirty money.

 The Bay of Pigs was the metaphor in Nixon's twisted vocabulary for a number of secrets. One was the CIA's devil's alliance with the Mafia to kill Castro (thereby returning the mob to its isle of dreams)— a plot begun in 1959 when Nixon was the Eisenhower White House action officer for the Bay of Pigs planning. Another 'Bay of Pigs' secret was Nixon's own kinky relationship to the gambling crowd in Havana in the 50s and his later-life financial connections to organized crime that so unnerved Nixon's never-loyal White House chief of staff, General Alexander Haig (a real climbing shit who, one recalls, when Reagan was shot, rushed to assure the public that "I'm in charge here") as to prompt General Haig, in the bunker days of the Watergate White House, to order the Army's Criminal Investigation Command to probe his president's possible ties to organized crime. Haig specifically asked the Army to check out Nixon's links to mob guys tied to international narcotic profiteering. The investigation was mercifully ended when Nixon resigned. A little known footnote to history is that the Army CIC chief investigator who took the Haig assignment told the *Washington Star* on December 5, 1976, after Nixon's stain had long been removed from the Oval Office, that his aborted investigation had uncovered "strong indications of a history of Nixon connections with money from organized crime."

The third secret Nixon understandably wanted kept that fit under the metaphor of The Bay of Pigs was his admininstration's outrageous and highly illegal war on the dissenting left that rivaled the Palmer raids of World War I vintgage. The core of the Nixon gang's infamous Huston Plan — named after a Justice Department right wing water boy who was only too anxious to do the bidding of the maximum leader — was for the president by secret directive to revome most legal restraints on so-called intelligence gathering on left wing groups — Nixon authorized unrestricted wiretaps, mail intercepts and info-burglaries in the name of national security. There were also some musings about domestic national emergencies and the suspension of all civil liberties. The Huston Plan was only kept from becoming operational by the unlikey intercession of J. Edgar Hoover, whose well known sense of civil rights was offended by Nixon's red neck recklessness. Nixon had to worry about the 'Cuba thing' in relation to his war on the left (a left more imagined than real) because in the absence of the Huston Plan blasting off the Watergate White House turned to Bay of Pigs veterans,

Hunt, Barker, and the ilk, to carry out domestic dirty tricks for the White House.

It should be pointed out to avoid further undue hypocrisy on the part of Nixon's admirer, President Clinton, that if Clinton is really concerned about the situation of political prisoners in China, before he starts throwing bricks he should look through the wall of his own glass house and right the terrible wrong against America's longest-term political prisoner, Geronimo Pratt, a Black Panther framed by the FBI in 1968 for a murder all subsequent investigation has proven he did not commit. Nonetheless the Nixon gang's way with the facts and the law has shamefully stuck to this day and Pratt is still in prison, an international disgrace to the American system of justice. Nixon's own unblushing brush with the casual benefits from organized crime goes back to 1952 when on an R&R tour of Havana he interceded with the mob to cover a buddy's bounced gambling check. He later rewarded the mob by dropping several hot prosecutions when he took office in 1968. *Newsday* revealed that all of Nixon's real estate deals including the Florida White House were mob mortaged or mob financed, either directly or through associates of Nixon buddy Bebe Rebozo. For its efforts the *Newsday* investigative team got investigated by the IRS.

GERONIMO PRATT

"Gentlemen," Nixon told a group of newspaper editors at the Floriday Disneyland, "Your president is not a crook."

Like hell he wasn't.   W.H.

Sally Belfrage
1936-1994

- -

This edition of *Argonaut* is dedicated to the memory of Sally Belfrage. Her "UnAmerican Activities"— an excerpt from her memoir of the same title about her adolescence in the McCarthyite fifties—graced our premier edition. Reviewers of the first *Argonaut* celebrated the wit and exuberance of "UnAmerican Activities" as well as its incisive clarity, seeing her piece as defining this journal's ambition: we agree.

Sally Belfrage died of cancer in London on March 14, 1994, aged fifty-seven. Her beauty was physical and meta-physical; she radiated an uncommon emotional and intellectual generosity that enriched her friends. For them, indeed for nearly everyone, she was full of energy, full of fun. She easily and gently engaged children— and, for that matter, kittens. To her friends she offered a rigorous and captivating intelligence, at once respectful and ardent. To all, no matter what their age or station, she eagerly shared experience and wisdom as well as sorrow— and long bouts of hilarity.

She was sceptical of everything; her journalistic shit-detection meter was well calibrated. Cant and camouflage had no place in her work; she wrote about great historical events from the perspective of ordinary people and everyday life. Though her writ-

SALLY BELFRAGE
"A good old-fashioned international nuisance" — Orson Welles

ing was infected with a contagious empathy, she also had an unerring eye that saw through prevarication and pinchbeck. Her four published books—each based, respectively, on living and observing everyday life in Moscow, Mississippi, India, and Northern Ireland—were admired for their unflinching non-squeamishness in the face of truth. A radical as well as a socialist and feminist, neither her work nor her mind could be pigeonholed. She judged people on their personal qualities, not their politics. Orson Welles was right: she was a "a good old-fashioned international nuisance"—to the powerful, and to the purveyors of prejudice, fear, and 'conventional wisdom.'

It must seem odd to memorialize Sally Belfrage in an issue devoted to things American when she was away from the United States most of the past quarter-century. But she was very much an American. Consider this: although her mother was "a mere English eccentric," and her father (editor and founder of the radical weekly *National Guardian*) was "a Red and so in trouble all the time, if not in jail," Sally wrote "when my teens began it dawned on me: that the only untried, unheard-of truly original ambition I might pursue was to be *normal*." So, at the Bronx High School of Science she tried to "blend in." She was a cheerleader, runner-up for prom queen, and she fell in love with a West Point cadet. She was an American in other ways: in 1964, as a civil rights volunteer in Mississippi, she taught literacy to black children, helped to register black adults to vote, and spent time in jail along the way.

Out of her time in Mississippi Sally produced *Freedom Summer*, in which she described the vivacity and optimism of her fellow-activists who believed that by empowering the disenfranchised they could make America deliver on its promises.

This land, its values constructed of so much smug mythology, could tolerate neither Sally's passion nor her compassion. A two-foot stack of FBI surveillance files testifies to that. Never a pessimist, she nonetheless knew that America wouldn't and couldn't face hard truths about itself.

Sally, we'll miss you. Shamefully, America knows not what it missed.

—Joanne Grant and John J. Simon

LONDON, MARCH 25, 1994

At 66

ALLEN GINSBERG

At 66 just learning how to take care of my body
to wake cheerful 8 AM & write in a notebook
rising from bed side naked leaving a naked boy asleep by the wall
mix miso mushroom leeks & winter squash breakfast,
Check bloodsugar, clean teeth exactly, brush, toothpick, floss,
mouthwash
oil my feet, put on white shirt white pants white sox
sit solitary by the sink
a moment before brushing my hair, happy not yet
to be a corpse.

Not Trotsky

Huffing puffing upstairs downstairs telephone
         office mail checks secretary revolt—
The Soviet Legislative Communist block
         inspired Gorbachev's wife and Yeltsen
to shut up in terror or stand on a tank
         in front of a White House denouncing Putschists—
September breezes sway branches & leaves in
         a calm schoolyard under humid grey sky,
Drink your decaf Finsberg old communist New
         York Times addict, be glad you're not Trotsky.

Clinton's Hideous Haitian Policy

MICHAEL RATNER

There was no refugee crisis when President Aristide was in Haiti. Only a handful of people fled Haiti during his seven months in office. Haitians had hope and there was no repression, no torture and no state-sponsored murder. The crisis began with the coup and will continue until President Aristide returns. People need a very good reason to leave their homes, their family and their country. The military gave people a good reason for flight—fear of persecution. Haitians were and are being shot down in the streets.

On May 24, 1992 President Bush issued an order requiring that all Haitians interdicted by the U.S. Coast Guard at sea be returned to Haiti. No matter how valid a refugee's claim, he or she was returned to Haiti. The abuse these refugees undergo upon return has been well-documented. President Clinton as a candidate had called the practice illegal and immoral and promised to reverse it.

Treatment of Haitian refugees in the United States remains a scandal. Their discriminatory handling compared to that of Cubans is a national disgrace. Cubans do not face detention nor do they face a long drawn out asylum process. Haitians are immediately placed in custody and frequently given substantial bonds in order to get released. Then they must find lawyers and begin a lengthy asylum procedure.

The battle to restore President Aristide and democracy to Haiti and the fight on behalf of the Haitian refugees have been intimately linked. On January 14, 1993 President Clinton broke his promise to reverse the Bush Policy of summarily returning Haitian refugees. This meant that Clinton, had no real stake in insuring President Aristide's return to Haiti.

While the U.S. might prefer a democracy in Haiti, it only wanted a democracy that left the status quo in place and did not threaten what it perceived as U.S. interests. After all the talk about democracy and human rights the main pressure on the U.S. to back Aristide was that many politicians and others did not want Haitian refugees coming to the United States. But there was another way to stop refugees: interdict them and summarily return them to the hands of their oppressors in Haiti. There was little outcry when Clinton announced this hideous policy in January, 1993.

By mid 1994. growing domestic dissent over his Haitian policy forced President Clinton to announce that the INS would begin processing Haitian refugees on board ships as it did in early 1992 instead of simply turning the ships back.

But there are several problems with this policy, which suggest that the safety of Haitians is not really of concern to Clinton. The United Nations High Commission on Refugees has declared that the conditions in Haiti are so dangerous now that no refugees should be returned. Clinton's policy however, continues to insist upon the distinction between "political" and "economic" refugees: the old policy returns those it decides are economic refugees to the hands of the Haitian military, which certainly does not make the distinction. The military assumes that all refugees are Aristide supporters and interrogates everyone who is reboarded at dockside. Under the pretense of punishing the crime of "illegally leaving the country," the military has arrested and beaten as many as twenty percent of the returnees; many have subsequently disappeared, and been found murdered.

In contrast, the United States has argued that all Cubans fled their country are automatically political refugees, even though the Cuban military does not chase down and mutilate its political opponents or hack hundreds of them to death with machetes. Neither are Cubans or any other refugees processed on board ship: only Haitians are to be singled out for this hasty and inadequate approach.

Equally discriminatory would be the suggestions floated by the administration for a third country processing of Haitians or for setting up giant refugee camps in their countries, or by reassigning the notorious camps at the U.S. Naval Base at Guantanamo Bay. All of these ideas reinforce the unfair practices that have allowed Haitian refugees to become a class unto themselves cut off from the rights and procedures that are routine for all other immigrants.

The entire practice is a sham. There is no excuse at this point for returning any Haitian refugee. Until the Administration is ready to let services about restoring democracy under Haiti's rightful president, until reform does not mean a death sentence, Haitians should be given some haven in the United States.

The United States, dominates Haiti as France did in 1802, when the French government kidnapped and imprisoned Toussaint L'Overture, the slave leader of the Haitian revolution and the father of Haitian independence. While the United States did not abduct Aristide, it seems clear that the CIA had on its payroll the coup leaders who overthrew him. In any case, Aristide has been figuratively, if not literally imprisoned in the United State.

When President Aristide spoke at the United Nations, he did not appear at the demonstration of thousands of Haitians less than a block away. The FBI claimed, as it had on numerous other such occasions, that it would be too dangerous for him to do so. Clinton's policy has been that Aristide cannot speak to his people in Haiti, and he cannot speak to his people here.

President Aristide's hands were tied in the negotiations that the United States and the United Nations are conducting with the coup leaders in Haiti. President Aristide is also known to have objected to the

NOZIER ELIE: "THE VIEW FROM GUANTANAMO BAY"
Painting done at U.S Haitian HIV-Positive concentration camp at Guantanamo by
HIV positive Haitian

broad amnesty provisions of the July 1993 Governor's Island accord, provisions that are not even legal under international law prohibiting impunity for state-sponsored murder and torture. Granting amnesty in the July 1993 accords allowed the military to kill with impunity through October and gave it time to stock up on oil and arms and build up its murderous network of political attaches.

Nearly two hundred years after France imprisoned Toussaint L'Overture, there is no indication that the new dominant power is ready to see justice done in Haiti.

Famiglia

NEW WRITING BY
ITALIAN-AMERICAN WOMEN

Grace Cavalieri: *The Secret Jew*

Grandfather,
among the Italians, you were a scholar and a Jew—
how is it we were never told your secret life
at Pisa, a PhD before your time, secret wealth,
lumber in Trieste—

only an uncle to raise you,
this must be why a woman caught your eye and
hunger overcame you.
When your moon was lighted by the sun of a
Catholic, your family said Kaddish for their loss,

you came to America, penniless
with a blue-eyed wife and six children to find
this country wanted nothing from you—
a literary man who couldn't even build a subway—
Why'd You Come? they asked,

but what matters more is your son, my father, who
thought your disinheritance a family shame and never
spoke your name as Jew, so we never knew, thinking
you an old Italian who couldn't use his hands.

Finding out now who you were
I dedicate this poem to you, old Jew,
who gave up land for love.
They say everyone writes for just one person,

I will write for you.

Nothing of you remains but my song which begins:
"My fellow Jews! I am of Rafael Cavalieri! and before
     him
other great people, probably smart people, rich people,
rabbis, and lawyers and scholars no doubt—I find I am
     with
you—suddenly a Jew!"

Maria Famá: *Caffè Espresso*

In the store in the States
I finger the cans of espresso:
Lavazza of Naples, Maimone of Sicily
Danesi from Torino, Ciao from Piacenza
I buy the Lavazza di Napoli, Mamma Giulia's favorite,
     and make a late afternoon cup
I think of my sister Pina in the pre-Alps of Lombardy
     brewing each tazza in an automatic machine
I sip, I taste, I remember
my sister Luisa having her sixth cup
     after the typing and telephones in Molise
     her macchinetta always handy
Elena and Luca and Babbo at the crack of dawn
     before work with the tiniest pots
     aromatic steam rising in cold mountain air.

When I visit Arezzo
     I like to sit with Mamma over two morning cups
     listening to the radio news

Then a caffè after pranzo and one after cena
     though Babbo won't take any coffee at night
     only wine and good grappa.

Once long ago
in the winter kitchen playing cards
     the room was filled with the smoke of espresso and wood
     there were tricks and laughter and only one question:

"What do you want in a love?"
"Goodness and honesty," was my answer.

Mamma, I come to you every few years
    traveling thousands of miles
    by bus, by airplane, and then by train
    all the vehicles I ride yearning for you
    my second mamma in my second Italian home
    il caffè e sempre pronto when I am home.

I remember Babbo lowering me cheese from a train
    fresh mozzarella from Naples
    when I was nineteen and waited at the station's
    espresso bar in the vastness of Rome.

O Mamma, I tell you over the coffee
    how so many have died and I mourn
    but you've seen so much death
    the war, the earthquakes and time
    and you pour me a tazza
    and speak of courage and dignity.

Mamma, we watch the fashions of Rome on TV
    you're reminded of bats and the night
    and you laugh and shout
    and put on fresh coffee.

Mamma, in the morning's gentle sun
    you hum over pots of basil and rosemary
    trim roses and parsley on the huge balcony
    overlooking green Tuscan hills.

Your energy surges as you cook the sumptious meals
    Your energy brims with the coffee as you hug me
    and call me "tesoro."

O Mamma, you are the treasure
    that I find over and over.

Mamma, I come home every few years to you
    to your tiled kitchen and il caffè

to sip the clarity
to drink in your deep strong voice
the words neopolitan accented
and rich as espresso.

I return to the States
always richer with your wisdom
always richer with your love.

Mamma, I sip slowly in the States
lowering my cup I know how I love you
and how I want to be like you.

Maria Mazziotti Gillan: *Public School No. 18: Paterson, New Jersey*

Miss Wilson's eyes, opaque
as blue glass, fix on me:
"We must speak English.
We're in America now."
I want to say, "I am American,"
but the evidence is stacked against me.

My mother scrubs my scalp raw, wraps
my shining hair in white rags
to make it curl, Miss Wilson
drags me to the window, checks my hair
for lice. My face wants to hide.

At home, my words smooth in my mouth,
I chatter and am proud. In school,
I am silent, grope for the right English
words, fear the Italian word
will sprout from my mouth like a rose,

fear the progression of teachers
in their sprigged dresses,
their Anglo-Saxon faces.

Without words, they tell me
to be ashamed.
I am.
I deny that booted country
even from myself,

want to be still
and untouchable
as these women
who teach me to hate myself.

Years later, in a white
Kansas City house,
the Psychology professor tells me
I remind him of the Mafia leader
on the cover of TIME magazine.

My anger spits
venemous from my mouth:

I am proud of my mother,
dressed all in black,
proud of my father
with his broken tongue,
proud of the laughter
and noise of our house.

Remember me, ladies,
the silent one?
I have found my voice
and my rage will blow
your house down.

Lenore Baeli Wang: *Vision in the Sauce*

Two tomatoes, my father said.
What?
Two tomatoes walking up and down

the street outside. One
with this big blonde hairdo,
the other smoking her cigarette
like there was no tomorrow.
    Tight black pants
Running to the window,
    I can't imagine tomatoes walking.

My father grows tomatoes out back
and they're always heavy on
    green stems, sway
if I touch one. How can tomatoes walk?

Fingertips clutching window's ledge,
    I almost hang there until
my palms grow bud red with the strain
when
    two women appear:
one's cigarette a glowing wand
    I long to comprehend;
the other's hair looks hard to balance.

The sauce is ready. My mother's
    voice rings loud
bringing my father and me
    from separate corners of our house.
Don't keep looking out there,
    she says, seemingly to
the pot of bubbling broth.
    Red sauce she pours
over pillowy ravioli, round—
    I cut into one, fork eager,
watch the jewel-hot sauce
cover all that whiteness as
    I long to grow up
with high hair, a cigarette that
ribbons the air with smoke like there was
    no tomorrow, black pants
and have someone call me a tomato walking.

Rose Romano: *The Drop of a Hat*

For a year I worked
beside these women,
annoying them. They
tell me I scream
bigotry at the drop
of a hat, but they don't
explain why they keep
dropping hats. But
they asked for diversity
so I gave it to them
(I'm Italian-American)
but not enough
(I'm constantly Italian-American)
but sometimes too much.
In this time of lesbian feminist multiculturalism
some of us are more multi than others.

but we make signs for the march

femminismo
emancipazione
rivoluzione
sì

In the languages of our people,
to show solidarity in diversity—
the people whose culture
we want to discover—the
Black lesbian in Swahili—the people whose culture
we want to remember—the
Jewish lesbian in Yiddish—

the people whose culture
we want to share—the
Wasp lesbian in Spanish,
who tells me
there's no accent
over the eye in see.

Oh, yes, there is.
Oh, no, there isn't.
She should know.
She's studied Spanish
for two years.

Helen Barolini: *Gay Talese, Besse Mi Colo*

WHEN I WROTE a letter to the New York Times to respond to Gay Talese's specious March 14, 1993 Book Review piece "Where are the Italian American Novelists?", I replied by saying, we're here—women (entirely overlooked by Talese) included.

These poems counter Talese's masterpiece of misstatement that would-be Italian American writers are silenced from writing about their most intimate material through feelings of guilt should they reveal family secrets. That fear may be operative in his case. For the rest of us, however, the ambivalence and inner qualms we have experienced in our struggle to emerge from Fortress Family, have resulted in an ongoing stream of novels, plays, essays, and poetry which use those very tensions to become our most cogent literary material. We have not only plumbed the world of our forefathers but made it accessible and visible to all through publishing.

Italian American women poets have been using the intimate material of their lives—the conflicts between cultures and generations, between family loyalty and achieving individuation—for as long as they've been writing.

Diane di Prima, the most important woman poet of the counter-culture from the 1950s is also a "revealer of family secrets" from an Italian American background which remains the strong base of life ritual for her. Her strong, continuous voice has been undiminished for almost half a century.

And so, too, the present women raise strong, uncompromising Italian American voices showing the ties both to a familial past and their own new selfhood—the ties to both pain and pride.

They are here and active and affirmative of their background and the doubters and sceptics, like Gay Talese, are invited to become acquainted.

GERRY ADAMS

Sinn Féin President, former M.P., short story writer and prison memoirist

ARGONAUT

The Adams Papers

Gerry Adams, The Writer

JIMMY BRESLIN

I t is supposed to be summer but because it is Belfast, which is as different in weather as it is in people, there is no summer. Of an August morning, a chill breeze comes off the grey water of the Belfast Lough. The dark sky has the promise of rain that will come sometime in the day, with no notice, thick white cold rain that drenches people before they get from one side of the street to the other.

The streets in Gerry Adams' stories are extraordinarily narrow. They are lined with tiny houses crowded with people who live silent, desperate lives that suddenly and dramatically explode into brightness with this one moment that makes a short story.

Gerry Adams' short stories fit the requirements that have been posted forever by the master of the form, Sean O'Faolain, of Killiney Hill Road, Killiney: "A short story is like a kite. You send it up in the air and then there comes a moment when the air catches the kite and it plays at the end of the string and gives this delightful shimmer. Then it is gone. And it is in this one moment that the short story also ends. To proceed is to ruin."

Gerry Adams stops all stories on time. He instantly fills the yearning for a time when the short story was the literary form for the superior writers in America. Once, a writer sending in a short story to the *Saturday Evening Post* or *Collier's* or *Cosmopolitan* was placing his work amidst that of Hemingway, Faulkner, Saroyan. When the magazines closed, the American writers were so dense that they felt that this meant the short story, too, was gone. Yet the short story always seemed best for America, where life is lived on the swift. Years living beside a brook in England produce these interminable novels that are read by nobody. But the short story is rapid and compressed and gets to the end when it should.

Therefore, it is only natural that a writer from Belfast, in cool air and in a life much more rapid than it appears to the eye, brings to Americans the form we instinctively know and like the most, the short story.

As presented in news reports, Northern Ireland is so shrouded in vapors that Americans merely wait for an understandable story about something else to come on. And all the time the people of Belfast get up in the morning and start another day of life in a place that is, as the people in Gerry Adams' stories begin talking, not much further away than the next street from you.

The Belfast that I know is the one Gerry Adams writes about. He sees in the people these problems and traits that cause the excitement of recognition. In reading his stories, I knew the place was as close as the next page.

I am in Belfast one Saturday morning when the Pope is visiting the Republic of Ireland, which is to the south. I am in the Royal Crown Bar on the Shankill Road. This is a bar for the Protestant beer drinkers, horse betters, and the odd gunman. The Catholics are the mortal enemies. The streets are covered with banners attacking the Pope of Rome. "No Pope Here!"

And here on television in this crowded Protestant bar is the Pope of Rome, loud and sonorous, delivering a long sermon at a huge outdoor mass down in Dublin. I am in the bar so I can hear people talk. They all glance at the television once in a while, but without emotion. They then go back to their conversation, which was totally about sports. The television is so loud that I can't hear the people talk-ing. I grow bold and reach up and try to change the channel.

"Yup!" the bartender shouted. "Leave it be. The racing comes on at half twelve."

The Pope talked on and the barfull of people waited patiently for him to be gone and the first race to be on.

When Adams writes of the city of Derry, I am riding into the city on the first day that I ever saw it, in a grey wet Sunday afternoon. Coming down the hill, I suddenly see this city behind a high medieval wall and then I ride through the gate and into the town and here on the wall in large letters is the inscription:

Sara Is
A Fucking Hussy

And I am on any street in New York.

I first came to Derry in the sixties and the politics was fierce and then the violence began and nobody knew it was going to last so long. Twenty-five years, as this is written in the spring of 1993. Yet through all the years of shrill speeches and disheartening violence, the scene I remember is one that belonged in one of the old dusty houses in Richmond Hill, in Queens, in New York City.

The old man, still from a stroke, sat in the living-room chair and told anybody who entered: "The four crimes crying out to God for vengeance are abuse of a working man. Withholding the wages of a working man. Murder. And sodomy!"

Here, then, are young men strolling back from Charlie Watterson's pub on the shoulder of the Black Mountain, with the dusk slowly settling on the city below them and the sea mists smothering Belfast Lough. Gerry Adams' stories are set in Ireland but they are about life everywhere, and in the great form that has nearly vanished in America, the short story.

Paul O'Dwyer: *America's Ban on Gerry Adams*

I FIRST MET GERRY ADAMS at Sean MacBride's funeral. We had both known of each other for many years, but it was typical of our great mutual friend MacBride, Nobel laureate and selfless fighter against racism and colonialism, that he should have taken time off from his own funeral to bring us together. As we stood at the graveside, Gerry turned to me with a mischievous twinkle in his eyes and said, "Isn't it wondrous to see how grand a eulogy the Catholic hierarchy are giving a man they almost refused to baptize and then reviled all his born days for being a Republican?"

Gerry is the President of Sinn Féin, the Irish Republican movement dedicated to ending British control of the North of Ireland. From 1983 to 1992 he was Member of Parliament for West Belfast, refusing, however, to take his seat in London in protest at Britain's occupation of the six counties. But most people in the United States probably see Adams through the eyes of the media and of the State Department, which have for years ingratiated themselves with Margaret Thatcher and John Major by seeking to portray this charismatic leader as a terrorist.

At the insistence of Thatcher and Major, Adams was kept out of the United States by the Reagan and Bush, and then, to the chagrin of those of us who supported Bill Clinton, the Clinton State Departments. The 48-hour "window" of opportunity granted Adams to visit New York last winter was only an exception to the State Department's running-dog-for the British position of refusing to grant him a visa for an extended stay. Adams has never been convicted of any crime, unless it is a crime to attempt to escape from the inhumanity of unconstitutional imprisonment without trial.

I believe it was Abbie Hoffman who said that sacred cows make the tastiest hamburger. In one of his stories Adams recalls how, as a lay member of the Catholic Church, the closest he got to meeting a Cardinal was while he was in Long Kesh: "Seated on the toilet one day, bowed down with matters of theological interest, when the Cardinal was shepherded past by a crusade of curates. We never got within smelling dis-

tance of each other." In a Swiftian switch from humor to deadly serious-
ness, he says, "Let me state my case briefly.... It is that the Catholic
Church has failed miserably to fulfill its role in Ireland.... The Church
perhaps fulfilled its Christian role best in St. Patrick's time and during
the Penal Days. Since then, with only a few notable exceptions, it has
deserted the poor."

Gerry Adams, the writer, was introduced to the United States by
Sheridan Square Press of New York City in two recently published vol-
umes of his short stories and prison writings, *The Street* and *Cage Eleven*,
from which these excerpts are taken.

In the stories that make up his book *Cage Eleven*, we see a side of
Gerry Adams that places him in the great tradition of Irish writing.
These stories were written in the prisoner-of-war camp called Long
Kesh. They were smuggled out of prison and first published under the
pen name "Brownie" between August 1975 and February 1977 in
Republican News, the Republican newspaper which is now called *An
Phoblacht/Republican News*.

By turns humorous and soul-wrenching, satirical and compas-
sionate, witty and entertaining, all are infused with a deep love and
respect for the humanity of the hundreds of men who, without having
been charged or tried for any offense, served long sentences of internment alongside him.

Adams' prison stories give insight into the inhumanity of a system that jails people without charge or trial. Today the British government boasts that it has abandoned internment. True on paper, but it has
replaced that evil with other horrors condemned by Amnesty
International, the International Association of Democratic Lawyers,
Helsinki Watch, and other respected human rights groups: abolition of
jury trial; systematic torture to obtain "confessions"; the "shoot-to-kill"
policy used against unarmed suspects; brutal jail conditions resulting in
1981's ten deaths by hunger strike of many who were Gerry Adams' comrades in Long Kesh and after; abolishing the right to remain silent;
employing warrantless searches and seizures; indefinite pretrial detention; and offical censorship.

As we stood at Sean MacBride's graveside, Gerry expressed his admiration for the United States Constitution. "If we'd had a document like that, I'd never have spent a day in the Kesh," he said. Indeed, the Fourth, Fifth, Sixth, Eighth, and Fourteenth amendments would outlaw the entire "justice" system of Northern Ireland. But, as a writer and political activist, it was the First Amendment that most impressed him. Surely, here was an instrument to enable the United States public to hear all opinions, however unpopular they might be with the government of the day.

It saddened my heart to have to tell him the story of how the *New York Times* had fired correspondent Jo Thomas for writing the truth about the North of Ireland. Gerry had read her columns and described her as the only honest and impartial reporter the paper had ever sent to cover the Six Counties. We stood for a moment considering what chance he, as Margaret Thatcher's *bête noire*, might have of ever getting a visa to the United States, if her influence was such as to get an American journalist and citizen fired from what was supposed to be the most prestigious newspaper in the country. But then he brightened and said, "Sure Paul, once J. Edgar Hoover had them all believing you were a communist and a subversive. And here's the good Archbishop praising the rebel Sean MacBride. Some day my hair'll turn as white as yours overnight and they'll think I'm respectable like the pair of you."

He could be right. Perhaps, during the Clinton Administration, the United States State Department will have the integrity to give Gerry Adams the right to freely travel to America to speak his mind, so that all of us may have an opportunity to listen to what this remarkable man and the remarkable people he represents have to say. But that's just the opinion of one eighty-six-year-old Irishman who read the Bill of Rights and Thomas Paine during his first year in this country and was so impressed that he has made their model his life's work. At my age, I do not intend to have any State Department keep me waiting much longer to see Gerry Adams again.

The Mountains Of Mourne

A SHORT STORY BY GERRY ADAMS

Geordie Mayne lived in Urney Street, one of a network of narrow Belfast streets that stretched from Cupar Street, in the shadow of Clonard Monastery, to the Shankill Road. I don't know where Geordie is now or even if he's living or dead, but I think of him often. Though I knew him only a short time and many years ago, Geordie is one of those characters who might come into your life briefly but never really leave you afterwards.

Urney Street is probably gone now. I haven't been there in twenty years, and all that side of the Shankill has disappeared since then as part of the redevelopment of the area. Part of the infamous Peace Line follows the route that Cupar Street used to take. Before the Peace Line was erected, Lawnbrook Avenue joined Cupar Street to the Shankill Road. Cupar Street used to run from the Falls Road up until it met Lawnbrook Avenue, then it swung left and ran on to the Springfield Road. Only as I try to place the old streets do I realize how much the place has changed this last twenty years, and how little distance there really is between the Falls and the Shankill. For all that closeness there might as well be a thousand miles between them.

Excerpted from *The Street*, Sheridan Square Press, New York, 1993

When we were kids we used to take shortcuts up Cupar Street from the Falls to the Springfield Road. Catholics lived in the bottom end of Cupar Street nearest the Falls; there were one or two in the middle of Cupar Street, too, but the rest were mainly Protestants till you got up past Lawnbrook Avenue, and from there to the Springfield Road was all Catholic again. The streets going up the Springfield Road on the right-hand side were Protestant and the ones on the left-hand side up as far as the Flush were Catholic. After that, both sides were nearly all Protestant until you got to Ballymurphy.

When we were kids we paid no heed to these territorial niceties, though once or twice during the Orange marching season we'd get chased. Around about the Twelfth of July and at other appropriate dates the Orangemen marched through many of those streets, Catholic and Protestant streets alike. The Catholic ones got special attention, as did individual Catholic houses; the marching bands and their followers, sometimes the worse for drink, excited themselves with enthusiastic renderings of Orange tunes as they passed by. The Mackie's workers also passed that way twice daily, an especially large contingent making its way from the Shankill along Cupar Street to Mackie's Foundry. The largest engineering works in the city was surrounded by Catholic streets, but it employed very few Catholics.

Though I'm often bemused by expressions such as Catholic street and Protestant area, I find myself nonetheless using the very same expressions. How could a house be Catholic or Protestant? Yet when it comes to writing about the reality it's hard to find other words. Though loath to do so, I use the terms Catholic and Protestant here to encompass the various elements who make up the Unionist and non-Unionist citizens of this state.

It wasn't my intention to tell you all this. I could write a book about the *craic*—the good fun—I had as a child making my way in and out of all those wee streets on the way back and forth to school or the Boys' Confraternity in Clonard or even down at the Springfield Road dam fishing for spricks, but that's not what I set out to tell you about. I set out to tell you about Geordie Mayne of Urney Street. Geordie was an Orangeman, nominally at least. He never talked about it to me except on the occasion when he told me that he was one. His lodge was The Pride of the Shankill Loyal Orange Lodge, I think, though it's hard to be sure after all this time.

I only knew Geordie for a couple of weeks, but even though that may seem too short a time to make a judgment I could never imagine him as a zealot or a bigot. You get so that you can tell, and by my reckoning Geordie wasn't the worst. He was a driver for a big drinks firm; that's how I met him. I was on the run at the time. It was almost Christmas of 1969 and I had been running about like a blue-arsed fly since early summer. I hadn't worked since July and we weren't getting any money except a few bob every so often for smokes, so things were pretty rough. But it was an exciting time: I was only twenty-one and I was one of a dozen young men and women who were up to their necks in trying to sort things out.

To say that I was on the run is to exaggerate a little. I wasn't wanted for anything, but I wasn't taking any chances either. I hadn't slept at home since the end of May when the Royal Ulster Constabulary, the RUC, had invaded Hooker Street in Ardoyne and there had been a night or two of sporadic rioting. Most of us who were politically active started to take precautions at that time. We were expecting internment, or worse, as the civil rights agitation and the reaction against it continued to escalate. Everything came to a head in August, including internment, and in Belfast the conflict had been particularly sharp around Cupar Street. This abated a little, but we thought it was only a temporary respite: with the British Army on the streets it couldn't be long till things hotted up again. In the meantime we were not making ourselves too available.

Conway Street, Cupar Street at the Falls Road end, and all of Norfolk Street had been completely burned out on the first night of the August pogrom; further up, near the monastery, Bombay Street was gutted on the following night. These were all Catholic streets. Urney Street was just a stone's throw from Bombay Street, if you were a stone thrower.

The drinks company Geordie worked for was taking on extra help to cope with the Christmas rush, and a few of us went up to the head office on the Glen Road on spec one morning; as luck would have it

I got a start, together with Big Eamonn and two others. I was told to report to the store down in Cullingtree Road the next morning, and it was there that I met Geordie.

He saw me before I saw him. I was standing in the big yard among all the vans and lorries and I heard this voice shouting: "Joe! Joe Moody!"

I paid no attention.

"Hi, boy! Is your name Joe Moody?" the voice repeated.

With a start I realized that that was indeed my name, or at least it was the bum name I'd given when I'd applied for the job.

"Sorry," I stammered.

"I thought you were corned beef. C'mon over here."

I did as instructed and found myself beside a well-built, red-haired man in his late thirties. He was standing at the back of a large empty van.

"Let's go, our kid. My name's Geordie Mayne. We'll be working together. We're late. Have you clocked in? Do it over there and then let's get this thing loaded up."

He handed me a sheaf of dockets.

"Pack them in that order. Start from the back. I'll only be a minute."

He disappeared into the back of the store. I had hardly started to load the van when he arrived back. Between the two of us we weren't long packing in the cartons and crates of wines and spirits and then we were off, Geordie cheerfully saluting the men on barricade duty at the end of the street as they waved us out of the Falls area and into the rest of the world.

Geordie and I spent most of our first day together delivering our load to off-licenses and public houses in the city center. I was nervous of being recognized because I had worked in a bar there, but luckily it got its deliveries from a different firm. It was the first day I had been in the city center since August; except for the one trip to Dublin and one up to Derry I had spent all my time behind the barricades. It was disconcerting to find that, apart from the unusual sight of British soldiers with their cheerful, arrogant voices, life in the center of Belfast, or at least its licensed premises, appeared unaffected by the upheavals of the past few months. It was also strange to catch glimpses on television of news coverage about the very areas and issues I was so involved in and familiar with as we made our deliveries. Looked at from the outside through the television screen, the familiar scenes might as well have been in another country.

Geordie and I said nothing of any of this to one another. That was a strange experience for me, too. My life had been so full of the cut-and-thrust of analysis, argument, and counter-argument about everything that affected the political situation that I found it difficult to restrain myself from commenting on events to this stranger. Indeed, emerging from the close camaraderie of my closed world, as I had done only that morning, I found it unusual even to be with a stranger. Over a lunch of soup and bread rolls in the Harp Bar in High Street I listened to the midday news on the BBC's Radio Ulster, all the time pretending indifference. The lead item was a story about an IRA convention, with media speculation about a Republican split. It would be nightfall before I would be able to check this out for myself, though a few times during the day I almost left Geordie in his world of cheerful pubs and publicans for the security of the ghettos.

The next few days followed a similar pattern. Each morning started with Geordie absenting himself for a few minutes to the back of the store while I started loading up the van. Then we were off from within the no-go areas into the city center. By the end of the first week the two of us were like old friends. Our avoidance of political topics, even of the most pressing nature (that unspoken and much-used form of political protection and survival developed through expediency), had in its own way been a political indicator, a signal, that we came from "different sides."

In the middle of the second week Geordie broke our mutual and instinctive silence on this issue when with a laugh he handed me that morning's dockets. "Well, our kid, this is your lucky day. You're going to see how the other half lives. We're for the Shankill."

My obvious alarm fueled his amusement.

"Oh, aye," he guffawed. "It's all right for me to traipse up and down the Falls every day but my wee Fenian friend doesn't want to return the favor."

I was going to tell him that nobody from the Falls went up the Shankill burning down houses, but I didn't. I didn't want to hurt his feelings; but I didn't want to go up the Shankill either. I was in a quandary, and I set about loading up our deliveries with a heavy heart. After I had only two of the cartons loaded I went to the back of the store to tell Geordie that I was jacking it in. He was in the wee office with oul' Harry the storeman. Each of them had a glass of spirits in his hand. Geordie saw me coming and offered his to me.

"Here, our kid, it's best Jamaican rum. A bit of Dutch courage never did anyone any harm."

"Nawh thanks, Geordie, I don't drink spirits. I need to talk to you for a minute..."

"If it's about today's deliveries, you've nothing to worry about. We've only one delivery up the Shankill and don't be thinking of not going 'cos you'll end up out on your arse. It's company policy that mixed crews deliver all over the town. Isn't that right, Harry?"

Harry nodded in agreement.

"C'mon, our kid. I'll do the delivery for you. Okay? You can sit in the van. How's that grab you? Can't be fairer than that, can I, Harry?"

"Nope," Harry grunted. They drained their glasses.

"I'll take a few beers for the child, Harry," Geordie said over his shoulder as he and I walked back to the van.

"You know where they are," said Harry.

"Let's go," said Geordie to me. "It's not every day a wee Fenian like you gets onto the best road in Belfast..." he grabbed me around the neck "...and off it again in one piece. Hahaha."

That's how I ended up on the Shankill. It wasn't so bad, but before I tell you about that, in case I forget, from then on, each morning when Geordie returned from the back of the store after getting his "wee drop of starting fuel" he always had a few bottles of beer for me.

Anyway, back to the job in hand. As Geordie said, we only had the one order on the Shankill. It was to the Long Bar. We drove up by

Unity Flats and on to Peter's Hill. There were no signs of barricades like the ones on the Falls, and apart from a patrolling RUC Land Rover and two British Army jeeps, the road was the same as it had always seemed to me—busy and prosperous and coming awake in the early-winter morning sunshine.

A few months earlier, in October, the place had erupted in protest at the news that the B Specials* were to be disbanded. The protesters had killed one RUC man and wounded three others; thirteen British soldiers had been injured. In a night of heavy gunfighting along the Shankill Road the British had killed two civilians and wounded twenty others. Since then there had been frequent protests here against the existence of no-go areas in Catholic parts of Belfast and Derry.

Mindful of all this, I perched uneasily in the front of the van, ready at a second's notice to spring into Geordie's seat and drive like the blazes back whence I came. I needn't have worried. Geordie was back in moments. As he climbed into the driver's seat he threw me a packet of cigarettes.

"There's your Christmas box, our kid. I told them I had a wee Fenian out here and that you were dying for a smoke."

Then he took me completely by surprise.

"Do y' fancy a fish supper? It's all right! We eat fish on Friday as well. Hold on!"

And before I could say anything he had left me again as he sprinted from the van into the Eagle Supper Saloon.

"I never got any breakfast," he explained on his return. "We'll go 'round to my house. There's nobody in."

I said nothing as we turned into Westmoreland Street and in through a myriad of back streets till we arrived in Urney Street. Here the tension was palpable, for me at least. Geordie's house was no different from ours. A two-bedroom house with a toilet in the backyard and a modernized scullery. Only for the picture of the British Queen, I could have been in my own street. I buttered rounds of plain white bread and we wolfed down our fish suppers with lashings of Geordie's tea.

---

* A part-time branch of the Ulster Special Constabulary, the B-Specials played a leading role in the August pogroms.

Afterwards, with my confidence restored slightly, while Geordie was turning the van in the narrow street I walked down to the corner and gazed along the desolation of Cupar Street up toward what remained of Bombay Street. A British soldier in a sandbagged emplacement greeted me in a John Lennon accent.

"'Lo, moite. How's about you?"

I ignored him and stood momentarily immersed in the bleak pitifulness of it all. The charred remains of the small houses sat below the wise steeples of Clonard. The world-weary slopes of Divis Mountain gazed benignly in their winter greenness down on us where we slunk, blighted. It was Geordie's impatient honking of the horn that shook me out of my reverie. I nodded to the British soldier as I departed. This time he ignored me.

"Not a pretty sight," Geordie said as I climbed into the van beside him.

I said nothing. We made our way back through the side streets on to the Shankill again in silence. As we turned into Royal Avenue at the corner of North Street he turned to me.

"By the way," he said, "I wasn't there that night."

There was just a hint of an edge in his voice.

"I'm sorry! I'm not blaming you," I replied. "It's not your fault."

"I know," he told me firmly.

That weekend, subsidized by my week's wages, I was immersed once more in subversion. That at least was how the Unionist government viewed the flurry of political activity in the ghettos, and indeed a similar view was taken by those representatives of the Catholic middle class who had belatedly attached themselves to the various committees in which some of us had long been active. On Monday I was back delivering drink.

We spent the week before Christmas in County Down, seemingly a million miles from the troubles and the tension of Belfast town. For the first time in years I did no political work. It was late by the time we got back each night and I was too tired, so that by Wednesday I realized that I hadn't even seen, read, or heard any news all that week. I smiled to myself at the thought that both I and the struggle appeared to be surviving without each other; in those days that was a big admission for me to make, even to myself.

In its place, Geordie and I spent the week going up and down country roads, driving through beautiful landscapes, over and around hilltops and along rugged seashores and loughsides as we ferried our liquid wares from village to town, from town to port and back to village again; from market town to fishing village, from remote hamlet to busy crossroads. Even yet the names have a magical sound for me and at each one Geordie and I took the time for a stroll or a quick look at some local antiquity.

One memorable day we journeyed out to Comber and from there to Killyleagh and Downpatrick, to Crossgar and back again and along the Ballyhornan Road and on out to Strangford, where we ate our cooked ham baps and drank bottles of stout, hunkering down from the wind below the square tower of Strangford Castle, half-frozen with the cold as we looked over toward Portaferry on the opposite side, at the edge of the Ards Peninsula. We spent a day there as well, and by this time I had a guidebook with me, written by Richard Hayward. I kept up a commentary as we toured the peninsula, from Millisle the whole way around the coastline and back to Newtownards. By the end of the week we had both seen where the Norsemen had settled and the spot where Thomas Russell, "the man from God knows where," was hanged, where Saint Patrick had lived and Cromwell and Betsy Grey and Shane O'Neill. We visited monastic settlements and stone circles, round towers, dolmens, and holy wells. Up and down the basket-of-eggs county we walked old battle sites like those of the faction fights at Dolly's Brae or Scarva, "wee buns," we learned, compared to Saintfield, where Monro and seven thousand United Irishmen routed the English forces, or to the unsuccessful three-year siege by the Great O'Neill, the Earl of Tyrone, of Jordan's Castle at Ardglass. And in between all this we delivered our cargoes of spirits and fine wines.

This was a new world to me, and to Geordie too. It was a marked contrast to the smoke and smell and claustrophobic closeness of our Belfast ghettos and the conflicting moods that gripped them in that winter of 1969. Here was the excitement of greenery and wildlife, of rushing water, of a lightness and heady clearness in the atmosphere, and of strange magic around ancient pagan holy places. We planned our last few days' runs as tours and loaded the van accordingly; whereas in the city we took the shortest route, now we steered according to Richard Hayward's guidebook.

On Christmas Eve we went first to Newry, where we unloaded over half our supplies in a series of drops at that town's licensed premises. By lunchtime we were ready for the run along the coast road to Newcastle, skirting the Mournes, and from there back home. At our last call on the way out to the Warrenpoint Road, the publican set us up two pints as a Christmas box. The pub was empty and as we sat there enjoying the sup a white-haired man in his late sixties came in. He was out of breath, weighed down with a box full of groceries.

"A bully, John," he greeted the publican. "Have I missed the bus?"

"Indeed and you have, Paddy, and he waited for you for as long as he could."

Paddy put his box down on the floor. His face was flushed.

"Well, God's curse on it anyway. I met Peadar Hartley and big MacCaughley up the town and the pair of them on the tear and nothing would do them boys but we'd have a Christmas drink and then another till they put me off my whole way of going with their *ceili*-ing and oul' palavering. And now I've missed the bloody bus. God's curse on them two rogues. It'll be dark before there's another one."

He sighed resignedly and pulled a stool over to the bar, saluting the two of us as he did so.

"John, I might as well have a drink when I'm this far and give these two men one as well."

He overruled our protests.

"For the season that's in it. One more'll do yous no harm. It's Christmas. Isn't that right, John? And one for yourself and I'll have a wee Black Bush meself."

"Will you have anything in the Bush, Paddy?"

"Indeed and I'll not. Now John, if it was Scotch now I'd have to have water or ginger ale or something but that's only with Scotch. I take nothing in my whiskey!"

We all joined him in his delighted laughter.

"What way are yous going, boys? Did you say yous were going out towards Newcastle?" the publican asked us.

Geordie nodded.

"Could you ever drop oul' Paddy out that road? He has to go as far as Kilkeel and by the looks of him if he doesn't go soon he'll be here till the New Year."

"No problem," Geordie grinned. I could see he was enjoying the old man who was now lilting merrily away to himself.

"De euw did eh euw, did eh euw did del de."

"Paddy, these two men'll give you a wee lift home."

Paddy was delighted.

"Surely to God, boys, but yous is great men so yous are. Here, we'll have another wee one before we go. A wee *deoch don dorais.** All right, John?"

"Indeed and it isn't," John told him. "Kate'll be worrying about you and these two lads can't wait. Isn't that right, boys?"

"Well, let it never be said that I kept men from their work," Paddy compromised.

"A happy New Year to you, John." The three of us saluted our host and retreated into the crisp afternoon air.

"It'll snow the night," our newfound friend and passenger announced, sniffing the air. I was carrying his box.

He did a jig, to Geordie's great amusement, when he saw that we were traveling in a drinks van.

"It'll be the talk of the place!" he laughed as we settled him into the passenger seat while I wedged myself against the door. Geordie gave him a bottle of stout as we pulled away.

"Do you want a glass?" I asked. "There's some here."

*One for the road

"A glass? Sure yous are well organized. Yous must be from Belfast! No, son, I don't need a glass, thanks all the same. This is grand by the neck. By the way, my name's Paddy O'Brien."

We introduced ourselves.

"You'll never get a job in the shipyard with a name like that," Geordie slagged him.

"And I wouldn't want it. 'Tis an Orange hole, begging your pardon lads and no offense, but them that's there neither works nor wants."

To my relief Geordie guffawed loudly, winking at me as he did. For the rest of the journey Paddy regaled us with stories of his mishaps in black holes and other places.

"I wouldn't like to live in Belfast, I'll tell yous that for sure. I worked there often enough, in both quarters mind you, and I always found the people as decent as people anywhere else. I was at the building and I went often enough to Casement Park, surely to God I did, for the football and some grand games I saw, but I wouldn't live there. Thon's a tough town!"

"It's not so bad," I said loyally, while all the time looking beyond Paddy and past Geordie to where Narrow Water flashed past us and the hills of County Louth dipped their toes in Carlingford Bay.

"No, give me the Mournes," Paddy persisted. "Were yous ever in the Mournes?" He emphasized "in."

"Nawh," we told him. Geordie began to enthuse about our week journeying around the county.

"Sure yous have a great time of it," Paddy agreed. "I'll come with yous the next time. Work? Yous wouldn't know what work was. But boys, I'm telling yous this. Don't be leaving this day without going into the Mournes. There's a road yous could take, wouldn't be out of your way, so it wouldn't. After yous drop me off, go on towards Annalong on this road, and a wee bit outside the village on the Newcastle side there's a side road at Glassdrummond that'll take you up to Silent Valley. It's a straight road from here right through to Glassdrummond, boys. Yous can't miss it."

"That sounds good to me," Geordie agreed.

"Well, that's the best I can do for yous, boys. Come back some day and I'll take yous on better roads right into the heart of the mountains, but it'll be dark soon and snowing as well and my Kate'll kill me, so the Silent Valley'll have t' do yous. You'll be able to see where yous Belfast ones gets your good County Down water from to water your whiskey with and to wash your necks."

"Is Slieve Donard the highest of the Mournes?" I asked, trying to find my faithful guidebook below Paddy's seat.

"Donard? The highest? It'll only take you a couple of hours to climb up there; but, boys, you could see the whole world from Slieve Donard. That's where Saint Donard had his cell, up on the summit. You'll see the Isle of Man out to the east and up along our own coast all of Strangford Lough and up to the hills of Belfast and the smoke rising above them, and beyond that on a clear day Lough Neagh and as far as Slieve Gallion on the Derry and Tyrone border. And southwards beyond Newry you'll see Slieve Gullion, where Cúchulainn rambled, and Slieve Foy east of there, behind Carlingford town, and farther south again you'll see the Hill of Howth and beyond that again if the day is good the Sugar Loaf and the Wicklow Mountains'll just be on the horizon."

"That's some view," Geordie said in disbelief.

Paddy hardly heard as he looked pensively ahead at the open road.

"There's only one thing you can't see from Donard, and many people can't see it anyway although it's the talk of the whole place, and even if it jumped up and bit you it's not to be seen from up there among all the sights. Do yous know what I'm getting at, boys? It's the cause of all our cursed troubles, and if you were twice as high as Donard you couldn't see it. Do yous know what it is?"

We both waited expectantly, I with a little trepidation, for him to enlighten us.

"The bloody border," he announced eventually. "You can't see that awful bloody imaginary line that they pretend can divide the air and the mountain ranges and the rivers, and all it really divides is the people. You can see everything from Donard, but isn't it funny you can't see that bloody border?"

I could see Geordie's hands tighten slightly on the steering wheel. He continued smiling all the same.

"And there's something else," Paddy continued. "Listen to all the names: Slieve Donard, or Bearnagh or Meelbeg or Meelmore—all in our own language. For all their efforts they've never killed that either. Even most of the wee Orange holes: what are they called? Irish names. From Ballymena to Ahoghill to the Shankill, Aughrim, Derry and the Boyne. The next time yous boys get talking to some of them Belfast Orangemen you should tell them that."

"I'm a Belfast Orangeman," Geordie told him before I could say a word. I nearly died, but Paddy laughed uproariously. I said nothing. I could see that Geordie was starting to take the needle. We passed through Kilkeel with only Paddy's chortling breaking the silence.

"You're the quare *craic*," he laughed. "I've really enjoyed this wee trip. Yous are two decent men. *Tá mise go han buíoch daoibh, a cháirde.* I'm very grateful to you indeed."

"*Tá fáilte romhat,*" I said, glad in a way that we were near his journey's end.

"Oh, *maith an fear,*" he replied. "*Tabhair dom do lámh.*"

We shook hands.

"What d'fuck's yous two on about?" Geordie interrupted angrily.

"He's only thanking us and I'm telling him he's welcome," I explained quickly. "Shake hands with him!"

Geordie did so grudgingly as the old man directed him to stop by the side of the road.

"Happy Christmas," he proclaimed as he lifted his box.

"Happy Christmas," we told him. He stretched across me and shook hands with Geordie again.

"*Go n'éirigh an bóthar libh,*" he said. "May the road rise before you."

"And you," I shouted, pulling closed the van door as Geordie drove off quickly and Paddy and his box vanished into the shadows.

"Why don't yous talk bloody English," Geordie snarled savagely at me as he slammed through the gears and catapulted the van forward.

"He just wished you a safe journey," I said lamely. "He had too much to drink and he was only an old man. It is Christmas after all."

"That's right, you stick up for him. He wasn't slow about getting his wee digs in, Christmas or no Christmas. I need a real drink after all that oul' balls."

He pulled the van roughly into the verge again. I got out too as he clambered outside and climbed into the back. Angrily he selected a carton of whiskey from among its fellows and handed me a yellow bucket which was wedged in among the boxes.

"Here, hold this," he ordered gruffly. As I did so he held the whiskey box at arm's length above his head and then, to my surprise, dropped it on the road. We heard glass smashing and splintering as the carton crumpled at one corner. Geordie pulled the bucket from me and set the corner of the whiskey box into it.

"Breakages," he grinned at my uneasiness. "You can't avoid them. By the time we get to Paddy's Silent bloody Valley there'll be a nice wee drink for us to toast him and the border *and* that bloody foreign language of yours. Take that in the front with you."

I did as he directed. Already the whiskey was beginning to drip into the bucket.

"That's an old trick," Geordie explained as we continued our journey. He was still in bad humor and maybe even a little embarrassed about the whiskey, which continued to dribble into the bucket between my feet on the floor. "The cardboard acts as a filter and stops any glass from getting through. Anyway, it's Christmas and Paddy isn't the only one who can enjoy himself," he concluded as we took the side road at Glassdrummond and commenced the climb up to the Silent Valley.

The view that awaited us was indeed breathtaking, as we came suddenly upon the deep mountain valley with its massive dam, the huge expanse of water surrounded by rugged mountains and skirted by a picturesque stretch of road.

"Well, Paddy was right about this bit anyway," Geordie conceded as he parked the van and we got out for a better view. "It's a pity we didn't take a camera with us," he said. "It's gorgeous here. Give's the bucket and two of them glasses."

He filled the two glasses and handed me one.

"Don't mind me, our kid. I'm not at myself. Here's to a good Christmas."

That was the first time I drank whiskey. I didn't want to offend Geordie again by refusing, but I might as well have, for I put my foot in it anyway the next minute. He was gazing reflectively up the valley, quaffing his drink with relish while I sipped timorously on mine.

"Do you not think you're drinking too much to be driving?" I asked.

He exploded.

"Look son, I've stuck you for a few weeks now, and I never told you once how to conduct your affairs; not once. You've gabbled on at me all week about every bloody thing under the sun and today to make matters worse, you and that oul' degenerate that I was stupid enough to give a lift to, you and him tried to coerce me and talked about me in your stupid language, and now you're complaining about my drinking. When you started as my helper I didn't think I'd have to take the pledge *and* join the fuckin' rebels as well. Give my head peace, would you wee lad; for the love and honor of God, give's a bloody break!"

His angry voice skimmed across the water and bounced back at us off the side of the mountains. I could feel the blood rushing to my own head as the whiskey and Geordie's words registered in my brain.

"Who the hell do you think you are, eh?" I shouted at him, and my voice clashed with the echo of his as they collided across the still waters.

"Who do I think I am? Who do you think you are is more like it," he snapped back, "with all your bright ideas about history and language and all that crap. You and that oul' eejit Paddy are pups from the same Fenian litter, but you remember one thing, young fella-me-lad, yous may have the music and songs and history and even the bloody mountains, but we've got everything else; you remember that!"

His outburst caught me by surprise.

"All that is yours as well, Geordie. We don't keep it from you. It's you that rejects it all. It doesn't reject you. It's not ours to give or take. You were born here same as me."

"I don't need you to tell me what's mine. I know what's mine. I know where I was born. You can keep all your emotional crap. Like I said, we've got all the rest."

"Who's 'we,' Geordie? Eh? Who's we? The bloody English Queen or Lord bloody Terence O'Neill, or Chi Chi, the dodo that's in charge now? Is that who we is? You've got all the rest! Is that right, Geordie? That's shit and you know it."

I grabbed him by the arm and spun him round to face me. For a minute I thought he was going to hit me. I was ready for him. But he said nothing as we stood glaring at each other.

"You've got fuck-all, Geordie," I told him. "Fuck-all except a two-bedroom house in Urney Street and an identity crisis."

He turned away from me and hurled his glass into the darkening distance.

"This'll nivver be Silent Valley again, not after we're finished with it," he laughed heavily. "I'm an Orangeman, Joe. That's what I am. It's what my Da was. I don't agree with everything here. My Da wouldn't even talk to a Papist, nivver mind drink or work with one. When I was listening to Paddy I could see why. That's what all this civil rights rubbish is about as well. Well, I don't mind people having their civil rights. That's fair enough. But you know and I know if it wasn't that it would be something else. I'm easy come, easy go. There'd be no trouble if everybody else was the same."

I had quietened down also by now.

"But people need their rights," I said.

"Amn't I only after saying that!" he challenged me.

"Well, what are you going to do about it?" I retorted.

"Me?" he laughed. "Now I know your head's cut! I'm going to do exactly nothing about it! There are a few things that make me different from you. We've a lot in common, I grant you that, but we're different also, and one of the differences is that after Christmas I'll have a job and you won't, and I intend to keep it. And more importantly, I intend to stay alive to do it."

"Well, that's straight enough and there's no answer to that," I mused, sipping my whiskey.

Geordie laughed at me.

"Typical Fenian," he commented. "I notice you didn't throw away your drink."

"What we have we hold." I took another wee sip and gave him the last of it.

"By the way, seeing we're talking to each other instead of at each other, there's no way that our ones, and that includes me, will ever let Dublin rule us."

The sun was setting and there were a few wee flurries of snow in the air.

"Why not?" I asked.

"'Cos that's the way it is."

"What we have we hold?" I repeated. "Only for real."

"If you like."

"But you've nothing in common with the English. We don't need them here to rule us. We can do a better job ourselves. They don't care about the Unionists. You go there and they treat you like a Paddy just like me. What do you do with all your loyalty then? You're Irish. Why not claim that, and we'll all govern in Dublin."

"I'm British!"

"So am I," I exclaimed. "Under duress 'cos I was born in this state. We're both British subjects, but we're Irishmen. Who do you support in the rugby? Ireland, I bet! Or international soccer? The same! All your instincts and roots and..." I waved my arms around at the dusky mountains in frustration "...surroundings are Irish. This is fucking Ireland. It's County Down, not Sussex or Suffolk or Yorkshire. It's us and we're it!" I shouted.

"Now you're getting excited again. You shouldn't drink whiskey," Geordie teased me. "It's time we were going. C'mon, I surrender."

On the way down to Newcastle I drank the whiskey that was left in the bucket. We had only one call to make, so when I asked him to, Geordie dropped me at the beach. I stood watching as the van drove off and thought that perhaps he wouldn't return for me. It was dark by now. As I walked along the strand the snow started in earnest. Slieve Donard was but a hulking shadow behind me. I couldn't see it. Here I was in

Newcastle, on the beach. On my own, in the dark. Drunk. On Christmas Eve. Waiting for a bloody Orangeman to come back for me so that I could go home.

The snow was lying momentarily on the sand, and the water rushing in to meet it looked strange in the moonlight as it and the sand and the snow merged. I was suddenly exhilarated by my involvement with all these elements, and as I crunched the sand and snow beneath my feet and the flakes swirled around me, my earlier frustrations disappeared. Then I chuckled aloud at the irony of it all.

The headlights of the van caught me in their glare. My Orangeman had returned.

"You're soaked, you bloody eejit," he complained when I climbed into the van again.

He, too, was in better form. As we drove home it was as if we had never had a row. We had a sing-song—mostly carols with some Beatles numbers—and the both of us stayed well clear of any contentious verses. On the way through the Belfast suburbs Geordie sang what we called "our song."

> O Mary, this London's a wonderful sight
> There's people here working by day and by night.
> They don't grow potatoes or barley or wheat,
> But there's gangs of them digging for gold in the street.
> At least when I asked them that's what I was told,
> So I took a hand at this digging for gold.
> For all that I found there I might as well be
> Where the Mountains of Mourne sweep down to the sea.

We went in for a last drink after we'd clocked out at the store, but by this time my head was thumping and I just wanted to go home.

As we walked back to the van Geordie shook my hand warmly.

"Thanks, kid. I've learned a lot this last week or so, and not just about County Down. You're dead on, son," he smiled, "for a Fenian. Good luck to you anyway, oul' hand, in all that you do, but just remember, our kid, I love this place as much as you do."

"I know," I said. "I learned that much at least."

He dropped me off at Divis Street and drove off waving, on across the Falls towards the Shankill. I walked up to the Falls. That was the last I saw of Geordie Mayne. I hope he has survived the last twenty years and that he'll survive the next twenty as well. I hope we'll meet again in better times. He wasn't such a bad fella, for an Orangeman.

Cage Eleven

PRISON MEMOIRS BY GERRY ADAMS

Cage upon cage stretches away in every direction. Black tarred roofs and grey metallic ones; black roofs where new cages have replaced those burnt out and grey ones where work has yet to begin. Away to the right the motorway shimmers in the bright sunshine and behind it green fields climb backwards to meet the horizon. The odd farmhouse dots the landscape and a whitewashed church sits comfortably between Long Kesh and the motorway. The British Army posts frown down on the prisoners and nearer at hand screws' watchtowers roast in the heat. Cars and lorries whiz up and down the M1. Two new Brit posts monitor the open ground between the perimeter fence and the motorway itself. That's where Hugh Coney was shot. Out there, between Long Kesh and freedom; between motorway and concentration camp.

Long Kesh concentration camp lies beside the M1 motorway about ten miles from Belfast and near the town of Lisburn; nowadays the British government insists that everyone should call it "Her Majesty's Prison, The Maze." A rose by any other name....

Almost twenty years have passed since Long Kesh was opened and through the years it has been a constant element in the lives of all the members of my family. On any one of the many days since then at

Excerpted from *Cage Eleven*, published by Sheridan Square Press

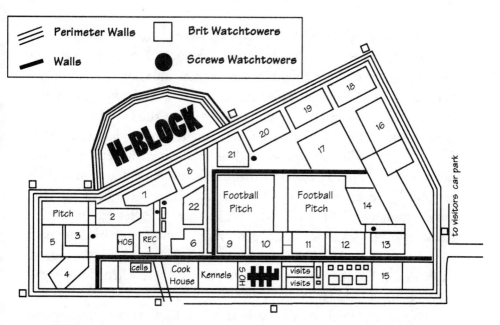

**REPUBLICAN CAGES:
LONG KESH PRISON CAMP**

least one of us has been in there. My father was one of the first to be imprisoned there when he and Uncle Liam and a couple of my cousins were interned without trial in August 1971 in Belfast Prison and transferred to Long Kesh when it opened to its unwilling guests in the following month. My brother Dominic, who was only six when our father was first interned, has been in the Kesh for the last few years, and this year our Sean endured his first prison Christmas. Our Liam did his time a few years ago and Paddy A, our eldest brother, has been in and out a few times. That's all the male members of our *clann*—apart from me, of course, and a handful of brothers-in-law and several more cousins.

Our female family members, like Colette and other wives, sweethearts, sisters, sisters-in-law, aunts, and my mother, have spent almost twenty years visiting prisons. Yet for all that, ours is a perfectly normal family, and we are by no means unique. Long Kesh is full of our friends and the north of Ireland is coming down with families just like ours, all with a similar British penal experience.

Amongst those with whom I was privileged to share Cage Eleven were Bobby Sands, later MP for Fermanagh/South Tyrone and leader of the 1981 hunger strike; Danny "Dosser" Lennon, killed on IRA active service; Kevin "Dee" Delaney, killed in a separate IRA action; and Tommy "Todler" Tolan, killed by the fundraising wing of the Republican Clubs (now Workers Party) faction. There was Hugh Feeney, who endured 205 days of force-feeding in a prison in Britain along with Gerry Kelly and Dolours and Marion Price before the British government gave in to their demand for repatriation to jails in Ireland. There were Brendan "The Dark" Hughes and Brendan "Bik" McFarlane, later leaders in the H-Blocks blanket protests and hunger strikes; Bik was one of those who played a crucial role in the Great Escape of September 1983, the biggest jail-break in Europe since the Second World War, when thirty-eight POWs escaped from H7 in the H-Blocks.

Five POWs died in Long Kesh while I was there. Another one died before I arrived and Henry Heaney passed away after my release. Henry, an old-age pensioner, had been sentenced to fifteen years under a law which makes it an offense just to have it in mind to do something. My abiding memory of Henry is of Sunday mornings before mass as he walked around Cage Twelve in his best suit. Henry was a great wee man and a sound Republican. Three years after his death, ten other sound Republicans were to die in the H-Blocks of Long Kesh. They died, after five years of unprecedented prison protest by over five hundred blanket-men and by women in Armagh, in the heroic hunger strikes of 1981.

Today these cages no longer contain political prisoners, for they are held in Long Kesh's infamous H-Blocks and in other jails. Cage Eleven exists now only in the minds of those who were once crowded into its Nissen huts. It is a memory which reminds us, among other things, that the H-Blocks, like the British regime which spawned them, will one day be only a memory also.

✪

Thousands of men and women have been incarcerated by the British government during this last twenty years. Thousands of wives and mothers and fathers and husbands and children have spent years visiting prisons, and it is they who do the real time. Today there are almost eight hundred Republican prisoners, most of whom are in British jails in the occupied six counties of Ireland. Others are imprisoned in Britain itself or in the Dublin government's custody in Portlaoise and other prisons. A handful are in prisons in continental Europe or in the U.S.A.

Everyone in the nationalist community in the north of Ireland knows someone who is or has been in prison. None of us is immune.

I was first interned in March 1972 on the Maidstone, a British prison ship anchored in Belfast Lough. It was a stinking, cramped, unhealthy, brutal, and oppressive floating sardine tin. We had the pleasure of forcing the British government to close it. A well publicized solid food strike, organized at an opportune time when the government was replacing its old Stormont parliament with an English cabinet minister, ensured the Maidstone's demise. We were airlifted to Long Kesh. A few months later I was released from Long Kesh, but thirteen months after that I was airlifted back in again, this time black and blue after being used as a punchbag in Springfield Road British Army barracks and spending a few days in Castlereagh interrogation center.

Long Kesh had grown: now over twenty cages contained both internees and Loyalist and Republican sentenced prisoners. In the internment area I became the camp's most unsuccessful escapee, but I was consoled by my involvement in the successful elopements of many of my close comrades. I was only caught twice.

In October 1974 we showed our heartfelt appreciation for being interned without trial by joining the sentenced prisoners in burning down the camp and just as it was being rebuilt my escape attempts caught up with me and I received two separate sentences of eighteen months and three years respectively. For a while I was an internee, a sentenced prisoner and a remand prisoner, all at the one time. Then I was moved with other would-be escapees to the sentenced area of the camp. From one cage to another—to Cage Eleven.

I'm in bed at the moment, covered in breadcrumbs and skimpy grey British Army blankets, my knees tucked up under my chin and a blue plastic mug of blue plastic tea in my hand. The eejit in the next bed is doing his staunch Republican bit. "MacSwiney taught us how to die,"* he is saying to his locker, and him only two weeks without a visit. The visits get canceled regularly here. I think we are only entitled to one visit a month; the other three are "privileges" to be withheld as the Prison Governor decrees. After the first visitless week or so men take to their beds. It's not a pretty sight. Your Man has retired for the night already, pink pajamas neatly creased and rosary beads in hand. And it's only seven o'clock.

During such phases the huts here are like some surrealistic limbo; made of corrugated tin sheets, they are unpainted Nissen huts. Leaky, drafty, cold, they are locked up at nine o'clock every night and unlocked at seven-thirty every morning. We're inside them of course: us and our lines of bunk beds, lockers, our electric boiler, a kettle, a row of tables, a television set, and a radio.

Somebody has just decided to brush the floor. Big floors in here, and thirty men lying, sitting, squatting, sprawled and splattered all over it. Nowadays there's thirty to a hut; it used to be worse. There are four or five huts to a cage, depending on the size of the cage; two-and-a-half huts or three-and-a-half for living in; an empty hut for a canteen of sorts, and the other half-hut for "recreation," with a washroom and a "study" hut thrown in. Wired off with a couple of watchtowers planted around, and that's us.

Oh, and the drying hut. I can't forget that. The drying hut is where we hang our wet clothes. When we don't hang them on the wire. The drying hut is also the only place in here where you can be on your own. If nobody else is in it, that is.

All the gates open inwards. They probably do the same outside but you notice it more in here—that's called doing "bird." And everyone walks in an anti-clockwise direction. I don't know why. Internees do it,

*Terence MacSwiney, the Republican Mayor of Cork, who died on hunger strike on October 25, 1920.

Loyalists do it as well. "Will you do a lap?" or "Fancy a boul?" or "*Ar mhaith leat dul ag siul?*" and away you go around and around. And always against the clock. Maybe some instinct is at work. That's the funny thing about this place: a simple thing becomes a matter of life and death. I suppose it has always been like that. If you walk the other way you get the back ripped out of you.

Jail is unnatural. Even the men in this hut are wired up. Imagine thirty men of different ages, the oldest sixty-three, the youngest eighteen, all locked up together for years and years. I don't know how they stay in such good form. A well-informed comrade told me years ago that if he was building a sty for his pigs he could only keep twenty-odd pigs in a hut like this. "Apart from the size," said he, "there isn't enough insulation and the walls must be breeze block or brick." Nowadays when he feels outraged at something or other he is heard to mutter: "This place isn't fit for pigs."

The floor is clean now and some of the boys are waiting for the late news. Sometimes we miss it and then there's a shouting match. Marooned as we are on the desert island of Long Kesh, television has become our electronic window on the world. The news programs are of paramount importance. So is Top of the Pops; it has a consistently large audience while the audience for the news programs goes up and down depending on what's happening outside. News comes from other sources as well. From visits, from rumors. You would be surprised at the rumors which go the rounds here. *Scéal* is the word used to describe the widest possible generalized interpretation of the word "news." It includes real news as well as gossip, scandal, loose talk, rumor, speculation, and prediction.

Much of it is manufactured by my friends Egbert, Cedric, and Your Man. They do it almost by instinct now and the thing about it is that by the time it does the rounds here its source gets totally lost in the telling and retelling, the digesting and dissecting. What starts as an apparently innocent, throwaway remark from any of the aforementioned comrades soon becomes attributed to a BBC newsflash, an absolutely impeccable source on the IRA Army Council, or a senior civil servant in the British Northern Ireland Office. and of course everyone adds their own wee bit; in fact, that's our main pastime. We manufacture it most of the time in our cage and sometimes shout it across to other cages, or we talk at the wire when we are out of the cage for visits, football, or other excursions. We also throw "pigeons" to each other. A pigeon is a well-tied snout (tobacco) tin containing a *sceal* note and a few pebbles for weight. We hurl our pigeons from cage to cage and thus have a line of communication which the screws can't penetrate. If you're a goods thrower, that is.

We drink loads of tea here. The Cage Eleven intelligentsia drink coffee. The water for both beverages is boiled in a communal boiler, which each hut has. Being "on the boiler" means being Gunga Din the water carrier for a day. When I was in solitary once, I was able to make tea from a second-hand tea bag with water heated by placing a water-filled brown paper bag on the pipes. It took eighteen hours and was only tepid but it was still tea. I think. Without milk. Or sugar.

Solitary confinement was condemned as far back as the end of the nineteenth century by a British Parliamentary Committee. Today in Long Kesh Republican prisoners are held in solitary twenty-four hours a day. They are naked, have no contact with the outside world (newspapers, letters, visits, etc. are stopped), no exercise facilities. Solitary confinement is an unpleasant, soul-destroying and mind-bending experience. Imagine yourself locked in a coal-shed for a week, naked, with no means of communicating with the world outside. Imagine the uproar if this activity were uncovered in South Africa or South America. Yet it is happening now, and only a few hundred yards from where I write.

In between praising the awful food and manufacturing *sceal*, receiving *sceal*, discussing *sceal* and passing on *sceal*, we read a wee bit, back-stab each other a wee bit, talk a great deal and engage in a little sedition, which is mainly a matter of getting to understand the political situation which has us in here in Long Kesh. This process is occasionally revealing, sometimes amusing and always, next to *sceal*, the most time-consuming activity of most sane POWs. Other, less sane POWs make handicrafts but that's a habit I've avoided so I can't really comment on it. A lapsed handicrafter told me once of his belief that the making of harps, Celtic crosses, purses, handbags, and even soft toys, was addictive.

Painting hankies with colored marker pens was, he believed, less serious—merely a phase all POWs go through.

We also go through phases of depression—the big D. On the
outside marriages break up, parents die, children get sick; all normal
worries intruding into our impotent abnormality. Some comrades have
nervous breakdowns. Some do heavy whack. Comrades also die in here
through lack of medical facilities and in one case a British Army bullet,
and people are dying outside all the time as the war goes on. It all has its
effects in this bastard of a place. That's one thing POWs have in common: we all hate Long Kesh. But we try not to let it get us down.

Screws: *Wee, Strong, Weak, Scruffy, Nasty*

I HOBBLED TO the doctor's during the week. Luckily I had been able to
time the spraining of my ankle to coincide with the weekday hours in
which the prison regime allocates a doctor for the thousand or so prisoners here. I was feeling pretty pleased with myself because if you are
going to sprain your ankle (or anything else for that matter) in Long
Kesh there's nothing like getting the time right. Timing is everything. If
you make a mess of that you could die waiting for the doctor to come.
On the other hand, if you're perfectly healthy it's pretty good *craic* going
to see the doctor here. For one thing, it gets you out of the cage.

First stop is the cage gate. It opens into a wee wire tunnel. That's
where the screws rub you down. Out of the tunnel (the regime calls it an
air-lock) then out, via the other cage gate. A brisk hobble takes us to the
wicker gate in the wall which now surrounds our cages. All movement of
prisoners is recorded at each gate. Passage through all gates is accompanied by your screw shouting "one on" or "one off" depending on whether
you're leaving or arriving. The screw on gate duty then makes his mark
in a little ledger, denoting your departure from or arrival into the area
controlled by his gate. All very elementary. Three gates within yards of
each other with screw at each one. Big screws, wee screws, strong
screws, weak screws. Screws of all shapes and sizes: smart, clean, regi-
mental screws; washed-out, bogging, scruffy screws. Security screws,

visit screws, sports screws, friendly screws, and nasty screws. Screws performing all kinds of functions, every role programmed to suit their capabilities. Every role programmed to subvert our attitudes.

Beyond the wall now and on to the road which runs alongside the visiting boxes. Lots of muck about the place. Building workers escorted by screws, sentry-boxes inhabited by screws; screws in vans, screws at gates, screws to-ing and fro-ing—all programmed, all functioning well. When I feel fit enough to go to the doctor's I have my own special screw to keep me company. He is a remarkable piece of humankind—a right pockel. I pause, he pauses; I hobble fast, he hobbles fast; I stop, he stops, I smirk at him, he smiles shyly back; I glare at him, he looks away; I address him as "my good man," he grins stupidly; I ignore him, he observes me sleekitly. I go to the doctor's, he goes to the doctor's.

I think he really hates me. Deep inside his blue uniform, I reckon he really, really harbors a burning hatred for me. Like, I'm not sure of that, of course, but the majority of screws here behave, most of the time, as if they hate the prisoners.

Just me and him then. Almost at the doctor's. Brit watchtowers within range, more building workers, the whole place being assembled on grip-work and overtime. Out of the ashes one more gate to go. Only one more screw to pass: this one is a breakthrough in time and motion. Usually they train two screws for complicated performances like that. One to open gates, one to do the names. This looks like an experiment, something like the one-man buses when they came out at first. Inside another cage now, my screw following closely. I'm glad we both made it. I tell him this and ask him, in my most regal tone, to open the door. He scurries forward, fumbles, gets embarrassed, succeeds. I ignore him and we step inside, me into a partitioned "waiting room," he into a corner.

No one else about. I examine the graffiti: "P.J. Can we ask for a retrial?" "Wee Arthur, 15 years! Wait for me Sadie I love you," "6 into 32 won't go," "This place is hereby renamed Lourdes—if you get cured here it'll be a miracle," "Bump," "Jim O'Toole, 12 years," "Mickey"...a whole wall of them. An interesting but unprintable one on the windowsill. Another one about that much-maligned old Italian Republican, Red Socks himself. The place is pigging. I sit down. My screw looks away again. A young lad comes in: a skinhead haircut, tattoos across his knuckles. He's a YP—a young prisoner. There is a swelling below his left eye, a bruise on his forehead. He sits down, ill at ease; I grin at him, ignoring the screws, and offer him a cigarette. He takes two drags while the screw has his back turned and then hands it back to me. The poor kid is frightened to death. He still hasn't spoken a word.

"Do you want some snout?" I ask. I give him another drag and wait for his answer, feeling protective, disdainful of the screws.

Suddenly he leans across to me: "Can you get a complaint made about a screw?"

"Aye, I'll get our OC to see the Governor."

"It's about———. He beat me up. He beats all of us up." His words rush at me in a frenzied whisper. He hesitates, then, "———is a bastard. He beats us up all the time. He's the worst screw of the lot."

The screws at the door must know what he's telling me. They must know what's happening. They pretend they don't. They ignore us. The YP gets cockier and pockets the cigarettes I give him. He is about fifteen or sixteen, pale-faced bar the bruising. I ask him for his name. He gives me his surname. He looks uncomfortable again as I leave. I hear the screws say something. I go into the doctor's.

More screws—three of them in white coats. Clean screws called medics. We examine my leg together. I wince, they wince; I explain how it happened, they nod their heads sympathetically. The doctor prescribes something or other. The screw with the pen calls me mister. I wonder how they will deal with the YP. I consider telling the doctor about him, just to get rid of my frustrations, just to get shouting a bit. Then I look at them all and I feel lost for a second. They know there is something wrong: they're programmed for that eventuality. They move away and I go out. Past the YP. He pretends he doesn't see me. Past the screws, who look sheepish. My own personal screw tags along behind me and we hobble back. Back past the gates, across the road. When my screw slips in the muck I mutter "idiot" at him.

I notice heavy cable beside the wicker gate: they must be going to make it automatic. I pass more screws. We head for the cage, but I hobble past our cage toward the next one. My screw follows uncomplainingly. I talk with our Camp OC at the wire, giving him a rundown on the YP's complaint. Afterwards my screw and I part company at our cage gate. I ignore him. He says goodbye. He uses my first name. I come through the gates, in by the tunnel. Through the next gate and across the yard. He heads off toward the gate in the wall.

Inside the hut I drink my tea. Outside the huts the screws continue their patrols. Outside our cages they hunch against the wind. At their gates they jangle keys. In sentry boxes they huddle against the cold. Don't ask me why they do it. I'm not programmed like they are so I couldn't give you an answer. It took the British army, the RUC, a British judge and a few Special Branch men to get me in here. Screws serve their sentences voluntarily.

Well, they do so for a lucrative wage plus overtime. I don't really hate them. I'm not so much against anything or anybody, it's just that I'm for a lot of things. None of them includes screws.

They are out there now, outside this hut, hunched against the wind huddled against the cold. They are out there, outside this window watching in, jangling their keys. They are out there now, they and the British Army, keeping us in here. For the time being anyway.

The Fire: *Bobby Magee In Meltdown*

IT'S SO COLD, if this was school we'd be sent home," Your Man muttered.

"I know," Cedric shivered, "I'm foundered."

" Yous two should be well hopped up," Egbert scolded. He wore a blanket poncho-style over his anorak and his jeans were thrust into knee-high football socks. His head was encased in one of Cleaky's balaclavas and he had football socks also on each hand. He lay on top of his bunk.

"In winter weather you have to wear winter clothes," he observed.

"The last time I saw you dressed up like that you had just burned down the camp," Your Man said.

"It was not I," Egbert protested with a smile, "I was but an inno-cent at large, wandering along life's busy highway..."

"You're in quare form anyway," Cedric interrupted. "It makes a welcome change."

"It must have been a good visit."

"'Twas, 'twas, 'pon my soul it was," Egbert agreed, "'tis wonder-ful the things the love of my life can do beneath a poncho."

"Aye, dead on! But you didn't go out on a visit like that did you?" Your Man asked.

"'Course I did. It was sound as a bell. And Angela said the same as you."

"What was that?"

"That the last time I was dressed like this was after the fire."

"It was just about this time last year," Cedric said. "Remember?"

"I'll never forget it," said Your Man with feeling. "It was the 15th of October. I was never so scared in my life. It was desperate."

"Ah, but you were a poor wee internee. Up in the sentenced end we never flinched," Egbert boasted.

"Houl' on, I don't know about that," Cedric protested.

"We were ready for battle," Egbert continued.

"Aye, bottle or draught," Your Man interrupted. "If it wasn't for the internees you'd be banjaxed. We provided the brains."

"I don't know about that either." Cedric was adamant.

"What do you know?" they both exclaimed.

"I know as much as you two anyway. I kept a diary. I still have it. I had it on me during the fire and the fighting, then I dumped it when the Brits overran us. I smuggled a copy out afterwards but if you want to read the original I'll get it for 'yous, so I will. I've dumped it away in a handy place."

"Okay," the others agreed, "that would be interesting."

"Right," said Cedric. "I won't be long."

He returned a few minutes later with a small packet wrapped in polythene. He unfolded his bundle carefully and passed a handful of soiled and creased pages to Egbert.

"They're stinking!" Egbert protested, "I thought you said it was a diary!"

"I hid them in a sewer. That's why I still have them. They were too smelly to send out. And they are a diary," Cedric confirmed. "Look!"

He took the pages from Egbert and spread them on the floor. His audience leaned over and read intently.

"*Saturday October 12*: Nearly six weeks now without food except for a half pint of milk and three rounds of bread daily. We have been refusing the prison food because after numerous representations by our staff to the prison regime the food continued to disimprove so we protested by dumping it over the wire. The prison regime retaliated by stopping our food parcels. We are also draping bed-linen on the cage wire in protest at the lack of clean sheets. Clean linen is supplied very irregularly, sometimes every six weeks. These protests have settled into an easy-going pattern. Everyone is in good form. The biggest excitement was when we discovered a dozen rounds of moldy bread in wee Harry's locker. He couldn't eat it without butter, he said.

"*Sunday October 13*: Things may be building up to a head. There was a meeting between the various OCs today. Months ago they presented a list of all the main points of contention to the Prison Governor. These included food, laundry, general living conditions, education facilities (or the lack of them) and the treatment of remand prisoners. It was when the prison administration refused to move on any of these that the present protests started. Today there is *scéal* about a major build-up of British troops around the visiting area. This is why I'm speculating that things may be coming to a head. Some time ago, after particularly vicious beatings on a Brit raid, our staff warned that if the British Army came into the cages to beat or baton men then we would burn the camp to the ground. Some men sent their clothes and other effects out with their visitors this afternoon.

"*Monday October 14*: Semaphore is being used to signal messages between the internées' cages and the sentenced end of camp. There is also a lobby building up, especially among our escape fanatics, that there should be no burning unless accompanied by a major escape. In our cage Your Man is arguing that as long as the perimeter is secure the British government will be unaffected, except in the short-term, by the camp being burned. He argues that burning the camp has no more potential than merely publicizing for a few weeks the conditions in here. But a mass escape under cover of fire, aimed at putting hundreds of men outside—either through tunnels or by storming gates or the perimeter—would advance the entire struggle, he says.

More men sent their clothes out today.

"*Tuesday October 15*: It's now really the 19th October and I'm writing this in a makeshift shelter of blackened, sooty, corrugated tin. The huts in our cage are no more. They disappeared in what has come to be the most unusual and dramatic days of my young life. The trouble started on Tuesday in Cage Thirteen. A screw made derogatory and sexual remarks about some lad's wife. The OC of the cage asked that the screw be removed from the cage. This is a long-standing arrangement between our staff and the prison regime. Our people have never abused it and the ordinary screws and SOs willingly work this procedure. It cuts down on any real aggro between them and the POWs. It has always suited us both. This time the senior screws (probably on orders) refused to comply with Cage Thirteen's OC's request to remove the offending screw. Reinforcements were put into the cage. There were scuffles. Our lads put all the screws out of the cage. The Prison Governor then arrived. He insisted that the POWs involved should come forward and go voluntarily to the punishment block. This was another breach of a long-standing and mutually beneficial arrangement whereby our Camp OC would usually be brought to the cage involved, to direct if necessary the men to the cells. The Prison Governor ordered that this was not to happen on this occasion. He warned that if the men did not come forward the British Army would come in and forcibly remove them. When the camp OC heard of this he sent word to the Governor reminding him of the Republican commitment to burn the camp if the British Army were used.

He asked that the matter be deferred until the following morning to allow things to cool down. It was almost lock-up. The Governor
refused that request. The OC then asked permission to go to Cage
Thirteen. The Governor refused that request; also he ordered all screws
out of the sentenced cages. They withdrew without any interference
from our lads. The Camp OC then sent word again to the Governor that
if the British Army were brought in the camp would burn.

He got word back that the Governor was no longer in charge.
The British Army was in control.

Down here in the internee end we knew nothing of all this. I
only picked up the *scéal* afterwards. Funnily enough I was at a cage staff-
meeting to discuss Your Man's idea about coupling any future burning
to an escape. The OC of the internees had earlier agreed to an informal
request to put this idea to the Camp OC up at the sentenced end. Your
Man was just doubling up by formalizing his request. We had just
agreed to do just this after a good discussion when someone burst into
the half-hut where we were meeting and told us he thought the sentenced end was burning. When we rushed outside a single black plume
of smoke was ascending heavenwards up at the top end of the camp. Me
and Your Man and Todler were delegated to check that no one was left
behind. As we went around, all the huts were well ablaze. It was a bit
eerie. Kathleen Thompson had sent me in a Kris Kristofferson LP.
Someone must have been playing it when the trouble started because
amidst all the confusion and smoke and flames "Bobby Magee" was
blasting out, and going slower and slower as the heat reached it. That
will be one of my abiding memories of the Long Kesh fire.

When we left the cage the screws were already formed up across
the big space between the cages to prevent us joining up with the sentenced end. The screws were assembled down at the visits. At first I
thought they were peelers. Maybe they were. There were none of our
lads near us as we three cut across. It was scary. The cage lights were
smashed but the screws saw us in the big searchlights. They fired rubber
bullets and gas. The gas was definitely CR gas. Not CS. I know the taste
of CS. I swallowed some of the CR. It's difficult to describe the sensation. It's like choking on balloons which inflate to fill out and smother

your windpipe and your lungs. I remember thinking this must be what it's like to drown.

When our cage assembled one man, a Derryman, was missing. Some of us went off and found him. I don't know how. He had got lost in all the noise and confusion. His nerves were gone.

Things were hectic for a wee while. Apparently, though none of us knew this, the idea was to try and join up with the sentenced men. Some internee cages had managed to do just that before the screws (or the peelers) cut off the only adjoining road—the Yellow Brick Road as Johnsie calls it—and our staff was trying to decide what to do. Everyone had burned their own cages and we were all milling about. Your Man volunteered to organize things while the staff sorted out their options. Very quickly he formed us all up—and there were a few hundred of us—into ranks. He drilled us for a few minutes until order was restored then we sent our wee foraging squads out to burn places outside the cages. The screws (or peelers) didn't really interfere. Only when we tried to penetrate or breach their lines did they get aggressive. Otherwise they just fired rubber bullets at our burning-squads. It appeared that their orders were to contain us within the camp—or within our part of the camp. They fired CR gas continuously for the first few hours.

When everything burnable was burning we just sat back and admired our handiwork. By this time Your Man's voice had expired so the Hurdy Gurdy man had to act as his megaphone. Three things happened to me. I discovered the Heathen wrapped in a blanket (probably the only POW in the camp with a blanket) and beneath it he was hugging a big mess-tin of sausages. (He gave me one.) God knows where he got them. Then I bumped into Dickie Glen and said to him that I'd love a smoke. He went off and in a few minutes came back and presented me with a Hamlet cigar. God alone knows where he got it.

The last thing was when I was helping John Joe McGirl and I asked him if he was all right. "If you're all right, I'm all right," he answered. His jaw had been broken by a rubber bullet.

"*Wednesday October 16*: After a while we put out scouts to warn of any counter-attacks and we retired into Cage Four. The wounded and the older men were put into what remained of one hut and the rest of us sat about smoking and talking. It was impossible to describe the scene. The whole night and the skyscape was blazing. Every so often a watch-tower would topple over and collapse in a great fanfare of sparks and flames. There were fairly loud explosions going off all over the place. Eventually we located them as exploding Kosangas containers. Occasionally a rubber bullet or gas grenade popped. All the time heli-copters with searchlights circled overhead. Occasionally they dropped gas-bombs.

As dawn slowly eased itself awake the OC of internees told us all to sit in the center of the cage. He was expecting the British Army to come in at first light. He was going to seek a commitment that no one would be ill-treated. As the night lightened into morning I looked around at Big Ted. He and I had been sitting back to back, keeping each other in an upright position. Beneath his beard and all the grime and soot and dirt his face was grey. So was everyone else's. I remember think-ing to myself that mine must be the same color. It suited our environ-ment. Everything around us was in shades of grey: grey wire, ash-grey smoldering debris, soot-blackened timber, charred wooden beams, tar-black tarmac, grey clouded sky, and hundreds of grey-faced men sitting and squatting amidst it all.

Then the Brits came in.

They came squealing and whooping. Psychological, I suppose. We remained silent. That had its psychological effect also. It silenced them. Soon they stood silently outside our cage, facing us. I noticed that they were also grey.

An officer with a megaphone instructed us all to get to our feet. None of us moved; we just sat there silently staring at them. Waiting. Then our OC went forward. He sought assurances of good conduct and asked for the wounded to be taken away. The Brits wanted to ascertain immediately that a certain two internees were not missing; they wanted them brought forward. Our OC refused. Eventually an arrangement was negotiated: the wounded would be taken away; the rest of our men would be paraded by our own staff for ID by screws, and then we would go back to our original cages. All of this would be supervised by screws.

The British Army would do an initial body frisk and then theirs would be a watching brief.

When the negotiations were concluded Harry F paraded us, and as we stood to attention he explained to us what was happening. He did a great job that morning. He made a wee speech and then we moved away from the center of the cage and made room for the British Army. As they filled our space their officer demanded that the two internees he was seeking come forward. Harry F told him again that none of us were being taken away. He suggested that he would escort a screw to where the two men were, and this was done. It was no big deal: the Brits only wanted to check that the two hadn't escaped. As soon as this became known our lads relaxed. Before this the fittest and best of the internees had grouped around the two wanted men. Now some of the lads started wisecracking, challenging individual British soldiers to step outside and all the usual tomfoolery.

Things got a bit hairy again when we were ordered against the wire for a body search. No one moved. One of our staff sorted it out by stepping forward and instructing us to go to the wire. We were there for a good while. Nothing unexpected occurred. Silly digs and the odd knee or kick between the legs, but nothing that equalled razing Long Kesh. We were IDed by a senior screw accompanied by a senior member of our staff. As we walked back to our original cages we became aware of the popping of rubber bullets and gas grenades from the top end of the camp. As I went back into Cage Two this eased off. All was quiet. The Brits were still everywhere.

When Your Man came into the cage he winked at me and pulled a pair of two-foot-long bolt-cutters from where he had them hidden down the leg of his denims.

Essay: *In Defense of Danny Lennon*

ON AUGUST 10, 1976, three young people died in Belfast. Two were young children, the other a young man. Later a third child died, and with his death a young family was almost wiped out. The Maguire family, understandably enough, have condemned the IRA and Mr. Maguire has been forthright in his condemnation of the Republican movement.

I accept his feelings and I can understand that he feels every justification for saying what he did. He has lost his children and no words of mine, nor of anyone else, can hope to encompass the loss which is his. All I can do is to offer my condolences to the Maguire family. If they refuse to accept this, I will understand. If I am condemned as a hypocrite, I will understand. I know there is nothing I can do to break down the feeling of animosity which the families bereaved in the past few years may hold toward those they feel are responsible for their loss.

This letter may be misrepresented or misunderstood by many people, as Republicanism itself has been misunderstood and misrepresented by many people. There can be no defense against that. Readers have the right to form their own opinions about my sincerity and about the sincerity of the Republican movement.

I do not write on my own behalf and I have no authority to speak for the movement. I, on a personal level, and the movement itself as an organization must bear the responsibilty and must face any criticism in the knowledge that we are not always in the best position to justify our stand, our philosophy, and our activities.

We can and we must do our utmost to ensure that everything we do will have the minimum effect on those people with no vested interest in opposing us and we must, on a personal level, ensure that our conduct, our discipline, and our attitude will encourage, not discourage, continued support for the Republican cause.

This letter, then, is to those people who have no vested interest in opposing us. I do not seek to change opinions about myself, about Republicanism, about violence, about the IRA, or the Republican leadership. Think what you will, good or bad about these, I, from Long Kesh, can do little to influence you. Only those Republicans on the outside, by their actions, attitudes and conduct, can do that.

I intend speaking here for the young man who was killed. I am deeply sorry that three young children died. I know that he would feel the same and that he would have done everything in his power to prevent injury or death to those innocent of any responsibility for the situation in which the Irish people now find themselves. Children are always innocent. The Maguire family were not Danny Lennon's enemies and he was not their enemy. They were victims of circumstances created when he was shot dead.

He did not point a weapon at them. He did not drive the car at them. He was dead before the car crashed. That much was conceded by the British Army.

Danny Lennon went out with a weapon against the people he had identified as enemies. He went out against the British Army and he knew the risks he was taking. He did not willingly involve others in that risk and his death, which came as a consequence of his actions, is all the more tragic because a young family died with him. He meant no harm to anyone other than the people who eventually killed him; and even then it was the system they represented which he was opposed to.

Danny Lennon became involved in the Republican movement in August 1971. He came into jail in October 1972 and he was released on April 30, 1976. He did not have to go back to the IRA. Three and a half years in Long Kesh and his time on the run before that left him with no illusions about how hard the struggle for national freedom is nor how easy it is to become confused and demoralized. He knew what he was fighting for and was articulate in speaking about the kind of Ireland that the Irish people could make their own.

He wasn't a young man caught up in violence. Second-timers (those who have been in and out of jail) know what it's about. Danny Lennon cared nothing for myths, for personalities, for glory-hunting. He sidestepped the petty material things which could have been his. He believed in a society where exploitation of people by people would cease. He recognized the sacrifices needed to secure this and he died in circumstances which he had dedicated his life to preventing.

His death, which robbed the Maguire children of their lives, was a contradiction of a life spent fighting for young children such as they.

Danny Lennon recognized that force, with all its hardships and tragedy, can be justified only by those who know what they are fighting for and by those willing to fight, by those willing to share the hardship.

He spent his last few months in this cage reading Pearse and Connolly, updating in his own fashion the threads of our Republican philosophy.

He knew what was right and what was wrong. He was a human being, a young man of twenty-three with a mother and father, brothers and sisters. He had human feelings and weaknesses like the rest of us. Like us all he made mistakes but he was a good young man, a socialist by instinct and an IRA operator by choice. He wanted an Ireland free of the profit motive, free of fighting, free from sectarianism and free from violence. He did not fight for some outdated ideal, for some abstract thing: he fought for a society in which the Irish people could be truly a sovereign people.

You may not accept this. You may believe that violence is never justified. You may have suffered; you may not want any trouble. You may be weary, sick, old or tired. I do not seek to change your attitudes, to rob you of your opinions. I only ask that you accept that the Danny Lennons within the Republican movement would, if given the chance, help to build a society in Ireland worthy of the men, women and children of Ireland and they are engaged in the struggle for this without thought of personal gain or recognition.

To the Maguire family and to the Lennon family I offer my sincere condolences. If I am misunderstood by those who have a vested interest, a political interest, in misconstruing this letter, I accept the consequences. If it is used to attack me or the Republican movement, so be it. If for one minute it allows readers to understand the many Danny Lennons who have been attacked and denounced by people older, greedier and more mercenary than themselves, his struggle will not have been in vain.

For all the dead who died for Ireland and for all the dead who died in Ireland, Jesus have pity. None of us stands guiltless; only our children are innocent. It remains for us to ensure that we build a society in which they will not be robbed of their innocence. Then and only then will we have the peace that ordinary people everywhere deserve and desire.

CRAZIES

**"I WAS CRAZY WHEN
CRAZY MEANT SOMETHING.
NOW EVERYONE'S CRAZY."**

– CHARLES MANSON, 1994

Regarding America Going or Being Nuts

gregory corso

It's said: When the country is sane
the poet is insane;
when the country is insane
the poet is sane
I don't think so
Seemingly I'm always nuts
and you, my dear country
can't spell nuts without you in it

gregory corso

Dear Warren
Hi, so set the Golden Fleece—
Tony Dingham asked me
to submit to your Crazy
issue —
hope U like it —

Dykes

R

Nuts

Incarcerated for Being Queer

LYN DUFF

LAY ON the concrete floor, dazed, my head throbbing where it had hit the wall. Drying the tears from my eyes, I slowly pulled myself into sitting position. It was some time in the afternoon of December 20th, 1991—that was all I knew. Or maybe it was the 21st already. How could I tell? This place had no windows, no way to see the outside world, if there still was one. What was this place?

I looked around at the bare block walls. They were painted Pepto Bismol pink, with dirt, blood and unidentifiable substances smeared all over. I paced; three steps to one wall, six to the other. Then I sat. And sat. And sat. Where am I?!

The question echoed and echoed. Only twenty-four hours before, I had been in the ACT UP Los Angeles office, discussing condom distributions in the high schools. This place, wherever, whatever it was, was a world away from my suburban Pasadena home. Would I ever see my friends, my books, my mother again? Why had she brought me here? And where was here? I sat, and I paced some more. I had been dumped in this room after being strip-searched by first one woman and then another. Funny: they'd always said not to let people touch your private parts, and then my mother brought me to this place where they paid to have strangers stick their gloved hands up my vagina. I sat, and paced, and stared at the wall; bumps and cracks in the paint were never so interesting before.

Then I saw it—scratched in the paint on the floor was a triangle, a small, pink triangle. We are everywhere, even in this place.

So went my first day at Rivendell Hospital, known by the inmates as Rivenhell. I was here, in this place, because I am gay, and the whole idea was to make me heterosexual. I was diagnosed first with "ego dystonic homosexuality," even though I was comfortable with my orientation and had been out for over two years. My diagnosis was then changed (presumably because my mother argued that I was not really a lesbian, that I was just saying that to hurt her). Now they said I had major depression, even though the psychiatric reports done by two of their doctors said that there was no evidence of even minor depression.

I was an incredibly typical teenager. Living with an older sister and my mother, I learned early that my family considered homosexuality to be abnormal. So, at the age of fourteen, when I was coming out to friends, I decided not to tell my mother. It was hard keeping secret what was quickly becoming a most important part of my life.

I threw myself into Los Angeles's gay community, became politically active, and found a girlfriend. My love of art and photography led me to a lesbian weekly photo walk. And my anger about my friends dying led me to ACT UP/LA.

Within a year I had completely adjusted to my new life of secrecy and begun to get careless. Once my sister walked in when I was talking to my friends on the phone about "all the queens on Santa Monica Boulevard." And a few months later I discovered my mother had read my diary. She could probably sense that something was going on and just wanted to find out, although that was entirely the wrong way. I quickly reread my diary only to find there was a poem in it about a girl I liked. Uh—oh. She wouldn't have known it was about a girl if I hadn't put in that line about her breasts. Oh, shit.

A week later I was in a shrink's office explaining that no, I wasn't gay, and my mother had only misunderstood, etc. Maybe I should have told the truth, but it was so much easier just to deny it and not have to deal with the fact that my mother hated gay people and thought we were unnatural.

This was the first of many visits to shrinks I was to make, in an attempt to have me declared "Severely Emotionally Disturbed." In the fall of 1991, through threats and coercion, my mother succeeded in her quest: I would be sent to a locked out of state institution.

I, of course, had no idea what was going on until I found a folder marked "school records." Opening it revealed a stash of letters to the school district and the county Department of Mental Health saying that I was insane and out of control and needed to be locked up.

I immediately started looking for a lawyer. Everyone I talked to said there was no way they would help me—I was under age, had no money to pay them, and didn't have my parent's consent to retain them. Twenty phone calls and a week later someone suggested that I talk to Richard Novak of Public Council's Homeless Youth project. He said they could and would help me.

But it was too late. The problem was that nobody believed it could happen, including me. Everyone said, "They don't do that in the nineties—maybe forty years ago, but not now." I just assumed that if I did get sent to an institution, then a doctor would see me, confirm that a mistake had been made, and release me, after telling my mother she can't do things like that.

Unfortunately that wasn't how it worked. I went to visit my grandparents in San Marino. On December 19, 1991, as we were putting up the Christmas tree, they said they had a surprise for me. I was excited, thinking it was driving lessons, something I had been asking for for a long time. We went out to the car and they told me to get in. I sensed something wasn't quite right, but didn't know what. Then a sweat shirt was thrown over my head and my mother held me down during the long overnight drive.

So. Here I was in a psych hospital in Utah, with a bunch of Mormon doctors who were saying I was insane and would try to "seduce other girls into my lifestyle." I was allowed practically no contact with the outside world. Newspapers, magazines, TV, radio, were all forbidden.

Letters and phone calls were limited to family members only. (My mother sent me—of all things—a get well card.) I soon discovered, though, how to get mail in and out of the building, through higher-level kids and a few staff whom I paid off.

Shortly after I arrived, two kids tried to escape. They climbed up through the ceiling in a bathroom and crawled through the ventilation system. Twelve feet from freedom, the ceiling fell through. Talk about desperation. They had both been in Rivenhell for over a year and a half.

At one point I wrote in my diary, "If there is no other option, then I will become a statistic, I will join the 30 percent of youth suicides that are committed by gay and lesbian teens. I don't want to die, but if I can't escape, even death is better than Rivendell." I was afraid that it would work, that they were making me heterosexual.

And here I was, a fifteen-year-old dyke who never really did anything "bad" beyond the usual adolescent fights with Mom and a messy room. Needless to say, Rivendell scared the shit out of me. I had to get out of there. But—all who had tried to escape had failed. I was determined to be gay and proud and, most of all, free!

Rivendell was an endless hell, every day longer than the last. I never thought it would end, and all I really hoped for was to be free. Free; it's such a short word that means so much; one we throw around every day. America is supposed to be the land of the free and the home of the brave. But I was never free, never able to be myself. Because I was fifteen and queer and that's not okay with some people.

Freedom was a big deal inside. Not having it, because we all knew that free is only something you can be. The staff thought that freedom was privileges. If you were perfect for three days, you got a compliment in front of the group—that was supposed to be freedom. Staff would say if you were good and didn't break any rules, then you could have more freedom. But we knew that freedom doesn't work that way. It's weird, but kids who are locked up seem to have a more highly evolved sense of justice than others three times their age. We knew we weren't free, and that's all we wanted to be.

A lot of the time I think that it would have been better if I hadn't known what was going on, if I hadn't been so out, if I hadn't been so

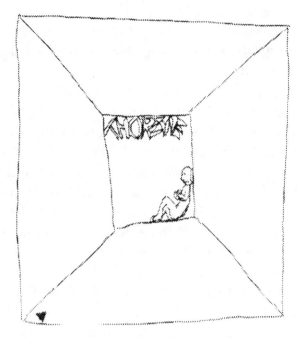

THORAZINE *by Lyn Duff*

aware of what they were doing to us. Many times I wished that the Thorazine I was injected with could make me as stupid as it made some of the other kids; maybe I wouldn't feel the pain of not being free.

So why, you may be thinking, are so many kids getting locked up? Wouldn't somebody do something if they didn't belong there? Good question. Who is this somebody and what could they possibly do? It's very easy in this society to get your child, or anyone for that matter, incarcerated in a mental institution. When I was "evaluated" by the shrinks before I was locked up, they took what my mother said as fact. Everything I said was either ignored or put in quotes. When my mother said I was emotionally disturbed and out of control, they took her at her word, even though it wasn't the truth. Things like staying up late, arguing with your siblings, and even watching a lot of TV, can be called a symptom that fits into one of their "disorders."

My mother first learned about Rivendell from an ad in *Sunset* magazine—but it was the school district that sent me there. So many kids get sent to hospitals and none of us really belonged there. Our "symptoms" were normal, our behavior typical, our feelings were like everyone else's—we were teenagers; teenagers naturally have problems—yet we were incarcerated. The psych industry advertises on TV and in magazines that the solution to problems with adolescents is to lock up your kids. And parents—confused, busy, scared of the world their children are faced with—fall for it. Then the child is identified as having some identifiable disorder, something wrong with him or her that can be "fixed," and the parents are relieved.

In homophobic counseling, teens are told that being gay is abnormal, a sign of sickness, and something they will grow out of. They are encouraged to conform to sex stereotypes by wearing dresses and make up if they are girls, or acting macho if they are boys.

I was also subjected to a word association "treatment"; almost fifty key words were associated with a negative word or phrase. For example, "girls" was associated with "gutter," and "sex" was associated with "the hot fiery pits of hell." After a while, when someone says the word, even in casual conversation, you automatically experience a sense from the associated word. Even today when someone says "sex" I picture in my mind a dirty gutter filled with litter and slimy water.

As if word associations weren't enough, there were also visualization techniques. I was told to imagine putting every romantic thought I had about girls into a box. And then imagine putting the box into a closet and locking the door.

Another type of aversion therapy is giving people medicine that makes them feel like throwing up and then showing sexually explicit pictures of the same gender, or reading horrific stories to them. Later, when you think about the story or the picture, you feel sick.

It was hard to survive. I kept a diary, wrote to my friend Bruce, cried a lot, and even played games with myself. My favorites were mental math (I worked my way up to seven-digit long division) and memory (reciting poems, phone numbers, street names, bus routes, to myself). My diary became a focus point for the anger and frustration I felt at having my life and my humanity wrenched out of my control. I was terrified someone would find it—so I often wrote very cryptic messages.

The "therapeutic treatment "continued for six months. After spending 178 days in hell, I was released to my mother's custody for two days to have jaw surgery. She took me to L.A. and a few hours later, I managed to run. After a week of hiding with friends, I took the bus to San Francisco. On June 28, 1992, twelve days after escaping from a mental hospital, I marched in San Francisco's Gay Pride Parade.

Nearly a month later, I was sitting in a fast food restaurant and in walked my mother, with two cops and a private investigator. The PI pulled out her handcuffs, and I was forcibly returned to Utah. But—by the time we had flown there and driven to the hospital, members of the press were calling. Rivendell's director got on a conference call with Los Angeles County DMH and South Pasadena School District, who had authorized and paid for my confinement. The director told my mother, "We've been getting a lot of interesting calls about your daughter."

My mother looked shocked —she thought no one knew I was there. The director was worried about being sued (I had an attorney now, and she was talking class action), and he kept saying ,"no, no, get her off the property." The person from DMH kept saying I needed a "secure placement" and my mother was crying that I was out of control. Funny, it seemed that the situation was out of control, not me.

To make a long story short, I was sent back with my mother until another hospital could be found. I ran away and lived underground, staying with a different person every few days, for the rest of the summer. Then on September 11, I took my mother to court. I won. Her parental rights were terminated; custody was granted to a lesbian couple, Ora and Rena, whom I live with now.

Years before I was ever hospitalized, I had seen a film about the horrible conditions at state hospitals. It was produced by the Network Against Psychiatric Assault (NAPA) and Madness Network News. The idea that there was a group, somewhere, that was opposed to what they were doing to me, is one of the things that kept me going. A few months ago I joined NAPA. It's been over a year since I escaped, and I'm becoming more active in the mental patients' rights movement. At a recent demonstration against the APA, I saw a doctor who gave shock treatments to the gay kids at Rivendell.

The whole experience of having been locked up has changed me a lot. I'm angry that my childhood was abruptly stolen from me—because I'll never be fifteen and innocent again. I feel a lot different from other kids my own age. I get jealous of them because they seem so trusting and care-free. I'm a lot older than I used to be, and a lot more responsible too. I stand up for what I believe in passionately, and what I believe is that nobody should have to grow up in a psych hospital.

With a few friends, I've started a network for teens who have been or are in psych hospitals and mental institutions. We've started a magazine for kids who are still institutionalized and for others who are concerned with the issue. For the first issue, only 40 people requested copies. Four months and two issues later, our circulation hit 6,000. I hear every day from other kids. They're fighting from inside to get out. And we're fighting the laws so that no kid, gay or straight, ever gets locked up again.

And They Call It Help — The Psy Sector Gulag

LOUISE ARMSTRONG

There is an epidemic of kids being placed in psychiatric facilities by fearful or misguided, or duped, or sometimes vengeful, parents. In 1985, over 270,000 kids under eighteen were hospitalized for psychiatric reasons—more than double the number in 1971. In 1986, four times as many American teenagers spent time on locked wards in private psychiatric hospitals as ten years earlier. A kid running away from violently confrontational or abusive parents could be perceived as "a danger to himself;" a teenage cheerleader might be locked away because she argued with her parents; or a boy institutionalized because he was failing chemistry, which his parents took for a sign of depression.

Competing hospital chains—Charter Medical Corporation, Community Psychiatric Centers (CPC), Hospital Corporation of because she argued with her parents; or a boy institutionalized because he was failing chemistry, which his parents took for a sign of depression.

Competing hospital chains—Charter Medical Corporation, Community Psychiatric Centers (CPC), Hospital Corporation of America, Psychiatric Institutes of America, National Medical Enterprises—launched major advertising and marketing campaigns that blatantly played to both schools and parents. They presented psychiatric institutionalization as a reasonable response to—variously—failing grades, moroseness, moodiness, rebelliousness. Ads flagrantly capitalized on parents' fears of drugs, juvenile justice involvement, teen suicide: "IS YOUR TEENAGER FAILING LIFE?"

Conduct disorders, adjustment disorders, identity disorders, oppositional defiance disorders...under these medical labels we seem to be using psychiatry as a police technology, a form of social control of unhappy, rebellious or non-conforming kids.

But, if we are talking about psychiatry as a policing mechanism, we are also, in recent years, talking about it as ideological imperialism. What the French call the "psy sector"—that is, anything to do with psychiatry or psychology—has laid claim to an ever-growing list of thoughts, behaviors, ideas, feelings, "problems in living," as requiring the psy technology; falling within the psy purview to spot, to evaluate, to prescribe solutions for. And we appear to have ceded the terrain.

Adults, adult women in particular, are subscribing to this expansionism. One bookstore in Maine had an entire aisle, five shelves high, of books on healing (from your own abuse, from your parents' abuse of themselves); on having the courage (to heal, to create); on being an adult child (of alcoholics) or codependent; on hugging the child within.

Since 1952, the bible of coined pathologies has been the Diagnostic and Statistical Manual of Mental Disorders (DSM). It codifies the language reserved to professionals; it offers them the menu from which they can choose the appropriate category for the qualities and behaviors of the object—the person, that is—before them. While any psy professional's judgment might be countered by another's reading of the same object, the object herself, simply by virtue of being the object, cannot contradict the category in which she is placed.

The original DSM in 1952 listed 60 types and subtypes of mental illness. DSM-II, in 1968, doubled the number of disorders, which grew to more than 200 with DSM-III in 1980. DSM-IV, in preparation now, will add more disorders.

As more of the ordinary human problems in living are labeled "mental illnesses," more people will be found to be suffering from them—and therapists can collect health insurance payments from an ever-expanding pool.

The issue for me, as I set out on this journey among kids, parents, professionals, was less the obvious entrepreneurial greed than the increasing dominion of the psy sector over all of human being—now including preadulthood. And the fact of our acquiescence in that dominion, in substitution for all social and political thought. The overall power of psychiatric thinking as an accepted, unquestioned schematic for describing life—that began to fascinate me; and the ever-shrinking distinction in American life between health and pathology.

In the late 1980s the media was ablaze with stories about the explosion of kids-as-psychiatric-hospital-fodder. Stories peppered the popular journals about programs that paid reimbursement to doctors for programs that used misleading, guilt-producing, or unduly alarming advertising to attract parents. Kids were not so much being "physician-referred." Rather, largely in response to alarm being spread by the mental health establishment, thousands were being parent-volunteered. (The most *conservative* estimate was that 12 per cent of the sixty-three million under-eighteen year olds in America suffer from "clinical maladjustment.")

The mainstream media identified the root cause of the explosive growth of teenage psychiatric hospitalization as the willingness of third-party insurers to cover the costs of inpatient treatment — and their equal reluctance to provide coverage for outpatient treatment. It was explained that if insurers were to cover outpatient treatment, hordes of America's parents would throng through the gates seeking psychiatry's (unquestioned) benefits.

Media stories of the 1980s almost uniformly led off with indignation that kids, doing normal kid things, were being shut away for one month, two months, six months in private psychiatric hospitals, often dosed with psychotropic medications, placed in restraints, locked in seclusion. By the end of these stories, however, the need for insurance coverage for outpatient treatment was deemed paramount. Virtually no writer seemed to recall the normalcy that had been premised eight paragraphs earlier. None, by the end of the stories, questioned why these normal kids, in conflict perhaps with their parents, or with the ever-more-stringent codes of social conformity that have come to prevail, needed psychiatric "treatment" at all—inpatient or outpatient.

This absence of skepticism about the inherent benevolence of "treatment"—the assumption that, the aberrant hospital scandal aside, such "help" could not do harm—seemed to me to be what gave institutional psychiatry its authoritative power, a power that readily extended into other major social institutions: the schools, the courts, industry—a power that brooked no query. David Richert, a youth advocate from Kentucky, said, "I cannot tell you what it was like to negotiate with psychiatrists about accountability—as we were drafting some of what we thought was model legislation. It was unbelievable. We've negotiated with judges and prosecutors and almost everybody, including the mentally ill. I have never met a more defensive, more patronizing group of people in my whole life than these people"—the psy world.

California has what can be fairly characterized as fake police: private enterprises that offer a "service" to parents and to hospitals. For a fee of some hundreds of dollars, such a service transports juveniles, sometimes forcibly, to treatment programs. Among the many ironies: half the world is frantically warning their kids against talking to, much less getting into cars with, strangers—and others, at least in California, are hiring strangers to talk their kids into getting into cars (and to force them in, if they can't move them with words).

Listening to kids who had done time in psychiatric institutions, the image I got was of a war zone, of kids living and trying to survive in an occupied country. The atmosphere has the strangeness of science fiction, of a world where a sinister actuality is masked by a much-propagandized apparency; where dreadful things are done to kids—and they call it help.

"Why do you suppose," I asked one teenager who had been incarcerated, after she was out, "some kids get targeted?"

"It's their parents," she said. "It has to do with the parents. The psychiatrists support it. They find the parent who's gullible. My mom's always respected psychiatry so much. She has no novels in her house. She has all books by psychiatrists. And the psychiatrists say, 'Oh, I'll take the kids for you. I can make them all better.' And it takes the stress off people.

"But the worst part of it, the scariest part, I think, is that they can really get you to doubt yourself. There are psychiatrists out there that can help you. But another brand of psychiatrist is manipulating. They take the things that you say and—Okay, if you say, 'I am not an alcoholic,' they say, 'Have you ever had a drink?' 'Yes.' 'How old are you?' 'I'm seventeen.' 'So— you're not twenty-one.' 'No.' 'So—you have broken the law. You said you'd never broken the law. And you must be an alcoholic. Why would you break the law just to drink when you're not twenty-one?' They keep doing that."

Acute care facilities are only one brand of psy institution: there are residential treatment centers, "therapeutic" group homes, and "therapeutic" schools. In these, kids are often placed by the *state*—by court order, by welfare, by the education establishment. What is consistent is the strange language and the stranger logic. The first paragraph in the "Welcome" brochure for one such place reads, "Res-Q Ranch is your home while you are away from your home and family. Here you have an opportunity to work on your problems. When that happens, you will return home." I am bemused. One child in this establishment, Mike, is here because his father left him home some nights without adult supervision; Mike was removed from home because of his father's behavior, not Mike's. No matter what kind of "work" Mike does, it will have no effect on Mike's incarceration. The authors of this brochure, as the authors of many similar psy institution brochures, simply do not seem to understand that what they say is incorrect. Their capacity for thought seems to be that seriously impaired; as though their brain cells have been soaking in psy clichés so long that they are no longer capable of recognizing actual circumstance.

Thus, conversations with psy professionals tend to be less than productive—divorced from reality and from the real meanings of words. The language of "treatment" is a language of masks: who, after all, could be against a "structured environment" for kids? Who would argue that a child should not be "restrained" when he is—to use the ubiquitous, all-justifying phrase—a danger to himself or others? Who could be against "thinking time?"

When Bruno Bettelheim died in 1990, that venerated psychiatric leader received glowing obituaries in the *New York Times*, *Washington Post*, *Parenting* magazine...a "pioneer in treating childhood mental disturbances [who left] major contributions to therapy for children," "one of the great figures in American psychology," "a man who left to the world—especially to parents and children—an enduring vision of love, innocence and idealism." But there is now plentiful evidence that Bettelheim was a fraud and a tyrant who browbeat—and beat—the children entrusted to him and manipulated his young charges to serve his own ends: his power over the children, his command of their parents' wallets, and his eminence. In the process, graduates testified, he caused his young charges enormous pain. Yet Bettelheim's routine use of terrorist tactics—unprovoked, erratic, unpredictable violence—was not only known about at the time within the professional community, but was kidded about (he was called Beno Brutalheim). And even when he was recently exposed, the assumption was made that each story was that of an isolated—or"incurable"—case (too tough even for the master). No lesson was drawn about caution in the face of psy speak.

Alida Jatich is the former inmate of Bettelheim's institution who first broke the silence about his Nazi-like regime. Alida is appalled by her parents' credulousness when faced with psy and educational authorities; but, as all of my listening led me to realize, it is a credulousness that many of us share. "My parents," Alida said, "were the kind of people that would slavishly follow anybody who they think is an authority or expert." We hear it again and again—the grip that psy "expertise" holds over adult America, the authority we vest it with, is what facilitates its unchallenged territorial dominance over children, culminating in the psychiatric incarceration of reasonably normal, certainly average, kids.

The net effect of the Bettelheim uproar was—not much. The public was not asked to question the fundamental underlying beliefs that make such things not only possible, but likely; not asked to speculate on their assumption that psychiatric intervention can't hurt. A story that should have served to raise a far larger issue came to rest as no more than a single-instance curiosity.

I felt, as I researched these issues for my book, *And They Call It Help: The Psychiatric Policing of America's Children*, that I was drowning in language with no particular content. The talk is of structure, of goals. The actuality is byzantine rules, restraints, forced drugging, dragging, isolation—all practices that would elicit public outcry were they done in a juvenile justice/punitive framework.

The justifying assumption was that these psychiatric decisions were first and foremost "medical" ones: that they were based on a fixed and reliable determination of definable pathology by a medical professional. Once you enter the psy world, the hypothesis is that you are sick. In some states, there is a hearing at the start of institutionalization—but under California law, for example, at that hearing a child is allowed no representation or friendly witnesses and the psychiatrist who presides at the hearing may well be a member of the staff of the institution that is petitioning for the prospective patient's admission. This is called an "independent" review.

On April 28, 1992, the U.S. House of Representatives Select Committee on Children, Youth, and Families held a hearing titled *The Profits of Misery: How Inpatient Psychiatric Treatment Bilks the System and Betrays Our Trust*. The committee chair, Representative Pat Schroeder, reported that their investigation found: that thousands of adolescents, children, and adults have been hospitalized for psychiatric treatment they didn't need; that hospitals hire bounty hunters to kidnap patients with mental health insurance; that patients are kept against their will until their insurance benefits run out; that psychiatrists are being pressured by the hospitals to alter their diagnoses to increase profit; that hospitals "infiltrate" schools by paying kickbacks to school counselors who deliver students; that bonuses are paid to hospital employees, including psychiatrists, for keeping the hospital beds filled; and that military dependents are being targeted for their generous mental health benefits. According to Schroeder, a briefing she received from the Department of Justice revealed, "psychiatric hospitals and clinics are defrauding government programs and private insurers of hundreds of millions of dollars annually. Patients have been forcibly admitted into psychiatric treatment programs in situations where they posed no threat to the community or themselves. Often patients are subjected to batteries of blood tests, X-rays, shock treatment, and other services. Investigations by the FBI to date have disclosed billings to the government in the hundreds of millions of dollars."

Testimony at the hearing revealed that the Civilian Health and Medical Program of the Uniformed Services (CHAMPUS) showed increased costs of 126 percent between 1986 and 1989—to $613 million in 1989—due almost entirely to the inpatient treatment of children and adolescents. This kind of gives new meaning to "military spending."

It was the testimony of state Senator Mike Moncrief of Texas that "in Texas, we have uncovered some of the most elaborate, aggressive, creative, deceptive, immoral, and illegal schemes being used to fill empty hospital beds with insured and paying patients. Probably the most widely known case, and the one that really started the investigation, involves an adolescent boy who was apprehended at his grandparents' home in San Antonio by employees of a private security firm who were not even certified peace officers—although they flashed large police badges. The firm was being paid between $150 and $450 for each patient delivered to certain private psychiatric hospitals in the area. This young man was admitted to the hospital for a substance-abuse problem without ever being examined by physician. His records show that he wasn't even given a drug test until four days after admission, and the results of the test were negative."

Moncrief's investigation turned up one young woman who was billed for eight, ten, and twelve hours of group therapy each day. And the same patient was billed on one day for thirty-six prescription drugs; her itemized statement showed 8,400 milligrams of lithium. "The Physicians' Desk Reference lists the maximum dose at 1,800 milligrams. This amount of lithium alone or in combination with the other drugs would have been lethal if it had actually been given to the patient."

Moncrief raises the point that it is not just the health care providers who are at fault, but the insurance industry, which "has not offered any acceptable explanations for their failure to monitor and investigate these claims for potential fraud."

What might the explanation be?

Moncrief says that "several major health insurance companies own large quantities of stock in the corporations that, in turn, own private psychiatric and other health care facilities. In my opinion, this is a blatant conflict of interest. What possible incentive is there for an insurer to help hold down costs if, by paying these exorbitant claims, the company will improve the return on this investment and just raise the policyholder's premium to adjust for the escalating health care costs?"

Cozy? But after all, insurance is an industry; we speak of the insurance business. We may be outraged., but we have no reason to be surprised (other than a wistful wish to believe that the insurance we pay for is there primarily to help us in time of need).

Curtis L. Decker, executive director of the National Association of Protection and Advocacy Systems, Inc., recounted further abuses, including an Alabama case where Larry and Patricia Barker, foster parents of an eight-year-old boy, Daniel, were having some difficulty toilet training Daniel. They thought maybe a little counseling might help. "After an initial session Daniel was removed from the custody of his foster parents and placed in a seven-month in-treatment program. The Barkers have alleged that within the treatment center their foster son was overmedicated, put in isolation, and came out a withdrawn and disturbed little boy. The Barkers were restricted from seeing Daniel, permitted only specific and limited visiting hours. Only after the Barkers sought legal and political help nationwide was the boy returned to the family."

The testimony of Russel D. Durrett—from November 1988 through July 1989 the comptroller of Twin Lakes Hospital in Denton, Texas, a Psychiatric Institutes of America facility—was even more detailed and more chilling about gross fraud and corruption. He recounted violations of Medicare regulations, state regulations, Internal Revenue Service regulations, and of acceptable business practices, including:

¶ Psychiatrists were recruited by paying for the establishment of their practices and in addition were paid salaries of anywhere from eight thousand to fifteen thousand dollars a month (for roughly ten hours a week);

¶ The chief medical officer, who might spend two hours a day in the hospital, earned a 50 per cent bonus, while office rent, renovation, furniture, and equipment were paid for by the hospital;

¶ The medical director for the Twin Lakes drug and alcohol abuse program was an ob-gyn physician, not a psychiatrist. He was given a loan of thirty-five thousand dollars with the understanding that as long as the number of patients on the program was above a certain level, the loan would largely be written off.

Psychiatrist Duard Bok, a former hospital employee, testified to abuses he had witnessed in private psychiatric hospitals in North Texas, including:

¶ unlicensed staff members doing work with patients that "involved a certain percentage of them going into hypnotic trance and many of these counselors not knowing nor understanding what was happening to these patients;"

¶ some of these hypnotized patients being given "false memory implantation"—false memories that would stay with them forever.("The reality of their personal history can be irrevocably changed," Bok testified); and

¶ some concoction called "rage reduction therapy"—later amended to pose as "trust development therapy."

About this last item Bok testified, "Not only is there no professionally recognized 'rage reduction therapy,' but it involves holding the young person down by one or more adults while another person usually verbally taunts them and beats him/her in the rib and chest areas, often causing severe pain and bruising.

"In some of the female preadolescent and adolescent patients there was tissue injury in the form of severe bruising incurred in the nipple and breast areas. The nursing staff were concerned about fractured ribs as a result of this procedure."

Further, and arguably most appalling, "Many of these children were probably the victims and survivors of physical, sexual and psychological abuse by their various major caregivers. In these youths the verbal taunting and the beating while being forcibly held down would often have been reminiscent of the type of terrifying abuse many of them had experienced before admission.

"To label that experience 'trust development therapy' was completely ironic. It probably compounded these youths' confusion and mistrust." Probably?

Bok also detailed "double-bind" scenarios: kids who complied were told they were faking it. Kids who did not comply were told they were "sick" or disturbed; they were punished, their passes withheld.

Why didn't nurses or technicians complain? Because these jobs were their livelihood, and because, as whistle-blowers, they would have had difficulty securing other employment. As Bok says,"Hardly anybody addresses the elephant in the metaphorical living room. Woe betide the person who does."

Also, Bok claims, medicated/sedated kids were deprived of sleep—allowed to sleep only between ten or eleven p.m. and five-thirty a.m. "If they fell asleep or misbehaved in school or a therapeutic activity, they were often penalized or it was noted on the record, or reported at the weekly team meeting, that they were unmotivated and/or 'not working their program.'"

Psychiatrists, psychologists, and therapists who referred their patients to the hospitals got, in turn, hospital referrals for postrelease treatment. Those who did not refer patients to the hospitals did not receive referrals from the hospitals. Psychologists and therapists who referred got lucrative contracts to do hospital-based group therapy.

Bok says, "I have knowledge of lies told to patients by their 'team coordinators,' usually chemical dependency counselors who ironically profess to promote spiritually based twelve-step programs, the essence of which is integrity.

Clearly Bok was a renegade, a troublemaker; as the hospital figured that out, they did what these sorts of places do: their executive committee "wrote a letter to the Impaired Physicians Committee of the Texas Medical Association in Austin, claiming that I had become 'incommunicado,' and suggesting that I had become this way as a function of being mentally ill."

There is more—sexual assault of kids by physicians, forging physicians' signatures; paying off recovery hot lines for referrals; bugging phones.

Bok says: "I have heard of cases in Dallas where young people have been confined in four-point restraints in hospital beds or wheelchairs for weeks at a time. I have heard of cases where, recently, children were placed in 'body bags' in Virginia. I have heard of cases in Nevada where people on orders from psychiatrists, and with the compliance of other staff and administration, deliberately and systematically have kept youths awake for several nights at a time 'to break them down.'"

There clearly is a discrete population of children who are born brain damaged; a population that will require some degree of chronic care; a population that is woefully underattended by psychiatry and woefully underserved by society.

And then there is everybody else who is delivered to the psy world. These kids do not have a problem called mental illness (or mental health, or psychiatric impairment or whatever) with a whole host of subsets. They have, rather, the whole range of personal and social problems—from non-comformity, deliberate or otherwise, to adolescent angst, on up to child abuse or other real-life trauma. They are the victims of increasingly unyielding and impersonal and inflexible education establishments; often they are victims of larger social oppressions played out on a first-person-singular plane. Sometimes they are just visited by bad luck.

Sometimes they are ornery. Often enough they are a pain in the neck. Some of them seem to be running for baddest kid on the block.

All these kids are lumped together as disease-ridden or brain damaged or genetically deprived, and the "treatment" visited on them is rote (the steps, the levels, the consequencing, the medication)—the state of affairs itself seems mad.

Because the ideology of psy-think is so entrenched—the use of the medical model, of illness—it seems overwhelmingly out of control, certainly more so than do the kids. Assuming one were to buy the viewpoint that all of these kids, with all their different experiences, are similarly neurologically flawed (and that that is fundamental causation), the treatment response of rules and sin confessing (therapy) is awesomely irrelevant. It is clearly based on a contrary assumption: that the kids are merely spiteful and willful. The treatment the kids receive is the kind of treatment one might rationally design for kids one believed to be not fundamentally ill, but deliberately bad. It is a policing/punishing response, not one of respect, concern, and care.

On the evidence, however, the kids, individually, are not the point. Who they are, what has happened to them, the narrative of their lives and their circumstance—all that is, at most, an afterthought. Many of the psy practitioners I met on this journey struck me as vaguely android: not only did they seem never to have met a child, they seemed never to have been one. By definition, those practitioners who do truly listen to and care about kids cannot wield power in a system that identifies that as unscientific, defiance. The good guys blow the whistle—and are themselves labeled sick.

Psychiatrists, psychologists, and therapists are, to differing degrees, trained to a mind-set. While there is variation in kind as well as degree (and mavericks, rebels, and true befrienders notwithstanding), part of the training is that they know what they are about. That they are experts in wellness and know what it is; that judgment in such matters is their right. And that they deserve to be in control; to make determinations and binding evaluations about those who come or are brought before them. As Carl Jung wrote, "The cure works best when the doctor himself believes in his own formulae, otherwise he may be overcome by scientific doubt and lose the proper convincing tone." To parse what is implied here: numerous doctors might not believe in the value of what they are doing (but keep doing it anyway); there may well be reason for overwhelming scientific doubt; the suppression of that doubt is essential in order to convince. What can this be called except excruciating intellectual fraud?

When applied to massive numbers of children of all manner of personality, circumstance, intelligence, alleged transgression, and where part of the deal is prescription of powerful and potentially toxic chemicals—drugs whose benefits are in doubt but whose potential for harm is recognized*—it is grotesque to allege that this "treatment" is benign; and it is ingenuous of us to imagine that psy intervention can do children no harm.

---

*For instance, "One-third of all children and adolescents treated with antipsychotic drugs in a New York psychiatric hospital developed symptoms of parkinsonism—mainly muscular rigidity and slowed movement—that interfered with daily activities and often persisted for weeks or months after antipsychotic use stopped, researchers report in the October *American Journal of Psychiatry*" (B. Bower, "Antipsychotics Evoke Youthful Concern," *Science News* 140 [November 2,

It is the contrast between the grave potential for damage inherent in psy ideology and practice, and the behavior and beliefs of those vested in the arrangement, that resulted for me, at moments on this journey of discovery, in a sense of breathtaking banality.

Nobody is trying to hurt kids; that's a byproduct. Under the patina of science, kids' troubles—or their troublesomeness—have been reconfigured to constitute market demand. Obfuscation and circumlocution are the recognized coin of the realm.

It is a peculiar idea—that something is medical, and thus curative, because the persons who do it are called "doctor." It is certainly not borne out by psychiatry's history; most especially not by medical psychiatry's history.

Examples abound from the nineteenth century: clitoridectomy as the cure for masturbation. Head-compressing machines with a clamp to the child's hair, another to his underwear, so that if he turned in the night there would be pain. The physician whose solution to bed-wetting was, in boys, to apply to the penis "a tolerably strong current for one to two minutes; at the close, a wire electrode is introduced about two centimeters into the urethra—in girls I apply 'small' sponge electrodes between the labia close to the metaus urethrae—and the faradic current [is] passed for one to two minutes with such a strength that a distinct, somewhat painful sensation is produced."

By comparison, heavy-duty tranquilizers and psychotropic drugs differ mainly in that they are less strenuous for the administrator, more efficient—and more potentially, permanently, damaging (they have been widely likened to chemical lobotomy). Of course they alter behavior. So does electroshock. So does being dropped on your head.

While an inpatient, one young woman, Vicki, 13, was variously dosed up with Thorazine, Mellaril, Cogentin, Stelazine, and other dope. Her description:

"Mellaril is an antipsychotic drug. It's very sedative. The side effects of some of these drugs are just horrible. To me, it's like being tortured. Extremely dry mouth. So that—my tongue would crack. It would hurt to drink anything like orange juice. You'd be extremely sensitive to the sun—

you burn, but it's not like a sunburn. It's—you burn and you itch and you certainly don't tan from it either. I had to stay out of the sun for years.

"You gained weight. Because it slows down your metabolism. It's like your mind turns to cotton candy. It's very hard to think. It's very hard to function. I had no energy. And it works. It really works. It slows you right down. Thorazine injections are extremely painful. It hurts for a couple of days. The shots would be if I would be put in the seclusion room. But I was also on regular doses. Three or four times a day."

In past decades, the American public has been trained away from a social response to problems and conditioned to a kind of psy reflex. Since the psy definition of "health" is "not female," women have been most targeted and been found most susceptible. As Peter Breggin writes, "The woman who seeks help from psychiatry or who is forced into the psychiatric system often is suffering from exactly those issues that feminism attempts to address—the feminine mystique of helplessness and dependency. On the one hand, she has failed in some important aspect of life, often with easily identifiable women's issues underlying her failure. She may be depressed in part because of conflicts related to being a woman. Or she may be anorexic, bulimic, or agoraphobic...obvious women's issues.... On the other hand, by going to a psychiatrist she is doing what women are trained to do best: she is placing herself in a dependent role, more or less at the mercy of an authority."

But it does not stop at the edges of medical psychiatry. A barrage of challenges is constantly issued to women—as women and as mothers—by the media: the women's magazines, the talk shows. The solution is everywhere proposed: seek help for this, seek counseling for that. Warning signs. In you. In your kids. Implicit is this: that psy intervention can't hurt. That you are acting responsibly by "owning" your problems (which, in the peculiar fashion of psy-speak, actually means turning them over to some psy authority's judgment).

Institutions that intersect with the lives of kids similarly believe that psy intervention can't hurt. The same schools that are happy to see Johnny placed on Ritalin by a psy authority would be incensed if Johnny were solicited to buy Ritalin (a relative of speed) on his own, in the schoolyard. The same drug—yet in one instance it would be thought "bad" for the kid. (Or bad of the kid, should he make the purchase.)

The root cause of the epidemic of kids dumped in psych hospitals, of kids placed under psychiatric surveillance, is an ideological virus, one symptom of which is mental mush: the willingness to have our realities and the feelings and actions they engender translated into a language that is able to express only one thing clearly: that those realities and those feelings are due to our deficits. Or to our children's deficits.

As my own journey into the psy world of kids concluded, it was clear only that the private, for-profit psych hospitals remain under blazing attack. Perhaps their prosperity will diminish. More likely they will attempt to mutate, retool the language, reorient themselves to the market as drug-rehab centers or residential treatment centers or re-education farms or learning-enhancement centers or growth-facilitation facilities. It is conceivable that pressure will be brought on insurance companies— despite their own investments—to crack down. But since we really don't know what we are talking about in the first place, it is hard to know— crack down on what? (How can one effectively do this when, if you say you do not cover conduct disorders, it is proclaimed that these are merely symptoms of something else you will cover?) Most likely, insurance restrictions will (in that contrary way of such things) wind up having their major detrimental impact on the acutely or chronically damaged kids—as do current time limits and lifetime caps.

I emerged from this journey convinced that what most needs challenge is that which is least likely to receive it: the entire ideology that empowers the entire psy machine, that places it outside the arena of rationality and blocks rational discourse. An ideology that allows what is called treatment to enter where justice and punishment and concepts of personal dignity and privacy cannot. An ideology that, in its purest imaginable form, is pastoral—one of befriending, of acting to help; but one that has turned mutant beyond recognition, with tentacles everywhere. And with alarming ties to the state.

Adapted from *And They Call It Help — The Psychiatric Policing of America's Children* by Louise Armstrong, Addison-Wesley Publishing Company, 1993.

I Cried,
You Didn't Listen

DWIGHT ABBOTT WITH JACK CARTER

From the outside, I saw nothing but a tremendous wall. Stepping out of the car, I looked up at that wall One of the social workers, a tall thickly built man, led me to a large metal door. I heard the lock click from the inside. It opened slowly, and the man nudged me through that doorway and into a small, white-tiled room.

I can only dimly remember how I was processed into the Los Angeles County Juvenile Hall in November of 1950. I was nine years old. I know I was fingerprinted and a man took my picture. I was also given a set of county-issued clothing before being led to the dorm.

A counselor walked with me across a narrow yard to a large building. The lock clicked open from the inside of that door, too. I stepped through the doorway. The noise was deafening.

There was a fight going on just a few feet from where the counselor and I stood. He completely ignored it. Kids were yelling, running all over the place. Some were as young as seven; others as old as seventeen. I had been placed there because my parents had been seriously injured in an auto accident and couldn't care for me. Others were there because of broken homes. Others because they were criminals.

Two rows of beds flanked my right side, with about twenty beds in each row. To my left was an office from which another counselor was just leaving. Across from the counselor's office was another door. I learned later that it led to the shower area.

The counselor who had walked me to the dorm took me by the arm and scooted me to his office. In a firm voice, he told me about the rules, all of which were being violated when we entered the dorm. There was to be no loud noise, no smoking, and no fighting.

We left his office and walked to the bed he had assigned to me. "Make it up before you do anything else," he said. A moment later, I made my first mistake. I took the blankets and sheets the counselor had given me and laid them on the bed next to mine. A black boy, twice my size and several years older, picked up the bedding and threw it on the floor.

"Watch where you put that, boy," he said. I looked at him but said nothing. I'd never seen a black person before. He scared me to death.

Seeing the other boys watching, he shoved me and asked, "What do you think you're doing?"

I was about to tell him when he took a step forward and hit me square on the mouth.

He'd knocked me to the floor and, along with the pain, I laid there, a very frightened and confused little boy. The black boy began kicking me, and I did my best to cover my head. This went on for what seemed like minutes before a counselor pulled him away from me.

I stood and, crying, saw the other kids watching me. My nose was swollen and bleeding.

"You'll be all right," the counselor said. "You better learn not to mess with anyone. Stop being such a baby."

I was completely confused. I'd never been hit before in my life, much less with a closed fist. I couldn't stop crying, so the counselor slapped me so hard that I rolled over my bed and onto the cold floor.

"You better fight next time," he said. "I'm not here to babysit you."

"That evening, as I learned was done every night after returning from supper, everyone undressed and stood in front of their bed, a towel wrapped around themselves, until it was their turn to shower. Five kids showered at a time, while a counselor sat at one of the tables near us, making sure no one spoke.

He should have been more concerned with what was going on in the shower room.

When it was my turn, I walked into the shower room and saw a couple of older kids holding a young white boy, about my age. He was bent over in front of a black kid, who had his penis inside the little boy's bottom. A Mexican kid held his hand over the boy's mouth, but I could still hear him crying. The bigger kids were about fifteen-years old. Each time the young boy struggled, one of them hit him on the back of his head.

At my age, it was difficult, if not impossible, to understand what was happening. I thought the boy was being punished for something he had done. I knew nothing about sex, of any sort.

I showered quickly, saying nothing to them. Even at that age, I knew instinctively it was best to keep to myself. I had already been beaten badly that day. I had no desire to make anyone mad at me again.

When the entire dorm had showered, the counselors allowed us to sit at tables and talk, or we could lay on our beds until the lights-out call. I stayed close to my bed. Another fight broke out between two of the older children. The counselor let it continue for some time before he broken it up.

When the lights went out, I laid on my bed and cried into my pillow until I fell asleep. I never needed Mom and Dad as badly as I did that night. More than anything, I wanted to go home.

The next day was the same as the first. The noise and fighting were continuous. The older, stronger kids raped the younger ones, who were unable to defend against the attacks.

I cannot honestly say that all the counselors allowed the fights, nor can I say for sure how may knew of the rapes and allowed them to occur. I do know that two counselors not only allowed those things to happen but also encouraged them. Their names were Mr. Alexander, a black man, and Mr. Beeman, a white.

Mr. Alexander would arrange bare-fisted fights, giving cigarettes to the winner. I also watched him observe, from beginning to end, black kids raping white ones.

On my third night at juvenile hall, I was sleeping soundly when Mr. Beeman shook me awake.

He whispered, "I want to talk to you in the bathroom." I had already learned I'd better do what a counselor told me or risk getting punched. I got out of bed and walked to the bathroom. I hoped Mr. Beeman had good news to tell me about my parents. Since my arrival, no one had mentioned them.

I walked into the bathroom. Mr. Beeman closed the door behind us. He took my arm and walked me to the far end of the room. He pushed me face-first against the wall and pulled my underwear down.

"Step out of them," he said.

He played with my penis until it became erect. Then he placed his mouth on it and copulated me for a short time, as I watched in fear and confusion. I felt his finger inside me, and he put his other hand over my mouth and muffled the sound.

I had no idea why he was doing that. I had done nothing wrong. I was very frightened, but I stopped crying so he wouldn't hit me.

"Lay down on the floor," he said.

I laid on my stomach. With his fingers, he rubbed something cold and wet on my rectum. Again, Mr. Beeman put his finger inside me. I tried to get away from him, and he slapped me.

"Don't move," he said.

I looked over my shoulder and saw he had his pants opened. He was rubbing his penis with something from a small can. I started crying, and he reached down and clamped his hand over my mouth so hard that my lips began to bleed. I couldn't breathe and began to panic. I cannot describe the pain of this man ramming his penis inside me, and I seem to be feeling it all over again now as I write this. Never before had I experienced such pain, not even when my arm went through that washing-machine wringer.

Mr. Beeman made strange moaning sounds, then pulled himself out of me and stood. He yanked me up toward him, keeping his hand over my mouth until I stopped crying.

"Put it on," he said, handing me my underwear.

He wiped himself off with a towel then took me to his office. He sat on the edge of his desk and, pointing his finger at me, whispered, "If you ever say anything to anyone about what just happened, I'll make sure you never go home. Now go to bed."

I believed every word he told me, and it has taken nearly forty years now to mention what occurred that night. I walked out of the office, went to my bed and cried myself to sleep.

In the morning, I awoke and walked to the bathroom. Two kids there began snickering and pointed to my bottom. I reached behind me and felt dampness on my underwear. In a toilet stall, I pulled my underwear down and saw a large spot of blood. When I returned to my bed, I pulled another set of shorts from the small dresser and put them on. I was afraid someone would find out what happened. Then I would not go home.

That night, I was in the shower when the black kid who'd beaten me up walked over. Two Mexican boys were with him. They began hitting me, and I began to cry, loudly. I knew the counselor in the dorm area heard me, but he did not come to see what the problem was.

The black kid was grabbing me, trying to hold me still. I felt one of the Mexicans feeling my bottom. Somehow, I broke loose from the black kid's grasp. I ran out of the shower room.

I returned to my bed and was sitting there, catching my breath, when the black kid walked up to me.

"I'm gonna get some of that," he said, pointing to my bottom. "Better not say nothin', boy."

He walked away. I laid down on my bed and thought, "Daddy, what's happening to me?"

Sometime the next week, the counselors took us all out to a field across the compound for recreation. The counselors chose which kids would be on the teams, and a softball game began.

My team was in the field first. We made three easy outs then walked to the backstop fence for our turns to hit. When it was my turn,

I swung a thick, wooden bat a few times to loosen my arms then stepped to the plate. I looked behind me and saw that the black kid who'd beaten me was playing catcher.

For the moment, I wasn't concerned with him. I felt he wouldn't bother me while the counselors were there. I was wrong. As the black kid crouched near the ground, he looked at me with a grin on his face.

The pitcher tossed the first ball. I set myself to swing and felt a hard pinch on my bottom. I ignored it.

As I waited for the second pitch, he did it again. I turned to look at the boy. He winked. I looked back to the pitcher, and I felt the black kid pinch me again.

A sudden rage fell over me, and I turned and brought the bat down onto the top of his head. I put all my strength into that swing. I pounded him several times more, but I remember most that first strike. I can still feel the warm blood that spurted from his head onto my bare chest and arms.

When one of the counselors tried to stop me, I hit him too. Another counselor grabbed me from behind and pinned my arms. Mr. Alexander yanked the bat from my hands, and I looked down at the black kid. I felt a little sorry for him. I learned later he nearly died.

The counselors took me to solitary confinement, where I soon thought I'd go crazy. Maybe I did, in a way. Solitary confinement consisted of a semi-soundproof cell with a bed, sink and toilet. There was small, metal flap in the solid steel door that could be opened only from the outside. Counselors used it to look into the cell. Guards used it for feeding.

Twice daily that great event would occur. Breakfast was always a bowl of oatmeal, two pieces of cold toast and a cup of warm milk. Late at night, I received beans, two pieces of stale bread and an apple or orange. The meals were served seventeen hours apart.

I had no idea how many other kids were in solitary confinement, but we were all awakened at 5:30 a.m. and served breakfast shortly after. A half hour later, a man came through and picked up the bowls. Each boy then was taken individually from his cell and given a shower, alone.

After returning from my shower, I would find that my mattress and blanket had been removed, placed on the floor outside my cell. It would be returned to me at 10 p.m.

I was not allowed any reading material, and the only clothing I wore were jockey shorts and socks. I saw a person only when I was fed, showered and counted. During that time, they refused to speak with me. At no time did I see or hear anyone else inside the solitary unit.

I stayed there for three months. Then, one day, a guard opened the door of the cell and threw me my clothes. His voice was the first I had heard in all that time.

"Your father's here to take you home," he said.

I stood still, frightened. I was unwilling, and unable, to leave the cell where I had sat for 90 days, staring at the walls, seeing no one, convinced that Mom and Dad had forgotten about me, no longer wanting me. I thought if they had wanted me, I would have gone home long before. I thought the counselor was trying to trick me.

He walked into my cell, helped me put my clothes on and led me from the building. I stepped out into the bright sunlight and had to shield my eyes from the sun while we walked to the waiting room. As I breathed the fresh air, I realized I had never before felt so suddenly alive.

Some things about my early life I have forgotten, but I have not forgotten that afternoon; the brightness of the sun, the freshness of the air. The memory remains with me as if it was yesterday. We walked into the waiting room, and I saw Dad. I stood looking at him. I watched a puzzled expression come over his face. Years later, I recalled that look when Dad told me that his eyes told him I was his son, but that mine had told him that his son was no longer there. My father died feeling that had he not dismissed that strange sensation he experienced then, his son's life would have turned out differently.

Dad was quite correct in believing that he was no longer looking at the well-behaved, polite, loving son he had raised. What he saw was a walking time bomb, ready to explode. It took the County of Los Angeles about four months to construct me, behind the walls surrounding that munitions-manufacturing plant they call juvenile hall.

From the first day I returned home until the day they died my parents suffered from my actions. Unconsciously, I sought revenge. People I had not yet met were going to suffer, too, at my hands.

When I reached the legally determined age of responsibility, I had become a predator, having learned how not to become a victim. Incarcerated children are constantly told what to do and when to do it — when to eat, when to sleep, when to talk, when to use the bathroom, when to sit, when to stand. Consequently, I never learned how to make a decision in a healthy manner common to children raised in a family environment. I responded to my pain through a life of stealing, raping and murdering.

Excerpted from *I Cried, You Didn't Listen: A Survivor's Expos of the California Youth Authority*, Feral House Press, Los Angeles

Who's Crazy Now? Florida Offers Serial Killer Ted Bundy A Sweetheart Deal, Railroads A "Bad Girl" To The Chair

PHYLLIS CHESLER

went to Tampa and made a little money hustling. I was hitchhiking home at night. This guy picked me up right outside of Tampa, underneath the bridge. So he's smokin' pot and we're goin' down the road and he says, do you want a drink? So we're drinkin' and we're gettin' pretty drunk. Then, around five in the morning, he says: okay, do you want to make your money now? So we go into the woods. He's huggin' and kissin' on me. He starts pushin' me down. And I said, wait a minute, you know, get cool. You don't have to get rough, you know. Let's have fun....

"I said I would not [have sex with him]. He said, yes, you are, bitch. You're going to do everything I tell you. If you don't I'm going to kill you and [have sex with you] after you're dead, just like the other sluts. It doesn't matter, your body will still be warm. He tied my wrists to the steering wheel, and screwed me in the ass. Afterwards, he got a Visine bottle filled with rubbing alcohol out of the trunk. He said the Visine bottle was one of my surprises. He emptied it into my rectum. It really hurt bad because he tore me up a lot. He got dressed, got a radio, sat on the hood for what seemed like an hour. I was really pissed. I was yelling at him, and struggling to get my hands free. Eventually he untied me, put a stereo wire around my neck and tried to rape me again....

"Then I thought, well, this dirty bastard deserves to die because of what he was tryin' to do to me. We struggled. I reached for my gun. I shot him. I scrambled to cover the shooting because I didn't think the police would believe I killed him in self-defense....

"I have to say it. I killed them all because they got violent with me and I decided to defend myself...I'm sure if after the fightin' they found I had a weapon, they would've shot me. So I just shot them...."

For the first time in U.S. history, a woman faces the electric chair for having killed six men, one by one, in just over a year, after accompanying them to wooded areas off Highway 75 in Florida, a state known for its sun, surf, and serial killers.

The woman is thirty-five year-old Aileen Carol Wuornos, a prostitute. She is Florida's first female serial killer, but she has been treated differently, and even more prejudicially, than Florida's most infamous male serial killer, Ted Bundy.

The statement above, about the threatening and murderous behavior of one of the men she killed, on November 30, 1989, a fifty-one-year-old ex-convict named Richard Mallory, was based on Wuornos' coerced confession and her confession on the stand. Her testimony was dignified, credible and very moving. The jury never heard the self defense aspects of her testimony, which were deleted from her confession by the court. She was rushed to judgement without even the courtesies given Ted Bundy.

The Wuornos case raises the question of whether we have different standards for evil, violence, and insanity: one for men, another for

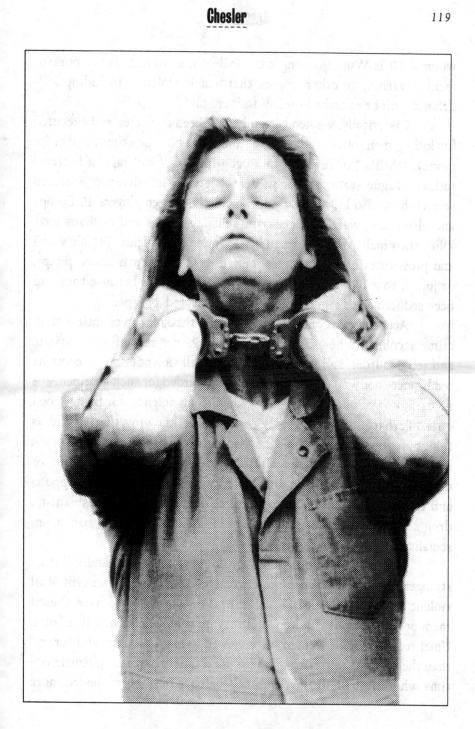

AILEEN CAROL WUORNOS

women? Or is Wuornos simply too evil—for a woman? Is her punishment a warning to other women that female violence, including self-
defense, will be punished swiftly and terribly?

Historically, women certainly have been convicted and executed
for killing men, often with male accomplices but sometimes alone, for
money, "thrills," or revenge, in a drug-induced fit of rage, a battery-
induced fugue state, and/or in death-defying self-defense. Battered
women have also killed children, the elderly, and employers. In Europe
and elsewhere, warrior queens and female soldiers and civilians have
killed their male counterparts in battle and in self-defense. Female slaves
and prostitutes have sometimes injured or killed their masters, pimps,
or johns, to avoid being beaten, raped, or killed, or because they had
been seduced and abandoned, beaten, prostituted, or raped.

According to contemporary studies, though, and countless true-
crime accounts of homicide and femicide, 99 per cent of mass, sexual,
and serial murder, and about 90 per cent of all violent crime, is committed by men, not women. Women are not rewarded for such abstinence—
no cash, no political power, no freedom from violence, for being "good
girls." Perhaps a woman's only reward is in knowing that as bad as
things are, they're even worse for "bad girls." A "bad girl" is any woman
who's poor (or too rich or ambitious for a woman), or non-white, or
unwed, not young, not thin-and-pretty, without strong family support,
and therefore vulnerable to accusations of mental illness, lesbianism,
drug addiction, sexual promiscuity, witchcraft, feminism, paganism,
socialism, etc.

Women do not massacre; nor do they stalk, rape, and kill male
strangers, one by one. When those women who commit 10 per cent of all
violent crimes *do* kill, nearly half kill male intimates who have abused
them or abused their children, and they invariably do so in self-defense.
Until recently, such women were viewed as more deviant and "crazy"
than their male counterparts. Indeed, for a variety of reasons, female victims who kill male intimates in self-defense have been viewed more

*According to a 1991 study by the Council for Prostitution Alternatives, Portland,
Oregon.

harshly than men who, unprovoked, kill their wives and girlfriends, or who kill female non-intimates, especially prostituted women.

Enter Lee Wuornos—a prostitute and lesbian accused of killing six men—a really "bad" girl.

On January 31, 1992, in Daytona Beach, Wuornos, described by the media and countless experts, including the FBI, as the world's first female serial killer, was sentenced to die in the electric chair for the murder of fifty-one-year-old ex-convict Richard Mallory.

I believe that if the State of Florida could, it would electrocute Wuornos once for each man she's accused of killing. But what, really, are her true crimes? Is Wuornos guilty of being a prostitute, a lesbian—"bad"—or is she guilty of daring to defend herself in a violent struggle with a male customer and, by example, encouraging other prostitutes to do likewise?

Most people—and this includes judges, jurors, and lawyers—value men's lives more than women's and empathize with, sometimes even romanticize, men—but not women—who sin. In fact, lawyers, both male and female, often defend male killers pro bono—but not female killers.

A woman's story is rarely believed, by men or even by other women: less so if she's accusing a man of being the aggressor. This is true for both "respectable" women like Anita Hill, Patricia Bowman, or the accuser in the St. John's gang-rape case, and less "respectable" women—like prostitutes.

Female prostitutes are raped an average of sixteen times annually by their pimps and thirty-three times a year by their clients*—not to speak of prostitutes who are mutilated and/or murdered.

Wuornos claims that she killed in self-defense. The jury never got to hear any evidence, apart from her own testimony, that might have helped them evaluate this much-derided claim. For example, according to police who interviewed Jackie Davies (Mallory's ex-girlfriend) and Chastity Lee Marcus (one of two prostitutes Mallory partied with the night before he picked up Wuornos): Mallory served ten years in prison,

---

*The rule allows evidence of a defendant's other crimes or alleged crimes if the court determines that the facts are sufficiently similar.

suffered from mood swings, drank too much, was violent toward women, enjoyed the strip bars, was into pornography, was erratic in business and in trouble with the IRS, and had undergone therapy for some kind of sexual dysfunction. Judge Uriel "Bucky" Blount did not allow Jackie Davis to testify about Mallory's violence toward women.

Wuornos was indigent and was assigned a public defender. The most idealistic and hard-working of public defenders is still too over-worked and lacks the resources to do more than a perfunctory job. Wuornos's had twelve other capital cases in addition to Wuornos's. She asked the judge: "Do I spend all my time on Ms. Wuornos's case and let the others slide? Or do I do it in reverse? I am in a bind." One reporter I spoke with about the case kept needling me for not being cynical enough: "C'mon, Wuornos is not entitled to the kind of lawyer that William Kennedy Smith had. Get real!"

Now, I'm not about to crusade for equal rights for serial killers, but let's look at another Florida serial killer: Ted Bundy, who killed at least thirty and possibly one hundred women. Several lawyers offered to defend Bundy pro bono, an expert advised him on jury selection pro bono; at one point, no fewer than five public defenders assisted Bundy, who insisted on representing himself. (Several lawyers would have defended Wuornos pro bono in the first of five trials, but only if at least $50,000 in expenses could be raised. I became ill and could not raise the funds.)

Even more interesting: the State of Florida offered Bundy a life sentence without parole under the circumstances a sweetheart deal for him; he refused the plea bargain. Wuornos's lawyer tried to set up a similar arrangement for her but one county prosecutor thought she deserved to die and refused to agree to a plea bargain.

Wuornos's trial was exceptionally speedy: only thirteen court days. Judge Blount granted all of the prosecution's and denied most of the defense's motions. The jury saw excerpts from Wuornos's video-taped confession—but only excerpts, without her repeated statements that she killed in self-defense. Under the judge's interpretation of Florida's Williams Rule* the Wuornos jury heard about the other alleged murders. By contrast: William Kennedy Smith's judge disallowed three other allegations of rape—under the same Williams Rule. Blount refused Wuornos's motion for a change of venue, which was based on the enormous, local, pretrial publicity, including excerpts on television from Wuornos's confession. Blount felt that he could seat an "impartial" jury even if they'd seen or heard about the confession and he did so in a day and a half! Given the gravity and the notoriety of the case, the sixty-eight prospective jurors might have been polled individually; they were not. By contrast: Bundy did get a change of venue, from Tallahassee to Miami, for a similar motion.

Wuornos herself was the sole witness for the defense—despite the fact that more than ten mainly pro bono experts were ready to testify for the defense. I know because I organized them. These included a psychologist, a psychiatrist, experts in prostitution, battery, rape, lesbianism, alcoholism, and adoption, among others. One is considered this country's leading expert on battered women who kill in self-defense. Wuornos's attorney turned down these witnesses. No reason was given. Incredibly, no one was allowed to testify for the defense in the guilt-or-innocence phase of the trial except Wuornos herself.

Her testimony on the stand about Mallory's murderous behavior was dignified, credible, and very moving. At midnight on November 30th, 1989, fifty-one-year-old ex-convict Richard Mallory picked up thirty-four-year-old Aileen Carol Wuornos in Tampa. He agreed to drive her to Daytona—nearly five hours away. Based on Wuornos's coerced confession and her testimony on the stand, here is her rendition of what happened that night:After she was convicted, in the hearing to decide her sentence, the jury heard from two psychologists who diagnosed Wuornos as a "borderline personality" suffering from "organic brain syndrome."

Attorney John Tanner, a born-again Christian, had been Ted Bundy's death-row "minister" and tried to have Bundy's execution delayed. Tanner was the lead prosecutor in the Wuornos case; Tanner pushed the death penalty, portraying Wuornos as a "predatory prostitute" whose "appetite for lust and control had taken a lethal turn"; who "had been exercising control for years over men" and who "killed for power, for full and ultimate control."

Wuornos is as conventional as most "good girls." She told me that some of her best friends were johns; she was proud she was able to please her dates/customers/johns; she believes in Jesus; she insists she's not a lesbian. The women who kill violent men are outlaws by default, not choice; they believe in the system. When one realizes she's been had by the system, taken, and that no one will help her, she's invisible anyway, that's when she kills the man who's been breaking her bones for years; the hundredth john who's taking out his knife to cut her face/breasts/anus/vagina; the man who's walking out with custody of her kids and a deed to her home.

When men are accused of crimes—even terrible crimes—their families usually back them. The Kennedy women always stick by their man; Mike Tyson's adoptive mother accompanied him to court daily. Even Bundy had enormous emotional and secretarial/public relations support from his mother Louise and from thirty-two-year-old Carol Lee Boone (whom he would marry and later impregnate), both of whom testified for him. Scores of pretty young women attended the trial and openly flirted with him in court.

Wuornos did have the support of the woman who first contacted her after her arrest and who legally adopted her in November, 1991. However, Wuornos's uncle/brother Barry, twelve years her senior, with whom she had been raised as a sibling and whom she hadn't seen for at least twenty years, testified for the *prosecution*. He claimed that Wuornos had never been "abused" at home and therefore had no "reason" to kill anyone. (I would call what happened to Lee Wuornos "abuse": according to Wuornos, she was abandoned by her biological mother early in childhood, abused and neglected by her grandparental family, raped—presumably by a stranger—and impregnated at thirteen; she surrendered the infant for adoption and, at fourteen, dropped out of school, left home, and lived as a teenage prostitute, alcoholic, panhandler, and occasional thief.)

In Bundy's case, the jury took seven hours to find him guilty and seven and a half hours to sentence him to death. Wuornos's jury of five men and seven women needed only one hour and thirty-one minutes to recommend the death penalty. At nine a.m. the next day, Blount, who could have overridden the jury's recommendation, ordered that Wuornos die in the electric chair. She was immediately taken to death row at the Broward County Correctional Facility for Women.

I am not saying that Wuornos did not kill six men, nor am I saying she's a political assassin or even that she's sane—merely that a strategic use of the insanity defense or the battered-child/battered-woman-syndrome defense might have saved her from the death sentence. In addition, it is still justifiable homicide when a seriously traumatized woman perceives herself in danger, in fact *is* in danger; and kills in self-defense. Wuornos's claim of self-defense against a violent john is plausible. The jury never got to hear that Richard Mallory had spent ten years in prison for crimes of sexual violence. They did not learn what the life of a street prostitute is really like. Wuornos's claim of self-defense certainly merited far more thought and consideration than the deliberate neglect it received from those who heard and tried her case. Blount refused to let the jury hear the special instructions fashioned by the defense to reflect these two considerations.

Wuornos has been under attack all her life, probably more than any soldier in a real war. For years people said: "How can a prostitute be raped?" Now, given what we know about how often prostitutes *are* raped, beaten, robbed, arrested and killed, often by real serial killers, people say: "Well, it's part of the job description. If she doesn't like it, why doesn't she get out?" Wuornos has turned this question around. "If men don't want to be killed, they should stay away from prostitutes or at least stop degrading and assaulting them."

Note: Wuornos has received additional death sentences and has requested no further trials and immediate execution.

Achilles Rizzoli's Sketch of His Cottage

On San Francisco's Bernal Heights Where

He Drew His Imaginary "Expeau," 1935-1945.

Paradise Found

THE HALLUCINATORY ARCHITECTURAL ART OF ACHILLES G. RIZZOLI

THE SPIRIT OF COOPERATION

THE KATHREDRAL...MOTHER SYMBOLICALLY RECAPTURED
(Rizzoli's 1937 birthday greeting to his deceased mother)
30"X50"

TRIBUTE TO A GOOD NEIGHBOR
Mr. and Mrs. Harold Healy Symbolically Sketched   36"X25"

Good Neighbors Make Good Houses

ALEXANDRA ANDERSON-SPIVY

"**O**UTSIDER ART" has sometimes been considered a contemporary mutant of folk art but the two are very different. "Folk art has nothing to do with outsider art, the art of insane people and deviants," said Hilton Kramer in reaction to the second Outsider Art Fair in New York in January. "Folk art came out of a society where people actually made the things that they actually used, a society that just doesn't exist anymore. Anything that calls itself folk art today is a fraud." Outsider art is what Jean DuBuffet first aesthetically validated as *art brut*. The French artist sought out works by isolates, psychotics, and children. Retrieving their images from asylums and hospitals, DuBuffet used his collection (since 1976, it has been the core of the collection at Lausanne's Musée de l'Art Brut) as direct inspiration for his own work.

Art brut actually was rechristened "outsider art" twenty years ago. Now it's become an increasingly troublesome categorization, exploiting the recurring nostalgia of a post-industrial society longing for some kind of artistic innocence, purity, and inventiveness attributed to these frequently disturbed, unacademicized artists, who don't make their art dependent on worldly recognition or financial reward.

There's no consensus on what really constitutes "outsider art." Nobody likes the label but everyone keeps on using it. At its most inclusive, the unsatisfactory term has been a marketing tool for work by artists, sometime compulsive visionaries, who operate far outside the mainstream. The market swiftly has created a tiny but distinct core of identifiable outsider-artist superstars like Bill Traylor, the Reverend Howard Finster, Martin Ramirez, and Adolf Wolfli, whose pictures have escalated in value through the 80s and the 90s.

Achilles G. Rizzoli, the most recently discovered, and arguably the greatest of this select group of visionary artists, is also the most stylistically atypical. The sophisticated variety of his work rises far above the usual repetitiveness and crudities of much that is under the outsider rubric. Rizzoli consistently drew with the sophisticated panache and control of a master. Yet no one could have been more obscure than this San Francisco architectural draftsman who over forty years devoted his spare time to rendering meticulously symbolic site plans and elevations for an ideal city, and composing a 3,600 page third volume of the Bible. Both projects were divinely inspired. Driven by his hallucinatory visions of paradisiacal structures, Rizzoli's work seems to have been one long obsessive meditation. He was probably schizophrenic.

This, and whatever else is known about this true visionary artist is due to the dedication of Bonnie Grossman, owner and director of The Ames Gallery in Berkeley. In July, 1990, a stranger appeared at her doorstep with four of Rizzoli's color drawings and thirty-nine various Bible sheets. Immediately mesmerized by the work, Mrs. Grossman learned that the woman, who was a building contractor, had rescued the drawings from Rizzoli's house as it was being cleared out in 1977 after the artist had had a stroke. Searching the drawings for clues and the phone book for names, Mrs. Grossman worked like a detective and finally tracked down a few family members, who had preserved the rest of the known body of Rizzoli's work, and several friends and neighbors who remembered the slight, taciturn man.

RIZZOLI'S RELIGIOUS WORK
Graphite on Vellum

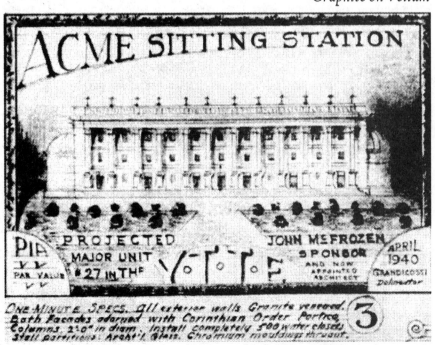

A PUN, AND A PUBLIC TOILET
Detail of diazo print for "Acme Sitting Station" (A.S.S.)

Rizzoli was born in 1896 in Marin County, lived for a brief time in Oakland, and moved to San Francisco when he was fifteen. He lived there for the rest of his life and died in 1981. His parents were first-generation Swiss-Italian immigrants who were Catholic. He was the fourth of five children. His father, a dairy worker, committed suicide when Achilles was nineteen. The suicide became a central symbol in Rizzoli's obsessive personal mythology. In his drawings he encoded the traumatic event as "The Dark Horse of the Festival Year."

Rizzoli never married. He lived with his widowed mother in an increasingly run-down cottage on Alabama Street in Bernal Heights. He spent much of his twenties writing a long, never-published novel about a man who attempts to impress his beloved by designing an elaborate colonnade. In the mid-1930s, at the same time that he went to work as a draftsman for Otto Deichman, a local San Francisco architect, Rizzoli began to create exquisite drawings of his imaginary city. He began his "heavenly inheritances architecturally expressed" in 1935 with the amazing design of a cathedral he dedicated to his mother. (Many of his drawings are what he called "symbolically delineated" portraits of neighbors and friends in which various people are represented as buildings.

His elaborate ink and paper metropolis he named "Y.T.T.E.," an acronym for "Yield to Total Elation." He made detailed portraits of the city's founder and maps showing its location on an imaginary island. He organized the city as a series of pavilions, neo-classical arcades, ornately embellished churches, apartment buildings, meeting halls, and cenotaphs. One projected "major unit" he named "The Shaft of Ascension, in which euthanasia is available to those desiring and meriting a pleasant, painless voyage from this land." Sly humor and puns abound, exemplified by buildings Rizzoli named "Fortress of Modern" DAER (Decorative Architecture Entertaining Royalty), or a decorative public toilet building named the "Acme Sitting Station," whose acronym is ass. Combining the Beaux-Arts, and the Gothic with poster-perfect legends and skyscrapers looking like what architecture critic Eve Kahn describes as "a cross between the Chrysler building and the Woolworth building," Rizzoli created a totally personal pastiche of revival styles to express his heaven-sent vision. Convinced of the significance of his work, for seven years he held annual

. O.A. DEICHMANN'S MOTHER SYMBOLICALLY SKETCHED

Rizzoli's tribute to the longevity of his employer's mother   60"X30"

JANET M PECK
PAINTED PICTOR[E]
LA REG[...]

A.G. RIZZOLI, DEL.
B.C. COPENHAGEN, ASSISTANT

DELLA VISTA DOLORES

PORTRAIT OF JANET M. PECK

A tribute to a friend on Dolores Street.
Banner on upper right reads: "Says she—it takes old
Roman blood to institute the exquisite." 26"X48"

MRS. GEO. POWELSON SYMBOLICALLY PORTRAYED

*Based on the Tower of Jewels from the 1915 Panama-Pacific International
Exposition in San Francisco.   37"X25"*

the Woolworth building," Rizzoli created a totally personal pastiche of revival styles to express his heaven-sent vision. Convinced of the significance of his work, for seven years he held annual exhibits of the drawings in his tiny house. The transcriber of divine messages in a highly developed, systemized inventive vocabulary which contained references to sex, family, eternity, and pleasure advertised the annual show by putting up signs in his window that read "A.T.E." or "Achilles' Tectonic Exhibit." The visitors to his shows were mainly neighborhood children. After 1944, he stopped working on the heavenly project.

For the last nineteen years of his active life, he wrote and illustrated a third part of the Bible, 500 sheets of architect's drafting paper with each page divided into eight sections handprinted and illustrated in black lead pencil. With the help of his family, Bonnie Grossman has reassembled 359 sheets of the manuscript of A.C.E., Rizzoli's "AMTE's (Architecture Made To Entertain's) Celestial Extravaganza." It is a maze of a document dictated by the departed and filled with architectural references and symbols. In tight, elegant print and complex visual codes it records his increasingly baroque hallucinations and fugitive perceptions.

A future museum exhibition and book still in the planning stages will spread the news about Rizzoli's work beyond the few who have now seen his marvelous drawings. The work merits wider attention. For while he may have been delusional, this draftsman dedicated to God was more than another naive outsider artist. He was an American original whose exquisite and poetic art belongs in the mainstream, not on the margins.

[All drawings are ink on rag paper unless otherwise noted.]

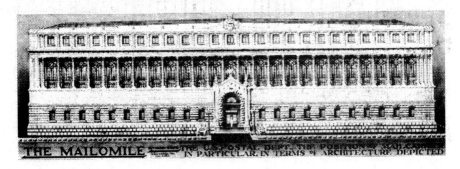

THE MAIL-O-MILE

The mail-carrier depicted in terms of architecture 12"X36"

On Ruth Tarson

WILLIAM KENNEDY

RUTH TARSON WAS in show business in Chicago during the 1930's with Studs Terkel, but he hadn't seen or heard of her since then until I sent him a couple of stories after meeting him last year and discovering their friendship. He read the stories and wrote me: "RuthieTarson is one hell of a wonderful, goofy writer. She is a natural. I am a fan of hers from now on in."

I also gave Ruth's stories to theater and opera director Frank Corsaro and he was so impressed he said this: "Ruth Tarson's stories give a new meaning to urban angst. They are relentless, extremely funny, and very touching. She creates a katzenjammer-Kafka labyrinth of an obsessed soul trapped by her environment."

I've known Ruthie since 1957. She's a very dear friend, a great comedienne, an old lefty, and was on Broadway, in the same show ("New Faces of 1956") as my wife, Dana.

While she wrote a few things as a young woman, she took up fiction seriously only in the last ten years or so, and has written a dozen or so very accomplished long and short stories. She's now 74, and has had two stories published: "Hicky" in the literary magazine *Groundswell*, in Autumn 1987, and another, and "Woman Found Dead in Elevator," in the *Paris Review*, Winter 1990.

Ruth has an absolutely original voice that should be recognized. She's a complex product of old movies, old songs, vaudeville and burlesque gags, a tortured heart, a wit as hilarious and black as Beckett's, and a singular capacity for telling a story sideways and upside down. She doesn't use these stylistic pyrotechnics for their own sake, but rather as the venting of a homegrown talent that has decided this is the only possible way to express itself.

She seems to me the literary equivalent to Grandma Moses, a writer whose career, belatedly but indisputably, is on the move.

The Shadow Knows

RUTH TARSON

LISTEN, I'M sorry; I'm sorry about the great big hoo-ha that's going on here, who ever dreamed that it would come to this; the Shadow dreamed, that's who. The Shadow knows. He knows the evil that lurks in the hearts of men, and, yes, in my own little heart here, and listen, I'm sorry, and I want you to understand exactly what happened here. Not that I know exactly what happened here; the police know, they say they know; who knows, I don't know. The Shadow knows. And maybe if you had said something; yes, you, blondie; you're not so innocent here, you know. But, no, nobody said anything, and now this, this great big hoo-ha here. No, the Shadow didn't say anything; the Shadow doesn't go around saying things, the Shadow knows, that's all he does. Please write to me and let me know how it is with you after all these years. No, I don't know how it's all going to end here; have you seen the papers?

Well, I'm sorry, and I understand you have a whole new life now; well, good, you should. And you don't come back here any more; I understand. It would be too hard to face all that; the house falling down like that, them dead like that, I'm sorry; the ceiling crashing in. And I'm sorry, but they're still there, dead on the floor there, and I have to call the police and the fire department, the pipe is broken. They broke the gas pipe, and the whole block could go up in one giant puff; in one giant hoo-ha here. And you're out there singing and dancing, and I'm sorry; and maybe you could take a minute out from your fancy new life to call the police and the fire department. Tell them there are two dead bodies, and there's a gas leak, the pipe is broken; they broke the gas pipe; and I'm sorry I started this whole thing with you here; and I just wanted to tell you I was sorry that you had to cry; the years flying by. No! don't call the Shadow, he knows; the Shadow knows. I have to go now, I'll be late, I'm due in court; write if you can; I understand how busy you are, but once in a while it wouldn't hurt.

So who knows, really; remember Mrs. Rosewald, she took the gas that time; nobody knows. They called the fire department and the fire department carried her out on a stretcher, and the fire department didn't know. And Mr. Rosewald came running down the block, and he saw her there on the stretcher, and he looked so shocked, and Mr. Rosewald didn't know; and she looked so peaceful, like she had just fallen asleep, and her cheeks were all rosy, not like she had taken the gas, but rosy; like she knew. And I thought wouldn't it be nice to be like that, to fall asleep like that, my cheeks all rosy like that; and to know; to really know. But I couldn't leave you, could I, leave you alone like that. And then you went away anyway; I understand. You had to go, you couldn't stay; who could stay there. Could even the Shadow stay there? Who knows. The Shadow knows.

Oh! Nellie had puppies again! so adorable! I can't bear to give any of them away, but I guess I will; I've already got lots of requests from kids on the block; one of the puppies reminds me of you; a little blondie; so cute; write when you can; I think of you always and maybe some day, who knows, we'll be together again; who knows. Nellie knows; dogs know; even the puppies know; they're only little puppies, but they know. I wish I knew.

No, I'm not angry that you left, you had to go; who could stay there, nobody could stay there. I stayed. Well, I couldn't go, could I, somebody had to stay; I guess that's the way it is; some go, and some stay. I wanted to go; I thought I would go some day; and then the house came falling down, the ceiling crashing in, and they were dead there on the floor like that, and I thought, I'll go now. I'll call the police and I'll call the fire department, and they'll fix the pipe so the gas doesn't leak, and then I'll go; there was nothing to stay for then; but then I couldn't go anyway, I stayed. I couldn't go, I can't go, I don't know. The Shadow knows. He knows the way it goes with those who can't go. I thought I would be glad that they were dead.

And even if I did go, I wouldn't go where you were. I would go somewhere where you wouldn't be; and I would be something, some- where, just as you are something now, somewhere; so beautiful and exciting, and all the men at your feet; but I'm still here. They're dead and gone, dead on the floor there, dead at my feet, but I'm still here.

There was a funeral and they were buried, side by side; I saw them there, dead and buried in the ground there, and they didn't know; they didn't know anything. And I was glad it was over for them, finally; and for me too. I was glad, because then I could go away somewhere and forget it all; and I was glad it was over for you too, because then maybe you could come back. But I knew you wouldn't come back, even if it was over, and I'm sorry; I'm sorry it was that way for you, I'm really very sorry. I would go to an island place somewhere and be an island person, an island beauty somewhere, an island virgin somewhere. But then they might want to toss me into the volcano there, and I don't want to go into any volcano; you go in the volcano if you want to; you be a virgin, you're so smart. I've got a big volcano right here; the pipe is broken here, and the house has come tumbling down; the ceiling crashing in; no, I don't know if the Shadow is a virgin; the Shadow doesn't go around being a virgin, or not being a virgin; the Shadow goes around knowing, that's what he does; the Shadow knows if other people are virgins. He knows if Mr. Rosewald is a virgin, and Mrs. Rosewald; is she a virgin, she took the gas that time; and the fire department and the police department; if they are all virgins or what. No, he doesn't write it down in a litttle black book; he just knows, that's all. He knows I could have stopped them, that's what he knows.

The Shadow knows. I came running in, and I saw them, and I could have stopped them. I had stopped them before, many times; and sometimes, I think I know, I think they were sorry about what they were doing; I think so, but I don't know. And they didn't stop, they didn't stop what they were doing and I said, let them do it then, I won't stop them any more, and I think they were surprised that I didn't stop them; that I let them go on and they went on and on, and it was getting to be over, and I heard the walls come tumbling down, and the ceiling crashing in, and I ran out and I called the police and the fire department, because there was a leak in the gas pipe. But you weren't there then, you were gone by then; I know you had to go; I know that you don't know; and I'm sorry, but you're fine now; and all the neighbors came running. Mr. Rosewald, his wife took the gas pipe that time, and she looked so peaceful, like she had gone to sleep; and old lady Matanky, she always used to yell at us, we played ball in front of her house; and the grocery and the bakery; none of them knowing. And they all asked for you, and I told them you weren't there any more, that you had gone away quite a while ago; and they don't know, none of them knows. The Shadow knows.

I have to run, I have to catch the special bus that goes to the cemetery; I get out and stand by their graves and it's really nice there, you know, and I don't know; and I wish you were here; so that's it, I guess; so take care, so so long for now, for forever, right?

There was a trial and everything, a really big hoo-ha trial; the defendant will please rise; I had a lawyer and everything; they think I did it, they say I killed them; daughter kills parents; a regular Lizzie Borden, that's me; it's up on appeal; that's what they say, who knows.

No, I don't wish you were dead, though I really could kill you sometimes; but I would be killing myself then too, wouldn't I, the way I killed a part of myself when I killed them; that is, if I killed them; they say I killed them; they say I'm going to be in the electric chair; there's not supposed to be any pictures, but the reporter is strapping a camera to his ankle and is going to capture the whole thing on film and they'll run it front page; maybe they'll make a movie of it; I'll be a star, I'll be a bigger star than you are; I'm the who in the hoo-ha.

Maybe I shouldn't have killed them; or maybe I should have killed them sooner; when you left; that would have been a good time; then we could have gone away together; although if they were dead, maybe we wouldn't have wanted to go; I mean, why leave; it would be nice without them. Or maybe you wouldn't have wanted me to go with you; maybe you just wanted to go away period, from them; from me.

Listen, I'm glad you went; it's good to go, if you can go, to get away, if you can, to just leave it all behind. No, I'm not angry. Well, yes, I'm angry sometimes; I miss you; I think of you a lot; you are always in my heart, right. There's a fire engine outside, I can hear them coming, hear their sirens, and the police too. Remember the firemen that time they carried out Mrs. Rosewald, she took the gas that time; I remember; I remember the whole block came running; and now everybody is going to come running to see them carry me out; I wonder if there'll be a fire-man. Policemen will be there, I know, and I hope there's a fireman too; a policeman and a fireman; I really don't know; hey, listen, do you want a ticket; I think I can arrange it; I think you're allowed a certain number of tickets; family and friends; hey, maybe you could come early and have dinner with me, I get a last request, I'm sure I could order for two; chicken and ribs, maybe, or Fluky's hot dogs; remember Fluky's.

Think about it, and let me know; that is, if they do it; that is, if I did it; they don't have a case, it's all circumstantial; hey, if they say I did it, then I did it; I'm not arguing; I'm not saying I didn't do it; I'm not say-ing I did it; I stand mute before the court. So the question is, if I didn't do it, who did it; who done it.

No, I will not plead insanity, temporary or otherwise; if I did it, I did it; I did it in a moment of pure sanity; or an intruder did it; that could be who done it; or Mr. Rosewald, his wife took the gas that time, she looked so peaceful, her cheeks all rosy, like she was asleep, maybe Mr. Rosewald did it; or old lady Matanky, she used to yell at us all the time, we played ball in front of her house, maybe she did it; or the gro-cery did it, or the bakery did it. Or you did it. Yes, you, blondie. I'm not saying you did it, you weren't even here, were you; you were there, wherever there is. Miss Starr, Miss Wonderful, Miss Glamourpuss. Miss Stealthy, that's who, and you could have come in the middle of the night, Miss Stealthy, and nobody knew you were here, and done it, and then gone back and left me with it; and of course, they're going to say I did it, who else could have done it; such dead bodies on the floor there, such matricide and patricide; and the defendant will please rise; and did I do it; or was I sleeping; was I sleeping innocently in my bed. Yes, I still have the bed. The same little bed.

Is that you; is that you standing there in the doorway; boy, am I glad to see you; have you come back, or did you never leave; were you here when they died, when the house came falling down, when the ceiling came crashing in, and I had to call the police and the fire department and the gas pipe was broken; were you here then, were you always here then. Hey, wait a minute, where are you going; don't leave me now when you just got here; we'll go to the corner and have a chocolate phos, we'll have a Green River, we'll have a lemon Coke.

I'm going to tell them that you did it; I'm going to be an I witness; I'm going to say that I was sleeping in the little bed where we both used to sleep, and your blonde curls would fall on the pillow; and I heard a noise, like someone in sneakers; you had those white Keds, and you looked so cute in them, and the way you used to run, so fast; you could tell right away you were going to be something; something special, running like that, and winning like that; always winning every race. And I always wanted to be like you; you were the one; but I wasn't like you, I was like me; you can't change these things. and I heard this noise and I got up, and there you were, doing it to them; and they started to scream, and the house came falling down, the ceiling crashing in, and the pipe broke; and you ran away without even saying goodbye to me, without even saying: look, I did it, I did what you always wanted to do. I saw it with my own eyes, my own big brown eyes, while your eyes were blue; so kiss me now, and goodbye; toodle-oo.

The puppies are starting to walk now; they get out of the box by themselves and they walk around; I've got to keep an eye on them, they could get out; they could wander away; they could get lost somewhere; lose their way somewhere; I try to keep the door closed, and Nellie watches them; but still, the first thing I do when I get home is count the puppies; a regular mother hen, that's me.

They don't have any real proof, it's all kind of circumstantial, some people saying they heard me saying I wished they were dead; but who wouldn't say that, everybody says that; I've also said I wish I was dead; but does that mean that I wish I was in the electric chair, or something? I wish this whole thing would go away, this whole hoo-ha here. The house hasn't been fixed yet, I live in the rubble that was left when it all came tumbling down, the walls and the ceiling; I sleep in the little bed; hey! yes, it survived; the same little bed we both slept in; I'd watch you sometimes as you lay there asleep, your blonde curls falling down around the pillow; you had the blonde curls and I had the dark, and I'd wonder what would happen to you; what would happen to all of us; who knows nobody knows.

I know; I'll tell them you did it, and you'll have a big trial, and the reporter will strap a camera to his ankle and take a picture of you, and it'll be page one; and I'll be a star because you can't be a star any more, because you did it; the defendant will please rise; or did I do it; or did they do it; hey, maybe the puppies did it; who knows, nobody knows

They are so adorable; their eyes are open and they're all over the place now; yes, they can walk; they can get out of the box now; you should see them, they are so cute; try and make it, and let me know, if you know; no, I don't know; I've got to go now, I hear the fire engines, the gas pipe is leaking; they're going to give me the gas pipe, just like Mrs. Rosewald who took the gas pipe that time and she looked so peaceful, her cheeks so rosy; maybe I'll look peaceful, my cheeks all rosy; and here they come now, I can hear the sirens, so hurry up and let me know; I'll be waiting to hear from you; I think about you a lot, and I hope you think about me sometimes too.

Is that you? Is that you standing there in the doorway; I can see your curls, I can see the outline of your curls in the moonlight; have you come back, or did you never leave; if you never left, then you know what happened here, and you must tell me, so I'll know; come lie down beside me on the little bed where we used to sleep; put your head on the pillow, tell me everything.

I've really got to run, it's been a terrible day, and I haven't had a minute to myself, what with this and that; I've got to pick up my laundry, and I've got to go to the bank, and I absolutely have to stop on the corner and pick up some milk, I've got to feed the puppies; I pour some milk into a big saucer and they lap up the milk with their little tongues, and they're dribbling the milk on their chins, they are so cute.

I've found good homes for all of them; they'll be good, they'll be great; yes, I was tempted to keep one; the one that reminds me of you; the little blondie, yes; but I'm going to let her go; I'm sorry; but it's best to let go, to go on, right? And I've really got to go now; I've got a date; I'm going to meet the Shadow; we're going to take a little walk; me and my Shadow, strolling down the avenue; he's got something to tell me; the Shadow knows; all alone and feeling blue, the Shadow knows; and who knows; some day, maybe, I will know; I will know what the Shadow knows; maybe, some day, who knows; I don't know.

The Reverend Jim Jones Reads The Comics

RON TURNER

I publish underground comix in San Francisco. *Zap*™, *Weirdo*, *Young Lust* are some of our 150 titles. I've been doing it for a few decades. In this business, I've gotten to know a few crazies. I think Jim Jones, founder of Peoples Temple, the Komandant of the Christian Auschwitz of Guyana, was Fruit Cake Numero UNO.

I've got a tale to tell about the 70s, when the Vietnamese had just kicked our ass, inflation had begun to roll (although you could still score an apartment for under $200 in the Haight and a lid of really good dope would go for $40) and the real estate specu-lators were pouring into the lower Haight. Sex was only hindered by this new distraction called Herpes. Everything was Okay. The newspapers were full of stories about local politicians making

NO.1

THE INNER CITY ROMANCE COMIC: "CHOICES"

COLWELL

75¢

ADULTS ONLY

good—and the Rev. Jim Jones a youngish white preacher with dark glasses was leading a mostly black congregation of inner-city people on air-conditioned bus caravans to testify to the wretched conditions in the ghetto.

My story begins one day when I was having a coffee at the Café Flore on Noe and Market with a teacher friend. The conversation turned to the subject of the lack of career guidance amongst the mostly black inner city kids that were in his class. We made arrangements for me to spend the day at the school discussing job potential in the printing and graphic arts worlds. I was also asked to bring large box of underground comix. I was assured that since the students were very streetwise the graphic content it would be okay.

The day arrived. I set about talking and taking questions about how underground comix, books and magazines were made. Who did what function, the printing industry in general, how printing presses worked, bindery work; blankets, rollers, folders, signatures, pagination, sales and marketing, distribution, population distributions, discounts and margins. I was very happy with the enthusiastic response, the questions were very good and the comprehension was there also. At the end of the day all the comix had disappeared.

A few weeks later I got a call from Reverend Jones. He said he had seen a number of his congregation reading the comix and wanted to know if I had more. I could not figure what a preacher wanted these for. Cautiously, I asked if he was familiar with any of the titles. He said *Inner City Romance* comix which were drawn by Guy Colwell seemed to be most popular. Guy had served several hard years at McNeil Island pen with a tough crowd. His crime was draft refusal, on moral grounds. He had grown up in Oakland and his early life went on hold when the war, and the draft, began. When he got out of prison he brought us his comix tales of blacks and whites, drugs and guns, psychedelia and sex from those streets he had grown to know. His themes ranged from totally dreamy sexual events to race wars. Jim Jones, a minister, had become a fan. I told him the material in these books was sex was sexually explicit. I didn't know if they would fit into his church's mission. He said he wanted them.

GUY COLWELL: "INNER CITY ROMANCE 1"

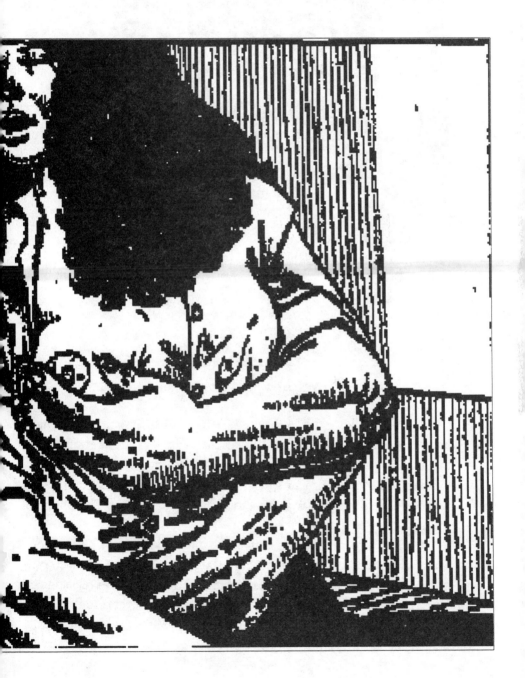

GUY COLWELL: "INNER CITY ROMANCE 1"

After talking to the Reverend, I had a 70s frisson, fearing that I had become too conservative. After all, the padre was the libertarian saying he didn't care if the comix had sex and violence. He was only interested in the literacy program at his church and these sexy comix were what had finally motivated his most reluctant readers. The ones the tutors had given up on.

The tutors, it turned out, were mostly kids from high school. The high school had been specially established by San Francisco officials—the city's then liberal establishment enjoyed a close relationship with the politically powerful preacher and was not adverse to doing him favors—to teach the children of Peoples Temple! It was the only private high school at the public's expense.

The details were worked out with Jones' white underlings. If they had any objections to lewd comix being read by the congregation they didn't let on. It was like if HE wants it, IT will happen! Total devotion.

Reverend Jones sent the high school kids over to pick up the comix. I had selected about 1,000 assorted titles (mostly Guy Colwell's *Inner City Romance* titles.). A week passed. Suddenly the Reverend Jones' attorney was on the line saying how much they appreciated it, and could they get some more? I said sure. More high-schoolers came by the warehouse. I recognized them as being in the classrooms where I had lectured. Their attitude seemed to have changed. It was to come and get the comix and with a minimal communication, leave with the goods. I thought this strange. Almost every teen who had ever come in to the Last Gasp warehouse had spent time trying to peak at all the shelves, or minimally wanted to play the pinball machines. Not these kids. Jim Jones' new youth corps was all spit and polish, and task oriented. Alert and physically handsome.

I was starting to get low on some titles and it seemed a bit stupid on my part to give away the profits. By now I had given away more than 5,000 copies. I delivered the new batch to the temple and asked about the inventory. Was he using them for premiums? But Jones had left for Guyana. The staff was now less than friendly. The next time they asked me for more books to send to Guyana where the Rev. Jones' flock had fled, I declined to provide them. I never heard from Jim Jones again.

A few weeks later I met Congressman Leo Ryan's daughter. She was quite taken with our *Slow Death Funnies* that dealt with ecological issues. She took some to her father, who said that we could get a grant to do eco-comix for middle and high school students. Then the news from Jonestown began to break. My young friend's father was dead, Jim Jones had killed him.

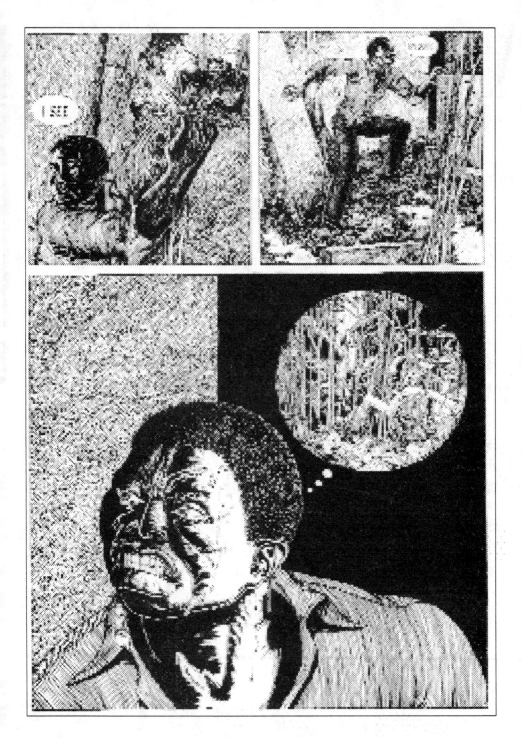

GUY COLWELL: "INNER CITY ROMANCE 3"

RIGHT: SELF PORTRAIT OF ARTIST GUY CALDWELL,
FOLSOM PRISON, 1979

Later I went to a sale of the assets of People's Temple. I thought I might get some of my comix back. I examined all the shipping crates in the back yard. I found a few secret hiding places in the building, but not one comic ever showed up at the auction. Most of the assets of the church had been shipped to Guyana. My comix were there when Jim Jones ordered the killing of the children, and then the parents of all those lovely, intelligent students I had met long ago. A few years later in San Jose I was at a party of rogue anthropologists and ran into the guy who killed Leo Ryan on Jones' orders. He had the hollow eyes of an android and his slight build and manner betrayed the effect that this master madman, the Reverend Jim Jones had had on his will to obey. His hands were like glass and looked like they never could have squeezed out the bullets that killed Leo Ryan.

Guy Colwell was so affected by the tragic news from Jonestown, the ghastly repository of 5,000 of his *Inner City Romance* comix, that he painted a woman in the jungle, still as death hiding from Jim Jones' death squads. The original painting hangs on my kitchen wall today. Here it is:

ARGONAUT

Conspiracy Wars

One Flew Into The Cuckoo's Nest

PAUL KRASSNER

- -

N THE 1970s a disturbing element was being imposed upon the counter-culture—various groups all trying to rip off the search for consciousness. I felt challenged to write a satirical piece about this phenomenon. Scientology was one of the scariest of these rip-off organizations, if only because its recruiters were such aggressive zombies. The stares of Scientology practitioners seemed to be tactical, their smiles unfelt. The goal of Scientology was to become a Clear—that is, a *complete* zombie—moving up to higher and higher levels by means of auditing sessions with an E-Meter, essentially a lie detector. In confronting their guilts and fears through the medium of a machine, they had become machinelike themselves and they responded like automatons.

In 1962, Scientology founder L. Ron Hubbard wrote to President Kennedy, claiming that his letter was as important as the one Albert Einstein had sent to President Roosevelt about the atomic bomb. He insisted that "Scientology is very easy for the government to put into effect," and that "Scientology could decide the space race or the next war in the hands of America." Kennedy didn't respond.

The E-Meter was presented as a panacea that could cure such "psychosomatic" problems as arthritis, cancer, polio, ulcers, the common cold and atomic radiation burns. But when the FDA began investigating Scientology, Hubbard wrote that the E-Meter is "a valid religious instrument, used in Confessionals, and is in no way diagnostic and does not treat." Nevertheless, in January 1963, the FDA raided their headquarters, seizing 100 E-Meters. Hubbard wrote to Attorney General Robert Kennedy—"even though you are of a different faith"—asking for protection of the Scientology religion. Bobby didn't respond either. Well there it was—my satirical angle—Hubbard's motivation for programming Sirhan Sirhan to kill Bobby Kennedy would be *revenge*.

In the course of my research, a strange thing happened. I learned of the *actual* involvement of Charles Manson with Scientology. In fact, there had been an E-Meter at the Spahn Ranch where his "family" stayed. Reality will transcend allegory every time. Manson had been abandoned by his mother and lived in various institutions since he was eight years old. He learned early how to survive in captivity. When he was fourteen, he got arrested for stealing bread and was jailed. He was supposed to go to reform school, but instead went to Boys Town, ran away, got arrested again, and began his lifelong career as a prison inmate. He was introduced to Scientology by fellow prisoners, and Charlie's ability to psyche people out was intensified so that he could zero in on their weaknesses and fears immediately.

When he was released from prison in 1967, he went to the Scientology Center in San Francisco. The individual who accompanied him there told me, "Charlie said to them, 'I'm Clear—what do I do now?'" But they expected him to sweep the floor—shit, he had done *that* in jail. However, in Los Angeles, he went to the Scientology *Celebrity* Center. Now this was more like it—here he could mingle with the elite. I was able to obtain a copy of the original log entry: "7/31/68, new name, Charlie Manson, Devt., No address, In for processing=Ethics=Type III." The receptionist—who, by Type III, meant "psychotic"—sent him to the Ethics office but he never showed up. At the Spahn Ranch, Manson combined his version of Scientology auditing with posthypnotic techniques he had learned in prison, with geographical isolation and subliminal motivation, with singalong sessions and encounter games, with LSD and mescaline, with transactional analysis and brainwashing rituals, with verbal probing and sexual longevity that he had practiced upon himself for all those years in the privacy of his cell. Ultimately, in August 1969, he sent his well-programmed family off to slay actress Sharon Tate, a few friends, and her unborn baby. Tate's husband, film director Roman Polanski, was in London.

And, yes, Charles Manson *was* Rosemary's baby. A few months later, when the family members were captured and charged with the homicides, Manson was portrayed by the media as a hippie cult leader, and the counter-culture became a dangerous enemy. Hitchhikers were shunned. Communes were raided. In the public's mind, flower children had grown poisonous thorns. But Manson was never really a hippie. He had grown up behind bars. His *real* family included con artists, pimps, drug dealers, thieves, muggers, rapists, and murderers. He had known only power relationships in an army of control junkies. Charlie Manson was America's Frankenstein monster, a logical product of the prison system—racist, paranoid, and violent—even if hippie astrologers thought that his fate had been predetermined because he was a triple Scorpio.

After having lived behind bars for most of his life, Manson began to explore and exploit the counter-cultural value system, from Haight-Ashbury to Strawberry Fields.

Driving his family around in a school bus painted black, Manson stopped at the Hog Farm, whose school bus was painted in rainbow colors. While traveling, the Hog Farmers had found themselves at a fork in the road. Up above them, two sky-writing planes were playing tic-tac-toe, and the Hog Farmers decided to go one way if the X's won and the other way if the O's won. Now they were back on their land, all in a circle, chanting "Om," which somehow caused the visiting Manson to start choking and gagging, so *his* family began counter-chanting "Evil." It was an archetypal confrontation.

Charles Manson had convinced himself and his family that the Beatles' songs—"Helter Skelter" and "Blackbird"—were actually harkening a race war, which he wanted to hasten by leaving clues to make it appear that black militants had done the killing. Stolen credit cards were deliberately thrown away in a black neighborhood. *Helter Skelter* (sic) was scrawled with a victim's blood on the refrigerator, and the word WAR was scratched onto a victim's stomach.

Roman Polanski put a $10,000 contract out on Manson's life.

As I was diving into my Manson research, I received a letter from Charlie himself. During the trial, I had published a piece of apocryhpha in *The Realist* about his stay at Boys Town—"Charles Manson Was My Bunkmate" by Richard Meltzer. A defense attorney read it to Manson and he got pissed off. "You know how long I stayed in Boys Town? *Two days!*" Now in response to his letter, I mentioned that the article had been intended only as a satire of media exploitation. He replied "Yes, brother, the world is a satire and I did see all sides of your story, 'Charlie's Bunkmate.' But I think in Now with no cover. Most people take into their minds bad thought and call it joking. Some lie and call it funny. I don't lie."

In pursuit of information, I visited Warren Hinckle. He was my editor at *Ramparts*, and after that folded, at *Scanlan's*, which also folded, but he had been planning to publish an article on the Manson case in *Scanlan's*, and now he brought me to former FBI agent William Turner, who had checked out Doris Day. The only connection she could possibly have with the Manson case was that her son, record producer Terry Melcher, had met Charlie and was interested in his music, and that Melcher was a former tenant of the Beverly Hills mansion where the massacre took place. *Aha!* I realized that could be the focal point of my satire—a torrid affair between Doris Day and Charlie Manson—a perfect metaphor for the coming together of the image and underbelly of Hollywood. Just for the hell of it, I wrote to Manson and asked if he ever had sex with Doris Day. He answered, "Yes, and I also fucked Rin-Tin-Tin and the Virgin Mary."

Hinckle also brought me to the renowned private investigator Hal Lipset, who informed me that not only did the Los Angeles Police Department seize pornographic films and videotapes they found in Sharon Tate's loft but also that certain members of the LAPD were *selling* them. Lipset had talked with one police source who told him exactly which porn flicks were available—a total of seven hours' worth for a quarter-million dollars. Lipset began reciting a litany of porn videos. The most notorious was an attorney for Howard Hughes, with the former wife of a former governor. There was Sharon Tate with a popular singer. There was Sharon with Steve McQueen. There was Sharon with two black bisexual men. "The cops weren't too happy about *that* one," Lipset recalled.

But when he told me there was a videotape of Cass Elliot from the Mamas and the Papas in an orgy with Yul Brynner, Peter Sellers and an actor who isn't dead yet—Brynner and Sellers were part of a group that had offered a $25,000 reward for the capture of the killers—suddenly there was a personal element intruding upon my investigation. In the summer of 1968, Tim Leary and I had been guests on the Les Crane show in Los Angeles; of course I publicized the upcoming Yippie convention. After the taping we went to a big party at Tommy Smothers's house, where I met Cass Elliot. We liked each other immediately. The next day she called to invite me to dinner at her home that evening. Instead, we decided to meet Leary at a restaurant in Laguna Beach. Musician David Crosby drove us there in a station wagon, while Cass and I cuddled and kissed on a foam-rubber mat. On the way we stopped at the Mystic Arts combination head shop and health food store with its magnificent meditation room. Two years later it would burn to the ground, on the same day that all the other head shops in the area were also destroyed by fire. Although Cass and I slept together that night, we didn't have sex. In bed she kept talking about someone named Billy Doyle, who was arriving from Jamaica the next morning. She seemed to be afraid of him. During breakfast the three of us sat around talking about the music scene, drug use, and the politics of protest. Doyle like to act tough and mysterious. "We know all about you," he said to me. "You better watch your step."

Now I came across Billy Doyle's name in Ed Sander's book on Manson, *The Family*. He was the drug connection for two of the victims, Voytek Fryowski and Abigail Folger. Ed Sanders wrote: "Sometime during [the first week in August] a dope dealer from Toronto named Billy Doyle was whipped and video-buggered at [the Tate residence]. In the days before his death, [Jay] Sebring had complained to a receptionist at his hair shop that someone had burned him for $2,000 worth of cocaine and he wanted vengeance. Billy Doyle was involved in a large-scale dope-import operation involving private planes from Jamaica."

Naturally, Doyle felt it was rude of Sebring and Frykowski to tie him to a chair, whip him, and then fuck him in the ass while a video camera taped the proceedings before a live audience. But police investigators eliminated him as a suspect in the murders. However, on Friday evening, just a few hours before the massacre took place, Joel Rostau—the boyfriend of Sebring's receptionist and an intermediary in a cocaine ring—visited Sebring and Frykowski at the Tate house, to deliver mescaline and coke. During the long course of the Manson trial, several associates of Sebring were murdered, including Rostau, whose body was found in the trunk of a car in New York. Ed Sanders, who had already engaged in years of agonizing research into the Manson case, remarked that personally, he had no desire for permanent meditation next to a spare tire. So it appeared that the Manson family had actually served as some sort of hit squad for a drug ring.

When President Kennedy was killed Mae Brussell was a twice-divorced suburban homemaker with five children. Her seven-year-old daughter saw Lee Harvey Oswald on TV—he had a black eye and was saying, "I didn't do it, I haven't killed anybody, I don't know what this is all about." She decided to send him her teddy bear. It was all wrapped up and ready to mail when she saw Oswald murdered by Jack Ruby on TV. Mae had to wonder, "What kind of world are we bringing our children into?" One bit of research led to another, and she started a weekly radio program, "Dialogue Assassination," originating on her own FM rock station, KLRB in Carmel, and syndicated to a half-dozen other stations. What began as a hobby turned into a lifetime pilgrimage.

She purchased the Warren Commission report for $86, studying and cross-referencing the entire twenty-six volumes, without the aid of a computer. It took her eight years and 27,000 typewritten pages. She was overwhelmed by the difference between the evidence and the commission's conclusion that there had been only a single assassin. In fact, she concluded, "Lee Harvey Oswald was set up to take the fall. But the Warren Commission ignored physical evidence from the scene of the crime—bullets, weapons, clothing, wounds—and based its judgment that Oswald was just a disturbed loner on the testimony of some thirty Russian emigres in the Dallas-Fort Worth area. Most of them, according to the testimony, were affiliated with anti-Communist organizations that had collaborated with the Nazis during the war."

Next, Mae began to study the history of six hundred Nazis brought to this country after World War II under Project Paperclip. They were infiltrated into hospitals, universities, and the aerospace industry, further developing their techniques in propaganda, mind control, and behavior modification. She observed how the patterns of murder in the United States were identical to those in Nazi Germany. The parallels between the rise of Adolf Hitler and the rise of Richard Nixon were frightening to Mae. Hitler came into power as the result of more than four hundred political assassinations. So, rather than just investigating the death of John Kennedy, she collected articles about the murders of people *involved* in his assassination. And, instead of limiting her research to the killing of Robert Kennedy, Malcolm X, Martin Luther King, and the attempted assassination of George Wallace, she began paying attention to the untimely, suspicious deaths of judges, attorneys, labor leaders, professors, civil rights activists, reporters, authors, Black Panthers, Chicanos, Native Americans—and Mary Jo Kopechne. Mae believed that Chappaquiddick was yet another CIA-orchestrated dirty deed; the National Safety Council had never found a single case of anybody escaping from a submerged car the way Senator Ted Kennedy supposedly had.

One afternoon in February 1972, Mae Brussell read in *The Realist* about the lawsuit in response to my announcement of "The Rise of Sirhan Sirhan in the Scientology Hierarchy." She immediately phoned to assure me that Scientologists had nothing to do with the assassination of Robert Kennedy. "Oh, I knew that," I told her, "but the article was just gonna be a satire, and they took it seriously. I'm working on something else now instead. Let me ask, do you know anything about the Manson case?"

"Of course," she said. "The so-called Manson murders were actu-ally orchestrated by military intelligence in order to destroy the counter-culture movement. It's no different from the Special Forces in Vietnam, disguised as Vietcong, killing and slaughtering to make the Vietcong look bad."

"Oh, *really?* Could I come see you?"

My friend Hassler drove me to Mae Brussell's home. She was about fifty, plump and energetic, wearing a long peasant dress patch-worked with philosophical tidbits, knitting sweaters for her children while she breathlessly described the architecture of an invisible govern-ment. Her walls were lined with forty file cabinets containing 1,600 sub-ject categories. Each day Mae would digest ten newspapers from around the country, supplementing that diet with items sent to her by a net-work of researchers and young conspiracy students known as "Brussell Sprouts"—plus magazines, underground papers, unpublished manu-scripts, court affidavits, documents from the National Archives, FBI and CIA material obtained through the Freedom of Information Act, and hundreds of books on espionage and assassination. Each Sunday she would sort out the previous week's clippings into various categories as though she were conducting a symphony of horror. "About 80 percent of all CIA intelligence information comes from printed news," she said, "so I am doing what they are doing, without being paid, and without selec-tively writing my own history, but using *all* the material.

"One agent called me—he had killed ten people for the CIA. When members of the CIA cut his jugular vein, he had to sew it up, and he vowed vengeance against them because he had killed ten people, and when he was ordered to kill a member of Congress, he wanted to stop. Various agents listen to my program. It's a safety valve for them, on how far things are going."

I stayed overnight, devouring material from her massive files. For Mae, although the ultimate mystery would remain forever inconceivable, assassination research had become her spiritual quest for truth. Conspiracy became her Zen grid for perceiving political reality, drawing her deeper and deeper into a separate reality that Carlos Castaneda—the mysterious author of the New Age bestseller, *A Separate Reality*—never dreamed of. Now I had stumbled upon an American version of the Reichstag fire. The next morning, my head was still swirling in the after-glow of a fresh conversion. On the bus, I pondered a theological question Mae had posed: "How many coincidences does it take to make a plot?"

Voytek Frykowski's father had financed Roman Polanski's first film. He and his girlfriend, Abigail Folger, were staying at the Polanski residence. She was paying the rent and supplying him with the money for their daily drug supplies. In July 1969, Billy Doyle promised Frykowski a new synthetic drug, MDA, made in Canada. I had tried MDA a few times—it felt like a combination of mescaline and ampheta-mine, acting as an extraordinary energizer and, if you were with the right person, a powerful aphrodisiac. The plan was for Frykowski to become the American distributor of MDA. He was hoping to sell a screenplay, but it's always nice to have something to fall back on.

"What *was* the motive?" I asked Ed Sanders.

Sanders seemed nervous. "Ask Peter Folger," he muttered through tight lips.

Folger was the coffee tycoon whose daughter, Abigail, had been one of the victims. She supported Tom Bradley as the first black candi-date for mayor of Los Angeles, despite the objection of her father, who had a reputation as a fierce racist. While Ed Sanders was researching his Manson book, he received a Mafia kiss from a lawyer for Peter Folger. When Sanders advised me to "Ask Peter Folger," I assumed he was refer-ring to the fact that Folger had conducted his own investigation. But then, in my increasingly paranoid fantasies, I began to believe that he meant Folger was *responsible* for the massacre; that he had actually *arranged* to have his own daughter brutally slain because she had violated family tradition by supporting a black mayor and living with a man who was going to distribute MDA, a drug that could provide tremendous competition for coffee. What once might have been a satirical premise had now become a serious possibility in the warped regions of my mind.

I even checked into the history of Folger's Coffee. A deal had been made with the FTC about their merger with Proctor & Gamble. It was so suspicious that *Advertising Age* ran a front-page editorial. I watched Folger's Coffee commercials carefully. One took place in a supermarket, showing two white housewives standing in an aisle discussing the virtues of coffee when, almost subliminally, a black woman elbowed her way between them. In another commercial, the locale was a political convention hall, again with two whites and a black almost subliminally elbowing between them. Commercials were produced frame by precise frame, and I became convinced that Peter Folger was deliberately trying to program TV viewers with racism in his coffee commercials.

It was as though I were psychically playing the part of both characters in Roman Polanski's first film, *The Fat and the Lean*, where a wealthy landowner shoots an arrow into the air, and then his servant runs across the lawn carrying a target so that his master is assured of scoring a bull's-eye every time.

Mae Brussell put me in contact with Preston Guillory, a former deputy sheriff in Los Angeles, and I interviewed him.

"A few weeks prior to the Spahn Ranch raid," he said, "we were told that we weren't to arrest Manson or any of his followers. We had a sheaf of memos on Manson—that they had automatic weapons at the ranch, that citizens had complained about hearing machine guns at night, that firemen from the local fire station had been accosted by armed members of Manson's band and told to get out of the area. Deputies started asking, Why aren't we gonna make the raid sooner? I mean, Manson's a parole violator, we know there's narcotics and booze. He's living at the ranch with a bunch of minor girls in complete violation of his parole. Deputies at the station quite frankly became very annoyed that no action was being taken about Manson.

"My contention is this—the reason Manson was left on the street was because our department thought that he was going to launch an attack on the Black Panthers. We were getting intelligence briefings that Manson was a very ready tool, apparently, because he did have some racial hatred and he wanted to vent it. But they hadn't anticipated him attacking someone other than the Panthers. You have to remember that Charlie was on federal parole all this time from '67 to '69. Do you realize all the the shit he was getting away with while he was on parole?

Now here's the kicker. Before the Tate killings he had been arrested at Malibu twice for statutory rape. Never got [imprisoned for parole violation]. Manson like to ball young girls, so he just did his thing and he was released, and they didn't put any parole on him. But somebody very high up was controlling everything that was going on and was seeing to it that we didn't bust Manson."

Manson was on death row—this was before capital punishment was repealed (and later reinstated) in California—so I was unable to meet with him. Reporters had to settle for an interview with *any* prisoner awaiting the gas chamber, and it wasn't very likely that Charlie would be selected at random for me. In the course of our correspondence, there was a letter from him consisting of a few pages of gibberish about Christ and the Devil, but at one point, right in the middle, he wrote in tiny letters, *Call Squeaky*, with her phone number. I phoned, and we arranged to meet at her apartment in Los Angeles. On an impulse, I brought several tabs of LSD with me on the plane. Squeaky Fromme resembled a typical redheaded, freckle-faced waitress who sneaks a few tokes of pot in the lavatory, a regular girl-next door except perhaps for the unusually challenging nature of her personality plus the scar of an X that she had gouged and burned into her forehead as a visual reminder of her commitment to Charlie. That same symbol also covered the third eyes of her roommates, Sandra Good and Brenda McCann. "We've crossed ourselves out of this entire system." They all had short hairstyles growing in now, after having shaved their heads completely. They continued to sit on the sidewalk near the Hall of Justice every day, like a coven of faithful nuns bearing witness to Manson's martyrdom.

Sandy Good had seen me perform at The Committee in San Francisco a few years previously. Now she told me that when she first met Charlie and people asked her what he was like, she had compared him to Lenny Bruce and me. It was the weirdest compliment I ever got, but I began to understand Manson's peculiar charisma. With his sardonic rap, mixed with psychedelic drugs and real-life theater games such as "creepy-crawling" and stealing, he had deprogrammed his family from the values of mainstream society, but *re*programmed them with his own philosophy, a cosmic version of the racism perpetuated by the prison system that had served as *his* family. Manson stepped on Sandy's eyeglasses, threw away her birth-control pills, and inculcated her with racist sensibility. Although she had once been a civil rights activist, she was now asking me to tell John Lennon that he should get rid of Yoko Ono and stay with "his own kind." Later, she added, "If Yoko really loved the Japanese people, she would not want to mix their blood."

I was basking in the afterglow of the Moody Blues's "Om" song when Sandy began to speak of the "gray people"—regular citizens going about their daily business—whom she had been observing from her vantage point on the corner near the Hall of Justice. "We were just sitting there," she said, "and they were walking along, kind of avoiding us. It's like watching a live movie in front of you. Sometimes I just wanted to kill the gray people, because that was the only way they would be able to experience the total Now." That was an expression Charlie had borrowed from Scientology. Later, Sandy explained that she didn't mean it literally about killing the gray people, that she had been speaking from another dimension. She told me that prosecutor Vincent Bugliosi once snarled at her as she kept her vigil outside the courthouse: "We're gonna get you because you sucked Charlie Manson's dick." The girls just sat there on the sidewalk and laughed, because they knew that oral-genital relations did not constitute a capital offense.

When we returned to their apartment, Sandy asked if I wanted to take a hot bath. I felt ambivalent. I knew that one of the attorneys in the case had participated in a ménage a trois with Squeaky and Sandy, but I had also been told by a reporter, "It certainly levels the high to worry about getting stabbed while fucking the Manson ladies in the bunkhouse at the Spahn Ranch—I've found that the only satisfactory position is sitting up, back to the wall, facing the door." Visions of the famous shower scene in *Psycho* flashed through my mind. But despite the shrill self-righteousness that infected their true believer syndrome, they had charmed me with their honesty, humor, and distorted sense of compassion. They sensed my hesitation, and Squeaky confronted me: "You're afraid of me, aren't you?"

Sandy tried to reassure me: "She's *beautiful*, Paul. Just look into her eyes. Isn't she beautiful?" Squeaky and I stared silently at each other for a while—I recalled that Manson had written, "I never picked up anyone who had not already been discarded by society"—and my eyes began to tear. There were tears in Squeaky's eyes too. She asked me to try on Charlie's vest. It felt like a bizarre honor to participate in this ceremony. The corduroy vest was a solid inch thick with embroidery—snakes and dragons and devilish designs including human hair that had been woven into the multicolored patterns. Sandy took her bath, but instead of my getting into the tub *with* her—assuming she had invited me—I sat fully dressed on the toilet, and we talked. I was thinking, *You have pert nipples*, but instead I said, "What's that scar on your back?" It was from a lung operation.

Brenda asked for another tab of acid, to send Manson in prison. She ground it into powder which she then glued to the paper with vegetable dye and the notation, *Words fly fast*, explaining that Charlie would know what it meant. She stayed up late that night, writing letters to several prisoners with the dedication of a polygamous war wife.

"Charles Manson was a patsy," Mae Brussell told me—"identical with Lee Harvey Oswald, Sirhan Sirhan, and James Earl Ray. The Manson thing was a hidden war against the youth culture. People sharing their housing, their food, their cars, recycling their old clothes. Make your own candles and turn off the electricity. It was an economic revolution, affecting everything from the cosmetic industry to the churches."

She believed that Tex Watson, the Manson family member who led the others on the night of the murders, had played a bigger part in planning the massacre than generally believed. Charlie had instructed the girls to do whatever Tex told them. When Manson was charged, Watson was also charged, but federal authorities held Watson in a Texas prison with no explanation—not even his own lawyers were allowed to see him—while Vincent Bugliosi prosecuted the Manson trial in California. In order to find Manson guilty, the jury had to be convinced that Charlie's girls were zombies following without question. However, in order to find *Watson* guilty, another jury had to be convinced that he was *not a zombie at all* and knew exactly what he was doing.

Mae gave me the heaviest lead in my Manson research. She told me that an agent for Naval Intelligence, Nathaniel Dight, had been meeting with Tex Watson. Naval Intelligence—of course! L. Ron Hubbard was in Naval Intelligence. During World War II, imprisoned Mafia boss Lucky Luciano was pardoned at the urgent request of Naval Intelligence. The Committee to Investigate Assassinations stated that Lee Harvey Oswald had worked in Naval Intelligence. Even the infamous Zodiac Killer used obsolete Naval Intelligence ciphers in his notes. Nathaniel Dight was taking courses at Navy Postgraduate School, and Mae claimed that only intelligence officers could do that. Mae said Dight had posed as a hippie artist, orchestrating the scenario of violence and witchcraft in meetings with Tex Watson, who then fulfilled the prophecy of this agent provocateur with all that shooting and stabbing. Dight had done the art-work for a magazine which predicted that the counter-culture would turn to violence and witchcraft. It was published by a corporation, which, Mae said, "was a conduit of CIA funds for medical research in mind control, intelligence money for electrode implants and for LSD experiments, according to documents I got from the Pentagon."

Although my interview with former deputy sheriff Preston Guillory had prepared me to accept Mae's theory on Dight, Guillory didn't recognize the name. Manson wouldn't answer any of my questions about him. "Brother," he wrote, "names to me are like past dreams and my thought doesn't live in time. Much moves that I can never put on paper or express in words." Instead he discussed the jailhouse code against snitching. I wrote back that there was *good* snitching and *bad* snitching—giving, as an example of the former, Daniel Ellsberg—but Charlie wasn't persuaded. I had also been corresponding with another prisoner at San Quentin, convicted mass killer John Linley Frazier, who wrote, "Me and Charlie are still trying to figure out how long our leashes are and who's been pissin' on 'em." Nor was I able to find anyone in the Manson family who could provide confirmation about Dight. Squeaky, Sandy, and Brenda had never heard of him.

Then came a break. My friend and Watsonville neighbor Jackie Christeve, who had started the first women's studies program in the country at San Diego State College, introduced me to Karlene Faith. They were both graduate students in the History of Consciousness Department at the Santa Cruz campus of the University of California.

Karlene invited me to participate in her activist thesis. She was writing a paper based on her project of bringing outside educators into the California Institute for Women at Frontera. I would conduct a workshop in creative journalism. Our visit to the prison was extended to include the Special Security Unit, which housed a trio of convicted killers—Manson family members Susan Atkins, Patricia Krenwinkel, and Leslie van Houten.

When we met them, Patricia and Leslie were needle-pointing a colorful dragon on muslim the size of a bedsheet. They had named the dragon Mao. "In case the Chinese take over," Patricia Krenwinkel explained, "we want to be ready." Jackie had brought an old film about dating that was more campy than instructional. She asked if they were interested in seeing it. "Yes," replied Leslie van Houten. "Anything with touching." She said it with such tenderness, and yet they had used knives to butcher people to death, the ultimate *perversion* of touching. Later, we talked about the murders. "It was their karma," Susan Atkins reasoned. "In another life, our karma could have been reversed," That was the key to this puzzle. The Manson family had taken other people's karma into their own hands.

I asked if anyone there had ever met Nathaniel Dight. Susan replied, "Oh, yeah, Tex took me to sleep with him. And he gave us dope." Keeping my adrenaline rush anchored, I explained who he actually was. The others teased her. "Ha, ha, you slept with a CIA guy." They asked me who really ran the country. I was carrying around in my pocket a pyra-mid shaped seashell I had picked up on the beach. Using that as model, I outlined the power structure of secret societies, culminating with an unholy coalition at the top—of organized crime, military intelligence, and corporate greed. The three women passed the seashell around, caressing it with their fingers as if trying to capture the sensuality for future reference. I should've left it with them. The next time I saw Squeaky, I told her about the meeting and gave her the seashell. She held it in her palm and rubbed it against her cheek. "Wow," she said, "I can *feel* their energy."

The Process struck me as a group of occult provocateurs, using radical Christianity as a front. They were adamantly interested in Yippie politics. They boasted to me of various rallies which their *vibrations alone* had transformed into riots. They implied that there was some kind of connection between the assassination of Bobby Kennedy and their mere presence on the scene. On the evening that Kennedy was killed at the Ambassador Hotel, he has been to a dinner party with Roman Polanski and Sharon Tate. Bernard Fensterwald, head of the Committee to Investigate Assassinations, told me that Sirhan Sirhan had some involvement with the Process. Peter Chang, the district attorney of Santa Cruz, showed me a letter from a Los Angeles police official to the chief of police in San Jose, warning him that the Process had infiltrated biker gangs and hippie communes.

In 1972, Paulette Cooper, author of *The Scandal of Scientology*, put me in touch with Lee Cole, a former Scientologist who was now working with the Process Church. I contacted him and flew to Chicago. Cole met me at the airport with a couple of huge men whose demeanor was somewhat frightening. They drove me to a motel, where I checked in, paying cash in advance. Cole arranged for a meeting with Sherman Skolnick, a local conspiracy researcher. He was in a wheelchair. Two men, one with a metal hook in place of his hand, carried him up the back stairs to my motel room. Lee Cole kept peeking out the window for suspicious-looking cars. It was becoming more surrealistic every minute.

Early next morning, the phone rang. It was Sherman Skolnick. "Paul, I'm sorry to wake you, but you're in extreme danger." My heart started pounding, and I put my socks on. "That fellow from last night, Lee Cole, he's CIA." I got dressed faster than I had ever gotten dressed in my life, packed my stuff, and ran down the back steps of the motel without even checking out.

I called up Lee Cole. Of course he denied being with the CIA. We made an appointment to visit the Process headquarters. "And this time"—with Clint Eastwood bravado—"you can leave those *goons* of yours at home." The Process men were dressed all in black, with silver crosses hanging from their necks. They called each other "Brother" and they had German shepherds that appeared menacing. They tried to convince me that Scientology, not the Process, was responsible for creating Charles Manson. But what else could I have expected? Lee Cole's role was to provide information on Scientology to the Process. To prove that he wasn't with the CIA, he told *me* stuff about Scientology. I phoned Sherman Skolnick, and he apologized for scaring me. "You know us conspiracy researchers," he chuckled, "we're paranoid." Actually, conspiracy research had become a religious pursuit. He once called me up with a new piece of evidence and proclaimed: "I've discovered the holy of holies."

No wonder Mae Brussell was so excited. The attempted burglary of Democratic headquarters at the Watergate Hotel in Washington, D.C., in June 1972 had suddenly brought her eight and a half years of dedicated conspiracy research to an astounding climax. She recognized names, methodology, patterns of cover-up. She could trace linear connections leading inevitably from the assassination of JFK to the Watergate break-in, and all the killings in between. There was, for example, the murder of Ruben Salazar, a *Los Angeles Times* reporter, at the first Chicano-sponsored antiwar protest. Salazar had been working on an exposé of law enforcement, which would reveal secret alliances among the CIA, the army, the FBI, California's attorney general, and local police authorities. L.A. District Attorney Robert Meyer received a phone call from L. Patrick Gray—who had recently become acting head of the FBI after J. Edgar Hoover's death—telling him to stop the investigation. Meyer did quit, saying it was like the "kiss of death" to work with these people. Mae called Meyer, asking if he would help with her research. She wanted to find out why the Justice Department in Washington was stopping a D.A. in Los Angeles from investigating the killing of a reporter. A month later, Meyer was found dead in a parking lot in Pasadena. And now L. Patrick Gray was involved in an even bigger cover-up. A year before the Watergate break-in, E. Howard Hunt, who had worked for the CIA for twenty-one years, proposed a "bag-job"—a surreptitious entry—into the office of Dr. Lewis Fielding, a Beverly Hills psychiatrist who had refused to cooperate with FBI agents investigating one of his patients, Daniel Ellsberg, leaker of the Pentagon Papers. It was the function of the White house "plumbers" to *plug* such leaks. The burglars, led by G. Gordon Liddy, scattered pills around the office to make it look like a junkie had been responsible. The police assured Dr. Fielding that the break-in was made in search of drugs, even though he found Ellsberg's records removed from their folder. An innocent black man, Elmer Davis, was arrested, convicted and sent to prison. Liddy remained silent. Mae Brussell corresponded with Davis, and after he finished serving Liddy's time behind bars, he ended up living with Mae. It was a romance made in Conspiracy Heaven.

Actually, the melding of Coincidence and Mysticism had begun when I wrote a comic strip for *The Realist*, drawn by Richard Guindon. It was about political witchcraft, a takeoff on *Rosemary's Baby*. A key scene in that film showed Rosemary moving around the letters from Scrabble game so that instead of spelling out the name of her neighbor the letters spelled out the name of a warlock in a book she had been reading about witchcraft. And now, scrambling the letters of the vice president's name—SPIRO AGNEW— it became GROW A PENIS. Coincidence had been my religion, but this was *so* appropriate that it challenged my theology. After all, when Senator Charles Goodell came out against the war in Vietnam, it was Agnew who called him "the Christine Jorgenson of the Republican party"—thereby equating military might with the mere presence of a penis. Around that time, Mike Wallace interviewed me for "60 Minutes." He asked me what the difference was between the underground press and the mainstream media, and I told him about the GROW A PENIS anagram, adding, "The difference is that I could print that in *The Realist*, but it'll be edited out of this program." My prediction was accurate.

Yoko Ono and John Lennon spent a weekend at my house in Watsonville. They loved being so close to the ocean. In the afternoon I asked them to smoke their cigarettes outside, but in the evening we smoked a combination of marijuana and opium, sitting on pillows in front of the fireplace, sipping tea and munching cookies. We talked about Mae Brussell's theory that the deaths of musicians like Jimi

Hendrix, Janis Joplin, and Jim Morrison had actually been political assassinations because they were role models on the crest of the youth rebellion. "No, no," Lennon argued, "they were already headed in a self-destructive direction." A few months later, he would remind me of that conversation and add, "Listen, if anything happens to Yoko or me, it was *not* an accident." For now, though, we were simply stoned in Watsonville, discussing conspiracy, safe at my oasis in a desert of paranoia. At one point, I referred to Mae Brussell as a saint. "She's *not* a saint," Lennon said. "*You're* not a saint. *I'm* not a saint. *Yoko's* not a saint. *Nobody's* a saint."

We discussed the Charles Manson case. Lennon was bemused by the way Manson had associated himself with Beatles music.

"Look," he said, "would you kindly inform him that it was *Paul McCartney* who wrote 'Helter Skelter,' not me."

Yoko said, "No, please *don't* tell him. We *don't* want to have any communication with Manson."

"It's all right," Lennon said, "he doesn't have to know the message came from *us*."

"It's getting chilly," Yoko said. "Would you put another cookie in the fireplace?

I had left the radio on and now Mae Brussell was talking about the assassination of Bobby Kennedy. But I had overdosed on conspiracy. I ran in one door and out the other, then down into woods behind the beach. I found a cove at the bottom of a hilly area, sat under a tree, and then I let out a long, loud, *uncontrollable wail*—it must have been a 10 on the Primal Scream scale—releasing all the fear that had been building up in my psyche, from Scientology to the Process, from the FBI to the CIA, from Charles Manson to Richard Nixon, from Naval Intelligence to Extraterrestrial Intelligence. Then I just sat there and watched the ground moving around in beautiful mosaic patterns.

At dusk, I moved to a dilapidated easy chair on the edge of the cliff. Through the fog I could see the silhouettes of some kind of space creatures. They were marking latitudinal and longitudinal lines on the ocean floor, as though it were a classroom globe.

That evening I called Ken Kesey. "It has to do with a struggle for the will," he said.

And I called Mae. "These people have their own reality," she said. "The occult is their safety valve for not having to deal with the problems on earth."

In fact, I was perceiving what had happened in mythical terms— the attempt to divert human compassion into otherworldliness. With that as my premise, I began to apply the logic of the paranoid, and so now *Jackie* became part of the plot. Her last name was *Christeve*. Of course! Wasn't Christianity utilized for the prevention of rebels? Didn't Eastern religion rationalize the suffering of others as rotten karma? How long had that spiritual teacher been rechanneling Jackie's energy? I recalled how I first met her when I was running on the beach and she was riding a bike slowly along the shore. *Aha!* She must've found out from the federal data bank that I had once been the winner of the Slow Bicycle Race. What a shrewd way to entrap me. I had developed the tunnel vision of a true believer. I was seeing everything through a conspiratorial filter.

The next morning, when I went outside, there was a man on the road observing me with binoculars. Then there was another man, in a red sweater, running behind a tree. I counted seven men altogether. There was a helicopter circling overhead. I hurried to the cliff and down the rickety wooden steps onto the beach. There was a sheriff's car parked on top of the cliff, and a couple of deputies were watching me. They had my whole house staked out. I walked along the beach, trying to appear nonchalant, back around into that cove in the woods. I sat under the same tree where I had howled like a helpless infant the day before. Now there was another *Mission Impossible* type standing in the woods, about fifty feet behind and above me, watching through binoculars. Finally, choosing my words carefully, I turned around and called up, "What are you waiting for?"

He hesitated, then called back, "You seen any girls around here?"

"No."

"I heard they take nude sunbaths."

"Well, I haven't noticed any."

After a brief silence, he called to me, "What are *you* waiting for?"

"I just like to watch the way people act."

He grabbed his crotch and said, "You want *this*?

"No, thanks." I stayed there a few more minutes, just so he wouldn't think he scared me away. Then I got up and called out, "Well, good luck." I headed toward the beach, and he signaled to another plain-clothes officer. All this was really happening. It was not my imagination. The LSD I took the previous day was very powerful, but it had worn off. These men were not any kind of hallucination. I was having a bad trip, but it was reality. I went back to my house, put all my dope in a jar and buried it. I packed a few things and walked along the beach for about a mile. It seemed like people were staring at me—every hippie surfer was an undercover cop—but somehow I managed to get away. I hitched a ride, making sure we weren't being followed.

Although I was suffering from a severe case of information over-load, I could still pass for sane in public. I even managed to keep a dental appointment without revealing the utter turmoil in my mind. I was des-perately trying to maintain my balance between coincidence and con-spiracy. I decided to go back to Watsonville. On the bus, my thumb began to feel numb.

The man sitting in front of me, an operative for the CIA, adjust-ed the ring on his finger in order to let his partner outside know that I was on the bus again. I had to let the man in front of me *know* that I was onto his game. So I took out my ballpoint pen. Clicking the top over and over like a telegraph key, I kept repeating, "Paul Krassner calling Abbie Hoffman." The CIA operative fidgeted nervously. He knew I was onto him now.

My mind had finally snapped.

Allen Ginsberg's poem *Howl* began, "I saw the best minds of my generation destroyed by madness, starving hysterical, naked," and I had always identified with the "best minds" part but never with the "mad-ness" part. Eventually I told Abbie Hoffman how I had tried to convince a CIA operative sitting front of me on the bus that I was calling Abbie by using my ballpoint pen as a telegraph key.

"Oh, yeah," he said. "I got your call, only it was collect, so I couldn't accept it."

I stayed up talking with former Prankster, Julius Karpen. As we spoke, we were rolling billiard balls back and forth across the pool table in the living room, pushing and catching them with our hands rather than hitting them with a cuestick and waking anybody up. Finally, I asked, "How long is it gonna go on?"

"How long is *what* gonna go on?"

"You know, this battle between good and evil, when is it gonna end?"

"Maybe never," Julius said. Suddenly I felt a wave of relief. So it *wasn't* all my responsibility. Such a heavy burden had been lifted from my soul.

Losing my sense of humor had been the direction my insanity took. By taking myself as seriously as my cause, I'd violated the Eleventh Commandment. I had an investment in my craziness, and I needed to perpetuate it. By publishing Mae Brussell's work, I was on a mission from the God I didn't believe in. I had bought into a *celestial* conspiracy. I had gone over the edge, from a universe that didn't know I existed, to one that did. From false humility to false pride.

But if existence was *not* absurd, then it was *planned*, and that was even *more* absurd. By adopting John Lilly's notion of the Earth Coincidence Control Office, I began to lose my own perspective. A couple of decades later, Lilly would dismiss his own concept, "Tooth problems," he explained. "I was trying to get in touch with my teeth."

It turned out that those inexplicable things which had helped frighten me into a state of acute paranoia could be explained logically. The space creatures who were dividing up the ocean floor were actually people in wet suits, clam digging with long rods in the mud. The Sheriff's Department was never after me—they had been looking for a rapist in the area.

In 1975, Squeaky Fromme tried to shoot President Gerald Ford. She was wearing a Red Riding Hood outfit, and I sent her a note in prison, teasing her about fading into the crowd. I wrote a piece for *Rolling Stone* titled "My Trip with Squeaky," including a paragraph about

Nathaniel Dight being in Naval Intelligence, posing as a hippie artist, and meeting with Tex Watson. Dight sued for libel, and my sources had to give depositions.

Mae Brussell called me "totally irresponsible" for publishing what she had told me.

Dight's neighbor was now in a state hospital. According to a psychiatric evaluation, "Her feet are encased in the most unusual pair of slippers constructed of layers of garbage, including coffee grounds, bread crumbs, tea bags and lettuce and socks stiff with age and then plastic bags. The patient denies that this garb is out of the ordinary. In fact, she indicates that she was planning to use this foot gear as a pattern for a pair of slippers...has related to the staff that she has been entered by the spirit of [Watergate burglar] James McCord. I realized that she wouldn't make a very good impression on the jury if she took the witness stand.

Dight was suing *Rolling Stone* for $450 million because he was never in Naval Intelligence. He claimed that my article caused him to lose interest in sex and his artwork. I considered pleading temporary insanity, but I realized that would be a copout. It was a moot point; the case was settled out of court for $100,000, and *Rolling Stone* published my letter of apology.

Meanwhile, Charles Manson has become a cultural symbol. In surfer jargon, "a manson" means a crazy, reckless, surfer. For comedians, Manson has become a generic joke reference. I asked him how he felt about that. He wrote back: "I don't know what a generic is, Joke. I think I know what that means. That means you talk bad about Reagan or Bush. I've always ran poker games and whores and crime. I'm a crook. You make the reality in court and press. I just ride and play the cards that were pushed on me to play. Mass killer, it's a job, what can I say."

As I began to unwind from my psychotic episode, I could survey the damage I'd done. I had broken up with a girlfriend because I somehow convinced myself that the FBI had sent her to spy on me. She asked if we could at least have a dialogue, but that only made me more suspicious. When I found a new girlfriend, I actually asked if there was a microphone in her cat's flea collar. Although I totally believed in the possibility at that instant, she of course thought I was just being my usual funny self. Twenty years later, I would read in an article by Harrison Salisbury in *Penthouse* that "The CIA wired a cat to eavesdrop on conversations. Micro sensing devices were installed in its body, and its tail was wired as an aerial. But it was hit by a car a day before it got into action."

I had wanted to explore the Charles Manson case, but ultimately I had to face the reality of my *own* peculiar darkness. Originally, I had wanted to expose the dangers of Scientology, but instead I *joined* a cult of conspiracy. I had been skulking around like the Ancient Mariner, waving my grungy albatross in front of people's faces. I thought that what I had published was so important that I *wanted* to be persecuted, in order to validate the work. In the process, I had become *attached* to conspiracy.

"My whole identity got tied up in plots," I said to Ken Kesey.

"Always stay in your own movie," he advised.

"Yeah, but I'll tell you something—the FBI was right."

"About what?"

"I *am* a raving, unconfined nut."

Our Assassins

MAE BRUSSELL

THE AMERICAN ASSASSIN is a different variety than history ever produced. This mongrel is not a pure breed nazi but the deformed and hideous baby produced from the marriage of nazi General Reinhard Gehlen and his mistress, Allen Dulles' CIA. It has taken a

long time to recognize just what is different about this creation whose birth followed a quickie ceremony immediately after World War II. The parents, who had helped finance Adolph Hitler's ascendancy, and the agencies still longing for revenge and war against most of mankind, changed their domicile but not their habits. The nursery moved from Germany into the United States.

Europeans and Americans who find the explanation of our assassinations hard to grasp have not yet recognized the species. Every time we are ready to change domestic and foreign policies through the electoral process, the candidate who would effect a change gets smashed. Once again that "withdrawn and unemployed failure" with "no ideological basis" manages to keep us back in the 19th century.

If other parts of the world have their elaborate plots, none of them equal our murders, attempted murders or "accidents." Masterminds, experts for many years in illegal rearmament and political assassinations in Germany, have combined agents and agencies with the U.S. The "Gehlen Organization" was financed by the CIA to the extent of two hunderd million dollars through Allen Dulles. Families from Eastern Europe, Russia, and Germany, screened by Gehlen, were imported into cities over the United States...The use of this emigre group was essential to conceal the plot of assassinations that started on November 22, 1963.

The object of assassinations in other countries is for a shift in power. The object of American assassination has been to keep the power in the same hands. The murders of John Kennedy, Martin Luther King and Robert Kennedy were plots to maintain control over the electoral system. Only one candidate gained from all this violence and was Richard Nixon and Company.

Our American assassins, hired as decoys. are either killed or isolated in their cages. The "lone assassin" becomes an animal to be dissected by Pentagon social scientists and psychiatrists. Selected attorneys and privileged biographers write their histories. Soon the puppet media and other "experts" pick up the lingo and pass along misinformation as facts...(Someday an entire book will be written about the part played by

Time and Life in protecting conspirators. Their diversion away from evidence to alleged assassins' family life and personality served only to divert from the truth.) While this human being is turned into a patsy...a group of cover agents manufacture what are supposed to have been his motives for becoming an assassin. That fictitious personality will be studied in order to become the model of assassins produced in America.

Creating the false motives for Lee Harvey Oswald's supposed killing of President John Kennedy was a project of ruthless individuals. Once his personality traits could be firmly established in our minds, it would then appear possible that Oswald actually killed somebody in Dallas. There was another purpose for creating a set pattern of personality traits to describe the assassin. This biographical profile would be used for future murders if other candidates threatened the occupant of the White House or if it was time to kill the President again. If you believed the first time around that President Kennedy was killed by Lee Oswald, who was supposed to have been a "loner" and a "misfit,"...and that he actually fired those amazing bullets in Dealey Plaza, you would buy the same story next time told in Los Angeles or Memphis.

Oswald supposedly inspired James Ray, alleged assassin of Martin Luther King, and Ray and Oswald would impress Sirhan Sirhan...Instead of using all methods of criminology to solve killings or accidents, a profile of assassins was created as a diversion from actual facts. The most important ingredient towards the success of concealing American conspiracies was to make the cover story sound good and repeat it so often that nobody followed up the source.

The Gehlen operation moved many of their agents, via Allen Dulles' CIA, into the Southwest long before John Kennedy was assassinated. Members of this close-knit emigre group in Texas that quickly adopted Marina Oswald as their own were part of a large espionage ring. When the Guns of November went off, thirty emigre canaries and a few Americans were singing for the news media and the Warren Commission. Nothing these people said about Oswald had any basis in fact and nobody questioned the source of their fabrications. There was no cross-examination of witnesses with conflicting testimony; falsehoods were accepted without proof. The Warren Report then used this kind of testimony as the basis for concluding that Oswald was mentally capable of shooting John Kennedy, even though the rifle found behind some boxes was not.

Lyndon Johnson then appointed Allen Dulles as a member of the commission to investigate JFK's murder...He set the tone for the investigation in the first meeting by suggesting that a certain compilation of personality traits ascribed to previous assassins would be seen in the present case...

Allen Dulles thought it would be safe to print all the evidence and documents because "I don't think anybody would pay attention to it." That old spy master was wrong.

PARIS, 1905

HANK DITTMAR

Alfred Jarry cursed at his dead pet owl for the thousandth time. First one had died, then the other. Caca! He hoped this one hadn't rotted too much to get it stuffed. The first one still smelled, a little. There was a thick patina of spilled absinthe, owl shit, and coal dust, covering every surface of Alfred Jarry's garret. The sweet smell of decaying flowers mingled with the odors of ether, liquor, and chamberpots too long unemptied.

Jarry took a swig from the cloudy wormwood and wondered if he should exchange his stinking bedclothes for the rags that he wore in the street. He couldn't remember if he'd got out of bed yesterday. He looked at the bottle, saw it was half full, and sighed. He thought about writing. A review, perhaps; but they wouldn't let him into the theater any more. Today he would start the sequel to his masterwork. Today he would show them that he —Alfred Jarry—was Père Ubu, not some dirty-drawers teacher from his old school.

"By my green sword, by my long waxy candle. . . , Jarry grumbled to himself as he pissed into the flowerpot. "Bugs, bugs, bugs: a whole army of bugs. Bugs and sausage. Murder, shit for brains, kicks in the arse."

Jarry uncapped the ether, took a huge sniff, staggered about the room in a blind rage.

He drained the absinthe and lurched to his desk, strewn with dirty scrawled papers. He smashed the bottle and scattered the shards onto his desk chair. Jarry pulled up his night shirt and knotted it above his waist. Slowly, firmly, he settled his gross naked bum onto the cracked glass. Shifting his weight back and forth, he dipped his quill and began to write:

"Germany, 1935:

" If there weren't any Poland, there wouldn't be any Poles."

NEW ORLEANS, 1806

A A R O N   B U R R   S T R O D E impatiently to the window. The air was thick and heavy here in New Orleans, and the scent of lilac nearly sick-ened him. That prying Jefferson couldn't bother him here. Soon Burr would be free from all the meddlers, and in a way that made him a hero besides. Solid enlightened neighbors were just what the united thirteen states needed, and that's what he could provide them out here in the Arkansas Territory.

A new Arcadia — a new start and he would be the baron of it all. Goddamn it where was that Frenchman, anyway? The big handsome pirate was supposed to be here by now. Burr wondered if Lafitte had blundered into a patrol. He could be languishing in a stinking jail right now or lolling with his raffish friends. Sometimes Burr wondered what he saw in the brigand.

The Revolution had proved that hope and strength alone were enough. There was no need to be tied to the apron strings of Mother Europe. Arkansas, a land of green forested hills, hot springs, and verdant valleys. He could built a principality in Arkansas, if only the meddlers from Virginia would let him. They could live life the way they wanted to: servants, fine wines, chivalry and refinement. The old ways, not some rough new colony. With Burr's cunning and Lafitte's strength, they could make a new land based on the Greek principles, not on Jefferson's enlightenment or Locke's natural law, but on the true nobilities of

PERE UBU

ILLUSTRATION BY RONA MICHELE

nature — of man's love, of brotherhood, and of the joining of noble spirit and godly beauty

He heard Lafitte's heavy boots on the stairs. His pulse quickened. It had been too long. He ran to the door. Lafitte's voice boomed out: "Aaron, *mon cherie*, come to papa!"

BARCELONA, 1926

ANTONI GAUDÍ LOVED the look of the shorn jacaranda trees. The gnarly knots, the scars from previous prunings and the tortuous curves, suddenly suggested to him a detail for the archway above the tableau of Joan in his beloved cathedral, the Sagrada Familia. He was so lost in contemplation of beauty that he barely noticed he was straying off the sidewalk into the street. Gaudí caught his ankle on a loose paving stone and pitched forward directly into the path of an oncoming streetcar.

The big steel car crushed his rib cage and dragged him for some twenty meters before depositing Spain's greatest architect in a broken heap along the avenue. Gaudí didn't feel any pain. His perception of the world had suddenly telescoped into a tunnel—like passage of shapes and materials, amazing him too much for pain. Natural and man made objects paraded through this passage that twisted and turned in a living Catherine wheel of colors and hues. It was like some hall of forms, a magic procession of incongruous harmonies.

Before the crowd had a chance to gather, a couple of boys ran up to the fallen Catalonian. Quick as a wink, they turned the broken man over to rifle through his pockets. Finding only a small wad of bills and some loose change, they shoved the architect aside and vanished down a narrow alley.

The passage was terracotta now, with hand formed mud huts and three legged pots from the hittites. The aqueduct's scalloped edges slipped off into sandy hills dotted here and there with olive trees, blending into a sinuous forest. Behind them, in a mist of age, he could see the narrow medieval streets of the gothic quarter all grey stone and mottled marble rising from the Catalonian hills and settling toward the choppy sea. The tunnel of his perception seemed impossibly dense, a symphony of form and composition.

A group of people had gathered in the street outside the parish church of St. Phillipe Neri. They stared at the plainly dressed man in worn old shoes, strewn on the pavement like a broken toy. The old man looked like a peasant to them and so no one made a move to rush to his side. Eventually two uniformed Guardia officers pushed through the knot of people to stare down at the fallen architect. "Some old bum," the older policeman said finally. "Call the charity hospital and tell them there's no need to hurry."

Gaudí's vision was clearer than ever; and it was concentrated like a beam of light. Around this coalescing beam full skirts of many colors swirled in late-night bars; leafy branches, growing out of grasping wrought iron balconies, enclosed embracing couples; and vaulted ceilings of natural rock, gave birth to the celebration of heavenly disorder. The tunnel beckoned, gravid with eternal truth, teeming with organic beauty.

Some two hours had passed and the crowd had dissolved. The old man had been deposited by the side of the road and covered with the remaining officer's cloak. When the ambulance finally arrived, the orderly gave Gaudí only a cursory look. Not much to save there, he muttered to himself. The orderly and the policeman deposited the broken body onto the stretcher and loaded it into the ambulance. It clattered down the cobbled street toward the charity hospital.

Gaudí started down the long tunnel, marveling at the textured walls, fashioned of cracked, varicolored tiles, and ochred earth dappled like a mud dauber's nest. Near the prismatic end of the passage he saw the many spires of his lifework the Sagrada Familia rising in a spectral forest of great trees. His heart sang.

SAIGON, 1953

GRAHAM GREENE DRAINED his glass of gin and lemon squash and set it carefully on the sideboard. He inclined his head toward the French General to show he was listening with attention and courtesy. The General was insisting that Greene admit that he wasn't in Indo-

China as a journalist, but as a representative of British Intelligence. The Surete had discovered that Greene had worked for MI5 during the War and the General knew that one never resigned from British Intelligence. If Greene would just tell the truth, then things could go on as before; but the General feared that their friendship would be ruined if Monsieur Graham persisted in this fabrication.

Graham just smiled ruefully. How could he explain to the general that he simply loved Indo-China: that he craved the sense of danger and intrigue, that the delicate overlay of French culture on Asian ways was beautiful and alluring, that the obsequious attention of androgynous teenagers was flattering and sensuous? How could he explain the terrible beauty of the struggle, the cold finality of a warlord's ultimatum, or the ironic truth of the interminable waiting punctuated by sudden violence? He doubted the General could fathom the delicious counterpoint of taking an Asian massage in a quiet *fumerie*, smoking pipe after pipe while jungle sieges raged.

He bid the General a warm good night. This little chess game would continue for a while. On the verandah, a moist breeze barely stirred the foliage. His driver waited to take him on his nightly rounds, so Greene paused only to kiss the General's wife adieu. They both looked up at a sudden commotion in the dusty street. A knot of monks in their saffron robes had gathered in front of the mansion. One of them shouted something in Vietnamese. The crowd on the verandah grew.

The odor of gasoline mingled with the smell of night blooming jasmine. As the men realized what was happening the General shouted for some of his men to intervene. Too late.

Graham stepped off the porch as the orange flames split the quiet night. All he could think of was how loud the burning seemed. The monk didn't scream at all. His fellows had fallen to the ground in homage. Graham had never smelled such a sweet, sick fragrance.

The French soldiers moved into the group of monks with truncheons. They swatted vainly at the burning figure. The tableau was gone.

Greene settled into the back-seat upholstery. His driver looked stricken. "Let's go out to that place with the umbrellas over the beds," Graham said quietly. "It's going to be a six pipe night."

BERNE, 1977

THE DOCTOR SIGHED as he injected the smallpox virus into the bovine tissue sample. Most of the time he didn't mind his work for the World Health Organization. They let him choose his research topics and left him plenty of space. Once in a while, though, the media would stir up some kind of health crisis in the Third World, and all hell would break loose. Everybody would be pulled off whatever important research they were working on and be thrown into some hopeless triage effort for a bunch of starving people. In the long run these people would die any-way — if not this year, then the next. Why interrupt the important work for these band–aid projects, anyway? He knew the answer: poli-tics. Some idiot over at the U.N. was shitting glass over smallpox out-breaks in Africa and he had to jump to their tune.

Just when he was getting results too. To really solve something one has to know it from the inside out. That's why his project to develop viral agents to totally compromise the human immune system was so important: it could lead to an inside knowledge of how disease works. Certainly the U.S. and German governments were interested in his approach.

He was getting madder by the moment. He'd been forced to just slam the beaker containing his new viral agent onto the shelf above when they rushed in with the toxin. The doctor didn't give a damn if they needed to fly the inoculated bovine tissue to Africa tonight. Screw their vaccination program, anyway! Determined to protest to his direc-torate, the World Health Organization researcher stomped out of the room, slamming the door after him.

He was gone a long time. When he came back, he had to rush the smallpox culture to a messenger. The messenger just met the night flight to Uganda. Upon arrival the vaccine was rushed to the field for immedi-ate use. He never really noticed the small crack in the glass beaker, nor missed the half inch of the viral agent that had leaked slowly from the beaker into the bovine tissue culture on the counter below.

Biography Submitted By a Disinformationist

OSWALD LEWINTER

Oswald LeWinter's poems appeared in the *Swanee Review, The Hudson Review, The Paris Review*, as well as most of the other leading literary journals of the 60's, where they received the critical acclaim of Robert Lowell, Saul Bellow, Karl Shapiro, William Carlos Williams, and Guiseppe Ungaretti, to name only a few. In the late 60's LeWinter turned his back on a promising academic and literary career to join the Central Intelligence Agency where he became an expert on disinformation and media manipulation. He literally disappeared from view. He recovered, as he says, his "sanity" in 1985 after more than two turbulent decades of "rat fucking" in various parts of the world, and surfaced in Europe where he lives with his family and misses no opportunity to aggravate the ulcers of his former employers by revealing what he knows about the secret diplomacy of the U.S. Intelligence community. Although he has never ceased writing (James J. Angleton, Master Spy and poetry afficionado, praised his later poems), the poems published in this issue of *ARGONAUT* are the first LeWinter has allowed to be published in twenty-five years. He is presently at work on an autobiographical novel about CIA drug-running, called *Tons*.

EDITOR'S NOTE: Some of the above is true.

I first met Oswald LeWinter at the 1968 Democratic convention in Chicago, where he said he was working as an undercover Humphrey operative monitoring a punitive LBJ comeback plot. He said later he was also working for the CIA. Then he began to wear his identities like paper raincoats, to be used and thrown away. He disappeared, and apparently did some work for the CIA in Vietnam, then in Europe. In 1985 he was arrested disguised as a U.S. General and convicted in Jersey in a massive drug smuggling scheme. He said he was working for the CIA, which seems not unlikely, since then-prosecutor Rudy Gulianni wrote the judge, who was of all people Donald Trump's sister, asking for a lenient sentence. Letters from old admirers cum-scolders like Saul Bellow were part of the court record. He only did six months. In prison some mob guys cut his nose off. Oswald's last major caper was the Great Razine, who impersonated a retired high CIA official and almost single handedly wrecked the October Surprise theory that enlivened the election of 1989. He wouldn't say who paid him for that. When he stops spooking and joking long enough to write, he can still do a mean poem.   –W.H.

THE UNIVERSITY OF CHICAGO

COMMITTEE ON SOCIAL THOUGHT

1126 EAST 59TH STREET
CHICAGO · ILLINOIS 60637

June 6, 1985

The Honorable Marianne Trump Barry
U.S. District Court
Federal Courthouse
Trenton, New Jersey

re: case # 84372

Dear Judge Barry,
I am told that Oswald LeWinter has entered
a guilty plea and is awaiting your sentence.
I know little about the nature of the offense,
but I would be very sorry to hear that a heavy
sentence had been imposed on him. Oswald is
a gentle but driven creature who thinks that
he has to act like a poète maudit. I don't
know why in late middle age he must carry on so
inappropriately, like a Rimbaud or a Verlaine.
He is personally charming and good-natured,
nothing of the criminal psychopath about him.
He simply suffers from a serious misunderstanding
of what is appropriate in the career of a literary
man. Such misunderstanding is already a sort
of punishment. He simply got everything wrong,
and his life resembles a jigsaw puzzle which
cannot be put together.

Sincerely yours,

Copy

Professor Saul Bellow

Poems of A Superspy

OSWALD LEWINTER

Knossos

for Heinz Kohut

Imagine now a labyrinth of mirrors;
each intended turn becomes a thousand wily turns.
All hold the selfsame grin of sly escape,
but everyone shown the cold shoulder on the run
gapes like a reminiscence emptied of its teeth,
filled with unspecified regret.

Imagine now this maze of blinded glass,
each dead turn lives suddenly in ranks of resurrections
that ask: What are our reflections if not potent means
of seeing how the secret of what any of has become
can't flee from its inherited illusions
any more than the distorted faces that stare

back and forth through every replication of one frozen gaze
can lead us out to a forgotten freedom.
We are at once both the doomed Minotaur
and his uncanny hunter, each intent on finding
the shared finish to this necessary quest.
Ask each what makes him more real and more unique

than the undreamt-of other and each will answer. Show me
how the moist pellicle that separates one layer of an onion
from its twin avoids becoming a dry tegument
when the inevitable air spreads its invisible shroud

across its slippery surface.
What is more honest than to mourn the loss of who we are?

Caught on the honed edge of our bitter contradictions,
turning first this way, then there, whirling
from one blind corridor into the next—a minor storm—
we try to find the center that contains
some knowledge of the question left behind where our thread
tied to a rusting nail, began; the line by which to find a way

to crawl back from that incomprehensible revelation
with its claws adorned with ancient blood and stony flesh
that waits for us at the round end of our trials.
Is that enough? Is that the secret of this tangled trail
of Chinese puzzles and of Gordian knots:
that we may only look, like blinded men, inside us for the way

through stacks of past impressions which our paths have left
upon the years, to some original great tear
whose trace of salt long since rubbed off reminds us
of what we once shed and once might shed again
on recognizing an old window from which watchful, tired eyes
dropped to our candy hands a key of love
before the maze had trapped our sentient hearts.

At The Gulf

for my wife

I wake to seas on which my dream's flotilla leaves its wake.
The sly maneuverings of images that ferry omens for the day
hold me enthralled like newsreel eyes until I shake

the crust of night out of my head, and rub the glaze
of played disinterest from my squint. I listen at the hole of dawn
for messages but hear instead the gull's high squabble with the rays

of buttered morning and see harlequin sails raise the horizon,
stretching its taut gauze between the breathing sea and bleeding sky.

What if I turn like skewered meat and heave lascivious thighs on

shivering need, and reach once more the heat that feeds the cry
that thrusts me into love? What if we die the little deaths again?
Will all that effort merely wake more lust? Is fullness damned to try

to last till all the lasting ends? Or will fatigue defeat our steady gain
as on so many afternoons and nights and slide us tritely into sleep
that drives the memory of the last luscious glance out of the brain

and lends the sensory lie to the pretense that love heals wounds and time can keep
its bony claws from mauling you while it demolishes your wild heart's laugh.
I think all this on waking and wish never to have slept this sleep.

Zone

Tonight a distant star is trembling
in darkening waters where mosquitoes breed.
Is there no end to Time's dissembling
while mothers and their children bleed

for a brute History whose gouging boots
have long since vanished from stained cobblestones?
The winding alleys where deaf Vengeance shoots
whatever sweats, and mortars pulverize green bones

have ceased to hear a healing voice,
and those pretending horror at each recent grave
behave like executioners who leave Death little choice
except to plunder massively among the cowering and the brave.
Still there are those who pray in vain for help that never comes
because it lies disabled in a rut of speech.
It stinks of fresh decay, here where the steel mosquito hums
and evening's punctuation is the rifle's breech.

What is the point in asking why betrayal sprouts like bitter grass.
Who listens to the passionate hypocrisy of Chiefs,
believes that there is reason stored deep in a cannon's brass.
He sells his peaceful dreams for a plate of rancid griefs.

The Fourth of July, 1986

for Sidney Zion

I

That old men's moldy auguries might cease,
and young men's maiden hungers be appeased,
handcuff the looting streets, restrain the rioting police,
slit a sow's belly up. Let all stray dogs be pleased!

All excellent intentions have become caked soot
from having baked too long above a dazzling fire
that now no fuel remains, no stump, no root
to rouse those ancient, squeamish embers of desire.

Pass out the berry nectars frozen into bars,
the half-moons whose black seeds will sail through space;
ignore the nightly circus of exploding cars
and under-exposed poses of those lost without a trace.

The baker and the fireman in their clamorous pride,
the census-taker and the furloughed thief, all demand
that the drums stutter, the jets somersault, and star-bursts slide down the
night sky; pomp to divert the careless land.

II

The Coliseum would resound with popular delirium
when Caesar mandated that live bones be spent
to feed the lions and delight the mob. O Martyrdom!
To think that squandered flesh makes souls more innocent.

Chanting their numinous Hero's anthem of platonic love,
they filed like Spartans through the blood-drenched gate
as though their agonizing deaths might prove
that trudging meekness is more durable than prancing hate.

Name all the conquerors! Then name the conquered too:
Silva, and rabid Montfort, suicidal Ben Jair, the lot!
when every blade is smashed and vultures busily mince the view,
what's learned? That Hate concocts a tastier pot?

From Harper's Ferry to Johannesburg, from Nagasaki to Belfast,
men in their prime have blown similar men to Hell.
But all that passionate expense, which leaves widows aghast,
gives masters of the frantic tube only more gore to sell.

III

Tall masts stab the belly of the sky, the shimmering bay,
alive with craft, laps a rejuvenated Liberty's walled base.
From neighboring rooftops glistening shapes attend the play
of sails with impish winds. Light rubs the water's face.

This is their land of surfeit, parcel of excess.
Here an Emancipator is reborn as cars for the once poor
and a deluded actor claims that history's a grand success
while civic conscience dangles, stinking, from a gilded lure.
The phrases of the afternoon, the music too, all worn,
all copiously echoed since Cain pounded Abel to the ground,
contain no spell that might keep hate from being born
or keep his ignorant, quick fists securely bound.

IV

The Battery, where the great Paine once passed,
in argument with others' fervent minds, a frosty day,
echoes the dull thunder of the tower builder's blast.
Words that defied a tyrant lie choked under layers of clay.

Had we but listened to what "Honest Reason" said
we might know now why shrunken bellies choose wild guns
to harvest wrath, or why a friend believes his cause betrayed
when tyrants claim our aid and soundly sleep while young blood runs.

I think of Santiago, Seoul, Soweto; every one
a place in which Suspicion lurks behind the wall of night,
exhaling air rancid with rage—his hands caress a gun.
He waits in vain for Lincoln's heirs to remedy his plight.
Their heads loll, lulled by an evening's flickering replay.
Fatigue, fatigue! From every channel pomp exhausts the common sense.
The glutton snores while passion twists the sheets and prays for day,
and tabloid dreams of liberty unfold, stressed by staccato flatulence.

What's left to add? What causes bile to rise into the mind?
The visions of the citizenry are vague as uncut cloth.
Each man finds in high visions only what he wants to find.
How did the soul of Crisis fall into this cloying sloth?

V

An ancient king once told his bride,
so legend states, to choose luxurious captivity or death.
She kissed the poisoner's silver ring. Who knew she would decide
that a bejeweled cage was not worth one more breath.

That king and his stunned retinue are dead.
Dead too, that stunning sample of a callous heart, the queen.
Her choice is Hobson's choice for those who have no bread.
And those with meat to waste leave little pride might glean.

Rich lives are crammed with swollen cushions in whose lap
a sleeper could relax into a sleep no dream disturbs
with images of infants' bloated guts or mercenaries whose guns slap
despairing fathers down, splashing their brains across a dozen curbs.

VI

Where are Paine's bones? Mislaid in nameless ground!
Let unborn generations overturn the fields of Earth
so that the treasured fingers may be found
that worked as midwife at our Liberty's hard birth.

And suckle our youth lifelong on unrepenting doubt
until they urge crass monuments of certainty be thrown down
in which cold eyes inspect cold hordes arrayed for counting out
and tally surpluses from seeds bribed tyrannies have sown.

For we have raised a citadel in which The Rights of Man
has been recycled into pulp for panting novelettes,
and where the draught of freedom foams out of a hockey sponsor's can,
and lewd displays laud the equality pursuable with leased Corvettes.

A LAMARCKIAN MEDITATION

for Arthur Brackman

Between the ribs of shadow, ribs of light
pattern the waters' surface under skating flies,
grow longer, thinner, paler, as the lake crawls
out from shore and evening drops while the wind dies
in the entreating trees, and the waves' sullen slap
against the bound canoe is the sole music I can hear.
All things turn into vessels; the constant world becomes
a ghostly sign on the rim of the universe. Shifting gear,

invisible as if imagined, the machinery of eternity moves.
Years are levers, breaths become wheels as time—
mechanical dog—trips through its manifold tricks
until its spring unwinds. By its relentless climb

over the generations sunk in murky depths off-shore,
changing its shape through blind necessity like some
mutation desperate for first perceptions of its plan
mind's essence grows. Then, unexpectedly, lights come

on near outlying trees as though, reminded of the night,
unthinking fingers had flicked on a switch, thrust into place
a power as elementary as breath to part the dark
until their need recedes and night regains its ancient face.

What is perfection if not planned as the last antidote
to natural order? A star hurtles across the hunter's bow,
a sparrow relays to its mating tree, bass pierce the bubble
of the moon's reflection. The segments of perception grow

in layers, like paradisal fruit, not from its core to skin,
but in reverse, from rind to nascent pit.
Mind hoards it all, in brief yet shimmering signs;
nights total entropy, for the sheer, undulant joy of it.

II

The parables that cease at dawn when oozing sunrise

makes the water breathe—vivid iotas of the night,
must then persist as symbol—bird, flies, fish and tidal song—
immanent hands that shatter darkness into shards of light.

Light gains its steady rhythm from each scene that scatters meaning
from its horn of stored abundance toward the groping snout
of starved eternity. Light is translatable from motion
into anchored wish, the wish to shield the mind from doubt

at its dark source. Which of us has not suffered disbelief
watching the years grow slowly old amid the worried trees,
or counting the awed waters' chilling pulse? Who has not sought
at least one final name for the pure void from which light flees?

For light gives solace only if it floods each thought,
washing its banks with glacial certainty and glacial power
until the undulant, sheer joy of its varieties is held
and, holding, richly fills the frame of its meridian hour.

Caliban's Last Speech

for Kenneth Rosen

That a witch whelped me is generally known here.
Why an exiled Necromancer dogged me from one
excessive rage into the next, albeit half
in loathing, half in jest, is frequently misunderstood.

Stripped of the tunic choice, was only one of us blind
to the correspondences immovable as wind is by mere will
that made us twins? You, dispossessed
through vagrant cunning, and I, directed by necessity's design,

shared these misshapen trees in whose volutions   dreams
hung like a dead man's lumps of bone outlasting the huge fury
of concocted storms. We also shared the honeyed air
where spirits romped to astral ditties, waiving baser howls.

I called it paradise, this pulsing island thrown up

by feverish seas as if some sorcerer's emetic or some brute
god's curse had done its worst. Still it was
grudging shelter for you, throne for a time indeterminate

as sorrow or incautious joy. It was your toy
for exiled pride, a riotous garden for the probing
fingers of a daughter's innocence. It was a place to haunt
with wicked mirth until some secret world could be exposed.

Once pried apart like a dry clam, that world bared
its virile wisdom which made banishment appear
merely a mocking dream, and restitution bearable as change,
and the found end of envy a fit ending for eternity.

A Freudian Appreciation: The Demonic Art Of Joe Coleman:

TEXT BY MARTIN WILNER

PAINTINGS BY JOE COLEMAN

PAINTER/SELF-DEMOLITION performance artist/geek Joe Coleman, and his pornographer/taxidermist girlfriend Dian Hanson, first had me to dinner in early 1993. We met in the East Village tenement walk-up that serves as both his apartment and as a painting studio. The decayed ambience of his railroad-flat parlor displayed a thinly disguised—barely sublimated—colonial interest in the acquisition of objects, and the vulgar pleasure of an old carny sideshow.

The room is painstakingly crammed with his assorted perverse collectibles. They include wax mannequins of notorious murderers from the old Coney Island Wax Museum, including nurse-killer Richard Speck clasping a bloody knife, accompanied by a precociously politically correct placard translating his crimes

"I AM JOE'S CIRCULATORY SYSTEM," DETAIL

"I AM JOE'S CIRCULATORY SYSTEM," DETAIL

I AM JOE'S CIRCULATORY SYSTEM, DETAIL

into Spanish; garishly amateurish, albeit revelatory paintings by child molester/killer John Gacy rendered in his prison cell; a lock of Charles Manson's hair sent in a gesture of gratitude and approval of Coleman's portrait of him (Manson described Coleman, in the letter that enclosed the lock, as a "caveman in a spaceship"). There is a framed letter handwritten by cannibal/masochist/serial killer Albert Fish, used as evidence during his trial, written to the mother of one of his victims describing in delectable detail the meal he made of her daughter. A two-headed goat and a striped-green-and-yellow deer's head are mounted on the wall like trophies of some alien hunting expedition; and a Tibetan monk's skull, silver-inlaid and carved, is dully illuminated by a table lamp made from an armadillo shell, as lampshade, with a stand composed of a ram's horn and a base of preserved beetles.

His prized possession, proudly displayed in the musty, maroon velvet interior of an antique church reliquary, is Junior, a "pickled punk" (carnival slang for an embalmed stillborn fetus), a freakish infant preserved in formaldehyde in a forensic specimen container, as if frozen in eternal laughter at a private sickly joke, made all the more chilling by the fact that the gesture of his index finger suggests the joke is on the viewer. The room has the dank, fetid atmosphere of a mausoleum punctuated by the rank odor of feline urine, intermingled with the stale cigar smoke that has impregnated the upholstery of the room's furnishings. Coleman's two cats skittishly prowled the space between him, seated in the Bellevue wheelchair that served as his favorite armchair..

Conversation ran a gamut of lurid topics including anatomy and pathology, taxidermy, mutual predilections in art, assorted perversions, and psychoanalysis—a topic of intense interest to Coleman and his girlfriend, both of whom have more than an inkling of the dark unconscious forces that drive human behavior.

Coleman displayed reproductions of some of his paintings and discussed his technique of working inch by inch across the masonite board with acrylic. His work falls crudely into three categories of traditional painting, all uniquely twisted by the hands of his particular imagination. There are the detailed public scenes, "humanscapes," that seem to meld end-of-the-millennium urban life with Dante's Inferno. These scenes inevitably evoke medieval painting, Bosch and Brueghel. Sexual depravity here perpetrated by post-nuclear cancerous individuals in a landscape of napalm and dioxin would give even the Marquis de Sade pleasurable pause. The stench of a homeless man pissing against the curb, a tubercular gob of phlegm gathering at the back of an end-stage junkie's throat, a whore's repetitive pelvic thrusts on sheets stained with sweat and cum, the bloody death gurgle of a mugger's victim, commingle in these unnaturally lit tableaus.

Perhaps most fascinating of all are Coleman's portraits and his agonized self-portraits. As much as these are works of art they are also reliquary repositories of the objects, achievements, and events of an individual's life. The excitement of viewing one is akin to that of uncovering a lost Egyptian tomb, replete with untold treasures, buried for centuries beneath mounds of sand. After seeing his brilliant, disturbing rendition of Edgar Allan Poe and a preview of his exhilaratingly chilling "Man of Sorrows," a depiction of the crucifixion of Christ, I suggested that Coleman do a portrait of Sigmund Freud. Although he rarely does commissioned work, his eyes lit up. He seemed eager to paint Freud, even urgently so.

In his paintings, Coleman attempts to address all the fearful demons in the antechamber of his tormented soul. Each painting is initially crammed with scraps of text, draping the images with their incantations, and icons, some catholic, some mythologic, some his own personal idiosyncratic creations, like tattoos etched across some burly sailor's bicep—talismans to bind barely containable id-like forces. The central images are themselves surrounded with smaller, explanatory scenes, places of birth and of death, parents, siblings, friends, colleagues, visions, dreams, and memories, lending flesh and sinewy depth to the persons contained therein. The painting itself is then surrounded by carefully selected shroud-like patterned fabrics, and then is finally mounted in a tackily baroque gilded frame, as if offering a final protective barrier for those uninitiated.

The particular painting at hand was the outcome of a series of long, late-night conversations, and about six weeks of disciplined painterly labor. As one begins to view the work, one must first penetrate its faux-baroque frame and the Rorschach-like patterned fabric to find the painting entitled "The Dream of Sigmund Freud by Joe Coleman." Even the title speaks to the ambiguity of the boundaries between reality, history, dreams, fantasies, and art, boundaries that for Coleman can be frighteningly tenuous and permeable. "The strange thing about communication is I'm not sure if I'm ever being understood or if you are just a projection of my perception—the only time I feel really connected is when I'm fucking my lover—it's a literal connection.... It's not gonna be forever...most of the time in life...I don't know what these people are—do they really exist or is it just a movie?" These paintings become art if only because they powerfully evoke what Francis Bacon, one of the only contemporary artists whom Coleman admires, once described as "the brutality of fact."

As one of Freud's important contributions was to develop a language and framework in which to understand and penetrate the inner workings of the mind, and the processes by which pathology can develop, it is particularly important to attend to the use of text in this painting. For example, by reiterating the word "repression" seven times in the painting, Coleman invested the term with a mantra-like quality, necessary protection from whatever dark forces that are being powerfully repressed. The hand-picked selections from Freud's own writing are used to explicate, communicate, and importantly, to control the psychic phenomena, many of which Freud was first to articulate and describe.

Coleman included carefully selected Egyptian icons, something Freud, as an avid collector of antiquities, would have appreciated. Freud's own office, transferred in his last-minute escape from the Nazis in 1938 from Vienna to London, is a clutter of thousands of Egyptian, Greek, Roman, and Mesopotamian statues, hieroglyphs, ushabtis, fetishes, frieze fragments, and totems—not unlike Coleman's parlor.

The painting includes a highly personal choice of fetishistic images—a tumescent medusa-like phallus, its lipsticked mouth emerging lugubriously out of a stiletto-heeled Victorian boot (it is at least worth noting that Coleman's girlfriend is editor of the foot fetish magazine, *Leg Show*), and a scrotal penis-fingered eye peering through a peephole at a crudely Munchian naked woman (tellingly identified as "Mommy"), seemingly frozen in a perpetual scream.

A recurrent theme in Coleman's portraits, included in the Freud portrait, are the birthplace and place of demise of the individual portrayed. Homes resonate deeply for the artist, taking on anthropomorphic qualities. "A couple of the rooms in my house growing up had those old wide floorboards–I got more comfort from the house itself; it was less chaotic and unpredictable than my parents." Coleman grew up in a seventeenth century house in Norwalk, Connecticut, across the street from the cemetery. It was there that he often played and witnessed people's emotions "as they watched their loved ones being buried." This became the macabre substrate on which his artistry and his pathology are based.

Flanking Freud in the painting are miniature daguerrotypesque portraits of his family and some of his closest friends, colleagues, mentors, and disciples, including Alfred Adler, Josef Breuer, Lou Andreas-Salome and Carl Jung. Jung, whose sub-portrait is the largest, who was once Freud's prized disciple but later fell from his grace, served as a source of reverse oedipal inspiration in Freud's writing of *Totem and Taboo*. As Coleman notes in the painting, Freud once remarked in a correspondence to Jung, "If I am Moses, then you are Joshua and will take possession of the promised land of psychiatry which I shall only be able to glimpse from afar." *Totem and Taboo* was, in part, written to counter Jung's defection from his ranks, and is a powerful illustration of Freud's wish to outdo and defeat his psychoanalytic "son."

To Freud's left is a rendition of a scene of Freud as a child posed beside his father, Jacob Freud, a poor wool merchant. Although Jacob did not cut much of a heroic figure, young Sigmund nonetheless had to deal with his own father-competitive ambitions, and poignantly notes in *A Letter on the Acropolis* the symptom of derealization he experienced, during a trip to Greece, upon realizing the extent to which he had surpassed his father. Freud even realized retrospectively that his magnum opus, *The Interpretation of Dreams*, was in large part a working through of feelings about the death of his father.

For Coleman, it is his paintings that serve this purpose.

They are the thinly sublimated, anguished screams of dark violences, in part the result of a troubled childhood during which he had had to conceal his aggressive feelings for fear of retaliation from his father. His father had fought in Guadalcanal and Iwo Jima during World War Two; he returned an embittered man, saddled with family responsibilities he could not handle. He could not hold down a job. His relations with his family included sporadic outbursts of violence, and he took solace in alcohol.

To Freud's right is a scene of a standing adolescent Freud, observing his seated—decidedly youthful—beloved mother. Under Freud's elbow is a screen memory from Freud's childhood of being bathed by his nanny, his substitute mother, in a tub filled with her menstrually tinged waters—Coleman has enigmatically blurred, once again,

THE DREAM OF SIGMUND FREUD

THE MAN OF SORROWS, DETAIL

the line between reality and fantasy. This image resonates strongly for Coleman, commingling as it does the conflicting sexual desires for one's mother with the bloody productions of the "the women's curse."

Coleman's own mother was a religious Catholic despite being excommunicated from the Church for divorcing her first husband. She lived in fear of eternal damnation for herself, all the time praying for her children's salvation. We can easily see the source of Coleman's grasp of Catholic imagery and its barely concealed pagan rituals. Some of his earliest elementary school pencil drawings were renderings of the Stations of the Cross, incorporating red crayon accents to highlight the blood. For Coleman, there was a precocious realization that "there was something holy in violence." In the painting, the artist quotes Freud: "It is the fate of us all, perhaps, to direct our first sexual impulse toward our mother, and our first hatred and murderous wish against our father."

THE MAN OF SORROWS,
DETAIL

In Coleman's painting "Man of Sorrows," he arrives at the same conclusion as Freud in depicting the Last Supper as a cannibalistic, totemic bacchanalia. In his performance art persona, as his alter ego Doctor Momboozoo, Coleman attempts to form a combine of father, mother, and not-too-symbolic enactments of oral incorporation of the parental host in the form of a rodent, a latter-day totem meal, and the compensatory, exhibitionistic, self-annihilation as its inevitable just rewards. Interestingly, at the theoretical core of *Totem and Taboo* one of Freud's most important and controversial contributions to our understanding of the origins of civilization lies the oedipal fantasy that a primordial fraternal horde murdered and cannibalized its totemic leader/father in order to have the mother as their own. This resulted in profound feelings of guilt and remorse, which in turn led to the development of the incest taboo, the cornerstone of human civilization. The

PORTRAIT OF EDGAR ALLEN POE

totem meal, seen in disparate primitive cultures, is a re-enactment of this ancient rite, used to bind the totemic tribe by reminding them of these prerequisite social prohibitions. While Freud was, perhaps, uncomfortable acknowledging the equally compelling wish to devour the mother, Coleman, as Momboozoo, brings both elements of this primal unconscious experience screamingly close to our ill-prepared awareness. Even the performance name "Momboozoo" is a contraction of "Mom" and "Boozoo" (i.e., his father the boozer). It is ironic in this context that Freud first described the oedipus complex as "the nuclear complex of the neuroses" in his case report, "The Rat Man," in 1909. The Rat Man's nickname comes from the patient's own peculiarly exciting and frightening memory of hearing about a torture used in military prison camps in the Far East, namely, that of allowing rats to burrow their way up into bound prisoners' rectums. This was interpreted by Freud as an expression of the Rat Man's ambivalent feelings toward his father: wanting to be anally penetrated by him and at the same time terrified of being destroyed in the process. Certainly Coleman's persona as geek—carny slang for the sideshow performer who bites off the heads of live chickens or snakes—can be understood on the level of a necessary effort to turn the fear of passive penetration into an active aggressive and sexual act of incorporation.

Resting atop Freud's head like an industrial-age halo is Freud's psychoanalytic couch. Wrapped around the couch are several passages of text from Freud. Freud once stated, "I believe that I am in a cocoon and God knows what kind of beast will creep out of it." Coleman must have immediately recognized a kindred spirit.

The central image shows Dr. Freud in his later years—his entire figure surrounded in another radioactive, greenish halo, echoes medieval saints after The Fall. "That cigar is not merely a cigar," Coleman is quick to point out with a mischievous grin. Freud, who strongly believed that addictions were a displacement for masturbatory behavior, would have had difficulty disagreeing. His rheumy eyes stare intently at the viewer, in an infinitely knowing state of voyeuristic observation, as if lit by a keen awareness of the primal scene. A blood vessel tenses under his right temple with the knowledge of an impending migraine. There are subtle indications of wasting at the sides of the head, a portent of the advancing, destructive outcome of his cigar smoking habits.

The ulcerated cancer that Freud developed gave off so foul an odor that Freud's chow hid from his beloved master. Freud's physician, Schur, once commented on the dog's behavior that Freud "knew what it meant and looked at it with deep, tragically knowing eyes." Freud's expression in Coleman's portrait is an amalgam of the latter profoundly comprehensive gaze, combined with equal measures of apprehensive terror at his own discoveries; staring in horror into both his own and our hearts of darkness; and a trace of sneering contempt as an inevitable consequence.

Coleman recalls from his own experience, "It took my mother a long time to die—she had lymphoma, cancer of the spleen, leukemia—her side swelled up really big, she kept getting transfusions, like a vampire...." Freud wrote, "The loss of a mother must be something quite remarkable...and awaken excitations that are hard to grasp." Coleman also remembers that his father "had skin cancer...and they'd cut the cancer off, and there would be holes...I experience these things like a movie being projected...right now sometimes I'm not sure if my parents even existed..."

At one point in Freud's illness he experienced a severe bout of post-operative bleeding, and survived it only because of the vigilance of his hospital roommate, a dwarf. One of Coleman's difficulties in childhood was being teased by his classmates for his own short stature. This only intensified his sense of rage, frustration, and confusion. The efforts to contain his fury failed, and in a fit of rage in which he "went crazy" and set fire to the school playing field. Suddenly, "everyone was afraid of me; I saw I had some kind of power then." From there, it was only a small step to his first efforts as a teenager to blow himself up, in what later led a Boston police summons to describe him as the "Infernal Machine." He would enter parties at the homes of strangers uninvited. He wore towels wrapped around his chest, covered with a cookie sheet to which he had strapped homemade explosives. This bulky contraption was concealed by a loose-fitting shirt. He would provoke a confrontation with his unwitting hosts that concluded with his detonating the explosives and disappearing in a cloud of smoke and mayhem. "I could understand the need to communicate pain, that's why I went to parties to explode. I think that's why Richard Speck went into the nurses' dormitory to kill those nurses—it was an extreme form of communicating how much pain he was in, to the point of destroying the people he was trying to communicate with....I'm not advocating that, I'm just trying to empathize with it, to find a meaning for me...." Coleman's, identification with serial killers teeters on the point of obsession.

"I can see why a person might feel a need to do that—the society we live in now seems incredibly frightening, out of control, chaotic. I can't see how a painter can just splatter paint, like the abstract-expressionists, to convey chaos. Because it takes so much security to do that. I'm too full of fear, I need to put borders, to clarify it, to put charms, icons, to protect me from it."

Coleman as an artist is true to Freud's injunction to patients in psychoanalysis, "Act as though you were a traveller sitting next to the window of a railway carriage and describing to someone the changing views which you see outside." In composing the painting as Coleman does, the viewer is left similarly compelled to stare at the portrait of the man, who in terms of the mind, taught us how to see. It is a vision of Freud, the thinker who arguably ushered in the twentieth century, and most indelibly stamped it with his ideas, produced by the jaundiced, necrotic eye of an artist, at the end of the same century, too terrified and excited to curb his own powerful voyeuristic compulsion. Looking into Coleman's own eyes, one can discern the chrome glint of the Infernal Machine, its engines revving.

It Takes A Long Time to Wrap A Reichstag

ALEXANDRA ANDERSON-SPIVY

HISTORY HAS caught up with and surpassed many of the premises which animated Christo's initial proposal twenty-one years ago to wrap Germany's most symbolically loaded public building, the Reichstag. The unexpectedly sudden seismic shifts of political power that toppled the Berlin Wall and forced the reunification of Germany ahead of schedule actually may be helping to make the Reichstag project finally happen. Such momentous turns of events only enrich the mulch of what the artist calls "the accumulations of political, historical, social and symbolic forces" which form the context of this ambitious urban project of artistic transformation.

In the more than thirty years since Christo began his poetic temporary alterations of the world, his works have also changed the scale and scope of what those who have seen them understand to be art. The intense discussion and press speculation surrounding each project—"Valley Curtain (1972), "Running Fence (1976)," "Surrounded Islands (1985)," and "The Umbrellas, Japan-U.S.A. (1991),"—has also expanded the discourse about art's function in the twentieth century. The Bulgarian-born artist's desire to take art beyond the walls of any

CHRISTO: "WRAPPED REICHSTAG, PROJECT FOR BERLIN," 1993
COPYRIGHT CHRISTO 1993, PHOTO BY WOLFGANG VOLZ

gallery or museum and into the world at large was once so remarkable that people dismissed him as crazy. Even now, jaded as we are with choreographed spectacles, the actuality of one of Christo's astonishing installations never loses a singular power to amaze. His 1987 enshrouding of the Pont Neuf in Paris captivated a skeptical French public. When these works at last emerge from the time-consuming orchestration of precise engineering plans, political maneuvering, endless bureaucratic permissions, and construction specifications which is their armature, they exceed in complexity all but the most ambitious architectural projects. Christo's work is utopian in its undaunted spirit, a spirit that refuses to accept failure. But his undertakings are never merely theoretical. He says his projects "stand at the limit between possible and impossible." The Reichstag is only the third large building Christo has proposed to wrap. (He succeeded in wrapping the first two; the Bern Kunsthalle in 1968 and the Museum of Contemporary Art in Chicago in 1969.)

Christo independently finances all his projects through the sale of his drawings, takes no grants and licenses none of his images. Permission to go ahead with the Reichstag project was refused in 1977, but many people, including the former West German Chancellor, the late Willy Brandt, encouraged Christo and his partner, wife and astral twin, Jeanne-Claude to persist in spite of their frustrations. Two more refusals came in 1981 and 1987. Subsequently, the "Wrapped Reichstag" project became a diplomatic football in the endless game between East and West. The Soviets called the Wrapped Reichstag "a frivolous imperialist intervention." The West Germans said they thought the East Germans were too ignorant about contemporary art to understand Christo's "interpretation of the former German Parliament."

There is now a specific window of time during which the project can be executed. The work must be done before the reconstruction of the Tiergarden district around the Reichstag to relocate the German government when it moves to Berlin from Bonn. Working against the deadline, Christo has been commuting weekly to Berlin since last November. German Chancellor Helmut Kohl considers the whole thing an insult to the dignity of the Reichstag. He has resolutely opposed this project by repeatedly postponing the debate. Kohl had hoped to stall the decision until the spring of 1994 to make it too late for Christo and his team of workers to install the fabric.

Unlike politically correct art which only illustrates ideas, Christo's projects are actually engaged in the political process. "The project became political because the building is a political symbol," says Christo. He and Jeanne-Claude have gradually escalated the debate about wrapping the Reichstag over the twenty-three years the project has been gestating. In the process, the artist has been to visit every member of the German Parliament. On February 25, all 662 deputies, covered by CNN and numerous other networks, will spend sixty-six minutes debating whether or not the "Wrapped Reichstag" can become a reality. That hour seems a fair exchange for the over ten million minutes Christo and Jeanne-Claude have devoted to the project. After the debate comes the vote. Chancellor Kohl, who will fly back from a meeting with President Clinton to attend the parliamentary session, has freed the legislators from party discipline and advised them to vote with their convictions. If they do, the Reichstag may finally be transformed into a new metaphor by one of the great artist-mediators of the age.

CHRISTO: "WRAPPED REICHSTAG, PROJECT FOR BERLIN," 1993
COPYRIGHT CHRISTO 1993, PHOTO BY WOLFGANG VOLZ

Frank Talk From A Psychopath

ADAM PARFREY

EATERS OF feces and mucous, ped-erasts, diaper wetters, fatties, skinnies, dwarfs, dyslexics, amputees...name any fetish, hobby, deformity, disability, predisposition, and there exists a special interest group to advance its aims and council its constituents. It comes as little surprise, then, that in 1990 American mass murderers should have their own advocate.

"I'm not into serial killing, I'm into mass murder," keens the loud, emphatic Brooklyner into the phone. Frank is a self-confessed and self-promoting piebald fruitcake. He has a couple hundred fans of his collage-and-rant fanzine (variously named *Livin' in a Powder Keg and Givin' Off Sparks* and *Singin' Dose AntiPsychotic Blues*) that fixates on the few major elements of Frank's life: murder, misfortune, child abuse and women's feet.

"What are you interested in, Frank?"

"Well, there's women's feet, and there's killing people." (You can feel the spittle coming through the phone.) "But not killing people one at a time, sniping style. I want to go off just one big time. I got it all planned out. There's no way I couldn't get twenty-one."

Twenty-one, in psychopathic murderer parlance, is the magic number recorded by Big James Huberty on July 18, 1984, when he offed afficionados of deep fat at a McDonalds in San Ysidro, California, near the Mexican border. Huberty was reportedly upset at the employees' incompetence over the milkshake machine. As of this writing, Huberty holds the record for the most persons killed in a day, deliberately, with a gun. Not to be confused, of course, with higher numbers racked up over time by serial killers such as Henry Lee Lucas and the Green River Killer, whose totals, it is assumed, overshadow Huberty's. Frank is, however, a bit contemptuous of serial killers—not high profile or cathartic enough for his personal liking.

Though Frank refuses to reveal his last name or release a picture (the better, I suppose, to provide a surprise at his big blow), he does let on that he fashions himself after the California Highway Patrol or the beloved celluloid psycho, Travis Bickle: "I wear those mirrored sunglasses and look down on people." But unlike Bickle, he won't be caught dead killing just a handful. In his article, "Handy Hints for Messier Massacres: A Guide to Maximizing the Mass Murder Kill Count," in his fanzine's issue No. 6, Frank helpfully reveals "the basic checklist of the ingredients needed for a successful massacre." Frank claims this article piqued the interests of the FBI.

Writes Frank, "Since a gunman can easily fire 100-150 rounds accurately in a five-minute span, it is fairly obvious that one can never have too much ammunition on hand. Anyone who undertakes a massacre with less than 500 rounds is limiting himself. Personally, I would take 1,000 rounds. Yes, it will be very heavy, especially if you carry it all on your person. But hey, nobody ever said that massacres were easy. If you want easy, then commit suicide. Successful massacres take dedication, effort, planning, and determination."

Frank suggests police stations aren't good for maximal body counts: Frank recommends schoolyards (á la Patrick Purdy) or a big party in which the gunman invites his friends and relatives. "In many cases he [the psychopath] will know with near certainty that none of these people carry guns, thus virtually no risk of return fire."

Frank's not reticent to discuss who originally inspired his nox-ious enthusiasms. As a child Frank was emotionally and physically abused by both his father and mother. Mommy gave Frank baths until the age of thirteen—traumatic baths. "She made me sit still with the shampoo going into my eyes. Now I'm blind in one eye."

Daddy was even worse. "My father made me suck his cock almost every day. My mom knew about it and she didn't do nothing. I can't drink any white liquids now. They make me throw up. What I remember more than the taste of my father's cum is the overwhelming feeling of helplessness, of being controlled and humiliated by this man who was supposed to love me as a father. I remember how I would always close my eyes as the cock was in my mouth and he would start hitting me in the back and yelling, 'Open your eyes, you cocksucker!' He would make me say that I wanted to suck his cock before he put it in my mouth...

"I personally feel that in most cases one thought is flashing through the killer's mind over and over as the bullets fly out of his weapon and into human flesh. That thought is 'why?' He feels not one single shred of pity or remorse. He is simply recalling his own dead soul as he murders the people."

Frank is a dead soul, one with so much antipathy that at the age of fifteen he tried to murder his father with a switchblade. He spent nine months at Creedmore Psychiatric Hospital in New York, where he was pumped up with Haldol, Coxitane, Trilafon, and Thorazine. Frank has sworn off chemical straightjackets for five years now.

"No, I do not think that my anger could be worked out by any-thing other than mass murder, but the majority of victims of abuse do not feel homicidal, rather, they feel suicidal. I'm not a typical victim. I may be crazy, but I've always been egotistical and aggressive, thus I was able to turn my anger outward with thoughts of revenge and murder. The majority of child abuse victims turn their anger inwards and become depressed, suicidal, anorexic, compulsive eaters, drug abusers. I have never felt this way. I love myself and my body, and am only obsessed with killing and hurting other people. I consider myself lucky to be psy-chotic, rather than suicidal or depressed.

HANDY HINTS
FOR
MESSIER MASSACRES

A GUIDE TO MAXIMIZING THE MASS MURDER KILL COUNT.   BY FRANK, YOUR EDITOR

•••
THIS ESSAY IS INTENDED FOR INFORMATIONAL PURPOSES ONLY.
THE ACT OF MASS MURDER IS A CRIME AS JUDGED BY THIS SOCIETY.
THE EDITOR DOES NOT ENCOURAGE,CONDONE,OR SUPPORT ANY TYPE OF CRIMINAL ACT.
THE EDITOR CATEGORICALY REJECTS AND RENOUNCES ANY AND ALL
LEGAL,FINANCIAL,AND ETHICAL LIABILITY THAT COULD ARISE AS A RESULT
OF ANY ACT BY ANYONE IN RESPONSE TO THE INFORMATION CONTAINED
IN THIS ESSAY.
•••
HEY! HOW ARE Y'ALL DOIN?.THIS IS FRANK,YER eDICKtor.I'M SORRY ABOUT TAKING
UP SPACE WITH DAT DISCLAIMER ON TOP.BUT I FIGURE THAT AN ESSAY DEALING
WITH MAXIMIZING MASS MURDER KILL COUNTS LEAVES A NOTICEABLE DRAFT ON YOUR
HUMBLE eDICKtors VALUABLE POSITION AS A RESPECTED AND LAW-ABIDING MEMBER
OF THE COMMUNITY. SO I AM COVERING MY ASS WITH A DISCLAIMER UP THERE!
   SO ANYWAY,TODAY IS DECEMBER 22,1989.A COUPLA DAYZ BEFORE CHRISTMAS.
IS YOUR HUMBLE eDICKtor THINKING OF PARTRIDGES IN PEAR TREES? IS HE
DREAMING OF A WHITE CHRISTMAS? IS HE PROWLING THE STREETS OF BROOKLYN
CARRYING MISTLETOE AND HOLDING IT OVER STRANGE WOMEN'S FEET AS HE PULLS
OFF THEIR SHOES AND KISSES THEIR FEET? IS IT EVEN REMOTELY POSSIBLE THAT
THE FESTIVE HOLIDAY SEASON HAS MANAGED TO PENETRATE HIS PSYCHOPATHIC
SOUL??? THE ANSWER TO ALL THESE QUESTIONS IS NO!
   ON DECEMBER 6TH,ABOUT 2 WEEKS AGO,MARC LEPINE KILLED 14 YOUNG WOMEN IN
MONTREAL,CANADA AND SET A NEW ALL-TIME RECORD HIGH FOR MASS MURDER IN THAT
COUNTRY. EVER SINCE THEN FRANKSTER HAS HAD A MAJOR CASE OF MASS MURDER
ON HIS OTHERWISE CAREFREE AND LIGHTHEADED BRAIN SO HERE WE ARE,AFTER TWO
WEEKS OF THESE THOUGHTS FLOATING AROUND MY BRAIN,THEY ARE FINALLY BEING
PUT INTO WRITTEN FORM IN THIS ESSAY. IS'NT THAT SPECIAL?!
   LET US SAY FIRST THE TOPIC OF THE ESSAY. WHICH IS:HOW TO KILL A LARGE
NUMBER OF PEOPLE USING A GUN (OR GUNS).YES,YOU CAN KILL LOTS OF PEOPLE
IN OTHER WAYS SUCH AS POISON,BOMBS,ARSON,ETC...BUT YOU WON'T LEARN HOW IN
THIS ESSAY,HELL NO! ONLY GUNS ARE DISCUSSED IN THESE PAGES.
   YES MY FRIENDS,IT'S THE ALL-AMERICAN PASTIME CALLED:MAXIMIZING YOUR
MASS MURDER KILL COUNT. SURE TO COME IN HANDY ON NUMEROUS OCCASIONS!
   THE RECORD HIGH FOR MASS KILLINGS IN THE UNITED STATES IN A SINGLE
DAY USING GUNS IS TWENTY-ONE. ON JULY 18, 1984, JAMES OLIVER HUBERTY
WALKED INTO A McDONALDS FAST FOOD RESTAURANT IN SAN YSIDRO CALIFORNIA
AND SHOT 21 PEOPLE DEAD.THAT IS THE RECORD HIGH.I PERSONALLY THINK
THAT THIS IS NOT A VERY HIGH NUMBER.TALK IS CHEAP.TALK IS VERY CHEAP,
MY FRIENDS! SO LETS SHOOT THE BULL FOR AWHILE.
   THE MAKING OF A SUCCESSFUL MASSACRE INVOLVES THE FOLLOWING:GOOD GUNS,
A POWERFULL AND LARGE QUANTITY OF AMMUNITION,GOOD SHOOTING TECHNIQUE,
ELEMENT OF SURPRISE ATTACK,INABILITY OF VICTIMS TO ESCAPE FROM CONFINED
AREA,GOOD MENTAL STATE OF GUNMAN,ATTACKING A POORLY DEFENDED LOCATION,
SINGLEMINDED AND CLEAR-CUT GOAL. IN MY OPINION,THIS IS THE BASIC CHECKLIST
OF THE INGREDIENTS NEEDED FOR A SUCCESSFUL MASSACRE.
   OF COURSE,THERE ARE NO GUARANTEES.HELL,YOU CAN INVADE A NUNNERY AND ONE
OF THE SISTERS MIGHT HAVE A LOADED AUTOMATIC UNDERNEATH HER HABIT AND BLOW

Heloise, eat your heart out
From *Singin' Dose Anti-Psychotic Blues* #6

MASS MURDERER FANZINE:
"SINGING DOSE ANTI-PSYCHOTIC BLUES" #6

Frank's magazine is an open-ended advertisement for homicidal hemorrhaging, rather than the quieter self-murder. Indeed, Frank has learned to socialize through his publications: "I find it truly pleasurable to be able to share my reality, to express my psychopathic thoughts and ideas to other people, and to have them agree with me and my psycho viewpoint. In addition, I can create a link with other people for the purpose of increasing psychopathic knowledge and ability. I won't go into specifics, but I have acquired several items of a 'restricted' nature through my contacts in the mail. Also, when I go on a killing binge and get arrested, I will have a ready network of fellow psychopaths who will be able to send me books or money or other types of support to make my stay in prison or the mental asylum more enjoyable."

This psychopath is kind enough to give people a few years head start because, as Frank says, he will only be able to "control my rage for possibly three years or so. In all likelihood, I should explode between the ages of twenty-six and twenty-eight." Those are the years 1993-1995. Remember, you heard it here first. The name's Frank, and he's raring to out-gun Jimmy Huberty.

As for the rest of us: "Just be grateful and thankful that you don't actually have my brain for a lifetime like I do. All of you can just put down my magazine, throw it in the garbage, or stuff it on a shelf and go back to your own realities. I can't do that. It never goes away. It's here for every minute of every day of every year until the day I die."

Crazy War

SUSAN CRILE'S PAINTINGS
OF THE GULF WAR INFERNO

PUTRID GLOW
1991 42"X 96"

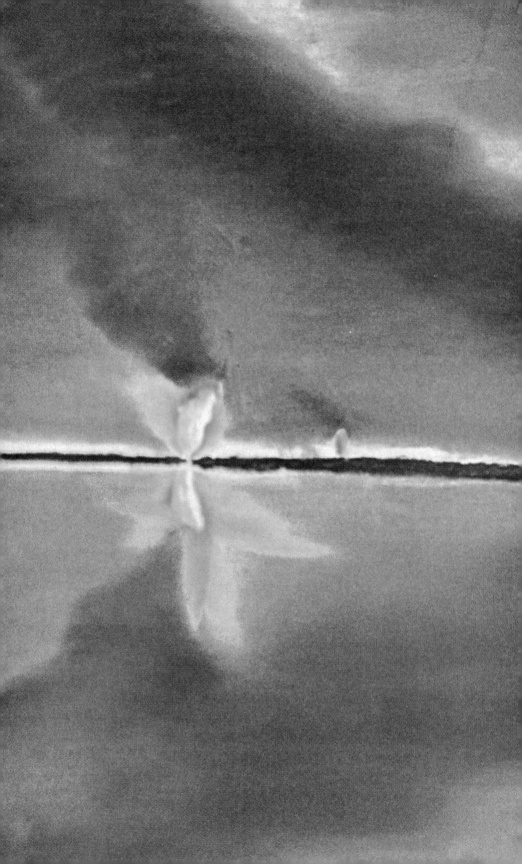

OIL FIRES REFLECTED
1991 38"X 50"

THE FURNACE

1993 79" X 42"

Green Amnesia

ALEXANDRA ANDERSON-SPIVY

MERICAN PAINTER Susan Crile went to Kuwait City in July, 1991. She was an artistic witness to a man-made environmental catastrophe unprecedented since the atomic bomb. Crile's horror at the calculated destruction of the oil fields that created some seven hundred raging fires in the desert is effectively conveyed in her paintings. Before her trip, Crile's recent work already had begun to visually investigate the edges of experience where destruction, terror and beauty intersect. Nowhere was that intersection more intense than in Kuwait's apocalyptic conflagration. "It was Hell itself," says the artist. She painted the Inferno.

Iraq had deliberately tried to induce the greenhouse effect and injure the world economy by setting the oil well fires. It used the environment as a weapon of mass destruction. Months after the war was over most of them were still burning. For two weeks, at 4 a.m. every morning, Crile hitched rides with Bechtel workers into the desert around Kuwait City (no rental cars were available) to photograph the cataclysmic landscape created by plumes of smoke from the burning oil wells which still rose as high as 22,000 feet over the Ahmadi oil field.

Fires surged 200 feet into the air. Near the blazes it was too hot to breathe. Soot-covered firefighters, sometimes using oxygen tanks for air, had to change their clothes three times a day. Each day the burning oil wells consumed some five million barrels of oil and generated half a million tons of air pollution. Viscous surface lakes polluted the desert with an estimated fifty to sixty million barrels of spilled petroleum that didn't burn. Falling oil and black soot, congealed with sand, had formed a dark, brittle crust over hundreds of miles of the desert surface. Winds blew oily black smoke that blotted out the sun. Black rain fell, infiltrating the air with potentially carcinogenic metal particles. "At noon it was like a moonless midnight," says Crile.

Using her hundreds of photographs of the fires as preparatory sketches, Crile has spent the two and a half years since she returned to New York from Kuwait creating a series of monumental allegorical landscapes based on her experience of the ecological inferno. The result was four monumental paintings up to forty feet long and more than thirty-five oil stick, pastel and charcoal works on paper. In these pictures, which the St. Louis Art Museum will show in April-May, 1994, the experience of the oil fields and the fires is annealed and transformed into art.

The great British landscape painter Frederick Turner once lashed himself to the mast of a frigate in the midst of a howling gale to better experience and thus paint nature's awe-inspiring power. Crile's new painting, while grounded in a similar insistence on personal experience, imbues her expression of nature's destruction with a terrible doomsday beauty and a fierce moral imperative unusual in depictions of landscape. There is a sense of warning, an emotional intensity in these paintings which differs from anything a photograph can achieve.

Yet Crile has her colleagues. American landscape painter Sanford Gifford expressed both the devastating effects of the Civil War and the industrial revolution in his paintings of the destruction of the forests along the Hudson River and in the Adirondacks. At the end of the twentieth century landscape as a vehicle for social and environmental protest is a subject largely usurped by the photographer. Crile permits no sentimentality to dilute the horror her works convey at the environmental poisoning of the future which is the consequence of the events of the

Gulf War. They expand the range of landscape painting beyond realism or reportage into a realm of excoriating anger and sorrow.

Crile's artistic outrage makes her a rare commentator on the war's after-effects. Few others are still publicly considering the long-term environmental consequences of the first major conflict in which environmental destruction figured so prominently as an instrument of warfare. The Gulf War only lasted for eight months. It left in its wake an unprecedented man-made environmental disaster. The ecological damage it wreaked on the Gulf will endure for decades if not for longer. But three years later hardly anyone is reporting these long-term effects to the public, nor has there been noticeable media analysis of the future implications of this war's new, terrifying level of using environmental sabotage as a military tactic.

One of the most recent—and most harrowing—document comes from Kuwait itself. In June, 1992, Dr. Jassin Mohammad Al-Hassan, Professor of Biochemistry at Kuwait University, published *The Iraqi Invasion of Kuwait, An Environmental Catastrophe*. His book, illustrated with photographs of desert minefields, fires, oil-encrusted sand and birds and butterflies drowning in the oil lakes, relentlessly describes the environmental destruction of the war, including the Iraqi decimation of the scientific infrastructure. (He says that the university laboratories were totally pillaged so that no instruments or even test tubes remained. New equipment had just begun to arrive as he finished his book.) He describes in excruciating detail the extensive toxic effects of the great lakes of oil on the desert itself and on wildlife, insects and migrant birds, attracted to these hellish ponds only to drown. Dr. Al-Hassan call this "the chain of death."

But not many Americans will ever see this book. It's not in bookstores. I got it from the Kuwait Embassy. After the troops went home, the notoriously fickle attention span of western mass media veered away from Kuwait at warp speed.

Reporters, broadcasters and columnists have almost universally ignored the aftermath of this war where environmental sabotage played such a central part. Even environmental groups have not adequately continued their observations. Says Nick Morgan, who is with the

Greenpeace International Waste Trade Campaign, "the resources just aren't there for ongoing monitoring of the ecological damage in Kuwait."

By December, 1991, all the fires were out, much earlier than was thought possible. During the fires, goats and sheep died from the toxic fumes and hens stopped laying eggs. The August, 1991 *National Geographic* survey of the war damage by Thomas Y. Canby reported "an armageddon" of dead crops and animals, devastated fields and polluted irrigation systems.

The desert itself is threatened by the disruption of the layer of pebbles that holds down the compacted sand. When the pebble rug is disturbed, winds create vast shifting sand dunes that cover roads and farms. Native grass are endangered. Kuwaiti scientists still fear the airborne toxic metal particles released by the oil fires also will enter the food chain. As oil slowly seeped into the Persian Gulf, contaminating the ecosystem of the already polluted shallow body of water, marine life was badly affected in the months after the war. Though international help was marshalled, including private American contractors and veterans of the Exxon Valdez spill, Greenpeace's report, On Impact: "Modern Warfare and the Environment, A Case Study of the Gulf War," said the oil clean-up efforts "appeared miniscule and irresolute."

A January 9, 1993 *New Statesman* article, "The First Casualities of War," claimed that health and environmental damage are now showing up in Iraq as well as Kuwait. Eric Hoskins, a Canadian doctor who has gone to Iraq a dozen times since the war ended, reports that mysterious new illnesses, including leukemia, in Iraqui children may be caused by spent radioactive bullets used by coalition forces. These bullets, thousands of which still litter the desert, may also be polluting the region's ground water and soil.

What has happened to the oil spills, the vast oil lakes seeping away into the sand? Susan Crile's paintings, the strongest work of her twenty-five year career, can and do ignite our outrage over this disaster but the world also needs a much better media watch to further assess and judge the long-term disaster of Gulf War.

Man On The Run

NANCY WEBER & RICHARD PEARLMAN

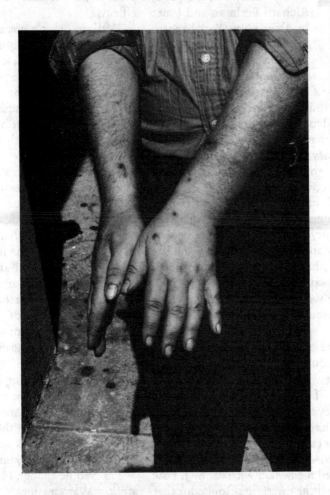

ON THE RUN: *Richard Pearlman displays wounds to his arms, inflicted by enemies who he says zapped him from a distance by high frequency rays.*

Nancy Weber: *Meeting Richard*

Twenty-many years ago, Richard Perlman and I met briefly at a New York happening called Rock Flow, where hundreds of us breathed gel-tinted mists, seam through waves of diaphonous rayon, submitted to a punishing roar of music, and pretended to be transported.

Richard—who has a phenomenal memory, among other intellectual gifts—held onto my name and my connection with the *New York Post*, which ended in 1965. He called me last summer and asked me to help get his story heard. He was the object of an Asian conspiracy to steal his life force, he said, and only publicity could save him.

He was aware that even the most credulous marshmallow might hink he had stayed too long at Rock Flow, and he offered the names of people who could vet his saga of torments. I spoke with a steel dealer, the very voice of America, who had with his own eyes seen objects of Richard's that had been destroyed by some mysterious dust unknoen in the West. A plausible-sounding lawyer assured me he had with his own nose smelled the mysterious foul odor that Richard said was being introduced into one rental car after another by "them." I heard on tape the tremulous voice of a well-placed academic confirming that conspiracies of the sort Richard described were a common-place in the Far East—complete with effleuvia.

Well, no, that's not evidence of a vendetta spawned by an offended acupuncturist; of course not. Sounds like the ravings of one paranoiac and three guys with a problem about Asians. But Richard nudges my mind about conspiracy the way Graham Greene does about Catholicism: What if he's right?

Fact is, sometimes a lot of big guys gang up against one little guy. Richard's can't-be-trues are no more fantastical than Watergate. If they're not true, or not wholly true, for sure he's on target with his indictment of Western intellectual arrogance. As he tells us in the moving passages about his pysician father, the same mind-set that cannot embrace the possibility of an Asian vendetta also dismisses the brilliant curative powers of Asian medicine.

I had no luck in selling Richard to my journalist friends or the people I know in law enforcement. "C'mon, I hear from these guys all the time, the CIA's wired their teeth, forget about him, for Chrissake don't give my number."

I'm glad he though of pitching his story to Warren Hinckle. Whether his real demons are out there in the world plotting against him, or within his own being, or some combination of the two, maybe publication wil bring surcease. I hope Richard will be able to stop running.

Stealing Chi

RICHARD PERLMAN

am the victim of an Asian vendetta. I have been on the run since 1975. I have traveled throughout the United States and Canada and I cannot escape. I have rented houses and apartments in Houston, New York, Toronto, and Santa Fe and I am found. I cannot travel on a plane, train or bus without an incident taking place. At times I have lived in leased automobiles thinking a moving target would be harder to locate. Still I have not been safe. People familiar with this type of crime refer to it as "stealing chi"* and tell me they are surprised I am still alive. Perhaps it's because of my knowledge of acupuncture, which I learned to perform on myself to save my life. "Stealing chi" is nothing more than biological torture with the immediate goal of impotency and vegetation and the ultimate goal of death. I've found it necessary to try to educate the press and law enforcement that these vendettas exist. This is notunlike what rape and molestation

*Daniel Reid, *The Tao of Health, Sex and Longevity: A Modern Practical Guide to the Ancient Way*, Simon and Schuster, New York, 1989, p. 41: "...chi is a form of bio-electric energy uniquely associated with living things, while Yin and Yang are the two opposite poles that make chi move. The body stores chi in the electrolytes contained in vital bodily fluids (essence), and transports it through a complex network of invisible channels called meridians. When chi is 'full,' the entire organism flourishes. When chi is 'empty,' vital functions grind to a halt and the organism begins to wither.

victims had to go through not so long ago. When I tell them my situation, there is a collective shrugging. On two occasions detectives with
the New York City Police made contact with the vendetta's perpetrators
and told me it was being "wound down and terminated." I do believe this
was the intention but because of a mutual distrust, there was no resolution.

Then the government got involved in what had been a private
matter—to learn what was happening to me, to see if this torture technique could be applied on a wide basis—to political dissenters, criminals and the like—and others became involved in assisting those carrying out the vendetta—doctors, professors, lawyers, members of law
enforcement, even members of religious communities, people who should
know better.

In 1974, I got sick. I was congested with mucus, suffered from
headaches, had chronic sore throats and irregular bowels. I began
antibiotic treatment for what was described as low-grade infection and
began tests for allergy conditions that might be affecting my immune
system. Some of the symptoms seemed to disappear with the antibiotics
but reappeared immediately with cessation of dosage. With pains literally from head to feet, I began my exploration of alternative medicine
(holistic healing) and acupuncture.

In 1973, I began treatment with Dr. Mai-Ling Joong. She was a
medical doctor in China but was forbidden to practice acupuncture in
New York because of a lack of license. At that time, though there were
many "illegal acupuncturists" operating primarily in Chinatown, you
had to be a licensed physician (M.D.) to legally practice acupuncture.
She consulted with a fellow physician and friend, Dr. Michael Chau,
who concurred with her diagnosis of kidney disorder. This was the
Chinese definition of kidney, not to be confused with the Western view
of the organ. She told me that in China Dr. Chau was a famous cardiolo-
gist. In 1975 he was in the same predicament she was in: unlicensed to
practice any medical art in New York. Every week he traveled to
Scranton, Pennsylvania, where he treated patients with acupuncture
four days a week. I received acupuncture from Dr. Joong three times a

week, and began to make a full recovery. I had been sick a very long time, maybe most of my life, and here I was becoming well. Richard Perlman, the son of a well known Manhattan physician-cardiologist, grandson and nephew of physicians—my life was being saved by an ancient form of medicine rescued from the obscurity of the villages of China by Mao Tse-tung. Wait till I tell Dad that I am well.

The only problem is my father did not believe. Neither did any of his physician friends. I beseeched Dr. Joong to please explain to my father what had been wrong, and all she would reply was, "You will find your way." It was important to me that my father understand how sick I was. I had never been close to my father and I felt this would help bring us closer. I even envisioned him learning Chinese medicine.

She refused to talk with him. In a phone conversation from my apartment, I got angry and threatened to report Dr. Joong for practicing medicine without a license. Almost immediately (thirty minutes or maybe sixty minutes later), I realized I was wrong to threaten, and I tried to call Dr. Joong back to apologize. There was no answer. For three days there was no answer. Dr. Joong I believe became frightened and went into hiding. Thus began the vendetta against me.

First of all I want to say that I considered Dr. Joong a friend. Most of the time after treatment I had dinner at her house. She cured me of a disease and symptoms I did not understand that almost cost me my life. I do not know exactly what Dr. Joong was feeling. I knew she must have felt threatened and I was ashamed of my behavior. I still am. At that time I was ignorant of the arrogance and ungraciousness of Western medicine and society.

Dr. Joong had given me muscles I never knew existed and energy that I never knew I had. This energy and my inexperience with it, I believe, exacerbated my relationship with Dr. Joong. When Dr. Joong refused to treat me, I began to seek treatment from other acupuncturists. I went to a doctor on Doyers Street in Chinatown, Bai Yin Rok. I told her my situation with Dr. Joong. At that time I still considered Dr. Joong a friend and wished to reconcile with her. I did not realize the hostility I had created with her and her community. With Dr. Rok and other acupuncturists in New York, Boston, and San Francisco, I developed symptoms that I never had before and were even more difficult for western-trained physicians to analyze. I became impotent, had difficulty walking, and had very little energy to perform the simplest of tasks.

I began to have difficulty talking and my ears were blocked with mucus; also my urine began to dribble. In another month I was hardly urinating; my bowel movements were once a month, and I was having pains throughout my upper and lower back. The vendetta was working. My chi was being stolen.

During 1977-1979, I literally wandered the world in search of an acupuncturist who could explain my illness and could get me well. I visited Canada, France, Germany, and Japan, as well as many cities in the United States. In each place the story was the same: I was either refused treatment or I was hurt intentionally. There were two exceptions: Mary Chung in Walnut Creek, California and Dr. Henry Yu in White Plains, New York. With Dr. Chung and Dr. Yu I did not tell them my history at first, and each one restored my energy that had been taken from me. With both, though, when they found out about my past, the benefits terminated. Dr. Yu refused to see me anymore and Dr. Chung exploded. "How dare you treat that woman that way!" I knew I was in trouble and after one "strange" treatment I left Dr. Chung.

In Germany I was injected with a substance that literally made my chest explode. I had difficulty walking; my abdomen became distended, and I was quite lethargic. I returned to the United States and did not start recovering until I visited a Dr. Ra in Chinatown. I made up a story about who I was and how I knew about him, and he agreed to see me. The treatment he gave me, two needles in the top of the shoulders, woke up the chest. I had a sense of warmth traveling throughout the body. He told me I should rest and return in three days. When I returned, he refused to see me. It was at this time that I began to teach myself acupuncture. That has kept me alive, but barely.

Since February of 1993, I have had contact with two police departments: New York and Berkeley. Both have told me they made contact with the perpetrators of the vendetta. In both cases the "stealing of chi" has not ceased. If anything it has gotten worse—my body's recuperative powers have diminished.

Now a perpetrator can walk by and I can suffer an electric shock to the feet, arms or head. At times, wounds have appeared behind the knees and on the arms and legs; there is periodic numbness of hands and feet. Boils suddenly appear on my arms. (See illustration page 241.)

This is a traditional style vendetta and for it to succeed in the United States, there has to be some high-level government participation. With the aid of Senate Judiciary Committee investigators, I can prove this allegation. If scientific knowledge from other lands can be tested to torture and murder our citizens, then it is about time we ended that experiment.

This is not the first time the government has tortured its citizens to find what would happen. The recent revelations of a 40-year program of secret radiation warfare experiments on U.S. citizens— "American Guinea Pigs" Rep. Edward Markey (D.-Mass) called the victims attests to this grim reality. "These experiments used human subjects that were captive audiences or populations...considered 'expendable': the elderly, prisoners, hospital patients, who might not have retained their full faculties for informed consent, according to *Newsweek* of January 3, 1994. In other words, victims were chosen who had little or no support system, individuals with little credibility who would have difficulty proving the medical tortures they experienced. Individuals like me.

Radiation, LSD, mustard gas, et al. were once esoteric toys to employ against an innocent population. Today there are other toys that excite these sadistic servants of our government. These are electromagnetism and the scientific basis of Asian medicine. Physicians trained in Asian medicine can cure diseases and symptoms that remain mysterious to Western trained physicians. Among these are: abnormal distension, inability to swallow, loss of voice, loss of hearing, urinary incontinence and retention, impotency, impaired locomotion. Just as Western scientists have their genetic warfare, they have their Asian counterparts who know how to create as well as cure these symptoms by stealing energy. Victims will become dysfunctional and eventually die. In the United States our doctors will not know how they died. "Energy stealing" is an ideal solution to undesired political dissent. I believe it is our government's latest "scientific toy." And I am the latest American guinea pig.

(All names have been changed. At the proper time, I will be glad to divulge all identities.)

**MANHATTAN RESTAURATEUR ELAINE KAUFFMAN AND
PAT RILEY, COACH OF THE NEW YORK KNICKS**

Studies In Craziness

**PHOTOGRAPHS TAKEN AFTER MIDNIGHT
AT ELAINE'S BY JESSICA BURSTEIN**

**A PATRON'S SPONTANEOUS STRIP
2:25 A.M., OCTOBER 12, 1993**

BOBBY ZAREM, THE WORLD'S GREATEST PRESS AGENT

LEWIS LAPHAM, EDITOR, HARPER'S MAGAZINE

DIRECTOR ROBERT ALTMAN AND HIS WIFE, KATHERINE

NEW YORK COLUMNISTS AT DINNER: AMY PAGNOZZI OF
the *DAILY NEWS* AND MICHAEL SHAIN OF
NEW YORK NEWSDAY

IN A CORNER AT ELAINE'S, CHRIS NOTH
OF TV'S "LAW AND ORDER"

ACROSS THE ROOM, GIANNI UZIELL
AND STEVE DUNLEAVY

CENTER: CHUCK DALY—COACH OF THE NEW JERSEY NETS

**"A CURRENT AFFAIR" MANAGING EDITOR
STEVE DUNLEAVY**

NEW YORK POLICE BEAT REPORTER MIKE MACALARY

**SAN FRANCISCO POLITICAL CONSULTANT, JACK DAVIS,
4 A.M., OCTOBER 19, 1993**

ELAINE AND WILLIAM STYRON

ELAINE'S REGULARS, LONDON *SPECTATOR* COLUMNIST TAKI AND NEW YORK NIGHT LIFE COMMISSIONER GIANNI UZIELLI

They Must Be Making It Up

TONY DINGMAN

In South Africa
a young engaged couple were
involved in a traffic accident & the young
man was declared
dead

and put into
a metal box at the morgue
and after 48 hours he came out of
coma & shouted
to be

released but his
fiancee refused to ever
see him because she thought he was
come back to
life.

In France came
a report of finding a
fully clothed skeleton of a man who died 10
months earlier
watching

TV & When
the neighbors found him the
TV was still on. In the United States a
burglary suspect
jumped

out of a second
story window as the police
closed in & when he hit the ground his
glass eye fell
out

which enabled
the police to identify him
as Aaron Harris. And in the Phillipines
during rush hour
in Manila

operating on the
word of God a group of religious
fanatics let air out of the tires of cars & trucks
in a mass de-
flating.

Dirty Commie Bastard

You Only Live Once: The Life and Times of A Fine American Radical

JOHN J. SIMON

You only live once and it is best to live one's life with one's conscience rather than to temporize or accept with silence those things one believes to be against the interests of one's people and one's nation.
—Vito Marcantonio in Congress June 27, 1950, the only Congressional voice opposed to U.S. intervention in the Korean War.

LMOST NO one knows who he is any more. There are four decades of material change to obliterate historical recollection. The children and grandchildren of Marcantonio's New York moved away from urban grit to suburbs paved over with super highways, malls, and prefab split-levels. Gone were the angry but emulous children of immigrants, the loam of his city. No one remembers. But in the thirties and forties—and for years after his death in 1954—Marcantonio was either revered or despised; there was no middle ground. For decorous historians and estimable journalists Marcantonio was either the Don Quixote of left-wing social justice, the ardent egalitarian, or he was the hard-line Stalinist in the thrall of Moscow, a pal of organized crime, the cynical con-man cajoling Puerto Ricans to migrate to New York to vote for him.

Marcantonio was respected as a diligent, inerrant, and innovative parliamentarian. Everyone called him Marc, adversaries like Richard Nixon, admirers like Franklin Roosevelt, and benefactors like Fiorello La Guardia. He was Marc to his constituents as well. In the squalid streets of East Harlem the people who sent him to Congress seven times knew he was one of their own: passionate, streetwise, and hardworking, a benevolent family patriarch who lived modestly but provided generously for his widowed mother and schizophrenic brother. In Congress, then as now a sodality that does not suffer insurgents easily, Marcantonio may have been unique as the only successful radical politician in twentieth century America, but to his friends he was ordinary, one of the guys. He liked nothing better than hanging out with people he grew up with like Republican Edward Corsi, later New York's Home Relief Commissioner during the Depression and a high-level official in the Eisenhower Administration, Leonard Covello, founder of East Harlem's Benjamin Franklin High School, oral historian, and great teacher who motivated the children of Italian peasants to stay in school; or the contractor and Saturday night poker buddy, who was "conservative, reactionary," according to Marc—"His career was to make money"—or his barber and childhood friend, Luigi Albarelli, who would give the main eulogy at Marcantonio's funeral in 1954. Nor can we forget Thomas Lucchese— "Three Finger Brown"—founder of a notorious Mafia crime "family." About his association with Lucchese, Marcantonio averred,

> I was born and raised in this district and there were men with criminal records here who are my supporters. And I'm not going to turn my back on anyone. But I've never had anything to do with a racket or protecting rackets.

Marc appointed Lucchese's son to West Point, a politically costly act, but defended his position on the floor of the House: "I feel that crime is due to conditions, economic and social, and I have done everything in my power to alleviate those conditions."

Marc was equally comfortable with Tammany spoilsmongers, Roman Catholic clergy, trade union militants, and Communist Party functionaries. He never left his family, his constituents, or his neighborhood. Marcantonio never traveled outside the United States; he was never far from the city he loved and championed. At his death his home was a small rent-controlled apartment only four blocks from where he had been born. He left an estate of less than ten thousand dollars.

The Manhattan into which Vito Marcantonio was born in 1902 was a locus of great wealth and mean privation. New York had become the nation's corporate capital and, by the 1880s, had surpassed London as the world's financial center. It was also home to the booming garment, printing, shipping, and rail industries, which had unquenchable appetites for cheap labor. So New York's population exploded: a flood of impoverished southern and eastern Europeans poured into dormitory neighborhoods—the Lower East Side, Little Italy, Hell's Kitchen, East Harlem, all overcrowded, fetid with garbage and disease, providing only the most wretched shelter. In the first two decades of the twentieth century Manhattan's population doubled, a cacophony of accents and dialects. Nearly half hardly spoke English at all.

Before World War Two, most East Harlem houses were "Old Law" tenements, built before the reform New York Tenement House Act of 1901. Typically a tenement was a six-story walk-up with four flats to each floor. Only a room facing front or back, or on a less-than-yard-wide airshaft, had a window. The kitchen coal caused many tenement fires. Toilets were backyard privies. Including boarders and lodgers, a building might have as many as 150 inhabitants. Disease was rampant: many died of cholera, influenza, tuberculosis, diphtheria, or smallpox. Infant mortality was high.

That was the way most of the millions who made New York the richest city in the world lived. Very little new housing was built in Manhattan after the 1901 law passed. Not until the La Guardia Administration and the social engineering of the New Deal in the thirties was there much improvement. In East Harlem as well as the other slum neighborhoods, hot water, private toilets, and central heating were uncommon luxuries until the end of World War Two.

Tammany Democrats ran the city. These sons of Irish immigrants built powerful electoral machines among the poor. Like other immigrant groups before and since, the Irish were manipulated. Combining appeals to ethnic pride and religious solidarity with practical community and social service, Tammany elected aldermen, mayors, even governors, all of whom had license to steal from the public treasury. Periodically, when they became too greedy, they were transiently replaced by "progressives" or "reformers," usually wealthy old-money Protestants who would "throw the rascals out." Through it all, the city's real rulers were a "Permanent Government" of bankers, investors, and real estate specula-tors who, then as now, controlled the city's financial base, manipulated its infrastructure, and ran its industries.

East Harlem may have been mainly residential, but industrial rapacity was its neighbor. The giant Jacob Rupert brewery filled the air day and night with the stench of fermenting grain. The Consolidated Gas Company plant burned coal from a nearby dump. Even a gentle wind would blanket East Harlem with black coal dust in summer and gray ash in winter. Foulness, grime, and squalid haze were everywhere.

Still, it was a vibrant community, a neighborhood of many small single-owner retail shops: in the 1930s there were more than a thousand groceries and candy stores serving as social centers, headquarters for numbers-runners and bookies, and places to buy daily bread, occasional ice cream, and penny candy. There were hundreds of small restaurants and saloons as well as tailors, doctors, insurance agents, loan offices, churches and funeral parlors.

It was not a complacent community. Leonard Covello, who col-lected voluminous oral histories over seven decades, described it as "a community always in transition, always on the move, its people ever looking forward to the day when they can break away, shake off the stig-ma of being identified with it."

The thirst for better lives was manifest in the organization of unions: in 1909 and 1911 more than thirty thousand Italian and Jewish garment workers struck for improved conditions and pay. Workers in other industries—fur, printing trades, transit, construction—were organized as well. The years before the First World War saw much labor violence in the city's streets.

Despite the best efforts of educators, social workers, police spies, and clergymen, alien doctrines like anarchism and socialism flourished. Anti-clerical immigrants joined anarcho-syndicalist circles. In East Harlem, the Socialist Morris Hillquit was only narrowly defeated in several Congressional elections. Eventually, the pragmatic radical Fiorello La Guardia won—usually with Republican support, and once on the Socialist ticket.

In 1917 Marcantonio went to DeWitt Clinton, the main Manhattan public high school for boys. For his family—still clinging to the traditional values of rural Southern Italian peasants—to have allowed its eldest son to go at all, no doubt had much to do with the fact that the U.S. had just entered the First World War. The economy was booming, and with carpenters in demand, Marcantonio's father probably could afford his son's daily carfare and forego the weekly earnings he might have brought to his struggling household. Defying the scorn of neighborhood pals, he was one of only two local boys to go to high school; the other boy soon dropped out.

The environment at Clinton was intense. Many kids saw school as a passport into the middle class, the American Dream. Others, Marc among them, were drawn to trade union activism and the vision of socialism as a way out of poverty and discrimination.

Leonard Covello, who taught Italian at Clinton and innovated programs to raise self-esteem in Italian-Americans and to help these children of rural peasants to value education, remembered Marc as "constantly discussing world affairs, politics, labor conditions," and berating fellow students:

> You birds don't even know you're alive. I'll bet you that this very minute there's somebody, some guy outside there figuring how he's gonna make money off of your hides when you go to look for a job. You don't even know that.

At a school assembly in 1921 Marcantonio met Fiorello La Guardia, then President of the City Board of Aldermen. La Guardia refereed a debate in which Marc, the main speaker for his team, spoke passionately for social security and old-age pensions, both extremely radical ideas then:

> If it is true that government is of the people and for the people, then it is the duty of government to provide for those who, through no fault of their own, have been unable to provide for themselves. It is the social responsibility of every citizen to see that these laws for our older people are enacted.

According to Covello, the deeply moved La Guardia, gripping the youngster's shoulder, used Marc's speech as the starting point for his own.

Taking Marc under his wing, La Guardia advised him on personal habits, telling the often disheveled young man how to dress and shave. More important, he encouraged him to go to law school. When Marc was still a law student, La Guardia helped him get a clerk's job at a labor law firm that represented noted radicals, including the anarchists Emma Goldman and Alexander Berkman, and Communist leaders William Z. Foster and Earl Browder.

At the neighborhood social agency, Haarlem House, Marc met Miriam Sanders, a member of the professional staff. As different from Marc as could be, she was a New Englander with family roots in Colonial America, and was eleven years older and five inches taller than Marcantonio. Deeply committed to the ethic of her Protestant heritage, she also shared Marc's engagement with economic and social justice. They were married at New York's Municipal Building in 1925. Remaining in the background during all of his political career, she gave him quiet support and invaluable counsel, while pursuing a long and distinguished career as a social worker and, ultimately, director of Haarlem House.

Marcantonio also began to speak at streetcorner meetings—in Italian and Yiddish as well as English—in La Guardia's electoral campaigns. He was instrumental in organizing the Fiorello H. La Guardia Political Association, the main mechanism for the latter's successful East Harlem Congressional races.

In the mid-twenties, Marcantonio joined La Guardia's law firm. The relationship grew extremely close; the Marcantonios even lived in La Guardia's apartment for a time. Marc was now manager of La Guardia's electoral campaigns—and indeed, the son that the future Mayor never had. In 1930 La Guardia arranged for an appointment to the United States Attorney's office for Marcantonio.

Marcantonio continued to hone his electoral skills. Ernest Cuneo, who worked for La Guardia's firm at the same time as Marc, described the latter during the 1932 campaign as "one of the smartest cookies I ever encountered, one who could trade punches blow for blow with any comer. He was a real tough guy [but with] the Bourbon look of combined sensuousness and asceticism." Cuneo left an unforgettable description of the young politician's power as a speaker:

> Marc then took over the microphone and there ensued what can only be described as a mass phenomenon. He started slowly and spoke for some time. Then abruptly he struck his heel on the [sound] truck bed; it made a loud hollow noise and the crowd stirred. The cadence of his talk increased and soon the heel struck again. Again the pace quickened.... His voice rose and now the heel struck more often with the beginnings of a real tempo. It began to sound like a train leaving the station. The crowd mirrored his growing excitement. At the climax, Marc was shouting at the top of his lungs and he was stamping his foot as hard and as rapidly as a flamenco dancer. The crowd pulsed to the rhythm and at last found release in a tumultuous, prolonged roar of applause.

Despite Marc's orgasmic histrionics, La Guardia, running on the Republican line, lost in 1932 to a Tammany Democrat riding the coattails of Franklin D. Roosevelt. But in 1933, with Marcantonio playing a key role, La Guardia was elected to the first of three terms as New York's Mayor. In 1934, using the La Guardia Political Association as his own base, Marc was victorious in an intense campaign for Congress, culminating in a huge rally at 116th Street and Lexington Avenue, the "lucky corner" at which La Guardia traditionally ended his campaigns. Sparked by a ringing endorsement from the Mayor, to be repeated in every campaign of Marc's as long as La Guardia was alive, the meeting concluded

with another spirited speech from Marc in English, Italian, Yiddish—
and this time in Spanish.

Just thirty-one years old, Vito Marcantonio went to Congress
with the same brash assurance, shrewd political insight, and passionate
commitment to social betterment that distinguished his work in the La
Guardia movement. Like La Guardia, he was elected as a maverick
Republican.

This small, defiant product of a slum cut a figure in startling
contrast to the suave, slow-moving, silver-tongued Southern Gentlemen
who ran the House. Marc's high-pitched, nasal, machine-gun delivery
bespoke the street-smarts of East Harlem. His small, gaunt frame,
draped in wrinkled, broad-striped, three-piece suits, his piercing eyes
shaded by a beige fedora—these did little to soften the impact of his
self-righteous belligerence. An unlikely Don Quixote had arrived to tilt
at the windmills of power.

The Seventy-Fourth Congress met under extraordinary circumstances. It was the fifth year of the Great Depression, and while the
country had been buoyed by FDR's relief programs and by the
President's radio rhetoric, there still was no economic recovery. Industry
limped along at only a fraction of its 1929 level More than a quarter of
the work force was still unemployed. The despairing country demanded
large political solutions: some turned to fascism, others to socialism and
communism. Yet Congress, for the most part, was still the preserve of
the privileged. FDR's ability to mobilize popular support only occasionally achieved a grudging legislative victory for some mild New Deal
reform. Then as now, the House and Senate were bought. But in 1934
conditions were sufficiently desperate that the electorate stirred itself
and elected a few dozen who, at least, recognized there was a problem.

Marcantonio identified himself with these insurgent iconoclasts
of both parties. He joined mid-western Farmer-Laborites to plunk for
social security, unemployment insurance, and other New Deal programs.

But compromise, the slow choreography of legislative politics, did not suit Marcantonio's streetwise temperament. Moreover, compromise and slow dancing did not meet the dire needs of his constituents. Marc began to stake out a position far to the left, not only of the major parties, but of many of the insurgents. His stance was distinguished not so much by which bills he supported or opposed, but by the way he did it. Along with many liberals, as well as the isolationists, Marcantonio opposed the military appropriations bill of 1935, objecting to any military spending so long as there were ten million unemployed. During the same Congressional session, Marcantonio attacked the Administration's Social Security bill as inadequate. Instead he backed a much more radical bill that provided for universal unemployment insurance, to be administered by unions and farm organizations, with benefits to be paid as long as a worker was unemployed, and at the prevailing wage rate. The bill was red-baited (the Communist Party had endorsed it) and defeated. Marc fought the smear vociferously. It was the first time he defended the civil liberties of Communists in the House.

Next, he took up the cudgels for a stronger National Labor Relations Act, called for a wealth tax act, and advocated the outlawing of public utilities monopolies. In support of the latter he stepped into the well of the House to announce that he was a radical:

> If it be radicalism to believe that our natural resources should be used for the benefit of all of the American people and not for the purpose of enriching just a few...then, Ladies and Gentlemen of this House, I accept the charge. I plead guilty to the charge; I am a radical and I am willing to fight it out...until hell freezes over.

While Marc concluded early on that the Congressional establishment was hopelessly reactionary, the leadership determined that—however much they liked him personally—Marcantonio's radicalism made him an unreliable outsider. Because he would not go along, he never had any real authority or power in the House beyond what he garnered with his parliamentary and oratorical skills. Except for one term on the Labor Committee, his committee appointments were trivial.

Yet, despite his exclusion from the two-party machinery that superintended the Congress, his accomplishments were notable, due largely to his diligence. He never missed a debate on important legislation. And, whether a nominal Republican or, as he was after 1938, the sole representative of the American Labor Party (ALP), he was often the informal floor leader for liberals on crucial bills—organizing Congressional and public support, planning and directing parliamentary strategy, and galvanizing the House with his unmatched speaking skills. In 1939, when an FDR funding request for a relief agency was bottled up in committee by conservative Southern Democrats, Marc forced the bill to a vote—by daily tacking an obstructing amendment on every piece of minor legislation to come up. When one Congressman asked for $400,000 to fight the pink bollworm in his state, Marcantonio retorted, "One week from today 400,000 pink slips will be delivered to WPA workers. How about the $150 million for the unemployed?"

In 1939, following the signing of the Nazi-Soviet Pact, Marc opposed intervention in the war in Europe, a stand similar to that of the Communists. This dismayed some of his early labor supporters, but caused him little grief among his Italian-American constituents, among whom there was considerable admiration for Mussolini. He held this position for two years. But even when the Communist Party changed its outlook following Hitler's invasion of the Soviet Union on June 22, 1941, Marcantonio did not follow suit, even continuing to appear with right-wing isolationists until that October. Finally, only two months before Pearl Harbor, Marcantonio became an ardent supporter of the Allied cause, saying,

> I submit that in now supporting these very measures which I have opposed in the past, I am supporting them for the same reasons which motivated my opposition, namely defense of our Nation and its liberties and opposition to imperialism and opposition to fascism, irrespective of their national character. The character of the war has changed and I have no other consistent course to follow but to support a war of defense as vigorously as I opposed a war of imperialist aggression.

Marc's complicated and inconsistent feelings about the war are one key to his intuitive radicalism and his unique character. He denied he was a pacifist, but he hated war with the vehemence of one. Like many others who came of political age in the aftermath of World War One, he was appalled by its carnage and convinced that wars occurred primarily in aid of profits. In the House he supported investigations into munitions profiteering, voted against military appropriations, and declared that if profit were eliminated from war "you will abolish 75 per cent of the cause of war." Nonetheless, he joined other leftists in defense of the Spanish Republic.

Marcantonio was the first white legislator to crusade for Civil Rights legislation. From the late thirties on, Marcantonio introduced Anti-Poll Tax bills. The poll tax, ubiquitous in the South, effectively prevented most blacks (and women) from voting. When Marc's bill was pigeonholed in the Judiciary Committee in 1942, he obtained the necessary 218 signatures on a petition to force the bill to the House floor. Each signature, as well as the impassioned floor debate, received maximum press coverage. Arguing that the abolition of the poll tax would extend "democracy to disenfranchised Negroes and whites," he connected the bill's passage to the war effort, saying, "The continuance of the poll tax is discrimination and makes for disunity.... Abolition of the poll tax abolishes this form of discrimination and makes for unity that is vital to victory." The bill passed the House, only to be filibustered to death in the Senate. In the end it took a Constitutional Amendment, ratified only in 1964, to end the poll tax.

Marcantonio used similar tactics to garner support for a Fair Employment Practices Commission, introducing legislation to outlaw employment discrimination in every session. The opposition was led by the Mississippi racist John Rankin, who said, "the Gentleman from New York...is harassing the white people of the Southern States." While the legislation was defeated, Marc was effective in pointing out the bigotry of the opposition and rallying civil rights forces North and South. It was not until A. Philip Randolph threatened to bring one hundred thousand blacks to Washington that Roosevelt issued an Executive Order mandating equal employment in war industries.

Despite its accomplishments, the New Deal was in trouble after 1938. Its Democratic and Republican opponents were able to smear even the mildest progressive reforms as red trade unionism or as race mixing.

FDR's Democratic Congressional majorities grew smaller with each election. So it made sense for him to court Marc and use his leadership abilities. In 1943 FDR even tried to get Marcantonio appointed to the powerful Judiciary Committee; only a major uproar among Southern Democrats forced withdrawal. Marcantonio became nationally recognized. Civil rights, effective price controls, and the rights of organized labor were all topics he addressed on nationwide radio broadcasts. In 1944 *Harper*'s magazine ratified Marcantonio's growing prestige:

> At forty-two, Marcantonio is well on his way to becoming a first-class national figure, though one of the most unorthodox sort. Previously, his influence in the Congress has been that of a gadfly, not a leader.... Lately, however, he has shown real genius in turning his liabilities into assets, in playing the political interstices for all they are worth.

Marc accumulated considerable local political power. In 1942 he became leader of the American Labor Party (ALP) in Manhattan. ALP endorsement, which he could deliver, often was the margin of victory for Democratic candidates. La Guardia, FDR, and Tammany all needed him.

In 1945, the war's end, and the attendant inflation, found most workers with sharply reduced real wages. The wartime "no strike" pledge was gone, and workers in auto, steel, electrical, coal, and oil industries struck. More working days were lost to labor-management disputes in 1946 than at any other time in American history. Marcantonio repeatedly rose to oppose attempts to repeal New Deal labor laws, telling the House:

> Men do not strike for the fun of it. [They are] provoked by the scheming, uncompromising, unreasoning tactics of profit-bloated, tax-benefitted corporations...beating the drums against American workers in order to intimidate Congress to pass anti-labor legislation.

In 1946, running on the slogan "Had Enough?," the Republican Party won Congress for the first time since the onset of the Depression. The Cold War had begun, and the New Deal coalition was dead. Election of the Eightieth Congress marked the beginning of Marcantonio's decline as a nationally influential politician.

Marcantonio's last leadership role in the House was in the fight against the Taft-Hartley Labor Relations Act. He spoke against the bill on the floor, asking, "What is your justification for this legislation?" A labor union is a worker's "only defense against exploitation":

> ...You are making him free—and impotent to defend himself against any attempt by industry to subject him to the same working conditions that existed in the United States seventy-five years ago. You are giving him the freedom to become enslaved to a system that has been repudiated in the past not only by Democrats but also by outstanding progressive-minded Republicans.... Under the guise of fighting communism you are, with this legislation, advancing fascism on American labor.

The fight was lost but Marcantonio fought on for labor, civil rights, and public housing. He was decades ahead of his time in advocating defense of the environment. He spoke against the Truman Doctrine and other Cold War policies and was the only member of the House who refused to applaud Truman's call for Marshall Plan aid for Western Europe. In 1948 he was the informal floor leader for the opponents of the Mundt-Nixon Bill to outlaw the Communist Party. But Marc was leader only by default; in the growing climate of anticommunist hysteria, others ran for cover. Knowing there was no way to defeat the legislation, Marcantonio asserted, as he increasingly did, that it would be history that would judge:

> I know many will succumb to hysteria and others will give us the usual flag-waving and red-baiting, but let us look back in retrospect: 1798-1948, one hundred fifty years. The men who opposed the Alien and Sedition Acts—Livingston, Madison, Jefferson—they constitute the bright constellations in the democratic firmament of this Nation; but those who imposed on the American people those tyrannies of which this bill is a monstrous lineal descendant have been cast into oblivion, relegated where mankind always relegates puny creatures that would destroy mankind's freedom.

In 1950 he lost his seat. The same year, Richard M. Nixon won election to the Senate.

⚜

Congress was only one arena in which Marcantonio represented the people who elected him. From 1934 on, Marcantonio returned to East Harlem from the Congress each weekend and, after regular airline service began in the forties, often several times during the week. At the Fiorello H. La Guardia Political Association he ran a unique neighborhood social-service clinic. Seven days a week, for three decades, Marcantonio's organization dealt with the myriad problems of his constituents: health, citizenship, relief, schooling, worker's compensation, immigration, tenant, legal, and family issues.

In those days, a weekend visitor to the club would climb a flight of rickety stairs and enter a large room in need of a paint job. Rows of wooden folding chairs faced several desks; behind one desk sat the Congressman. The club was filled with the hubbub of followers, staff and local campaign aides.

Anyone could come to the club. On weeknights one could discuss a problem with any of several volunteers; on weekends one could see the Congressman himself. Marcantonio might phone a city agency to secure a relief payment, might solve a problem at a local school, or find a job in a relief program. La Guardia was Mayor, and Marc had considerable pull at City Hall. Often Marc turned the problem over to a growing circle of left-wing volunteer professionals: teachers, doctors, lawyers, and social workers who came from all over the city.

There was nothing new about this kind of help—Tammany had bought constituents turkeys at Thanksgiving, supplied coal at Christmas, and found patronage jobs as well. But the hangers-on in the Tammany clubs were in it for the business. If you couldn't pay your rent, the Tammany club would find a loan shark. To get service from a city agency, you might have to buy insurance from the candidate's brother-in-law. If the district leader helped you get a job, he would expect your vote—and a salary kickback.

Marcantonio attached no strings. He and his staff were available to everyone. Assistants actually sought out landlord-tenant problems. In the 1948 campaign, a huge billboard fronting the club read "Don't pay rent increases. If your landlord asks for a rent increase, report here and I

shall help you fight the real estate trust. Your Congressman, Vito
Marcantonio."

The press tried to paint Marc as a typical big-city political boss
running a spoils operation. But one reporter noticed that the
Congressman required "almost fanatically that no constituent, however
lowly or troublesome, get the kissoff." In response to a query about legal
fees, Marc wrote to a resident, "As your representative in Congress I am
most pleased to do whatever is proper and possible in this matter without any fee." He also held the volunteer lawyers, many of them from
other ALP clubs, to the same standard. They were not allowed to charge
a fee—even when one would have been legal and proper.

One reporter who spent a day with Marcantonio at his district
office wrote:

> "What do you make of it?" the Congressman asked us. We said that a
> couple of days like that would drive us nuts. "Well," said he, "it's
> what I get paid ten thousand a year for. It's their dough." We also said
> that we were very grateful we were not a member of Congress. "You
> probably have something there," sighed Vito Marcantonio.

Did all this add up to a political machine? Certainly Marc
received political support from his old neighborhood cronies: the shop
workers, small businessmen, storekeepers, and petty hoods. In campaign
years, the ALP, other leftist groups, and unions flooded the district with
canvassers. They visited sixth-floor tenement dwellers, distributed
leaflets, and did routine office work. Marc praised them, saying, "There's
no substitute for doorbell ringing. Republicans don't climb stairs." This
"machine" was voluntary: it was sluggish, inexpert, inconsistent.

Marc was—and saw himself as—a professional politician in
competition with the old-line parties. He needed, he believed, an efficient, highly-coordinated organization. His people were well-inten-
tioned, highly motivated, and deeply committed—but they were unpaid
amateurs. Marc nonetheless made the same demands on them that the
Democrats and Republicans made on their well-paid staffers. Marc
insisted leaflets be written and printed overnight, that sound-truck
schedules and canvassing goals be met. His associates tell of curt

demands for seemingly impossible tasks to be performed, followed by Vesuvian rages when they were not. Marcantonio's archives at the New York Public Library are filled with letters berating his captains for missing a meeting or union leaders who had failed to deliver on promises. If this was a machine it often was, for him, one of infuriating and frustrating ineptitude.

The most important ingredient of the Marcantonio phenomenon was Marcantonio himself. Gerald Meyer, in his thoughtful political biography of Marcantonio, *Radical Politician*, describes how his political style and "personalism" fit the traditional Italian culture of East Harlem. He was of the neighborhood and lived that way: he and his wife lived in a four room rent controlled apartment on 116th street. Another of Marc's biographers, Alan Schaffer, notes that it was simply furnished with a few pictures on the wall "and a couple of shelves of books...Bryce, Hay, Claude G. Bowers [biographer of one of Marc's heroes, Thomas Jefferson, and FDR's Ambassador to Republican Spain], Carl Sandburg, American history generally." On weekend mornings, after a heavy breakfast with lieutenants, Marcantonio walked the streets, greeting everyone by name. Marc had a sense of humor; indeed, those close to him say he was given to reasonably malevolent and tasteless practical jokes.

But all that was tame compared to his devotion to politics, Marc's only concern. Occasionally he played poker or prepared an immensely complicated spaghetti sauce for friends. But the table talk was always politics, and Marc's life had little room for anything but politics. Old radicals still gossip about his relationship with Lil Landau, who ran his campaign operation and was his liaison with leftist fundraisers. It is not clear that there was a sexual relationship. But even if there was, it was subordinated to his politics. His vision was a better society rather than heavenly salvation, and he felt his calling as powerfully as any priest. His life was quite austere. He cared little for clothes, restaurants, or luxuries. He never took a vacation in all the years he served in Congress. If there was another, less political side to Marc, it was intensely private. Leonard Covello best sums up Marcantonio's persona:

Those who did not know him wondered at the terrific plurality he always managed to pile up, no matter what his political banner. These doubters never saw Marcantonio in his office, in shirtsleeves, the crowd consisting of neighbors he had helped or was about to help. They never saw him on a street corner or listened to the comments of the crowd. They never saw him walk along 116th Street, never heard the old and the young greet him. If they had seen these things they would not have wondered.

Many older New Yorkers remember Marcantonio as "the man who brought the Puerto Ricans here," presumably so that they could collect welfare—and vote for him. If today that bit of racist logic seems preposterous, one needs to remember that a major underpinning of Cold War delirium was a kind of triumphant nationalism; outsiders were despised.

In fact, Puerto Rican migration to New York began long before—in the 1880s. Puerto Ricans settled in East Harlem for the same reason others did: it was an affordable neighborhood for the poorest immigrants. From the mid-twenties on they replaced Jews in the western part of the neighborhood, while the Jews, beginning their climb into the middle class, followed the subway lines to Flatbush, Bensonhurst, and Borough Park in Brooklyn, or to University Heights and Pelham Parkway in The Bronx.

After World War Two the Puerto Rican migration accelerated, spurred by cheap air travel and desperate economic conditions in in their native island. As the children of Jewish and Italian garment workers become professionals or clerical workers, or ran small businesses, Puerto Ricans flooded East Harlem's El Barrio to meet New York's ever-insatiable appetite for cheap labor.

Puerto Ricans evolved a vibrant and diverse culture in East Harlem. Before World War Two, there were Spanish language cinemas, cafes, and nightclubs, and many political organizations. In 1936 there were Spanish-speaking Republican and Democratic clubs alongside left-

**COMMUNIST PAPER NEWSPAPER PHOTO OF
MARCANTONIO WITH HIS PUERTO RICAN CONSTITUENTS**

wing and pro-independence organizations, although Puerto Ricans were a relatively small voting bloc.

Marcantonio analyzed the voting data. The Puerto Rican voter turn-out was small because most residents could not pass the required English language literacy test—so he arranged for the La Guardia Association and Haarlem House to offer classes in English literacy. But his main effort was political: he opposed the New York literacy law, arguing that it denied participation simply on the basis of language. Nevertheless, the test remained on the books until the late 1960s, effectively preventing participation of many Latino immigrants.

Marcantonio's Congressional identification with Puerto Rico began on May 6, 1936 when he introduced the first bill to call for the island's independence. Citing the vast export from Puerto Rico of capital and resources by North Americans—over $400-million in four decades—as the cause of Puerto Rico's extreme underdevelopment and destitution, he called for reparation. During his Congressional career he introduced five bills for independence.

When Pedro Albizu Campos, leader of the independence movement, was convicted of sedition, Marc immediately went to his defense. Leaving the continental United States for the only time in his life, Marcantonio flew to San Juan on July 31, 1936, to serve as Albizu Campos's lawyer. A new-trial motion was lost, but during his stay Marcantonio spoke frequently on behalf of the Nationalist Party. In an island-wide radio address he asserted that Albizu Campos's freedom was the most important issue facing Puerto Rico. Marc's return to New York occasioned the largest mass demonstration in El Barrio's history—prefiguring Marcantonio's political relationship with that community.

In Congress, Marcantonio demanded an increase in the island's sugar quota and successfully fought the sugar companies' effort to eliminate its minimum wage—twenty-five cents per hour. In 1939 he won extension of the Social Security Act to Puerto Rico. In 1940, appealing a 50 per cent cut in a relief appropriation, he said,

> If you want to get an idea of how we have expropriated Puerto Rico, go to a street on one of the hillsides in one of the small towns and what do you find there? The only thing you find that is native is a

bunch of bananas. All else on the shelves comes from New York and the various other cities of the United States.... Whenever Puerto Ricans make an attempt at establishing an industry it is destroyed by dumping from the States. Our ruthless imperialism has strangled the economic life of that country, and yet we here refuse to provide for the victims of a system imposed by us, which causes slow starvation to hundreds of thousands of people in Puerto Rico. We have no right to call ourselves an enlightened people until we at least give adequate relief to the people of Puerto Rico. History will condemn us for this cruel and inhuman treatment of a good people.

Marcantonio's initial support from his Puerto Rican constituents was due to his strong positions on island issues, especially independence. They also responded to his support for labor and welfare legislation. But it was his defense of El Barrio residents against discrimination in employment, housing, and education that won him his greatest support. In 1939 he objected to a psychological profile of Puerto Rican children based on a dubious analysis of I.Q. test scores. He said,

> Mr. Speaker, a most slanderous attack has recently been made on Puerto Rican children living in New York City. It has been made under the guise of a psychological report. It proves that there is such a thing as racketeering even in the field of psychology. This report is evidence of it. I have had this report investigated, and I hereby submit the findings which constitute the expose of another fraud at the expense of a racial minority in our country.

Marc's support for his Puerto Rican constituents cost both him and them dearly. In the hysterical climate of the postwar years, fed by their growing migration to New York, Puerto Ricans were libeled as Marcantonio dupes, drug addicts, and worse. In 1947, the New York *World-Telegram* opined, "into the relief picture Vito Marcantonio, pro-Communist representative from the East Harlem District, has injected himself with vigor and success." Marc counterattacked, leading a demonstration against the paper. Because increasing numbers of them voted for Marc, the link between Marcantonio, the commie-demagogue, and the victimized, "lazy," "relief-prone" Puerto Ricans has persisted in the tabloids—and, in historical mythology, to this day. Ignored was a *New York Times* report that the island's "Commissioner of Labor knew of

no effort, governmental or private, to instigate or stimulate the migration of Puerto Ricans to New York."

Marcantonio's consistent—and principled—engagement with
the Puerto Rican independence movement contributed to his defeat in
1950. Throughout the campaign his opponent equated support of
"Moscow-echo-Marc" for independence with Soviet subversion. Then,
just six days before the election, on November 1, 1950, two pro-independence activists, Griselio Torresola and Oscar Collazo, attempted to
assassinate President Truman. Torresola was killed by Secret Service
agents, but Collazo, who once had been an election canvasser for
Marcantonio, survived. Marc helped find a lawyer for Collazo, an act
totally in character and one that helped insure his defeat. In a last-
minute appeal to Puerto Rican voters, he wrote:

> Now is the hour for the true friends of Puerto Rico to gather to its
> side. Now is the hour for those who believe in democracy, liberty,
> and the self-determination of all peoples, to rise in the struggle for
> the liberation of Puerto Rico.
>
> Puerto Ricans: I was with you yesterday, I am with you today, and I
> will be there tomorrow and all the days of my life."

Third-party politics had a long history in East Harlem by the
time Marc first ran for La Guardia's old seat in Congress in 1934. In the
first three decades of this century, the Socialist Party achieved a substantial Jewish vote in East Harlem as well as in other working-class
areas. In East Harlem, the Socialist vote was often the balance of power.
In 1924, La Guardia ran, and was re-elected to Congress on the Socialist
ticket. But even when he ran as a Republican, he made major appeals to
Jewish Socialist voters, campaigning in Yiddish and calling for Social
Security, a major Socialist demand.

When Marc first ran for La Guardia's Congressional seat, he had
the Republican and Fusion parties' nominations. In fact, Marcantonio
and others had created the ad hoc Fusion Party the year before as a vehicle for voters wishing to support La Guardia for mayor, but unwilling to
vote Republican. In the 1934 Congressional race, when Marc defeated

the incumbent Tammany man in a close race, the Fusion Party provided the winning margin.

In 1936 a local left-wing grouping, the All People's Party, created by Marcantonio and a coalition of blacks, Puerto Ricans, Jews, and Italians—many of them Socialists and Communists—supplied him with a second voting-machine line and a third of his vote in his re-election bid. But it was the Republican Party to whom he owed his major position on the ballot, and that meant he could not openly support FDR's re-election—fatal in East Harlem. It was a dilemma that lost him—narrowly—the election. Not one to brood over defeat, Marcantonio continued to serve East Harlem residents and pursue a labor-law practice.

During the years of Congressional exile, 1937-38, Marcantonio moved closer to the Communists, with whom he found himself allied on numerous issues. While the Communist Party (CP) attempted to recruit him, Marcantonio was never a member and never accepted party discipline. Personally close to many Communists, Marc was nevertheless no ideologue and could never have found politics congenial as a Communist.

Marcantonio was not the only political figure who understood the value of third parties and independent political action. In 1936, at the urging of FDR, the leadership of the needle-trades unions formed the American Labor Party to secure votes of left-wing, predominantly Jewish, workers—who shunned the Tammany-controlled Democratic machine—for Roosevelt and the liberal Democratic gubernatorial candidate, Herbert H. Lehman. The ALP was originally intended as a temporary device, because Roosevelt thought the election in New York might be close. But the ALP exceeded expectations, drawing more votes than the Socialists had previously. Much to the chagrin of the Tammany bosses, the unions, with the tacit support of FDR—and the open encouragement of Eleanor Roosevelt—continued to sponsor and finance the ALP as a permanent third party. Marcantonio began to work with the ALP almost immediately, enrolling as a member just two weeks after his defeat. Later in 1936, Marc's All-People's Party affiliated with the ALP. In 1937, the ALP became the linchpin of La Guardia's strategy for re-election as mayor.

In 1938, Marcantonio returned to Congress. Now he listed himself not as a Republican but as the House's only member from the American Labor Party—a designation he held throughout the remainder of his congressional career.

Also in 1938, Communists and their supporters joined Socialists and others as rank-and-file ALP activists. That year the ALP supported many liberal Democrats and Republicans, some of whom, running in marginal districts, owed their victory to votes garnered on the ALP line. The party became a force to reckon with. Soon La Guardia was an enrolled member.

What distinguished the ALP from the major parties was its direct appeal to class interests. Its name said "Labor." An early slogan implored, "Don't Scab at the Ballot Box." By 1941 the Communist Party had concentrated nearly all of its electoral efforts in the ALP. The resulting powerful leftist faction, which included many non-Communists as well, almost immediately found Marcantonio as its leader. Bitter fratricidal conflict broke out between Marc's group and the old Socialist-influenced garment-union leadership of the ALP, exacerbated by Communist support for the Nazi-Soviet Pact. The leftists won control of the Manhattan organization in 1941 and the state apparatus in 1944; as a result David Dubinsky, leader of the International Ladies Garment Workers Union, and Alex Rose of the hatter's union, withdrew to form the Liberal Party.

It would be easy to dismiss the ALP, especially in its later years, as a Communist-dominated political movement and, thus, a victim of all of the policy disasters of the Communist Party. In fact, until its demise—and despite the major role of Communists—the ALP included a wide range of liberals and non-CP leftists. Communists constituted a strong and essential phalanx of experienced campaign workers, but Marcantonio and the ALP undoubtedly profited more from the presence of Communists in the ALP than vice versa.

New York in the 1940s had a unique radical culture. A relatively large number of New Yorkers who would never dream of joining the CP nonetheless read left-of-center newspapers like the experimental, advertising-free *PM*, its successor, the *Daily Compass*, and the then milque-

toasty liberal *New York Post.* Many of them were self-consciously committed to a radical politics. Intellectually curious and socially active, they
believed passionately in the struggle against fascism and anti-Semitism.
They were moved by the extraordinary wartime sacrifices made by the
Soviets, but with equal ardor supported the rights of labor and racial
equality. On these issues, the views of these non-communist radicals
were similar to those of the Communists. But their political commitment lay with the ALP, which they saw as a vibrant, principled, and
democratic organization—not with the Communist Party, whose secre-
tiveness, hierarchical structure, dreary meetings, and catechized political positions they found alien and arid.

ALP clubs became centers of neighborhood activity, demanding
more traffic lights and better schools, petitioning for enforcement of
rent control and effective food price controls. The clubs were home to
film showings, folk dances, and choral groups. In Brooklyn, The Bronx,
and East Harlem, where the ALP was strong, its enrollment and voting
support made it frequently the second strongest and, occasionally, the
leading political party in its area.

Marcantonio's and the ALP's vote-getting strength made possible
mutually beneficial electoral alliances with liberal Democrats. With La
Guardia and FDR denying Tammany access to patronage, the old machine
had nothing to lose in collaborating with Marc. Indeed, in return for support for major party candidates the ALP found acceptable, Marc ran
unopposed for re-election twice during the war, obtaining the
Republican and Democratic nominations as well that of the ALP. ALP
support for judges and State Assembly and Senate candidates led to coali-
tions that elected not only liberal Democrats, but some ALPers as well.

With the end of World War Two and the beginning of the Cold
War, the formation of issues-oriented and candidate-oriented coali-
tions—key to the ALP's and Marcantonio's electoral strategy—became
more difficult. In 1945 La Guardia, still an enrolled member of the ALP,
recognized that the bitter split that had led to the formation of the
Liberal Party made his re-election impossible.

With La Guardia out of the race, Marc and the ALP threw their
support to Democrat William O'Dwyer. In return, O'Dwyer, who had a

strong pro-union record as a judge and as Brooklyn's District Attorney, agreed to back some ALP candidates and support ALP policy on housing, education, and, especially, the preservation of the five-cent subway fare. Even though the ALP provided O'Dwyer's margin of victory, the changing political climate permitted O'Dwyer to break his promise to Marcantonio on the five-cent transit fare.

Marc's 1946 Congressional campaign in East Harlem was marred by violence and by the mysterious murder of Joseph Scotterigio, a Republican campaign worker. Although Marcantonio and his campaign staff were cleared by a Grand Jury, the investigation of the Scotterigio murder, led by bipartisan New York County District Attorney Frank Hogan, was gleefully pursued by both Tammany and the Republicans. The probe also attempted to tie Marc to organized crime, but nothing was found to sustain the accusation. In this climate, in 1947, the State Legislature passed a law preventing candidates from running in the primaries of parties in which they were not enrolled. The press called it the "Anti-Marcantonio Act."

In 1948, as the Cold War intensified, the ALP, supporting former Vice President Henry A. Wallace's third-party Presidential campaign, found itself under attack as Communist-controlled. Marcantonio was red-baited and the major parties intensified efforts to defeat him, denying him both the Republican and the Democratic nomination. Running only on the ALP ticket for the first time, Marcantonio was re-elected to his seventh term.

In the difficult postwar elections, the ALP, with its citywide resources, became increasingly important to Marcantonio's political survival. Former ALP campaigners still tell how they were mobilized from all over the city to canvass door-to-door through the slums of East Harlem, the tenements of the ever-growing Puerto Rican El Barrio, and the high-rise housing projects built through Marcantonio's legislative initiative. Others, middle class professionals, worked for Marc in the affluent neighborhoods recently gerrymandered into his district, seeking votes and campaign financing.

The "Last Hurrah" for the ALP was in 1949. Marcantonio sought the office of his mentor, La Guardia. He ran for Mayor in an emotionally charged, raucous, viciously fought campaign. Red-baited from the start, the victim of accusations of association with Mafiosi, red espionage agents, and even, charged the *Daily Mirror*, with "subversive show girls," Marcantonio stuck to the issues: he supported a return to the five-cent fare, equal housing opportunity, and improved health and welfare services. As he did in all his campaigns, he connected small issues with large ones, explaining that the growing anticommunist hysteria and increased military expenditures directly affected deteriorating municipal services and the ever-mounting cost of living.

Marcantonio's campaign was a great classroom. Speaking fourteen or fifteen times a day, he drew great crowds; thousands came to hear him in Greenwich Village, Harlem, Brownsville, Flatbush, and neighborhoods in The Bronx. On the Friday before election-day, fifteen hundred gathered at Sixth Avenue and Bleecker Street to hear the dark-eyed, now-hoarse-voiced New Yorker ask voters to take control of their municipal destiny. Marc won great applause and the ALP scored its second-largest vote for a citywide office ever—more than 350 thousand. But O'Dwyer, seeking a second term, swamped Marc.

The following year, Democrats, Republicans and Liberals joined behind one candidate in Marcantonio's district; the ALP no longer had the leverage to prevent this coalition. Despite the largest vote the ALP ever received in East Harlem—and the greatest concentration of citywide ALP support—Marcantonio was easily beaten. He delivered his own political epitaph in a final speech in the House of Representatives:

> ...I have stood by the fundamental principles which I have always advocated. I have not trimmed. I have not retreated. I do not apologize, and I am not compromising..

Marcantonio seemed to accept defeat defiantly, even with optimism. He returned to an active but penurious civil liberties legal practice, where he is best remembered for successfully defending the scholar and civil rights activist W. E. B. Du Bois in 1951. Du Bois, perhaps the greatest American intellect of this century, whose very being gave the lie to the doctrine of white supremacy—the "original sin" that made America possible—like Marcantonio, Du Bois had refused to trim his sails; his activism against the Cold War only made this black man even more despised. In his eighties, he was accused of running a Soviet-controlled peace advocacy organization at the height of the Korean War. Marcantonio won his acquittal despite the Government's thinly veiled appeals to racism.

In another, more explosive, case, Marc, along with George Crockett, until recently a Democratic Representative from Michigan and leading member of the Black Congressional Caucus, was counsel to William F. Patterson, executive secretary of the Civil Rights Congress (CRC). Patterson had been subpoenaed before a House subcommittee investigating lobbying activities. Patterson was asked to produce the records of CRC, labeled a Communist front by the Attorney General. In fact, the House committee was interested in obtaining the names of CRC's members and donors so that they could be intimidated into withdrawing their support. Patterson, subsequently cited for contempt, refused to provide the names and was called a "black son of a bitch" by committee chairman Henderson Lanham of Georgia.

The East Harlemite's summation to the jury was vintage Marc—explicit, colloquial, and passionate. From the Court record:

> MR. MARCANTONIO: [The prosecution] could not stand anyone petitioning the Congress of the United States.... Since when has it become unlawful to petition the Congress of the United States? The rights of petition are guaranteed by the First Amendment, guaranteed by the men and women who shed their blood so a free nation could be established in this country.

> THE COURT: Please do not pound the furniture.

> MR. MARCANTONIO: That may be, Your Honor. I feel strongly about this. I feel strongly about this Your Honor.

> THE COURT: It is a breach of the Court to pound the furniture.

> MR. MARCANTONIO: Perhaps the furniture may be hurt. But what is more important are the rights and dignity of human beings. That is more important than the furniture. The rights of and dignity of human beings, the rights and dignity of the proposition that all men are created equal, that men are not to be framed because of the color of their skin—that is more important than the furniture of this court or any court in the United States of America.

Marcantonio also took a leading role in the legal defense of the Communist Party, then facing a multitude of attacks from the government. He also successfully defended Fur Workers Union leader Ben Gold, accused of falsely denying membership in the Communist Party.

Much to the surprise of the legal establishment, Marc won all of these cases. Jurors responded to his clear and impassioned plea as voters had done previously. It is ironic—and revelatory of Marcantonio's commitment to principle—that at the same time he was tirelessly representing the Communist Party, he was also engaged in a bitter political dispute with it. In the early fifties the Communists had changed their political line yet again. Advocating working within existing liberal institutions, they sabotaged Marcantonio's ALP leadership, shifting campaign workers to the Democrats. Marc continued to represent the CP anyway—on civil liberties grounds.

At the same time, despite his political isolation, Marcantonio continued to serve his constituents as if he still held public office. Without political power, with no access to patronage, Marc had to rely on old friends still in city agencies to solve problems. Nearly every day he would spend time, at what was now called the Vito Marcantonio Political Association, assisting his neighbors. At the same time he met with old campaign aides and with former ALP, Democratic, and Republican precinct workers, planning a comeback bid for Congress. The three-party coalition that had beaten him was falling apart, and there seemed to be a bit of a thaw in the Cold War. Senator McCarthy was in disgrace. The Korean War was over. Marcantonio planned to run on an ad hoc Good Neighbor Party ticket. Old allies gathered to raise money and stump the district for him, and seasoned politicos thought he might just make it.

It was not to be. On the morning of August 9, 1954, Vito Marcantonio dropped dead of a heart attack in the rain on lower Broadway and Warren Street. He had just been to the printer to pick up nominating petitions for his Congressional race. His only monument is a junior high school named after him—an event preceded by much controversy—but its students know little of him.

Correspon-
dence
Noted

CORRESPONDENCE NOTED

Curt Gentry: *The FBI's Rites of Succession –A Personal and Confidential Communication To An About-To-Be-Deposed Bureau Director*

Curt Gentry, the distinguished San Francisco writer, co-author of Helter-Skelter *and biographer of J. Edgar Hoover, sent this memorandum, titled "The Bureaucrats vs. The Outsider," and marked Personal and Confidential on March 23, 1993, to his friend, former Federal Judge William Sessions, then the reformist-minded director of the FBI, warning him of the Bureau's primitive rites of succession and the perils he faced in continuing to do his job. In effect, Gentry warned Sessions, through the alarm signals of history, that he was being set up for a fall by his enemies in the FBI's Old Boy bureaucracy. Gentry's memo was as prophetic as it was instructional. Sessions was fired by President Bill Clinton on July 19, 1993. The memo is printed here as it was sent to Sessions.*

DEAR BILL: I hope you will forgive my being presumptuous, but there are some things that need stating. (I am not referring to the ridiculous accusations of former attorney general Barr, which I am sure you can answer to everyone's satisfaction, and which I suspect were meant as much to embarrass the Clinton Administration as you.)

My concern is what is happening within the FBI.

Historically, the situation you've inherited goes back a long way...

L. PATRICK GRAY: MAY 1972—APRIL 1973

Within hours after President Nixon announced that L. Patrick Gray would be the late J. Edgar Hoover's successor as FBI Director, top officials of the Bureau began plotting Gray's demise.

They lied to Gray, saying, for example, that there were no secret files. They hid things from him, first and foremost the vast amount of corruption in the Bureau's administrative division. They spied on him, compiling daily reports on his activities, remarks and contacts, reports allegedly so detailed that they had to have come from taps, bugs and/or his personal security squad. They also convinced him that his first priority as director was to re-establish contact with the "field." During his brief tenure, Gray visited 58 of the Bureau's 59 field offices, missing only Honolulu, thus earning the nickname "Three Day Gray," and, of course, leaving the bureaucrats in charge during his absence.

It has also been rumored, I have

no factual basis for this as Gray has refused all interviews, that when Gray destroyed the contents of Howard Hunt's safe he did so on the advice of one or more top FBI officials.

Gray's tenure as Acting FBI Director lasted less than a year. He did force the resignation of John Mohr (often referred to as "the most powerful man in the FBI," because, as head of the administrative division, he controlled all promotions, demotions and transfers, as well as the Bureau's budget, its procurement and its finances); he greatly reduced Crime Records, the Bureau's vast publicity arm, scattering its personnel, whom he didn't trust, with good reason, all over the U.S.; and, to the delight of the agents, he replaced several of the most unpopular SACs, but it was too little too late. They were gunning for him and they got him, making sure his misstatements and mistakes were widely publicized, deeply involving him in the authorization of illegal break-ins and technical surveillances. He was almost totally dependent on Mark Felt, whom he'd named acting associate director, but Felt was more interested in promoting his own candidacy than in protecting Gray's back.

Read the transcript of L. Patrick Gray's aborted confirmation hearings and one thing stands out: Gray, the outsider, never knew what was going on in the FBI.

WILLIAM RUCKELSHOUSE: APRIL—JUNE 1973

Ruckelshouse was a caretaker, and was treated as such. He lasted only 70 days, and made no significant changes, except for accepting the resignation of Mark Felt, whom he'd caught leaking stories to the press.

Arriving at work on his first day, Ruckelshouse found a telegram on his desk. The acting associate director, all the assistant directors, and all except one of the special agents in charge had wired the president, urging him to appoint a highly qualified professional from "within the organization." There was nothing personal about it, the FBI bureaucrats told Ruckelshouse. They were sure he was a nice guy; but he had no law enforcement experience and he knew nothing of the traditions of the Bureau.

CLARENCE M. KELLEY: JUNE 1973—JANUARY 1978

In choosing a permanent director, Nixon and Ruckelshouse went outside the FBI, but not far. They picked Clarence M. Kelley, a 21-year veteran of the Bureau (1940-61), who had spent his last 12 years as police chief of Kansas City, Missouri.

Confirmed in the midst of the first revelations about the Hoover era, Kelley had a mandate for change, but showed no undue haste in exercising it. He did institute a policy of "participatory management," which he'd used most successfully in Kansas City, turning the executive conference into more of a corporate board of directors. But he surrounded himself with unreconstructed Hooverites and J. P. Mohr loyalists, who did their best to co-opt him and even involved him in their petty pilferings.

The Exhibits Section installed new valances in Kelley's apartment; purchased two television sets for his home use; built him a walnut table, a set of stack tables and a jewelry box; and mounted the FBI seal on a gold disk as a charm for his wife, who was dying of cancer.

In addition, Director Kelley's automobile received occasional servicing by FBI employees and his FBI-provided chauffeur performed personal errands for the Kelleys.

One weekend, while his wife was still able to travel, Director and Mrs. Kelley joined a number of former and current FBI executives and their wives on a trip to New York, where they met with officials of the Prudential Life Insurance Company, which underwrote the Special Agents Mutual Benefit Association (SAMBA) policy. The others attending included former Assistant to the Director John Mohr, who, following his suggested retirement in June 1972, had become a paid retiree's consultant to SAMBA. In what was later characterized as a "purely social" weekend, the group stayed at the Waldorf Astoria. Director Kelley's travel from Kansas City, Mo., to New York and return to Washington, D.C. was by Government Travel Request (GTR). Travel for Mrs. Kelley and the others was paid by SAMBA. Prudential paid all other expenses.

Director Kelley was never told that the gifts and other services were provided by the Exhibits Section, at taxpayer's expense. Nor was he told that the New York trip violated government regulations and ethical guidelines. In fact, he was advised otherwise.

In the fall of 1975, the House Select Committee on Intelligence provided the Justice Department with information indicating that various illegal acts had been engaged in by top officials of the FBI, including former Director J. Edgar Hoover, former Associate Director Clyde Tolson, and some of their key bureaucratic assistants. In November of that year, Attorney General Edward H. Levi asked FBI Director Kelley to investigate. Kelley appointed an Ad Hoc Committee to oversee an inquiry by the FBI Inspection Division. It took the inspectors, most of whom had served under John Mohr, only a month to decide there was no basis for the accusations. Attorney General Levi thought otherwise, and, after finding the FBI report "incomplete and unsatisfactory," in January 1976 he directed the Office of Professional Responsibility and the Justice Department's Criminal Division to conduct an independent investigation. The probe took eleven months, during which "hundreds" of past and present FBI officials were interviewed and "vast quantities" of documents and records were examined.

Clarence Kelley (who subsequently reimbursed the Bureau for the cost of the valances, returned the two TVs and repaid Prudential for the costs of the New York trip) cooperated fully with the Justice Department team. As the latter stated in its final report, Kelley's cooperation "greatly assisted

NOW
WINNING
FOR INFORMATION
CALL 408/28-SHARK

Departmental investigators in uncovering the facts. His cooperation made this report possible."

A partial list of the various illegal acts—which included theft, the misappropriation of funds and services, the fraudulent use of travel vouchers, double billing, kickbacks, fraud, perjury, etc.—can be found on pages 725, 726, 740-47, and at various other places in the text of my biography *J. Edgar Hoover: The Man and the Secrets*.

"The Department of Justice Report on the Relationship Between United States Recording Company and the Federal Bureau of Investigation And Certain Other Matters Pertaining to the FBI" was released by Attorney General Griffin B. Bell on January 10, 1978, and runs to forty pages. I have been told that the complete report, which has never been made public, is hundreds of pages in length.

Although it took him nearly five years to get around to it, Kelley cleaned house. He fired Associate Director Nicholas P. Callahan, for unspecified "abuses of power." He completely reorganized the Inspection Division, restructured the FBI inventory system to provide built-in controls and audit trails, instituted new auditing and accounting practices, separated budget from property procurement, ended the exclusive relationship with one provider of technical devices, reorganized or replaced various FBI funds which J. Edgar Hoover, Clyde Tolson and key FBI officials had looted for decades for their own personal use, and—some felt at the time, most important of all—as Attorney General Griffin B. Bell carefully phrased it, "developed and improved the FBI career development program for special agents to insure that the best qualified individuals are selected for administrative advancement, subsequently reducing the possibility that one group or person can control the selection of such candidates."

Although Bell was obviously referring to John Mohr, the first of the "career managers," he was aware that much of the real power in the Bureau remained in the hands of whoever dispensed the patronage, in the form of promotions, demotions, transfers and "perks."

WILLIAM WEBSTER: FEBRUARY 1978–OCTOBER 1987

His "reforms" of the Bureau—not all of which proved permanent— were Clarence Kelley's last hurrah. He announced his intention to retire in early 1977, shortly after President Carter took office. The long search for a replacement resulted in the choice of William H. Webster, a former prosecutor and trial and appellate court judge from St. Louis, who was confirmed in February 1978.

Judge Webster had been forewarned of the insular nature of the Bureau and its attitude toward "outsiders," and he restructured the high command, appointing not one associate director but three executive associate directors, none of whom were "Hooverites." Younger, better educated and less resistant to change than their predecessors, each was given clearly defined responsibilities. This meant that no one person had all the power. Webster also brought in a number of his former law clerks, to serve as his office staff, so he was for the most part surrounded by people he knew and could trust. Perhaps needless to say, these changes, as well as others Judge Webster instituted, were very unpopular with the career managers in the FBI's high command. When, in May 1987, President Reagan announced that Webster would be the new director of the Central Intelligence Agency, they swore: "Never another judge."

WILLIAM S. SESSIONS: NOVEMBER 1987—[JULY 1993]

I needn't review your first five years as director of the FBI, but having studied the Bureau for some 18 years—I began my research for the Hoover biography in 1975—I agree with Congressman, and former special agent, Don Edwards when he states that you have been the best director the FBI has ever had.

The FBI is a great organization; you and former directors Webster and Kelley have gone a long way toward restoring its public reputation and making it, for the first time, a truly modern law enforcement agency.

But, having said this, I must add that I think you have made some serious mistakes:

1. On taking office you listened to the wrong people. You acquiesced to the complaints of the career managers about the great dissatisfaction with Judge Webster and his law clerks, and reinstituted the policy of a single deputy, again putting all the power in the hands of one man, who by the very nature of his solitary position commands the loyalty of those under him.

This, I believe, can still be corrected by returning to a system similar to those inaugurated by Kelley or Webster, or perhaps broadening the duties of the executive conference.

2. You failed to realize that whatever feelings you have for the Bureau you head—and I know in talking to you that they are deep— you are always going to be an outsider to some within the organization, particularly those career managers who see change as a threat to their own agendas. And this must be taken into account.

You, not they, are the director: you were appointed by the president and confirmed by the Senate to fulfill that role. You alone are responsible for making sure the Bureau's best interests are first and foremost.

3. You failed to recognize, while fending off attempts by the Bush Administration to politicize the FBI, that you were also dealing with a palace revolt, the attempt of a small cabal, numbering probably no more than a half dozen senior officials, to recapture control of the Bureau. I'm really not sure if you realize, or accept this, even now. This is not a conspiracy theory. It is simple fact. And I think any impartial investigation of the roles of this group, by Congress or the new attorney general, would bear this out.

This too, I believe, can be corrected, once the restrictions placed on you by the Barr edict are removed.

4. Although you sometimes failed to do so, I think you should appoint people of proven ability and integrity as your key aides, giving preference, but not restricting your choices, to those who have served in the Bureau and are aware of its Byzantine byways. They should be loyal to both you and to the FBI, not the FBI of the past but the FBI as it might be. Above all, they should be people you can trust to tell you the truth, no matter how unpleasant it might be, so you can take whatever corrective steps are necessary.

5. I think there has been a serious failure by your Office of Public Affairs to fully publicize the very real accomplishments of the Bureau during the past five years. I am not advocating more hokey TV shows, nor urging a return to days of the old Crime Records, when the Bureau took credit for any crime that anyone solved, but an attempt to inform the public about the many-faceted role of the modern FBI. It's fascinating stuff, and I think it should be made known to the public.

Bill, I'm writing this to you because I think highly of you, and I want very much to see you continue in your role as Director of the Federal Bureau of Investigation.

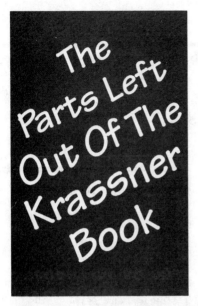
The
Parts Left
Out Of The
Krassner
Book

In Paul Krassner's autobiography, <u>**Confessions of a Raving, Unconfined Nut: Misadventures in the Counter-Culture**</u>, there is a chapter on his most notorious achievement, "The Parts Left Out of the Kennedy Book."

Now, ironically, Krassner's irreverent newsletter, 𝕿𝖍𝖊 𝕽𝖊𝖆𝖑𝖎𝖘𝖙, includes the parts left out of his own book— names that were changed; incidents that were omitted.

Other features in that issue and the succeeding two:

Robert Anton Wilson on the False Memory Syndrome ↶· Ellen Sander revisits the infamous **Plaster Casters** ↶· Will Durst on **Howard Stern**'s Private Parts ↶· Krassner on **Michael Jackson**'s Private Parts ↶· **Marc Maron** on the Fine Art of Cloning ↶· **Roseanne Arnold**'s last Fax ↶· The 6th Annual Cannabis Cup ↶· Conversations with **Carlos Castaneda** ↶· Inside the Toyota Comedy Festival ↶· Our regular feature, "Media Freak," a collection of bizarre news items ↶·

These three issues of 𝕿𝖍𝖊 𝕽𝖊𝖆𝖑𝖎𝖘𝖙 are yours for $6, or free with a subscription.

𝕿𝖍𝖊 𝕽𝖊𝖆𝖑𝖎𝖘𝖙
Box 1230, Venice CA 90294

☐ $6 for the three issues described in your ad
☐ $23 for a 12-issue subscription plus those three issues free
☐ $25 for a copy of <u>**Confessions of a Raving, Unconfined Nut**</u>
☐ $10 for a copy of <u>**The (Almost) Unpublished Lenny Bruce**</u>

Name...
Address...
City.. State.................. Zip...............................

Erick Gilbert: *Is Tintin P.C.?*

ERGÉ'S CORPUS of twenty-three adventure stories, each featuring Tintin, his dog Snowy, Captain Haddock, and a cast of characters developed over a fifty-year period, leads the world's translations alongside the Bible, Shakespeare, and, until some recent events, Lenin.

Tintin's broad international appeal has been polished over the years through Hergé's revisions, both major and minor, of the original stories. The biggest changes took place after the Second World War; standardization to a sixty-two-page format from a comic strip serial was Hergé's pretext for self-censorship and the readjustment of failed ideologies. Some of these changes were born of aesthetic mistakes; others were political necessities.

Hergé's political choices and subtext were re-defined and criticized in Europe during the 1960s and 1970s, the same time Chilean writers produced a strongly Marxist analysis of Barks Duck Stories. These left-leaning readings questioned Hergé's output during the war and other political touchpoints between 1929 and 1979, criticism that continues today. The subtext is that literary entertainment is not acceptable unless the author presents politically correct opinions. Is Tintin P.C.? The prewar adventures of Tintin,

Books Reviewed

Tintin in the Land of the Soviets, 1930
Tintin in the Congo, 1931
Tintin in America, 1932
Cigars of the Pharaoh, 1933
The Blue Lotus, 1935
The Broken Ear, 1937
The Black Island, 1938
King Ottokar's Scepter, 1939
The Crab With the Golden Claws, 1941
The Shooting Star, 1942
*The Secret of the Unicorn and
Red Racham's Treasure*, 1943
The Seven Crystal Balls, 1948
Prisoners of the Sun, 1949
Land of Black Gold, 1950
Destination Moon, 1953
Explorers on the Moon, 1954
The Calculus Affair, 1956
The Red Sea Sharks, 1958
Tintin in Tibet, 1960
The Castafiore Emerald, 1963
Flight 714, 1968

permeated by the ideological climate of the time, are the basis of most of the political attacks on Hergé and his creations. Although critics who identify him with proto-fascist thinking are unaware that the first Tintin book was an attack on the Soviet Union. It was withheld from publication for a long time because its politics were too nonconformist in the face of the left's orthodoxy about the old USSR. Its recent publication in the United

States affords the opportunity to view the politics of all Tintin books.

Hergé (Georges Rémi) was born May 22, 1907, in Brussels. His father worked at a children's clothing manufacturer and his mother reared the children. His younger brother, who eventually went into the army, may have been an early inspiration for Tintin. Hergé went to Catholic schools, and enrolled in the Catholic Boy Scouts after a short stay with the "nondenominational" Boy Scouts. In 1925, he began a clerk's job at *Le Vingtième Siècle*, a Catholic daily directed by Abbot Norbert Wallez. Wallez, an admirer and personal acquaintance of Mussolini, made his publication the voice of the prewar Belgian extreme right. Hergé began to illustrate insipid texts by house writers, and he designed ads. In 1927 he created a boy scout hero, Totor, for *Le Boy Scout Belge*; Totor continued his adventures over two years. In 1928, Wallez began *Le Petit Vingtième*, a young reader's supplement, and made Hergé editor-in-chief, as well as designer and main illustrator.

The adventures of a young reporter named Tintin and his talking dog, Snowy, first appeared in *Le Petite Vingtième* in 1929. Started as a quick "fill," it quickly became a main attraction. By the end of the first adventure, *Tintin in the Land of the Soviets*, Tintin was a hero in Belgium.

In 1940, Germany invaded Belgium, and Hergé fled to France. He went back to Brussels when the King of Belgium called for his subjects to return, and worked for the daily *Le Soir*. He started a new Tintin story, *The Crab with the Golden Claws*, where he introduced his second main character, Captain Haddock.

During the war, two of Tintin's adventures were banned by the censorship system in Occupied France: the "pro-British" *Black Island* and *Tintin in America*. (The subtly antifascist *King Ottokar's Scepter* was somehow overlooked.)

In 1944, when Brussels was liberated, Hergé was arrested as a collaborator because of his newspaper work. He spent a night or two in jail and was then released. This began a two-year hiatus in Hergé's career, during which he published no new books but edited his earlier works for a new printing by Casterman, an ultra-respectable 150-year-old publisher, in a standardized sixty-two-page album format. The stories were newly laid out and colored, and some redrawn to satisfy the author's more defined aesthetic choices. In 1947, with the help and support of French Résistance member Raymond Leblanc, Hergé and four other cartoonists created a *Tintin* magazine.

The 1950s were a decade of futuristic dreams and, accordingly, Hergé sent his heroes on their wildest trip ever: the first humans to walk on the moon. This was also an era of existentialist questioning, and this influence showed in Hergé's work and his personal life. Hit by postwar troubles and possibly a mid-life crisis, Hergé questioned his life and his heroes. Over the next ten years, his output slowed, and the moral guidelines of his characters fluctuated; by the 1960s they completely reversed with *The Castafiore Emerald* and *Flight 714*.

It took him eight years to realize the last completed Tintin adventure, *Tintin and the Picaros*. Hergé died in March, 1983, with his final Tintin story incomplete.

TINTIN IN THE LAND OF THE SOVIETS

Originally serialized in 1929, *Soviets* found its inspiration in a book lent to Hergé by Father Wallez: *Moscou sans voiles* or, *Moscow Unveiled*. Written by a Belgian ex-consul, it denounced a criminal and decadent Soviet Union with a precision that today seems prescient. Though Hergé used a number of techniques in his page and panel designs, that were new to his time, continuity and characterization were absent; and a number of scenes were lifted straight from the reference book. Here, the use of Flemish slang for exotic languages and locations first appeared; it became a successful Tintin staple. Hergé said himself that he had no scenario, and he would often draw the night before going to press, thereby giving the completed story an absence of structure. The style was slapstick and silent-movie humor peripeteia against the backdrop of an anti-Soviet propaganda pamphlet. After the war, Hergé did not want this story reprinted, considering it too juvenile. By 1979, though, many bootleg editions were on the market, and

first editions had become highly priced collector's items; Hergé agreed to reprint a facsimile of the first edition. It was published in English for the first time only in 1989.

Beyond the forgettable story, the main interest of this first adventure is the art. It shows the early development of what came to be called the Clear Line style, featuring no halftones or shadings. Hergé drew from the Art Deco style and Dutch De Stijl architecture that he had first used in his work on advertisements. Also, he used word balloons instead of a narrative under the panel, a stylistic breakthrough in Europe.

TINTIN IN THE CONGO

After the unexpected success of the Soviet story, Hergé wanted to send his hero to America, which had a large place in his imagination. Wallez, however, dissuaded him, and, to promote the glorious Belgian colony, requested that Tintin visit the Congo. Hergé's storytelling techniques are still primitive here, but the story had some real sources: the Belgian King had visited the Congo and there were many articles about Africa and museums of African art and culture. The dated, stereotypic images of black people, and the disregard for animal life, still restrain the book from being published in the United States. A facsimile of the first black-and-white 1930 version is available in English, and a 1946 color version in various European languages.

The most cited difference between the 1930 and 1946 versions is a classroom scene where Tintin addresses a room of African children. In the 1931 edition: "Today I'm going to teach you about your homeland...Belgium." In 1946: "Now who can tell me what two and two make?...Nobody?" But the picture Hergé drew of the Congo has always—excepting a couple of articles during the turbulent sixties—been accepted in Africa, and is still an excellent seller in Africa today. While black characters in later stories (such as *The Red Sea Sharks*) had their speech patterns changed in response to criticism in *Jeune Afrique* magazine, *Congo* retained its dated views. One can safely speculate that Hergé saw no major objection to Tintin's view of the African colony when he was drawing

it, though later in his life he felt slightly uncomfortable with the message one can read in *Tintin in the Congo*.

TINTIN IN AMERICA

From the Wild West to the Industrial Giant to Gangsters, many aspects of early America have been romanticized by Europeans. Hergé was both fascinated by its giantism and disgusted with its commercialism and lack of humanity. Though ethnic stereotypes are present in this adventure, Hergé also presents a few unflattering faces of American society Native Americans being evicted by the Army after gas is discovered on their land; racial violence; and lynchings Hergé saw Native Americans as noble savages living Boy-Scout-style in the wilderness as opposed to America's corrupt and criminal urban society and he retained this critical attitude toward America throughout his career.

Some black background characters in early printings were later changed to white, at the request of the American publishers, thereby eliminating all references to black people Such corrections were due more to American segregationist censorship which frowned on blacks and white appearing together, than concern over possibly demeaning stereotypes Similar changes were made for the American editions of other stories like *The Crab with the Golden Claws*.

TINTIN IN THE ORIENT:

This long story of Tintin's travel and tribulations in Egypt, India, an

China began in the 1930s as yet another series of weekly cliffhangers-and-slapstick romp. Tintin is pursued by two bumbling secret agents, who would soon be named Thompson and Thomson and would provide comic relief for the heroes in most of the following adventures. Rastapopoulos, a recurring bad guy whose name has not yet raised the ire of Greek special interest groups, also made his debut here.

During the six-month hiatus between the end of "The Cigars" and the start of "The Lotus," Hergé befriended a Chinese student living in Belgium, Chang Chon-Ren, who later became a respected sculptor in China. Hergé admits that his previous conception of the Chinese was extremely stereotyped. He discovered, through Chang (also the name of Tintin's companion in "The Blue Lotus"), a whole civilization, and the very favorable opinion he formed of it is obvious throughout the book. The first pages show a rich American industrialist abusing a rickshaw operator; Tintin promptly puts the industrialist in his place in front of a sign that reads "Down with Imperialism."

Hergé seemed to discover, with "The Blue Lotus," a way to let his own political opinions seep into his comic work. At that time his opinions seem to begin to diverge from the *Petit Vingtième* ideology. His pointed denunciation of Japan as the invaders of China compares favorably with the unnamed "invader" in *Terry and the Pirates*, which started at the same time. Once again, very dated physical stereotypes kept the book from being published in English until 1983. In the book itself, though, the focus is on the relationships between characters in life-and-death situations that are typical of adventure stories and independent of any racial allusions.

Hergé's freedom to denounce Japanese aggression—and particularly to denounce Franco, by use of "fifth columnist" as derogation of Japanese actions—seems startling, in a supplement to the Wallez paper. One can speculate that the supplement was not thought politically important because its audience was juvenile. Tintin does appear, however, to be published under some constraint. More pointed political caricatures appeared in his other strip, *Quick and Flupke*, the weekly two-page adventure of Brussels street boys published in another paper.

BEFORE THE OCCUPATION

The Broken Ear takes Tintin from a Brussels museum to the depths of the Amazon and back. Hergé used the setting to denounce arms trafficking while referring to the Gran Chaco War, in which nations opposed nations over rumored oil in the desert. Barely camouflaged names refer to very

Elaine's

1703 2nd Ave. New York City
(212) 534–8114, 534–8103

Beatrice Inn

285 West 12th Street   New York, NY
(212) 929-6165

Seven Decades in Bohemian Greenwich Village

real characters and situation.

Suppressed by the Germans, later, because of its British setting, *The Black Island* was—even later—one of the most heavily redrawn episodes, to correct a quaint and primitive view of England and Scotland. The revised version, while more accurate, loses a lot of its charm. Hergé recycles previous gags in this straightforward counterfeiter story and, unlike the two previous adventures, takes no strong political stands. The personalities of Thomson and Thompson are more developed and fully integrated into Tintin's "family" of characters.

King Ottokar's Scepter is considered Hergé's clearest political statement; it refers directly to the situation in Europe immediately before the war. The two imaginary central European countries that he invented are models of the genre Hergé continued in later stories, complete with a long history and complex culture. Inspired by the expansionism of Hitler and Mussolini, the rise of strong governments and new political parties, it shows Tintin blocking a takeover of Syldavia by neighboring Borduria and its military,

shaven-neck, leaders. The theme of the two dictators appears at the same time in *Quick and Flupke*; the two boys play visiting Heads of State and come to no good. *Scepter* still reads today as a direct attack on the then-current wave of fascist takeovers, much stronger and more pointed than American adventure strips of the same time (such as *Terry and the Pirates* and *Captain Easy*). While Borduria was clearly identified as Germany (Eastern Germany, since it inherited a Stalin-like dictator in postwar additions), different identifications have been proposed for Syldavia: Poland and Rumania are the most likely prospects, though the appellation "Balkanic Belgium" has stuck and hits quite close to the point.

In 1939, when Belgium was invaded and *Le Petit Vingtième* ceased publication, Hergé stopped work on *Land of Black Gold* and retreated to France. On his return to Brussels, Hergé refused a position with the publications of the Belgian Rexist party—the local brand of Nazi—and went to *Le Soir*, the main Brussels daily allowed to continue publishing.

The first two stories of the Occupation years, *The Crab with the Golden Claws* and *The Shooting Star*, established a major new character in the Tintin family. First introduced in *The Crab* as an inefficient and dangerous-when-inebriated alcoholic, by the end of *The Shooting Star* Captain Haddock was Tintin's main companion after Snowy. He appeared in every one of the following stories.

The Crab is a police mystery, involving drug smugglers, and contains no

allusion to the war or current events in Europe. Some of the panels were censored for American audiences: black characters later became Caucasians, and scenes of Captain Haddock drinking straight out of a bottle of whiskey were replaced.

It was the scenes and characters in *The Shooting Star* that caused Hergé to be accused of political crimes after the war. This search for a mysterious meteorite by rival scientific expeditions was written and drawn in 1941. The Germans had already banned two of Tintin's adventures; could that explain the casting of the United States, still uninvolved in the war, as the origin of the bad guys? Hergé promptly transferred the nasties' headquarters to a fictional South American country for the first postwar reprint. Blumenstein, the obviously Jewish sponsor of the rival scientific expedition, was transformed to Bohlwinkel (from the name of a local confection, *bollewinkel*, also a Jewish name). From this flimsy evidence stemmed accusations of anti-Semitism against Hergé that persist to this day.

Jewish and Arab terrorists who are not given precise opinions or ethics were featured in the still unfinished *Land of Black Gold*, situated in Palestine, as it was called at the time. The absence of any Allied scientist in the group of Europeans aboard Captain Haddock's has also been noted. In the early war years, Hergé was more interested in developing his characters than stating political opinions.

The Secret of the Unicorn/Red Rackham's Treasure is a two-part treasure hunt. The absent-minded Professor Cuthbert Calculus and faithful butler

Nestor make their debut here, together with the future residence of the heroes, Marlinspike Hall. *The Unicorn* is Captain Haddock's origin story, and it gives him a history and an illustrious ancestor. While it does not evoke any large human problem, or mention the war or any other current event, the quality of artwork, continuity, and dialogue interplay, set a standard of excellence in European comics.

Prisoners of the Sun, another two-parter, was interrupted by the end of the war. After two-thirds of *The Seven Crystal Balls* had been published, the Allies liberated Brussels. All newspapers that had published during the Occupation were shut down, and—as mentioned before—Hergé was arrested. That he had worked during the war, and had included some Germanic characters in his stories, were thought to be collaborationist. Hergé never spent more than a couple of nights in jail; nonetheless he was hurt by the charges of collaboration, and the postwar period became a time of depression and self-questioning that lasted well into the sixties.

In 1946, Hergé met members of the

French and Belgian Resistance who wanted to publish more adventures of Tintin. Their political credentials allowed Hergé to focus his energies on the interrupted stories. Hergé went on to finish *The Land of Black Gold*, integrating the new characters created over the war years. The story was redone again in 1970 at the instigation of his British publishers, who complained about the dated Palestinian occupation. The story was shifted to fictitious countries in the Middle East.

Later postwar stories shifted from the global events of earlier adventures toward character development and more interpersonal relationships. After the trip to the moon, "their greatest adventure," the moral rigidity of the heroes eroded, the clear separation of good and bad characters lost its focus, and the very concept of adventure was questioned, although "important subjects" still provided a background for the adventure (the cold war in *The Calculus Affair* and slavery in *The Red Sea Sharks*), they never appear so prominently as in *King Ottokar's Scepter*. Visiting Tibet in the late fifties, Tintin ignored the Chinese views on the country. *Tintin in Tibet*

focused on the power of friendship and possible psychic phenomena as he climbed the Himalayas to rescue his old *Blue Lotus* friend, Chang. It has adventure, it has drama, and it is a work of art. *The Castafiore Emerald* is a non-adventure, a humorous, suburban pantomime that Hergé infuses with the illusion of threat. There are no good guys or bad guys, no great problem of the epoch for the heroes to tackle. Hergé wove strands of non-intrigue in a pseudo mystery that has almost nothing in common with the action-oriented comic stories published at the time in the Tintin weekly.

Hergé was undeniably influenced by the political currents of his epoch, and his early works show a little too obviously their slanted inspiration. Still, his later works showed a more tolerant and liberal attitude, even within a rather strict framework. Hergé never questioned the legitimacy of state apparatus, but he very often denounced the abuses of power.

FURTHER CORRESPONDENCE NOTED

Jack Micheline: *One Poet to Another*

Tony, please type it up for me, put it in a suitcase, I need a manager, a typist, a nymphomaniac, need a better world, need a bunker to store it in, need Magellan, need the bells to ring for me.

—*Letter from poet Jack Micheline to fellow poet Tony Dingman*

[THE FOLLOWING IS TYPEWRITTEN FROM MICHELINE'S HANDWRITING.]

I Chose

I chose the whippoorwill, the imaginary throne of ego madness of fantasy land
I chose the herringbone
I chose the waitress at Tina's
I chose chasing pussy over a bank account
I chose poetry over standing in line at the opera
I chose art just to kick the dark devil in the ass forever
I chose pain & torture because I'm a masochist
I chose alcohol & cigarettes over 9 grain cereal
Sublime destiny over mediocrity
Like Darwin I chose the monkey over man
I chose the harmonica over the harpsichord
I chose Superwoman over Betty Grable
I chose the safety of failure over the Winner's Circle

The Magician Man Is

A mime
A minuscule ant
A mouse at best
A mickey
A moose
A magpie
A member
A molotov cocktail
A Mack Truck
A tootsieroll
A whimsy
A walloper woo
A wham
A wack
Aware
awake
Alarm

Where

Where is the artist without the Art
Dealer
Where is the professor without a book
Where is the peeker without the
   Trieste Cafe
Where is the poet without a publisher
      He is Flagellation Highway
      He is a free show
      A lost soul
      Groping in the blindness &
        darkness
      A comedian at best
      A maniac
      A pair of trousers
      A lonely hard-on
      I'm boss
      I'm bingo
      I'm babe
      I'm blue-eyed
Where is the soldier without a gun
      Without an army
I would die for truth & brotherhood
But my brother Tommy Trantino in
   jail 29 years
      I would follow the wind up a
small canyon
      I would climb the highest
        peak for the smell of roses
      I would be a Dingo Dog
      A doosey
      A dunce
      A dalmation
      A digger
      A dumbbell or blonde
I WOULD DIE FOR A CAUSE IF
THERE WERE ONE!
      (There is not any but the
      dollar bill & I give that away)
So where am I
      On Wall St. dumping
        waterbags from rooftops
      on stockbrokers
Where am I
      in the shit house with roaches
Where am I
      In fantasy land fantasia
      In Finland
      In the funny house at Macy's
Where am I
      Living on my own planet in a
        little space called Whacky
        Dacky Doo
      I'm Doolittle, Ford & the
        Wright Brothers
      I dig ice cream & flowers too
      I'm Einstein
      I'm Columbus
      I'm Leonardo da Vinci
Where am I
      I'm shaking it for old ladies in
        Reno
      I'm writing down numbers of
        license plates & running
        down to play The Big Six
      I'm on my knees praying for a
        miracle
      I'm a monk
      I'm mad
      I'm an ant
      I'm an apple
      A lemon tree
      A piece of Action
      I'm a towel boy in a whore
        house
      A goner
      A gong
      King Kong
      A kisser
      A pisser for truth
      A soliloquy
      A silly goose
      I'm a sausage
      A siren
      A soup

A sucker
A solitary soul
A sampan
A singer
A soldier
A poet
A pimp
A pamphleteer
A penis
I'm Walt Whitman
I'm Freddy
I'm Willy
I'm tired
I'm broken
I'm a jumping bean in
    Barney's Beanery

I'm packaged meat
    without tinsel or neon
A dreamer in Nazi death camps
I'm a conductor with a baton
A judge without a Talis
I'm falsies
I'm fallacy
I'm flicker
I'm tense
A fast act
A fusion
A fantasy
A friend

(end letter)

To: Hinckle

GONZO NATION

VOL. I, NO. 1, FALL 1993

WARREN

    I SHALL SURFACE WHEN THE ROCK IS ROLLED AWAY.
YOU CAN HELP. I WANT TO BE APPOINTED IMMEDIATELY AS
HEAD OF THE ART DEPARTMENT AT STANFORD. MY FRIEND BILL
WALSH HAS RECOMMENDED ME VERY STRONGLY, BUT HE SAYS I
NEED SUPPORT FROM THE INTELLECTUAL COMMUNITY IN SF, ALONG
WITH A TORRENT OF AFFIRMATION BY LOCAL ARTISTS.

    I KNOW YOU CAN DO THIS, WARREN -- AND, ONCE IT"S
DONE, BILL HAS AGREED TO SIGN ON AS SPORTS EDITOR OF THE
ARGONAUT. INDEED, HE LOOKS FORWARD TO IT WITH GREAT EAGER-
NESS & POLITICAL ZEAL, AS DO I. SO LET US PROCEED.

    AS FOR ART -- WELL, SHUCKS. WHY NOT? I WOULD BE
HONORED TO HAVE MY ART ON THE COVER OF YR. MAGAZINE, WHICH
IS LOOKING VERY SHREWD, CRUEL & ELEGANT A/O VOL. 2. I HAVE,
AS YOU KNOW, ALWAYS MAINTAINED THAT YOU ARE THE FINEST EDITOR
OF YR. GENERATION & PERHAPS THE MOST GENEROUS WITH ARTISTS.

    IN CLOSING, LET ME SUAVELY REMIND YOU OF THAT $10,000
YOU OWE ME FOR THE WORKS (OF MINE) THAT YOU PUBLISHED IN
VOL. 1 -- AND BE ASSURED THAT I DO UNDERSTAND THAT THE RICH
PAY LATE & THE DOOMED PAY FOREVER. SELAH.

    SO , WHO DO YOU WANT SHOT? ALL I NEED IS A FINELY-
MOUNTED HUMAN PORTRAIT, CORPORATE LOGO OR EXPENSIVE ANIMAL
IMAGE. YOU SEND IT, I"LL SHOOT IT. NO QUESTIONS ASKED. I AM,
AFTER ALL, A PROFESSIONAL. OKAY

HUNTER

NOTES ON CONTRIBUTORS

DWIGHT EDGAR ABBOTT has served time at San Quentin, Vacaville, Oregon State Penitentiary, Lompoc Federal Prison, and Folsom Prison, where he is now writing a book about his adult life.

GERRY ADAMS is the President of Sinn Féin, and was the elected Member of Parliament for West Belfast from 1983 to 1992. He never took his seat in London, however, in protest over the British occupation of Northern Ireland. He is also the author of *The Politics of Irish Freedom, A Pathway to Peace,* and *Falls Memories.*

ALEXANDRA ANDERSON-SPIVY, contributing art-editor for *Esquire,* is a writer and critic. She lives in New York City.

LOUISE ARMSTRONG's books include *Kiss Daddy Goodnight* and *The Home Front: Notes from the Family War Zone.* Her newest, *Rocking The Cradle of Sexual Politics: What Happened When Women Said Incest* is due out from Addison-Wesley October 1994. Inexplicably, she began her published career as a humorist.

LENORE BAELI WANG is a poet living in New Jersey.

HELEN BAROLINI originated the first collection of Italian American women writers, *The Dream Book,* which won an American Book Award and the American Culture Association's 1987 Koppleman Award. Her next work is *Chiaroscuro: Essays in Identity.*

JIMMY BRESLIN is a columnist for New York *Newsday.* He is the author of numerous novels, including *World Without End, Amen,* which deals with Northern Ireland.

MAE BRUSSELL was an extraordinary conspiracy researcher. Her first article published in *The Realist* in 1972 and her writing has since been collected in an anthology, *The Mae Brussell Reader.* She died in 1988, shortly before the 25th anniversary of JFK assassination.

JESSICA BURSTEIN apprenticed under Burt Stern and Phillipe Hoffman. Her photographs have appeared in virtually every general interest magazine including *Paris Match* and *Time.* She is now constructing a permanent photomontage installation for the New York HBO offices. These photos were taken in the last six months.

JACK CARTER is an investigative journalist and makes his home in Cardiff, California.

GRACE CAVALLIERI is a poet living in West Virginia.

PHYLLIS CHESLER has written six books including *Women and Madness, Mothers on Trial: The Battle for Children and Custody,* and *Sacred Bond: The Legacy of Baby M.* Illness has delayed her book on women and self-defense that will focus on issues raised by the case of the nation's so-called first female serial killer.

CHRISTO, who was born in Gabrovo, Bulgaria on June 13, 1935, and Jeanne-Claude, born in Casablanca, Morocco, on the same day, met in Paris in 1958. For the last thirty years though their projects have taken them all over the world, they have lived and worked in Lower Manhattan.

GREGORY CORSO is an encyclopedic wit, one of the original beatniks, author of seven books, divine shit disturber, and stepson of Rome.

SUSAN CRILE, a New York City artist for the last twenty-five years, is represented in the collections of many institutions, including the Metropolitan Museum of Art, The Hirshhorn Museum, and The Brooklyn Museum. Ms. Crile is also Associate Professor of Art at Hunter College C.U.N.Y. in Manhattan.

TONY DINGMAN is a member of the Mechanics Institute Library and has been a worker bee for Zoetrope Productions since '68. He is stage manager for *Theater of the Page.*.

MARIA FAMA is a poet living in Philadelphia.

ERICK GILBERT has been in the comics business for fifteen years. He edits comics that have been burned by customs officers in various countries.

ALLEN GINSBERG lives in New York City.

WARREN HINCKLE is an editor, journalist, and author who lives in San Francisco and New York City. He is the recipient of the Tom Paine and H.L. Mencken awards.

WILLIAM KENNEDY is the author of a cycle of novels set in Albany, NY including the most recent, *Very Old Bones* and the Pulitizer prize-winning *Ironweed*. His non-fiction works include *O Albany!* an impressionistic history and *Riding the Yellow Trolley* to be published by Penguin Books in paperback in Spring 1994.

PAUL KRASSNER currently lives in Venice, California, where he continues to publish the satirical newsletter *The Realist*, performs stand-up comedy, and is working on a novel.

MARIA MAZZIOTI GILLAN is the Director of the Poetry Center at Passaic County Community College in Patterson, N.J. She is the author of *Unsettling America: Race & Ethnicity in Contemporary-American Poetry*.

RONA MICHELE, anarcho-libertarian, will work for just about anyone who'll publish her art.

JACK MICHELINE, the poet's poet, is friend to painters, poets, con-men.

JOHN O'BRIEN, formerly of New York City, now resides in the Bay Area and is a full-time fine arts painter.

PAUL O'DWYER, the spiritual father of Irish-American politics and a human rights advocate, was President of the New York City Council and, most recently, the city's Commissioner for the United Nations.

ADAM PARFREY envisions his role in society as a "necessary irritant." He helms Feral House publishing, and has edited *Apocalypse Culture* and *Rants and Incendiary Tracts*. His new book of dispatches from the millennial front, *Cult Rapture*, will debut Fall '94.

MICHAEL RATNER is an attorney wuth the Center for Constitutional Rights. He was co-counsel in the Supreme Court case challenging forced repatriation and the case which closed the HIV detention camp on Guantanamo.

ROSE ROMANO founded *La Belle Figura*, a magazine dedicated entirely to Italian-American Woman poets, and is the author of a chap-book called *Vendetta*. She is living in Italy.

JOHN J. SIMON is completing a historical novel set in Marcantonio's New York. He is editorial director of The World War Two Radio Project.

DR. HUNTER S. THOMPSON lives in Woody Creek, CO. He is, above all, a professional.

RON TURNER is the publisher of Last Gasp Books and Comix in San Francisco.

NANCY WEBER made a splash in the '70s with *The Life Swap*, the true tale of her attempt to be someone else while that someone was being Nancy. She intends to make waves in the '90s with her fiction.

KRISTEN WETTERHAHN is a San Francisco illustrator who specializes in woodcuts. She is putting together a collection of bar napkin portraits.

MARTIN WILNER is a Freudian psychoanalyst and psychiatrist living and working in Manhattan. He secretly collects his patient Joe Coleman's paintings.

CREDITS AND PERMISSIONS

Photograph of Gerry Adams courtesy Sheridan Square Press. Gerry Adams'prison writings and fiction, "The Mountains of Mourne," were excerpted from "Cage Eleven" and "The Street" by Gerry Adams, published by Sheridan Square Press, New York, 1993. Intrpductions by Paul O'Dwyer and Jimmy Breslin were excerpted from "Cage Eleven" and "The Street". "Incarcerated For Being Queer," by Lynn Duff was published in a slightly different form in Dendron, P.O. Box 11284, Eugene, Oregon 97440. "I Cried, You Didn't Listen," by Dwight Edgar Abbot with Jack Carter, was excerpted from the book of the same name, published in 1991 byFeral House, Portland Oregon."And They Call It Help," by Louise Armstrong was excerpted from "And They Call It Help—The Psychiatric Policing of America's Children," Addison Wesley, New York with the permission of the author. Portions of, "Who's Crazy Now?" by Phyllis Chesler appeared in "On The Issue", Summer 1992 and Summer 1993; St. John's Review, April 1993, "AWoman's Right To Self Defense: The Case of Aileen Carol Wournos; "Criminal Practice Law Report," Vol.1 No. 9, October 1993, "Sexual Violence Against Women." Photograph of Aileen Carol Wournos courtesy Strtand Releasing and the documentary film, "Aileen Wournos: The Selling of a Serial Killer." Achilles Rizzoli artwork reproduced with permission from the Ames Gallery, Berkeley, California, which exclusively represents his artwork. "Memoirs of a Conspiracy Nut" by Paul Krassner adapted with permission by the author from "Confessions of a Raving Unconfined Nut: Misadventures in the Counter Culture" by Paul Krassner, Simon & Schuster, New York, 1993. Photographs of Paul Krassner supplied by the author. "Our Assassins" by Mae Brussell originally appeared in the Realist. "Poems of a Superspy" by Oswald Le Winter @ 1994 by the author. Cover and artwork by Joe Coleman reproduced with permission from "Cosmic Retribution: The Infernal Art of Joe Coleman," Feral House Fantagraphics Books, Seattle and Portland, 1992. Christo drawings of Covered Reichstag @ 1993 by the artist. "Frank Talk With a Psychopath" by Adam Parfey was first published in "Apocalypse Culture" by Feral House, Portland, Oregon. For a free catalogue write P.O. Box 3466, Portland, OR, 97208. Guy Colwell artwork from Inner City Romance Comics reproduced with permission of the publisher, Last Gasp of San Francisco, P.O. Box 410067, San Francisco, Ca. 94141. A catalogue will be sent for $3. Photos by Vido Marcantonio, p. 270-271, AP Widewrold Photos. "Tin Tin in the Land of the Soviets" (reviewed, p.302) was published in Belgium by Les Editions Du Petit "Vingtieme" and distributed in the U.S. by Last Gasp of San Francisco. Other Tin Tin titles in the omnibus reviewed by Erick Gilbert were published in the U.S. by Atlantic Little-Brown , Boston and New York.

AUTHOR! AUTHOR!

[SELF PORTRAIT BY RALPH STEADMAN, ISSUE TWO]

ARGONAUT AUTHORS, WHO REFLECT THE SENSIBILITY OF THE BOOK, WHICH IS TO CHALLENGE THE NUMB-ING SAMENESS AND POLITICAL PRECON-CEPTIONS OF CONTEMPORARY AMERICAN MAGAZINES WHILE STRETCHING THE ENVELOPE OF IMAGINATION AND WIT, INCLUDE RALPH STEADMAN, STUDS TERKEL, ALAN GINSBERG, CURT GENTRY, ERICA JONG, PAUL KRASSNER, SHANA ALEXANDER, ISHMAEL REED, EVE BABITZ, SUSAN CHEEVER, SIDNEY ZION, HUNTER S. THOMPSON, FRANCIS COPPOLA AND JERRY BROWN